5 Penny Blood A

GOTHIC HORROR

The Dark Nun's Church - Marie Laveau's Army
The Werewolves of London - The Mad Lab - Midwinter Vampires

Other Penny Blood Adventures:

- The Dark Nun's Church
- Maria Laveau's Army
- The Werewolves of London
- The Thirteenth Hour
- The Mad Lab
- Krampus
- Midwinter Vampires
- Gothic Horror - single volume that includes 5 Gothic Horror Adventures
- Walk the Plank

TABLE OF CONTENTS

5 Penny Blood Adventures

GOTHIC HORROR

The Dark Nun's Church · Marie Laveau's Army
The Werewolves of London · The Mad Lab · Midwinter Vampires
Compatible with D&D 5e

THE DARK NUN'S CHURCH

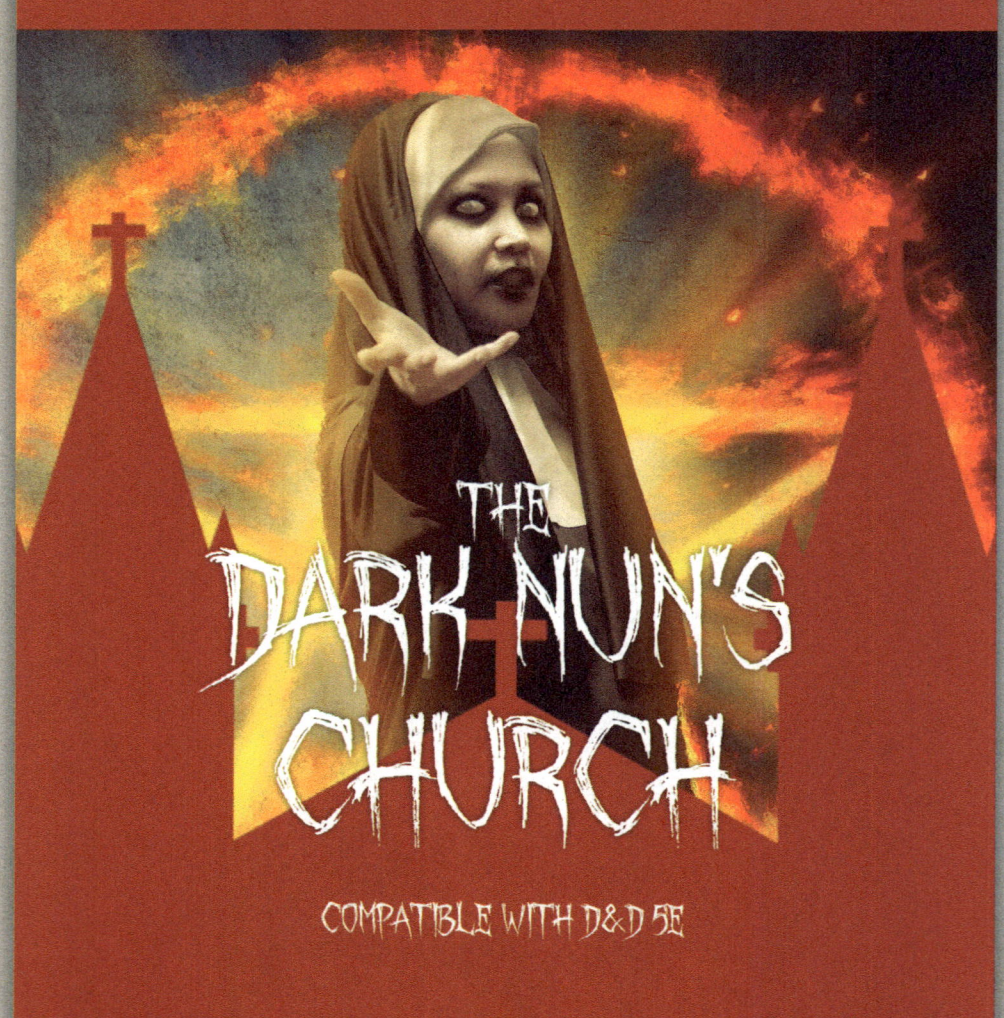

A Penny Blood Adventure

THE DARK NUN'S CHURCH

COMPATIBLE WITH D&D 5E

THE DARK NUN'S CHURCH

THE DARK NUN'S CHURCH

People are going missing. Religious chanting can be heard in the middle of the night. A foul smell rises from the depths of a dark and evil church!

The Dark Nun's Church is a 5E compatible adventure for groups of 2-5 people. The adventure is designed for fifth-level players but can be expanded to support players up to and beyond level 16.

Have lots of fun, and don't let the Dark Nuns get you!

RUNNING THE ADVENTURE

The adventure is written for 5th Edition Dungeons and Dragons. The D&D Player's Handbook will have detailed instructions on how to play.

The monsters, spells, and magic items are unique to this game. Each room will have a breakdown of the room description and a list of the monsters, traps, magic items, non-player characters, and treasure. Special items are highlighted in bold text.

Details for the **Monsters**, **Magic Items**, and **Non-Player Characters** can be found at the back of the book.

You should run the game how you like. There are no hard and fast rules for how your adventurers move through the game.

A **Random Encounter** table is located at the end of the adventure to ensure chance encounters happen.

You will see that there are several different versions of the Maps. Maps with a DM in the name are for the Dungeon Master (DM). The DM maps have labels for all the rooms that match the names in this adventure book. The maps without DM can be given to the adventurers. The maps are available in full color, night version (very cool when presented on a large screen TV), printer-friendly in black and white, and Sepia Tone version.

Finally, the game includes separate cards for the Maps, Monsters, Magic Items, and Non-Player Characters in both Black & White and color.

BACKGROUND

The Dark Nuns worship at a Church located outside of a small village. The church is run by the Dark Mother Superior. She is a powerful, dark half-elf using the "Books of New Living," three cursed books that contain horrific spells, to reanimate corpses back to life.

STORY HOOK

People from the village have been taken against their will to the church. The innkeeper, Grilia, an old tiefling, suspects that the Dark Nuns have taken his sister, Lena, and her husband, Tatum. He offers 100GP to anyone who can find and bring Lena and Tatum back.

THE DARK CHURCH

THE DARK CHURCH

The outside of the church is dark and forbidding. The church is located five miles from the nearest village. It sits on the top of a small hill in the middle of a thick wood. The fog is extensive. You can see 500 ft during the daytime, but this drops to 50ft at night.

Out of the clinging fog emerges the Dark Nun's Church. You see the twin towers capped with grotesque statues. The large, heavy doors are closed. On one side of the church is a small graveyard. On the other side is a small building. As you walk closer to the church, you hear the sound of rhythmic chanting. The Dark Nuns are home.

ENTRANCE

Before you enter the church, the adventurers will see that two huge ironwood doors are closed. High above them on the roof are gargoyles. The adventurers need to roll a D15 dexterity to check if they can open the doors without waking the gargoyles. If the adventurers fail, then a gargoyle will attack them.

Closed, twelve-foot ironwood doors prevent you from entering the Dark Church. Looking up, you see statues at the top of each tower. The fog somehow feels colder.

MONSTER
Church Gargoyles

NARTHEX

The Narthex is a small room between the church's front doors and the doors that lead into the Nave. To the right, a passageway leads to the Tower. To the left, a passage leads to the Facade. A trap is set into the floor directly in front of the doors leading into the Nave.

You step into the Dark Church and enter the Church's Narthex. In front of you, two more doors lead into the Church's Nave. Passageways lead to your left and right. As you stand inside of the Dark Church, the doors behind you close. There is no light. Chanting from the Dark Nuns can be heard.

TRAP
Under Pressure

This trap is triggered when an intruder steps on a hidden pressure plate directly in front of the door that leads into the Nave.

Effect: Targets all players **within ten ft., DC 10 WIS** save or become confused for 1 (1d4) rounds

Trigger: pressure plate activates when **20 or more pounds** are placed on it.

Countermeasures: A successful **DC 10 Wisdom (Perception)** check will spot the pressure plate and **wedging an iron spike** or other object under the pressure plate prevents the trap from activating.

FACADE

The Facade is a small room with no lights. Any member of the team with dark vision will be able to see that there is a D6 number of Blind Rats hiding in the shadows. Each rat has had its eyes burned from its skull. They are feral and will attack anyone coming into the Facade. There are three barrels filled with sweet wine in the Facade.

A foul urine smell hangs in the air as you enter the Facade. There are no lights. You hear tiny squeaks.

MONSTER
Blind Rats

TREASURE
Barrels filled with wine.

The wine in the barrels is delicious. The Dark Nuns make it themselves and use it as an offering to their dark gods. One glass of wine is the equivalent of 1 hour of rest. The wine is addictive. Each person must make a Wisdom Saving Throw or become drunk, causing them to sing loudly and dance in the darkness. Use the Random Encounter table to determine who hears the singer and comes to investigate.

TOWER

The tower has no stairs. It is the place where the Gargoyles will rest. Entering the tower can trigger a trap.

You enter the Tower. Oddly, there are no stairs or means of going up the Tower. A single candle burns on a small shelf on the opposite wall. You see a silver cross on a chain lying on the shelf.

TRAP
Splat Trap, a falling block

A taught length of string stretches across the diameter of the tower base. The trap is activated if the string is moved. Once activated, a large block will fall down the Tower and crush anything under it.

Effect: **DC 15** to find, **DC 10** to disable

Targets all creatures within a **10 ft. square area, DC 15 DEX** save or take 8 (2d10) damage.

Treasure: A Silver Cross

A silver cross lies on the shelf. The cross can be used to confuse the Dark Nuns. It is not magical, but the Dark Nuns are repulsed by the religious meaning of the cross. It can be used only once in an attack. The Dark Nun will be confused when she sees the cross and skip an attack round.

THE NAVE

The main entrance to the church is the Nave. A roaring fire lights the room, and Dark Nuns chant in the shadows cast by the light. Beyond the Nave can be seen rows of pews and at the front of the church is an altar where a powerful woman stands with her arms raised into the air. The Nave is a large area 20' wide and 30' long.

A massive 12-foot-wide fire illuminates a group of chanting Dark Nuns. You look further and can see pews lined up before an Altar. With her back to you, you see the feared Dark Mother Superior standing at the altar with her arms lifted into the air.

ENCHANTMENT

The song the Dark Nuns are singing is an enchantment. Anyone who is in the Nave will be too close to the sound of the Nuns Chanting and will fall under its spell. A **DC 12 INT** will be needed to shake off the effect of the chanting. If a player loses, they will immediately prostrate themselves on the floor and being chanting with the Dark Nuns. The Dark Nuns will see the new supplicant and attack. You will lose initiative and the Dark Nuns gain an extra attack round.

COUNTERMEASURE

Rolling a **DC 15 Dexterity** check will allow the adventures to sneak past the chanting Dark Nuns. A failed check will ensure the Dark Nuns see the adventurers. All Dark Nuns attack.

MONSTER

Dark Nuns

PORTAL

The left Transept reveals a cauldron boiling with a foul-smelling liquid. Bursting from the cauldron appears a ghost of a Dark Nun. The ghost will hurl insults at the adventurers and challenge them to a riddle. If the adventurers successfully answer the riddle, the ghost will tell them that there is a secret entrance behind the Altar to the Construct Room where Lena and Tatum are being kept.

Roll 1d6 to select a riddle.

1d6	Riddle
1	I am not alive, but I can grow. I have no lungs, but I need air to survive. What am I? Answer: Fire.
2	When set loose, I fly away, never so cursed as when I go astray. Answer: A fart.
3	Soft and fragile is my skin. I get my growth in mud. I'm dangerous as much as pretty, for if not careful, I draw blood. Answer: A thorn.
4	Lighter than what I am made of, more of me is hidden than is seen. Answer: Iceberg.
5	I go around in circles, but always straight ahead, never complain, no matter where I am led. Answer: Wheel.
6	Alive without breath, as cold as death, clad in mail, never clinking, never thirsty, ever drinking. Answer: A fish.

The Dark Nun Ghost will shout insults. Roll 1d10 for an insult:

1d10	Insult
1	You sagging piss-stained idiot
2	You're not a complete idiot. Some parts are clearly missing.
3	I thought breath weapons were supposed to come out of your mouth!
4	If ignorance is bliss, then why aren't you happier?
5	Putting teeth in your mouth ruined a perfectly good asshole.
6	You dim-witted chromosome collecting whelp.
7	Really, I'm doing you a favor by smashing up that dim-witted pile of rotten meat you call a face.
8	Should I be using smaller words so you can understand?
9	Were you hit by an acid arrow, or have you always looked like that?
10	You're like Rapunzel, but everyone else is the only thing you let down.

MONSTER

The Dark Nun Ghost

TRANSEPT

The right Transept contains two of the magic books used to reanimate bodies. These books should be destroyed or taken away from the church's sisters. Be careful when handling the books. There are two books, and the person picking up the books will need to roll a 1D4. If the number rolled is 4, the trap, a Close Shave, will be activated. The trap can only be activated once.

MAGIC ITEM

Books of the New Living

Magic books that hold the secrets to reanimating the dead. Three books are needed to ensure that the spells are cast correctly. Two are in the Transept, and the third is with the Dark Mother Superior at the Altar.

TRAP

Close Shave

Effect: **+11** to hit against all targets within a **5 ft. arc**, 9 (4d10) slashing damage

Trigger: when someone picks up either one of the "Books of the New Living."

Countermeasures: A successful **DC 15 Intelligence (Investigation)** check will know that the books are possessed. Wearing leather gloves will protect the player from activating the trap when handling the books.

ALTAR

The Dark Mother Superior is standing at the Alar, chanting her litany to the dark god.

There is an altar with the Dark Mother Superior standing at it. She has her back to the church and is facing the Altar. In one hand, she holds a Vampiric Dagger, and in the other, she is clutching one of the "Books of the New Living." The Altar is ablaze in ethereal light. The Dark Mother is chanting. She is calling on the dead to come back to life. "Hear me, all mighty dead, and join us in our dance!"

Behind the Altar you will see the secret passage if you have answered the ghost's riddle. If you have not spoken to the ghost, you can roll a **DC 15 Intelligence (Investigation)** to reveal the secret passage. To get to the secret passageway without disturbing the Dark Mother Superior, the adventurers will need **DC 12 Dexterity (Stealth)**.

The adventurers can try to speak with The Dark Mother. A **DC 15 Charisma** will be needed for her to talk to you. If you are successful, and she does speak to you,

she will try and convince you to join her Dark Sisterhood and become Dark Monks. If you choose to become Dark Monks, then your life is forfeit.

You can also roll a **DC 15 Intelligence (Religion)** to explain in religious terms to the Dark Mother Superior that she has lost her way. Your words soothe the Dark Mother Superior's tortured soul. She converts her beliefs to a neutral deity and retreats for prayer and contemplation.

If you fail, she will attack.

MONSTER

The Dark Mother Superior

MAGIC ITEMS

- Vampiric Dagger

- Charred Rosary (hung around the neck of the Dark Mother Superior)

TREASURE

- 1 of 3 Books of the New Living (the other two books are in the Transept)

- 1 Golden Chalice worth 50GP

- 2 upside down silver crosses, both worth 20SP each

SECRET PASSAGE

The darkness in the secret passage hides the Unholy Knight guarding the entrance to the Construct Room. The Unholy Knight has been waiting for a fight.

MONSTER

Unholy Knight

CONSTRUCT ROOM

The Construct Room is where the Dark Nuns cast their reanimation spells to bring back the dead. There is a private altar in the room with a partially mummified body. Gore-encrusted chains on the walls contain the remains of dead animals that are also used in the reanimation process. Two sets of stocks at the back of the room hold Lena and Tatum.

The construct room is a room directly from hell. A small altar has a mummified body wrapped on it. Chains, where people have been kept, line the walls. At the back of the room, there are two stocks with a man and a woman. These are the two people you have been sent to free.

The mummy will animate if the players touch it.

MONSTER
Mummified Body

TREASURE
A small, wooden box is in the corner of the room contains 5CP. The last money from an unfortunate victim.

OFFICE

The office has a warm fire, a comfortable sofa, and a desk with chairs around it. Sitting at the desk is a Dark Elf. Her name is Sister Alotel Galamin, and she is the scribe for the church. She talks a lot but loves to gamble. You can choose to play the game Dead to Rites against Alotel Galamin. If you win, Alotel will show you the secret door that takes you to the Construct Room.

The office is a stark contrast to the rest of the Dark Church. It is warm and comfortable, and a smiling woman sits at a table with accounting books open before her. She welcomes you in and introduces herself as Sister Alotel Galamin. She asks you "Would you like to win some money?" She shakes dice she holds in her hands and her smile broadens.

GAME OF CHANCE: DEAD TO RITES
How to Play: Each player must pay 1 SP to play. Sister Alotel will match the number of SP added.

Five D6 and paper to record players' scores are all needed. A player rolls the five dice, and if the throw does not include a 2 or 5, they receive the score of the total numbers added together. That player is also able to roll the dice again. When a player rolls the dice that contain a 2 or 5, they score no points, and the dice that include a 2, or 5 are excluded from any future throws they make. A player's turn does not stop until their last remaining die shows a 2 or 5. At that point, the player is "dead to rites," and it becomes the next player's turn. The highest total score wins.

The winner can choose to take all the silver or receive some information from Sister Alotel. The information is that she knows where a secret passage to the Construct Room can be found (right behind her desk) and that the people you are looking for are located there.

BEDROOM

It's a bedroom. Pretty much all it is. You can choose to rest here for 1d8 hours. No one will come in. If you stay longer than the time you roll then a random encounter will happen.

SIDE QUEST

SIDE QUEST - THE GRAVEYARD

To the side of the church is an unholy graveyard.

A foul, funky smell comes from the graveyard. Fog lies on the ground and you see a scattering of headstones and crypts. Some of the graves are still fresh. The dead feel very close.

There are graves the adventurers can visit. If they go to a burial, you will need to roll a 1D10 to determine what the encounter will be.

1d10	Encounter
1	A **Reanimated Hand** scuttles out of the grave and attacks.
2	Five CPs have been left to pay safe passageway to the dead. The coins are cursed! A character can take the money but will permanently lose 1HP per coin they take. They cannot give the coin back, lose it or get rid of it in any way other than having it stolen from them unknowingly at which point their HP maximum will be restored. At the DM's discretion, increase the HP loss for higher level characters.
3	A **Skeleton Nun** steps out of a new crypt and surprises the adventurers. The Skeleton Nun receives one extra attack before the group can respond.
4	A weathered map is pinned to a grave marker. It shows the church and has two rooms labeled. The DM can decide which two rooms they want to reveal to the group.
5	There is a flash of lightning followed by a distant rumble of thunder. Heavy rain is coming.
6	There is a small potion bottle. It is corked closed. A label on the side says "sleep." Anyone who drinks the potion will fall immediately into a deep sleep for 1 hour or until they take damage.
7	A small, pink box with 6 shortbreads are lying on a fresh grave. Eating a shortbread will restore 2 HP to a maximum of 4 per character.
8	You see a grave digger. He has just finished filling in a new grave. You can bribe (1SP) or threaten him (he is a coward and will back down quickly). He does not know much about what happens in the church. He can tell you that there is a trap on the floor when you enter the Narthex.
9	A **Blind Rat** leaps out of a fresh grave, its mouth oozing with congealed blood.
10	A single red flower rests next to the headstone. This is one sign that love can find a way in this world of terror.

RANDOM ENCOUNTER

There is room around the church for the adventures to wander. The following "Random Encounter" table will help keep things lively.

Roll a 1d10 for a Random Encounter in the Church.

1d10	Random Encounter
1	A Dark Nun attacks with both blades.
2	The party is attacked by 1d6 blind rats.
3	Sister Ervina Banksi finds them and asks for some food. In exchange, she will tell them one piece of information about the church. See Sister Ervina Banksi for details on her character.
4	Kethend stumbles onto the adventurers and asks to join them in fighting the nuns who kidnapped and killed her husband. See Kethend for details on her character.
5	A reanimated hand drags itself to the adventurers.
6	Grilia finds them and asks them to join their group. See details on Grilia's personality in the Non-Player Character section.
7	A potion is lying on the floor. The bottle has thick, viscous liquid and smells acrid. Strangely, if anyone is brave enough to drink the potion, they will receive total health and restoration. All HP returns to the same number as at the start of the game.
8	An old gardener is weeding the graveyard. He can be asked questions or bribed for 5CP. He will tell the adventures that the Tower has a trap in the base. "Watch out for the trip wire" he cackles.
9	Chanting can be heard from the church. After a few minutes, it is followed by a woman's scream. Are the adventures too late to rescue Lena? Short answer: No, but Lena will have a nasty cut on her side that will slow her down when she is saved.
10	A white dove lands on the ground. It is a good omen. A feather falls from the dove. It is a Holy Feather, and it can be used against the Dark Mother Superior. The Holy Feather can be used against any unholy or undead monster. Any unholy or undead monster will be repelled by the person holding the feather, allowing the holder to gain an additional attack each round. The feather will only last for three rounds.

RESOLUTION

The game's primary goal is to find and free Lena and Tatum. They are both found in the Construct Room inside of the church. Your team will need to get in and out of the Construct Room with Lena and Tatum. When they return to the village, they will receive their reward from Grilia. Grilia, even though he is a tiefling, is a man of his word and will pay the full 100GP. In addition, Grilia will give your team free night and board whenever they are in the village.

ALTERNATE RESOLUTIONS

Well done, you have rescued Lena and Tatum. You may have collected some treasure, a magic item, and good stories to impress your friends.

But that doesn't mean the game is over. After all, this would not be a Penny Blood Adventure if it was that easy. Here are additional ways (one of them twisted) your adventurers can end the game.

BRING HOPE TO THE VILLAGE

It is good that you have freed Lena and Tatum, but the village still lives in fear that the Dark Nuns will continue to kidnap people. To prevent this, your team must find and remove the "Books of the New Living" from the church. The books can be destroyed or kept.

RAISE THE DEAD

Your team finds and reads the "Books of the New Living." If you have someone on your team who can cast spells, they will learn the magic art of raising people from the dead.

With your new knowledge, you take control of the church and rule over the local village. The villagers must deliver a tax of 50GP each month, or you will send your Dark Nuns to kidnap a person, at random, and add them to your army of the dead.

MONSTERS

MONSTERS

BLIND RAT

Tiny beast, unaligned

Armor Class 10

Hit Points 3 (2d4 - 2)

Speed 20ft

STR	DEX	CON	INT	WIS	CHA
2 (-4)	11 (+0)	9 (-1)	2 (-4)	10 (+0)	4 (-3)

Senses darkvision 30 ft., passive Perception 10

Languages —

Challenge **0 (10 XP)**

Description. The blind rats have had their eyes burned from their skull. They are feral and will attack anyone. Roll 1D6+2 to determine the number of rats that attack.

Keen Smell. The rat has an advantage on Wisdom (Perception) checks that rely on smell.

Actions

Bite. Melee Weapon Attack: +0 to hit, reach 5 ft., one target. Hit: 1 piercing damage.

CHURCH GARGOYLE

Medium elemental, chaotic evil

Armor Class 15 (natural armor)

Hit Points 52 (7d8 + 21)

Speed 30 ft., fly 60 ft.

STR	DEX	CON	INT	WIS	CHA
15 (+2)	11 (+0)	16 (+3)	6 (-2)	11 (+0)	7 (-2)

Damage Resistances bludgeoning, piercing, and slashing from nonmagical weapons that aren't adamantine

Damage Immunities poison

Condition Immunities exhaustion, petrified, poisoned

Senses darkvision 60 ft., passive Perception 10

Languages Its speech is halting and raspy due to it spending most of its life as a statue, Terran

Challenge 2 (450 XP)

Description. The Church Gargoyle is covered in lichen and moss. It looks like a moving statue!

Actions

Multi-attack. The gargoyle makes two attacks: one with its bite and one with its claws.

Bite. Melee Weapon Attack: +4 to hit, reach 5 ft., one target. Hit: 5 (1d4 + 2) piercing damage.

Claws. Melee Weapon Attack: +4 to hit, reach 5 ft., one target. Hit: 5 (1d8) slashing damage.

DARK KNIGHT

Medium humanoid (any race), any alignment

Armor Class 18 (plate)

Hit Points 52 (8d8 + 16)

Speed 30 ft.

STR	DEX	CON	INT	WIS	CHA
16 (+3)	11 (+0)	14 (+2)	11 (+0)	11 (+0)	15 (+2)

Saving Throws Con +4, Wis +2

Senses passive Perception 10

Languages Common

Challenge 3 (700 XP)

Description. Dark Knights are Paladin initiates that have abandoned the path of good and now do evil.

Fearless. The knight has an advantage on saving throws against being Frightened.

Actions

Multi-attack. The Dark Knight makes two melee attacks.

Great sword. Melee Weapon Attack: +5 to hit, reach 10 ft., one target. Hit: 10 (2d6 + 3) slashing damage.

Short sword. Melee Weapon Attack: +3 to hit, reach 5 ft., one target. Hit: 5 (2d4 + 3) slashing damage.

DARK NUN

Medium humanoid (any race), Neutral Evil

Armor Class 11

Hit Points 16 (3d8 + 3)

Speed 30 ft.

STR	DEX	CON	INT	WIS	CHA
11 (+0)	12 (+1)	12 (+1)	10 (+0)	10 (+0)	10 (+0)

Senses passive Perception 10

Languages Common, understands Undercommon

Challenge 2 (450 XP)

Description. A Dark Nun has given her life to learning the arts of reanimating dead flesh. She preys upon the living, using their body parts for dark purposes.

Actions

Multi-attack. The Dark Nun can attack with two daggers. Roll a 1D6 to see if the dagger is a Vampiric Dagger (see Magic Items). A successful roll is 3 or 6.

Dagger. Melee Weapon Attack: +3 to hit, reach 5 ft., one target. Hit: 4 (1d6 + 1) slashing damage.

REANIMATED HAND

Tiny construct, Neutral Evil

Armor Class 9

Hit Points 15 (6d4)

Speed 25 ft.

STR	DEX	CON	INT	WIS	CHA
4 (-3)	9 (-1)	11 (+0)	3 (-4)	6 (-2)	1 (-5)

Damage Immunities poison, psychic

Condition Immunities deafened, poisoned

Senses blindsight 60 ft. (blind beyond this radius), passive Perception 8

Languages It does not speak

Challenge 1/8 (25 XP)

Description. The necrotic hand scuttles around the floor on long, razor-sharp nails like a crab searching for its next victim.

Actions

Razor Sharp Nails. Melee Weapon Attack: +3 to hit, tech 5 ft., one target. Hit: 2 (1d4 + 1) piercing damage.

ROTTING MUMMY

Medium undead, lawful evil

Armor Class 10 (natural armor)

Hit Points 67 (9d8 + 27)

Speed 20 ft.

STR	DEX	CON	INT	WIS	CHA
15 (+2)	7 (-2)	16 (+3)	4 (-3)	4 (-3)	4 (-3)

Saving Throws Wis -1

Damage Vulnerabilities fire

Damage Immunities bludgeoning, piercing, and slashing from nonmagical weapons

Condition Immunities necrotic, poisoned

Senses darkvision 60 ft., passive Perception 7

Languages the languages it knew in life

Challenge 3 (700 XP)

Description. Chunks of flesh fall from the body of this half-formed mummy as it moves towards you. The Rotting Mummy is a mistake gone terribly bad. The mummification process failed, and what this left is an animated body rotting on its own skeleton.

Actions

Multi-attack. The mummy can use its Necrotic Glare and make one attack with its Rotting Fist.

Necrotic Glare. The mummy targets one creature it can see within 60 ft. of it. If the target can see the mummy, it must succeed on a DC 11 Wisdom saving throw against this magic or become frightened until the end of the mummy's next turn. If the target fails the saving throw by 5 or more, it is also paralyzed for the same duration. A target that succeeds in the saving throw is immune to the Necrotic Glare of all mummies for the next 24 hours.

Rotting Fist. Melee Weapon Attack: +5 to hit, reach 5 ft., one target. Hit: 10 (2d6 + 3) bludgeoning damage plus 10 (3d6) necrotic damage. If the target is a creature, it must succeed on a DC 12 Constitution saving throw or be cursed with mummy rot. The cursed target can't regain hit points, and its hit point maximum decreases by 10 (3d6) for every 24 hours that elapse. If the curse reduces the target's hit point maximum to 0, the target dies, and its body turns to dust. The curse lasts until removed by the remove curse spell or other magic.

SKELETON NUN

Medium humanoid (any race), Neutral Evil

Armor Class 12 (natural armor)

Hit Points 11 (2d8 + 2)

Speed 30 ft.

STR	DEX	CON	INT	WIS	CHA
10 (+0)	12 (+1)	12 (+1)	4 (-3)	4 (-3)	2 (-4)

Senses passive Perception 7

Languages —

Challenge 2 (450 XP)

Description. Boney, pointy, and haggard, the skeleton nun wears her habit long after life has left her body. All that remains are her bones and her tortured soul.

Actions

Multi-attack. The Skeleton Nun can attack with two sets of boney fingers.

Boney Fingers. Melee Weapon Attack: +3 to hit, tech 5 ft., one target. Hit: 2 (1d4 + 1) piercing damage.

THE DARK MOTHER SUPERIOR

Medium humanoid (any race), Neutral Evil

Armor Class 11 (padded armor)

Hit Points 32 (4d8 + 16)

Speed 30 ft.

STR	DEX	CON	INT	WIS	CHA
4 (-3)	10 (+0)	7 (-2)	15 (+2)	15 (+2)	12 (+1)

Saving Throws Wis +5

Skills Deception +4, Persuasion +4, Religion +5, Stealth +3

Condition Immunities charmed, frightened, poisoned Senses blindsight 30 ft., darkvision 30 ft., truesight 20 ft., passive Perception 12

Languages Abyssal, Common, Infernal, Undercommon

Challenge 5 (1,800 XP)

Description. Ellyn Cloudfang, the Dark Mother Superior, is a 50-year-old female half-elf.

Life Giving Blood. Her blood is the cure for any sickness.

Spellcasting. The Dark Mother Superior is a 15th-level spell caster. Her spell casting ability is Intelligence (spell save DC 15, +7 to hit with spell attacks). The Dark Mother Superior can cast invisibility at will.

Actions

Leadership. For 1 minute, the Dark Mother Superior can utter a Special Command or warning whenever a non-hostile creature that it can see within 30 ft. of it makes an attack roll or a saving throw. The creature can add a d6 to its roll provided it can hear and understand the Dark Mother Superior. A creature can benefit from only one Leadership die at a time. This effect ends if the Dark Mother Superior is killed.

THE DARK NUN GHOST

Medium undead, any alignment

Armor Class 11

Hit Points 45 (10d8)

Speed 0 ft., fly 40 ft. (hover)

STR	DEX	CON	INT	WIS	CHA
7 (-2)	13 (+1)	10 (+0)	10 (+0)	12 (+1)	17 (+3)

Damage Resistances acid, fire, lightning, thunder; bludgeoning, piercing, and slashing from nonmagical weapons

Damage Immunities cold, necrotic, poison

Condition Immunities charmed, exhaustion, frightened, grappled, paralyzed, petrified, poisoned, prone, restrained

Senses darkvision 60 ft., passive Perception 11

Languages any languages it knew in life

Challenge 4 (1,100 XP)

Description. A visage of a Dark Nun reveals itself floating in the air as a ghost.

Incorporeal Movement. The ghost can move through other creatures and objects as if they were difficult terrain. It takes 5 (1d10) force damage if it ends its turn inside an object.

Actions

Withering Touch. Melee Weapon Attack: +5 to hit, reach 5 ft., one target. Hit: 17 (4d6 + 3) necrotic damage.

Possession. The Ghost can also possess a single person in their mind. The victim must make a DC13 Wisdom saving throw or become Frightened for one minute. On an unsuccessful saving throw, the Ghost must roll an Intimidation Check. If the value exceeds 18, the target takes (1d8) psychic damage.

SCALING MONSTER ATTACKS

The following chart scales the monster attacks by level of your adventurer. The table assumes a group size of 2-5 adventurers. Some monsters increase in number to form a swarm, most increase in HP but some gain additional powers and weapons for higher level adventurers.

	Level 1-3	Level 4-6	Level 7-9	Level 10-12	Level 13-15	Level 16+
Blind Rats	Determine the number of rats that attack: 1D6+2	Determine the number of rats that attack: 1D6+4	Determine the number of rats that attack: 1D8+4	Determine the number of rats that attack: 2D6+4	Determine the number of rats that attack: 2D8+4	A plague of blind rats attack. Determine the number of rats that attack: 4D6+4
Church Gargoyle	1 gargoyle will attack	2 gargoyles will attack	1D4+1 gargoyles will attack	1D6+2 gargoyles will attack	1D8+2 gargoyles will attack. The attack will come from both sides of the church. This is a 40' wide area.	2D6+3 gargoyles will attack. The attack will come from both sides of the church. This is a 40' wide area.
Dark Knight	Hit Points: 8D8 + 16	Hit Points: 8D8 + 32	Hit Points: 8D8 + 48	Hit Points: 12D8 + 16	Hit Points: 12D8 + 32	Hit Points: 12D8 + 20 + The Knight uses a Dark Flame Sword. HP is doubled when hit with the Dark Flame Sword.
Dark Nun	Number of Dark Nuns: 1D4+2	Number of Dark Nuns: 1D4+4	Number of Dark Nuns: 1D6+2; Dark Nuns receive 50% less damage when attacked inside of a religious building.	Number of Dark Nuns: 1D6+4; Dark Nuns receive 50% less damage when attacked inside of a religious building.	Number of Dark Nuns: 1D8+4; Dark Nuns receive 50% less damage when attacked inside of a religious building.	Number of Dark Nuns: 2D10+6; Dark Nuns receive 50% less damage when attacked inside of a religious building.
Reanimated Hand	1 hand	1 hand	2 hands (left and right)	2 hands (left and right)	4 hands	4 hands

Rotting Mummy	Hit Points: 4D8 + 27; bludgeoning damage plus 10 (3D6)	Hit Points: 6D10 + 20; bludgeoning damage plus 4D6	Hit Points: 8D8 + 21; bludgeoning damage plus 6D6+4	Hit Points: 9D8 + 22; bludgeoning damage plus 6D8+10	Hit Points: 10D8 + 20; bludgeoning damage plus 8D8+12; resists all flame spells and flamed weapons	Hit Points: 12D8 + 30; bludgeoning damage plus 6D12+20; resists all flame spells and flamed weapons
Skeleton Nun	1 Skeleton Nun	2 Skeleton Nuns	4 Skeleton Nuns	1D6+2 Skeleton Nuns	1D8+4 Skeleton Nuns	2D10+6 Skeleton Nuns
The Dark Mother Superior	Hit Points: 4D8 + 16	Hit Points: 6D8 + 24	Hit Points: 6D8 + 32; The Dark Nun has Dark Soul Prayer. She can use the prayer as her attack. The prayer casts black fire (1d4 Radiant or Fire Damage)	Hit Points: 8D8 + 40; Dark Soul Prayer + Summon Demon spell. She can cast the spell once during combat. The demon she summons has 120hp 10+0Str 18+2Dex 8+2Con 18+3Int 9+0Wis 19+0Cha its speed is 60ft. and armor class 12 and 150Xp for defeat.	Hit Points: 10D8 + 48; Dark Soul Prayer + Summon Demon spell. She can cast the spell 1D4 number of times during combat. The demon she summons has 120hp 10+0Str 18+2Dex 8+2Con 18+3Int 9+0Wis 19+0Cha its speed is 60ft. and armor class 12 and 150Xp for defeat.	Hit Points: 112D8 + 56; Dark Soul Prayer + Summon Demon spell. She can cast the spell 1D6+2 number of times during combat. The demon she summons has 120hp 10+0Str 18+2Dex 8+2Con 18+3Int 9+0Wis 19+0Cha its speed is 60ft. and armor class 12 and 150Xp for defeat.
The Dark Nun Ghost	Hit Points: 2D8	Hit Points: 3D8	Hit Points: 4D8	Hit Points: 6D8	Hit Points: 6D8+16	Hit Points: 6D8+24

MAGIC ITEMS

MAGIC ITEMS

BOOKS OF THE NEW LIVING

Weapon (magic book), very rare

DESCRIPTION

These three books are old and moldy with puss oozing out of the pages. There is only one reason these books exist: to reanimate the dead!

USE

The books contain the spells that can be used to reanimate the dead as well as other related spells.

DAMAGE

When you attack with any spells learned from the "Books of the New Living", you deal extra 1d6 necrotic damage.

Curse: If attack missed you take 1d8 necrotic damage.

CHARRED ROSARY

Religious Item (blessed)

DESCRIPTION

The rosary is hundreds of years old with 7 beads strung on it, each bead is burnt along the edges.

USE

The owner of the Charred Rosary is able to ask a demon one question and the demon, no matter what level they are, must respond with the truth. But be careful, the Charred Rosary can only be used once with each demon.

HOLY FEATHER

Religious Item (blessed feather, very rare)

DESCRIPTION

The Holy Feather is a delicate white feather of a dove that has been blessed.

USE

The Holy Feather can be used against any unholy or undead monster.

DAMAGE

The unholy or undead monster will be repelled by the person holding the feather, allowing the holder to gain an additional attack each round. The feather will only last for three rounds.

VAMPIRIC DAGGER

Weapon (dagger), rare

DESCRIPTION

This ornate dagger with an edge made of black steel casts a powerful aura of necrotic magic.

USE

Whenever you hit a creature with this magical weapon, the dagger deals an additional 1d6 necrotic damage as it endeavors to transfer the life substance of its prey to its bearer. If you succeed on a DC 12 Constitution saving throw, you gain hit points equal to the portion of necrotic damage dealt. However, if you fail the saving throw, your body rejects the creature's life force, inflicting the same amount of necrotic damage.

DAMAGE

Necrotic

Damage Immunities

Undead creatures or reanimated monsters are not affected by the necrotic damage, and you cannot gain hit points from them.

NON-PLAYER CHARACTERS

NON-PLAYER CHARACTERS

SISTER ALOTEL GALAMIN

DESCRIPTION

Alotel Galamin is a 167-year-old female darkelf scribe.

- She has a bald head and black eyes.
- She has soft black skin.
- She stands 162cm (5'3") tall and has a lean build.
- She has a triangular, slightly stunning face.
- She is missing three fingers from her right hand.

PERSONALITY

She openly worships Shar, Goddess of dark, night, loss, forgetfulness, unrevealed secrets, caverns, dungeons, and the Underdark.

She is quick to forgive.

She is very talkative. She collects iridescent feathers. She stretches the truth to tell a good story.

PLOT HOOK

She likes to gamble.

DARK MOTHER SUPERIOR

DESCRIPTION

Ellyn Cloudfang, the Dark Mother Superior, is a 50-year-old female half-elf.

- She has short, straight, blond hair and green eyes.
- She has rugged red skin.
- She stands 187cm (6'2") tall and has a lean build.
- She has an oval, awful face.
- She wears leather armor beneath her habit.

PERSONALITY

She proudly worships Cyric, God of murder, lies, intrigue, strife, deception, and illusion. (Chaotic Evil)

She is very pessimistic. She uses a beautiful walking cane.

PLOT HOOK

Her blood is the cure to any terrible and deadly sickness.

GRILIA

DESCRIPTION

Grilia is an 81 year old male tiefling innkeeper.

- He has extremely long, curled, gray hair and green eyes.
- He has soft red skin.
- He stands 177cm (5'9") tall and has a regular build.
- He has an edgy, stunning face.
- He has a lisp.

PERSONALITY

He doesn't worship any god.

He is very competitive.

He is materialistic. He cannot tolerate rough living conditions. He collects iridescent feathers.

PLOT HOOK

He needs help rescuing his sister who is one of the Dark Nuns.

KETHEND

DESCRIPTION

Kethend is a 23-year-old female Dragonborn armorer.

- She has a bald head and red eyes.
- She has smooth, ghostly, white scales.
- She stands 182cm (5'11") tall and has a fat build.
- She has a diamond-shaped, bland face.
- She is albino.

PERSONALITY

She discretely claims to worship the archdevil Asmodeus but secretly worships Torm, God of duty, loyalty, obedience, and paladins. (Lawful Good)

She is incredibly conceited. She works hard to play hard afterward.

PLOT HOOK

She has been hired to steal items from the PCs.

SISTER ERVINA BANKSI

DESCRIPTION

Sister Ervina Banksi is a 38 year old female lightfoot halfling acolyte.

- She has long, wavy, gray hair and blue eyes.

- She has soft golden skin.

- She stands 94cm (3'1") tall and has a round build.

- She has a sharp, cute face.

- She is very nimble.

PERSONALITY

She is very focused.

She can't keep a secret. She sporadically misquotes proverbs.

FOOD AND FUEL

FOOD AND FUEL

An army runs on food and fuel. Here you will find a recipe to feed your hungry hoard and an adult drink to quench their thirst.

FOOD - ROTTEN EYEBALLS

2 bags of frozen meatballs (Swedish are the best, but you can use any type)

2 cups of BBQ sauce

½ cup of grape jelly

1 tbs honey

1-2 tsp red pepper flakes (optional)

Combine the ingredients together in a slow cooker and cook on "low" for six hours. For a quicker meal, you can cook on "high" for 3-4 hours.

FUEL - THE DARK NUN'S TONIC

2 parts Dark Rum

2 parts Blackberry liqueur

Edible glitter

¼ tsp of sugar

Shake with ice and strain into a cocktail glass. Maybe say a prayer if you have too many.

MAPS

There are two types of map:

- DM/GM Maps with room names

- Game player maps with no rooms names

In addition, the maps are available in the following formats:

- Color

- Black and White printer friendly version

- Sepia Tone - when testing this game, the teams I worked with LOVE IT when I sent them the Sepia Tone versions of the maps as teasers for game night

THE DARK NUN'S CHURCH MAP (WITH LABELS)

Altar

Secret Passage

Construct Room

Portal

Transept

The Nave

Office

Bedroom

Facade

Narthax

Tower

Entrance

The Dark Nun's

Church

THE DARK NUN'S CHURCH MAP (WITHOUT LABELS)

The Dark Nun's

Church

THE DARK NUN'S CHURCH MAP (PRINTER FRIENDLY)

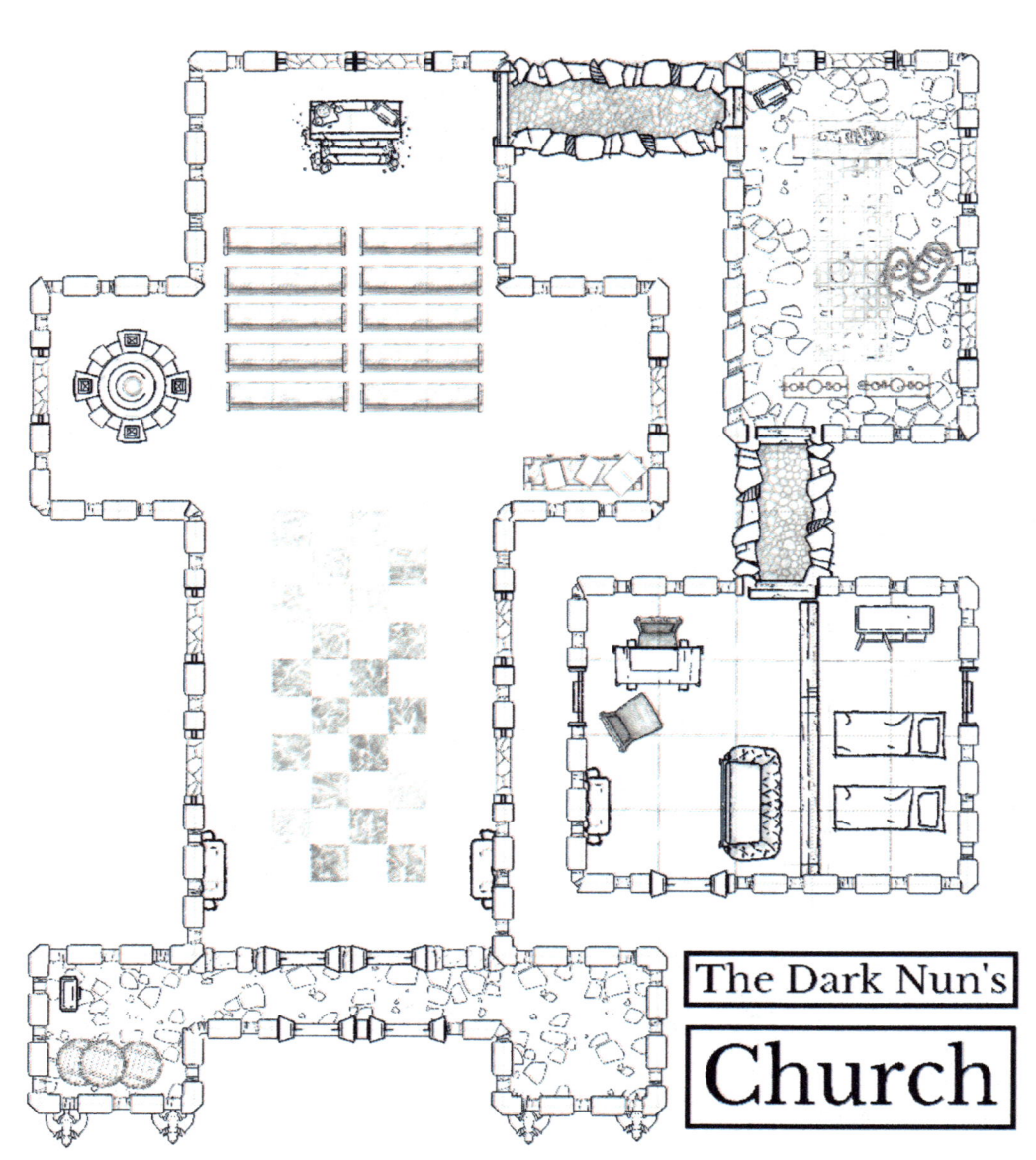

The Dark Nun's

Church

THE DARK NUN'S CHURCH MAP (SEPIA)

The Dark Nun's

Church

MARIE LAVEAU'S ARMY

MARIE LAVEAU'S ARMY

MARIE LAVEAU'S ARMY

A ghoul by the name of Black Crow has the town of Marais Fétide under his control. Zombies are wandering in the night and only an army of the dead can stop Black Crow. You need the Voodoo Queen, Marie Laveau, to summon her soldiers!

Marie Laveau's Army is a 5E compatible adventure for groups of 2-5 people. The campaign is designed for players level 1-5 but can be expanded to support players up to and beyond level 16.

Be careful in the swamp. There are monsters out there!

RUNNING THE ADVENTURE

The adventure is written for 5th Edition Dungeons and Dragons. The D&D Player's Handbook will have detailed instructions on how to play.

The monsters, spells, and magic items are unique to this game. Each encounter will have a breakdown of the encounter description and a list of the monsters, traps, magic items, non-player characters, and treasure. Special items are highlighted in bold text.

Details for the **Monsters**, **Magic Items**, and **Non-Player Characters** can be found at the back of the book.

You should run the game how you like. There are no hard and fast rules for how your players move through the game.

A **Random Encounter** table is located at the end of the adventure to ensure chance encounters happen.

You will see that there are several different versions of the Maps. Maps with a DM in the name are for the Dungeon Master (DM). The DM maps have labels for all the encounters that match the names in this book. The maps without DM can be given to the players. The maps are available in full color, night version (very cool when presented on a large screen TV), printer-friendly (black and white), and Sepia Tone.

Finally, the game includes separate cards for the Maps, Monsters, Magic Items, and Non-Player Characters.

STORY HOOK

Voodoo. It conjures up images of horror, possession, and fear. A zombie stumbling down the street. Dolls filled with pins. A queen controlling a preternatural army. Yes, this is Voodoo.

Exhausted from their last campaign, your team finds themselves at the edge of a small town. No people come out to greet you. Only a sign, the town's name, offers an eerie welcome. "This is Marais Fétide. May God forgive us for what we have done." Straw Dolls with pins in them cover the ground. It is a grim sight.

A moment of silence passes where all you can hear are the bullfrogs calling and feel the clawing heat sink into your damp clothes. You hear running feet and a young man appears out of the mist, his face contorted in fear. "My name is Bruno Michaud. Please help me find Marie! Find her and bring her army! A Ghoul called Black Crow has enslaved the town. We need her!" A screech fills the air. A curdling cry that causes everyone to turn away from the noise. Bruno, already on the edge of reason, turns and runs into the swamp, shouting, "Follow me, and I will take you to Marie's house!"

The sickly yellow hue of the ghoul, Black Crow, starts filling the air before you. Do you stay to fight, or do you find Marie Laveau in the swamp?

VOODOO QUEEN CLASS

VOODOO QUEEN CLASS

Voodoo is a powerful religious belief system with women rising to be leaders. The women are influential practitioners of magic. You will find specific spells for a Voodoo Queen in the section titled "Spells."

A Voodoo Queen will rely more heavily on magic, such as curses, as she rises through the levels. If she is to use a weapon, it will be a staff or dagger. Both the staff and dagger are frequently used as part of her spell-casting ceremonies.

The magic she learns will be to focus on two key areas in her life:

• Helping the sick and poor with potions for better health and mental well being

• Revenging the poor with curses and dark magic

In addition to helping the people in her community, a Voodoo Queen will also be a compelling storyteller. Frequently, she commands the attention of an entire room with her stories. A Voodoo Queen uses dramatic arm gestures, different voices, and sleight of hand to drive the narrative of her story. At the end of her storytelling, she will influence the room and convince everyone to do what she commands for an additional 30 minutes.

Marie Laveau, her daughter, and Sanité Dédé are all Voodoo Queen class. The level for each NPC is listed in their description. You can equip the NPCs with the following details. Ten Voodoo Queen spells are included in this campaign, but you supplement open Spell Slots with Druid and Warlock spells.

HIT POINTS

Hit Dice: 1d6 per level

Hit Points at 1st Level: 6 + your Constitution modifier

Hit Points at Higher Levels: 1d6 (or 4) + your Constitution modifier per Voodoo Priestess level after 1st

Proficiencies

Armor: None

Weapons: A staff

Tools: None

Saving Throws: Wisdom, Intelligence, Charisma

Skills: Choose two from Nature, Religion, Perception, Arcana, Intimidation, Performance

EQUIPMENT

You start with the following equipment:

• A Voodoo Doll

• Cowrie Shells

• Gris Gris

• Starting gold 1D4x6

RANK TITLE

Your character will gain news titles as they advance through the different levels from Voodoo Acolyte all the way to Voodoo Queen.

Level	Rank Title
1-3	Acolyte
4-6	Witch Doctor
7-10	Shaman
11-14	Priestess
Level 15-20	Queen

SPELL SLOTS

Spell Slots

Level	Proficiency Bonus	Cantrip	1st	2nd	3rd	4th	5th	6th	7th	8th	9th
1st	2	3	2	-	-	-	-	-	-	-	-
2nd	2	3	3	-	-	-	-	-	-	-	-
3rd	2	3	4	2	-	-	-	-	-	-	-
4th	2	4	4	3	-	-	-	-	-	-	-
5th	3	4	4	3	2	-	-	-	-	-	-
6th	3	4	4	3	3	-	-	-	-	-	-
7th	3	4	4	3	3	1	-	-	-	-	-
8th	3	4	4	3	3	2	-	-	-	-	-
9th	4	4	4	3	3	3	1	-	-	-	-
10th	4	5	4	3	3	3	2	-	-	-	-
11th	4	5	4	3	3	3	2	1	-	-	-
12th	4	5	4	3	3	3	2	1	-	-	-
13th	5	5	4	3	3	3	2	1	1	-	-
14th	5	5	4	3	3	3	2	1	1	-	-
15th	5	5	4	3	3	3	2	1	1	1	-
16th	5	5	4	3	3	3	2	1	1	1	-
17th	6	5	4	3	3	3	2	1	1	1	1
18th	6	5	4	3	3	3	3	1	1	1	1
19th	6	5	4	3	3	3	3	2	1	1	1
20th	6	5	4	3	3	3	3	2	2	1	1

ENCOUNTERS

MARIE LAVEAU'S HOUSE AND GROUNDS

Marie Laveau's grounds are extensive and surrounded by a massive swamp. A creek separates the property from the town. A walkway lined with wooden planks leads up to the house. On one side of the walkway is a hanging tree and cemetery. On the other, fey light fills the air. A Victorian house, its paint peeling and shutters falling off, looms in front of the players. A bridge made of rotting wood planks must be used to cross the creek.

You see the young man, Bruno Michaud, running through the swamps, across a broken bridge, and towards a large Victorian home. The sweet, rotten smell of flesh fills the air. The heat is intense, and you start to sweat while insects buzz around you, sucking blood from any exposed skin.

THE DEAD LAND

The Dead Land area is vile swamp land where zombies wander aimlessly, looking for their prey. Zombies are not fast and can often be evaded. If a zombie of any type attacks, the players can roll DC 8 Dexterity to avoid the zombie. If 3 Zombies attack at once, then they cannot be avoided.

Bruno will be in the Dead Land waiting for the players. He can be a guide or leave the players to find their own way. If the players choose to have Bruno as a guide, then the DM must keep the Side Quest "We Don't Talk About Bruno" running in the background.

A foul funk fills the air. Bruno Michaud is waiting for you in the swamp. Further on, you see a rotten bridge that connects to a wooden pathway. Dull noises from the walking dead drift in over the swamp mist.

MONSTER

Roll 1d6 to determine the type of encounter:

1d6	Encounter
1	Nothing happens - the players walk through the swamp, hearing only the buzz of insects
2	One Swamp Gator attack
3	1D6 Swamp Zombies attack
4	1D4 Swamp Zombies attack
5	1 Swamp Zombie attacks
6	1 Swamp Zombie Torso attacks

THE BRIDGE

The bridge is rotten and starting to collapse. Halfway across the bridge, the players must roll a DC 10 Dexterity to ensure they do not slip off the bridge. Players who slip off the bridge will disturb the Zombie Troll. Fortunately for the players, the Zombie Troll is decayed and moves slowly, but it is desperately hungry. It will attack the players.

A rotten bridge crosses the swamp. Each plank looks like it will snap in two. The creek below, thick with green ooze, has a stink that rises and hits your noses. Be careful as you cross the bridge. Plank by plank.

MONSTER

Zombie Troll

THE SWAMP

The swamp is massive and surrounds the boundaries of Marie's house and grounds. If players step into the swamp, they need to roll a DC10 Strength to stop them from being sucked into the fast-acting quicksand. If players do not go into the swamp, then 1D4+1 Swamp People attack.

Gators and snapping turtles slip into the stagnant waters of the swamp. The air is heavy with heat, and moisture. Your clothes stick to your skin. The swamp water is still. Dead trees lie half submerged. Occasionally, a plopping sound reaches your ears of something slipping into the water.

TRAP

Stagnant Water

Players must roll DC10 Dexterity. If the player loses, they are sucked into the water. The foul water will cause the player to vomit violently for two rounds and suffer 1D6 HP.

MONSTER

Swamp People

1D4+1 Swamp People emerge out of the swamp and attack! The Swamp People automatically have initiative and a bonus surprise attack.

FEY LIGHT

Swamp Fey are annoying but mostly harmless creatures.

Phosphorus green, red and blue light shines from tiny, winged creatures flitting about in the air. The creatures look like lightning bugs.

TRAP

Swamp Fey will annoy the players. Roll 1D4 to see how the Swamp Fey attack:

1d4	Encounter
1	A tiny Swamp Fey lands on a player's nose pulls out a small dagger, stabs the player's nose, and flies away. The player receives 2 HP damage, and blood runs down their face from their nose. It will be 15 minutes before the blood stops flowing. Mosquitos are attracted to the blood and will buzz around the players nose while it is bleeding.
2	Land on a player and stabs a small tattoo of a skull behind the players left ear.
3	One Swamp Fey lands on a player's head and urinates in their hair. The smell is repulsive, and the player's eyes will stream with water for 10 minutes until the urine evaporates. During this time, the player's speed is cut in half as they cannot see very well, and their Armor Class is reduced by 2.
4	Three Swamp Fey fly around the player's heads and light up the sky with green-blue-red light forming a message that reads, "Marie's daughter can help you."

HANGING TREE

As the name suggests, the hanging tree is where criminals were hanged until they died. Grim business. Spirits of the dead fill the air around the tree forming a strange fog. If Marie is not with the players, they need to roll DC10 Intelligence to detect the Spirit Fear trap.

If Marie is not with you, the Spirit Fear trap is sprung, and a Hanging Tree Spirit attacks.

If Marie is with you, add the following:

"Many have died by that rope," says Marie. "But their spirits are strong, and they would be welcome in my army."

Marie will step into the fog and embrace the flying spirits. Roll 1D6 to see if you recruit the souls:

1d6	Result
1-3	The spirits calm themselves and fall in line behind Marie. They will follow Marie and obey her. Roll 1D4 to determine how many Hanging Tee Spirits join Marie's Army. These spirits will now behave as NPCs and can be controlled by Marie.
4-5	The spirits laugh at Marie's request and trigger the "Spirit Fear" trap on the players.

| 6 | A lone spirit separates itself. A noose hangs around its neck, and it charges the players. They must defeat it. **Monster: Hanging Tree Spirit** |

A rope, greased with blood, sways from the hanging tree. A fog, formed from the spirits of the dead with nooses hanging around their necks, swirls in front of you. As you step closer, the spirits become more agitated.

TRAP

Spirit Fear

A thick fog that is 100 feet in diameter descends on the players. The mist is formed from the spirits of the dead who were hanged here.

Effect: +10 HP against all targets in the.

Countermeasure: a successful DC 15 Intimidation will alert the team, and they can step away from the spirits.

CEMETERY NUMBER 1

Cemetery Number 1 is where Marie's spirit rests. It is also where Crypt Zombies can be recruited. Only Marie can control the Crypt Zombies. If the players arrive at Cemetery Number 1 without Marie's daughter as their guide, then a Crypt Zombie will attack them.

This is the infamous Cemetery Number 1. All bodies are laid to rest in tombs that sit above the ground. Dig three feet down, and you will hit water. Bury a body down there, and it will reappear during the next heavy rains. There are six cracked tombs in the cemetery. The final tomb, close to the entrance, has many crosses drawn over it. Small offerings cover the ground. This is where the Voodoo Queen, Marie Laveau, rests.

To summon Marie, you need to have her daughter with you. She will sing and chant to invoke Marie's spirit. Following the chant, you must draw three X's on Marie's crypt, leave a magical item as an offering and shout out what you need. If the players do this, then the spirit of Marie will appear. She is a striking and powerful African American woman. The strength she had in life exudes from her spirit. You need to roll a DC 12 Charisma to convince Marie to help you.

"My army is spread across my land. Here, we start at the cemetery, but we must also visit the hanging tree, talk to my sister at the Dead Throne, and find my Voodoo dolls in my home."

Roll a 1d6 to determine the encounter:

1-3	A body shuffles out of the fresh coffin. It is a Crypt Zombie, a man pulled back from the edge of death to obey Marie. The Crypt Zombie will join Marie's Army and follow every word she says.
4-5	There is silence. Marie curses and shouts, "You did not wish hard enough!" You must shout your wish again and roll DC 12 Arcana. If you are successful, you can roll 1D6 against this table. If you fail, you must leave another gift for Marie.
6	A zombie lurches from an open coffin. It hurls itself at the players. It must be destroyed. See "Crypt Zombie." If the Crypt Zombie is defeated, the players must leave a magic item as an offering and roll 1D6.

MONSTER

Crypt Zombie

WISHING WELL

The Wishing Well is a mischievous place. When a silver piece is thrown into the wishing well, it will respond with a randomly generated insult. The voice will boom the name loudly so everyone can hear. For the next hour, the player must be referred to by the name the "Insult Generator" gives.

Behind the house is an old well. Walking up to the well, you see there is a sign. The sign reads, "For 1SP piece, I will tell you your true name." Do you want to know your true name?

ENCOUNTER

Insult Generator

"Your name is…" + choose one word from each column:

1d10	First Name	Middle Name	Last Name
1	Atomic	Knob	General
2	Steamy	Bum	Gremlin
3	Rusty	Turd	Pixie
4	Witless	Prick	Fiend
5	Lumpy	Bulge	Fungus
6	Shitty	Shit	Demon

7	Moist	Dong	Zombie
8	Chunky	Slug	Juggler
9	Bulbous	Pee-Pee	Fiddler
10	Crusty	Poop	Magician

DEAD THRONE

A throne made of stone sits behind Marie's ancestral home. A skeleton, dressed as a Voodoo priestess, sits on the throne. The skeleton is Sanité Dédé, who ruled as the first Voodoo Queen and is Marie Laveau's spiritual sister. The queen is still powerful and can be convinced to join Marie's army. She has the power to throw a Voodoo Curse on anyone during a battle.

Sanité Dédé will only participate if a riddle is solved. Sanité Dédé herself is powerful and casts magic. If the players do not solve the riddle, they can attempt to bribe the spirit. A DC15 Charisma will be needed to successfully charm Sanité Dédé. If the players fail, then she laughs and fades from the night.

A skeleton sits on a lichen-encrusted stone throne. This is Sanité Dédé, the original Voodoo Queen and Marie Laveau's spiritual sister. She is powerful and mischievous. Be careful how you answer her questions.

If Marie is not with you, Sanité Dédé will ask you a riddle. Solve the riddle, and she will give you one piece of information. The information is that Marie's daughter, who lives in the house, can be convinced to take you to Cemetery Number 1 and command the spirit

of Marie Laveau to join you and form an army to attack Black Crow.

If Marie is with you, then Sanité Dédé will join her army if a riddle is successfully answered.

ENCOUNTER
Sanité Dédé's Riddle

Roll 1d4 to determine what riddle is asked:

1d4	Riddle	Answer
1	It weighs nothing, it cannot be seen, but when put into a barrel, it makes it lighter. What is it?	A hole
2	What gets wetter as it dries?	A towel
3	What happens when you throw a green rock into a blue stream?	It makes a splash
4	I can be short or I can be long. I can be painted or left bare. I can be round, or square. What am I?	A fingernail

VISITING ROOM

Marie Laveau's daughter, also named Marie (this is a beautiful custom from France where mothers name their daughters after themselves), is sitting behind a large table. On the table are many of the tools and objects of Marie's Voodoo practice, including a wrapped body, spell books, charms, and a golden skull. Marie's daughter is a mighty Voodoo Queen herself. She is tall, muscular, and handsome.

A warm fire and the strong smell of incense greet you as you enter the house. A tall, muscular, handsome Cajun woman sits behind a large, wooden table covered in books, religious items, and a wrapped body. "Hello, children, welcome to my house," greats the woman, Marie Laveau's daughter. "Come, sit with me, and I will hear your troubles."

The players must convince Marie's daughter to help them find Marie Laveau and form an army to fight against the ghoul Black Crow. There are several ways to persuade Marie's daughter to support that, including:

- Roll DC15 Charisma. A successful player will receive help from Marie's daughter. A player who fails the roll will receive a sharp slap across the face from Marie's daughter, followed by some rude words in Cajun French.

- Marie's daughter requires money to help feed the homeless people living in the swamplands. You can pay 5 GP and ask a question. Marie will thank you for the donation and answer your question. If asked, Marie's daughter will be a guide and take the players to Cemetery Number 1, where Marie Laveau is interned. The cost of being a guide is 10 GP per hour.

- Marie's daughter is a magical woman. She likes to collect magic items. A magical item can be used to buy the answer to a question.

Marie will invite the players to look around her house.

Encounter: Visiting Room

The Visiting room has the following items in it that players can interact with:

Wrapped body: if the players poke the wrapped body, it will start to moan. Unwrapping the body will reveal an old man who is in the process of becoming a Voodoo Zombie. He can talk but cannot move. You find out that he died, and Marie is in the process of being brought back to that he can help as a mindless slave on his family's farm. He asks you to wrap him back up so that Marie can complete her process and make him a complete Voodoo Zombie.

Wine rack: players can drink the wine. It is a potent brew made with flowers collected from a vine that grows in the swampland. Roll 1D4. If the player rolls 1, they will start hiccuping for 5 minutes.

Spell-books: there are spell-books on the table. Reading them, the players will find that the spells are incantations used to cure people of sickness, help crops grow, and eliminate poverty. There is no evil magic here.

Golden Skull: a player who reaches for the Golden Skull will feel a buzzing in their hand as they go for the item. If they choose to take the Skull, they will need to roll a DC12 Strength as their hand is now fixed to the Skull. If they are successful, they can release their hand, leaving a red mark where the skull scorched their skin. The wound will clear in a day. If they fail, the skull sears a tattoo of a pentagon into the player's hand. The pentagon cannot be removed. If the player goes near a cemetery or graveyard, the pentagon tattoo flairs white hot, inflicting 1 HP and warning the player that they are near a place of the dead.

TAROT ROOM

Peronell Hillless sits on a chair in the room. She is a distant relative of Medusa. Snakes writhe on her scalp, replacing any hair she would have, but her gaze does not turn you to stone. She is here to read your Tarot. The Tarot is a three-card read (past, present, and future)

using conventional 52-card playing deck. The instructions for how to read the cards is in the section named "The Cursed Cards." Please note that it is to be fun. Some people become upset with a Tarot reading, so use your judgment, keep the reading positive and reflect the reading on the player's character.

There is also a tiny chest in the room Peronell. The chest contains a silver tiara. The tiara has no magical qualities but looks pretty when worn.

Peronell can also chose to tell the players about the Side Quest "Bargaining for Freedom."

A woman with snakes for hair greets you. "Welcome, my name is Peronell, and I would like to read you your fortune with my cards." She fans out a deck of cards onto her table.

The players can also elect to steal the Tarot Deck to run the alternate ending: Fortune Favors the Bold.

The Tarot room has a secret room next to it. Players can roll DC 10 Intellect to detect the hidden door on the wooden wall. The door will slide open and reveal the Secret Room.

THE CURSED CARDS

See the section "The Cursed Cards" to learn how to read the Tarot with a 52-card deck.

SECRET ROOM

Behind the Tarot Room, there is a hidden Secret Room. There are two ways to access the Secret Room:

- A panel on the wall can be opened to reveal a secret door.

- The players can choose to break through the wall. It is a thin wall; any melee weapon will hack a hole big enough to step through in three swings.

In the Secret Room, two bodies are covered with rags on the floor. Straw dolls lie next to them, with pins in each. The straw dolls are Voodoo Dolls.

If Marie Laveau is with you, she will clutch the Voodoo Dolls close to her chest as if they are lost children. They are clearly very dear to her. She can use them in the final battle with Black Crow.

If the players stay in the room for more than 1 minute then the bodies under the sheets will start to move. The bodies are two decomposed, zombie torsos.

Dust settles on two bodies lying beneath dirty sheets on the floor. Beside each are straw dolls stuck with pins. Blood oozes from the dolls.

MAGIC ITEM
Voodoo Dolls

The owner can point the Voodoo Doll at someone and start sticking pins into the doll when held. Each pin will inflict 1D4 HP of Piercing damage until all the pins are used or the doll is knocked out of the player's hand. Each doll has six pins.

Encounter: Two Zombie Torsos

PRIVATE CHAMBER

This is the private chamber for Marie's daughter. A cat sleeps on the bed. This is Marie's familiar. Marie's spirit will be delighted if you bring her the cat. She adores the cat and will call it sweet names.

You walk into the Private Chamber and see a comfortable bed, a roaring fireplace with green and gold flames, some cabinets for clothes, and a chest. An orange cat lies curled on the bed, purring, its eyes are fixed on you and follow you as you step into the room.

REST AND INFORMATION
The room has the following:

- **A larger, double bed**: players can rest in the bed. 1 HP will be restored for each hour they sleep.

- **Two sets of drawers**: there are clothes in the drawers. If the players search thoroughly, they will find a small pouch filled with honey-flavored sweets. The sweets are potent and infused with healing. One sweet will restore 1HP. There are 8 sweets in the bag.

- **A fireplace with green and gold flames**: the fireplace burns in tribute to Marie. A spell caster can roll DC 12 Wisdom to speak to the spirit in the fire. The spirit echoes Marie's whole spirit and will tell the players that Marie can be summoned at Cemetery Number 1. The spirit will also caution the players not to steal from the Trophy Room.

- **A small chest**: In the room's corner is a small chest. Within the chest is a game map with labels for each room.

CORRIDOR

Marie's house is protected by Voodoo herbal magic. Smudge sticks burn on the corridor walls to protect the home from evil. Sage smoke fills the corridor.

There are four doors in the corridor that lead to:

- The Visiting Room
- The Clairvoyant Room
- The Trophy Room
- The Shrine

All the doors are shut but not locked.

The thick scent of Sage and Lavender fills the corridor. Looking to the walls, you see herbal smudge sticks burning slowly to warn off any evil spirits. There are four doors in the corridor on each wall. All four doors are shut. The smoke from the smudge sticks irritates the taller players.

ENCOUNTER
Smudge Stick Smoke

Roll DC10 Intelligence for players over 6 feet to remember to lower your head and avoid coughing uncontrollably for 10 minutes due to the smoke. Players shorter than 6 feet are unaffected.

TROPHY ROOM

The Trophy Room is a place where players can buy items. Each item has a small label that lists the item, the price, and a short description of what it does. Payment is on the honor system. A table in the center of the room has a small box with a label that says, "pay here." The players can choose to leave the cost of each item in the box on the table. If the players look into the box before paying, they will see a red ruby (worth 10GP), 5 GP, 15 SP, and 32 CP.

Here is a list of items that can be purchased:

Item	Description	Price

Dead Bat	The Dead Bat is pinned in a glass case. If a player picks up the case, then the Bat will start to twitch. The Bat can protect the player; if the player is attacked and breaks the glass, a swarm of bats will fly at the attacker. For two rounds, the attacker is disoriented by the swarm of bats and will not attack the players. After two rounds, the bats vanish. The Taxidermy Bat can only be used once.	15GP
Gris-Gris	The Gris-Gris is a small amulet of a Voodoo Iwa spirit. These are wise spirits. The owner of the Gris-Gris can roll a 1D4 when encountering a trap. If they roll a 2 or 4, they will see the trap.	5GP
Spirit Offering Bag	It is believed that the spirit of Bondye, the supreme creator, resides in the Spirit Offering Bag. The bag contains sage that is soaked in olive oil. A player receives +2 Wisdom when they hold the bag. The bag can only be used once per day. After using the bag, the player must do one good thing as a payment for the Wisdom modifier.	25GP
Mojo Wish Beans	These pale beans allow you to make a wish. Seven days after the player makes the wish, they must plant the beans in the ground, or the wish will be undone. Be careful what you wish for.	50GP
Cowrie Shells	The shells represent a divine power, particularly from the ocean's mother Goddess, or spirit. The owner of the shells will be able to hold their breath underwater for 15 minutes.	10GP
Egg shell Powder	Cascarilla is a powder made from grinding white eggshells. It is used for psychic protection and guarding against harmful spirits. The owner will gain +2 Strength when attacked by either psychic or spirit.	8GP

The door opens to a small room lined with glass cases. A large candelabra swings from the ceiling above a wooden table in the center of the room. Inside the glass cases are Voodoo items. Stepping closer, you see each item has a price. An open chest on the table is where you pay for each item.

TRAP
Drowning in Swamp Water

If the players choose to steal the money and/or items, the door to the room will snap shut. The players will not be able to leave. Vile swamp water starts to flood the room from the bases of each trophy cabinet. The players have 2 minutes to pay for the items they have bought or return the money to the box, at which point the waters immediately recede, and the door to the room opens, inviting the players to leave. If the players do not return the money, the room fills with water to the ceiling. The players will start to drown, and each player will pass out. They lose 10HP each. The players wake up choking on swamp water, lying outside the Trophy Room back in the corridor. The door to the Trophy Room is closed and will not open again.

SHRINE

The shrine room is dedicated to Bondye, the supreme creator god of the Voodoo religion. Bondye cannot be seen by mortals and will communicate through an open book, titled "Voudou," on a pedestal. In the room, there is also:

- A Voodoo Warrior statue in the corner
- A small chest in the corner with a silver cross. The cross is worth 5GP.

The square room is clearly dedicated to Bondye, the Voodoo creator god. There is a small shrine at the back of the room, a giant statue of a warrior in the corner, and a pedestal with an open book. There is a strong smell of smoke in the air.

ENCOUNTER
Divine Intervention

Bondye is a benevolent creator but does not tolerate insolence. Players who interact with the book or the shrine must do so with respect. If they do not, the DM can roll 1D4 to determine the encounter.

1d4	Encounter
1	Divine light emits from the book in a cone shape. The tip of the cone is 1 foot wide and
2	A divine voice emits from the book and fills the whole room. Each player will need to roll
3	The voice of Bondye issues a warning to the group to respect the Voodoo religion.
4	The Voodoo Warrior in the corner of the room animates and attacks.

CLAIRVOYANT ROOM

The Clairvoyant room has a chaise lounge with a hand mirror. Korth, a lizard woman, sits in her chair next to the chaise lounge. She is an astrologer and clairvoyant.

She will offer to show the future to anyone at the party for 20GP or a magic item.

The room you enter is dominated by a comfortable-looking chaise lounge. In a chair sits a slender Lizard woman. "Hello," she rasps through her sharp teeth, "welcome to my Clairvoyant room. I am Korth, and I can show you your future for a price."

Korth can also tell them about the Side Quest "Bless the Children".

ENCOUNTER
The Seeing Glass

The player must lie on the Chaise Lounge and stare into the hand mirror to see the future. Their reflection will change to reveal the future. Roll 1D6 to determine their fate.

1d6	Response
1	A fierce battle is shown. The outcome is cloudy and uncertain.
2	A dream the player has will come true.
3	The player is standing victorious after a battle. Fortune favors the bold!
4	The player is holding onto something or someone. If you have something beneficial in your life, don't let it go.
5	The player is shown tripping over their own feet. Learn from your mistakes and live another day!
6	Be bold! You will step up in a battle. For your deeds, you will be rewarded.

SIDE QUESTS

SIDE QUESTS

As the DM, you can introduce the following side quests at any time in the game.

BLESS THE CHILDREN

There are Voodoo Dolls scattered throughout Marie's grounds. Each doll is cursed but the curse can be reversed. When the players meet Korth, in the Clairvoyant Room, she will tell them that if each doll is buried a small yellow flower will immediately grow and bloom. The flower radiant positive life. Anyone standing in a five-foot radius of the flower cannot be attacked by an undead monster.

BARGAINING FOR FREEDOM

Peronell Hillless needs help stealing the Cowrie Shells from the Trophy Room. She will use the shells to bribe the Zombie Troll on the bridge and enable her to escape. If she does, she will reward each player with 25GP.

WE DON'T TALK ABOUT BRUNO

Bruno Michaud is the person who leads you into the swamp to find help defeating Black Crow. What he does not tell you is that he is being blackmailed by Black Crow. Black Crow has his family and Bruno will do anything to help them. Black Crow has challenged Bruno to kill one of the players. It will be a surprise attack. If Bruno gets down to 2HP he will beg for his life and explain why he is attacking. Bruno has no money, but he does have knowledge of Marie's grounds. He will have a labelled map that he can share with the players.

RANDOM ENCOUNTER

RANDOM ENCOUNTER

Roll a 1d10 for a Random Encounter.

1d10	Random Encounter
1	A Crypt Zombie stumbles onto the path and attacks.
2	The mist from the swamp envelops you. For 15 minutes you cannot see more than 10 feet.
3	You hear whispers from the dead spirits that haunt Maria's grounds. Roll DC 10 Constitution. A loss will turn you mad and you will attack your own party for two rounds.
4	A Voodoo Doll is lying on the ground with one pin lying next to it. If a player takes the doll and sticks the pin into the doll, they will feel an intense pain caused by the doll. Lose 2 HP.
5	If outside, the ground is soft and a Crypt Zombie hand pushes through and grabs a random player. If in the house, a Crypt Zombie lurches into a room. Either way, the Crypt Zombie attacks.
6	You find Bruno Michaud, the young man who told you about Black Crow. He is frightened but wants to help. He will give you one piece of information that will help the players.
7	You stumble onto a small bottle filled with green liquid. The liquid has an herbal smell. If you drink it, you will restore 4 HP. This is Marie's Tincture of Life.
8	Lightning fills the sky followed by a crack of thunder. Black Crow is calling his army together. Roll DC10 Wisdom to check your fear. Fail, and you curl up into a ball, fear coursing through your veins as you think of the coming battle with Black Crow. The effect lasts for five minutes.
9	Green, insidious fog envelopes the players. Roll DC10 Constitution. If failed, the players will find that the fog is a mild acid that leaves a scar on any exposed skin. It will take 7 days for the scars to
10	Roll 1d4 Crypt Zombies attack!

RESOLUTION

Marie Laveau is dead, but her spirit is strong. You will need to conjure her spirit to ask for help. The only way to do this is to visit the house and convince her daughter, whose name is also Marie, to take you to Cemetery #1. At the cemetery you must conjure the spirit of the mighty Marie Laveau.

To conjure Marie's spirit, you will need to draw three "X" on her tomb, leave a precious gift, and shout out your wish to build an undead army and attack the Ghoul who has taken the town of Marais Fétide. Marie's Army is comprised of:

- Spirits from the Hanging Tree
- A long-dead Voodoo Queen located at the Dead Throne
- Any zombie you encounter
- Voodoo Dolls

With Marie's Army, you must then face Black Crow.

Black Crow can be summoned at any time. Black Crow has a strong army and will send his minions to attack. The number of attacks Black Crow will send is dependent on the average level of the players. Use the following table to determine how many "attacks" Black Crow will send:

Level	Number of attacks Black Crow sends before he attacks
Level 1-3	1 attack is sent
Level 4-6	2 attacks are sent
Level 6-8	3 attacks are sent
Level 9-11	4 attacks are sent
Level 12-15	5 attacks are sent
Level 16+	6 attacks are sent

You will need to roll 1D10 to determine what type of attack Black Crow sends.

1D10	Attack
1	1D4x2 number of Crypt Zombies attacks
2	A fine mist falls on the group. This is the Mist of Cowardice. Roll DC12 Intelligence to determine if you see the mist. Roll for each member of the team and army. Any who fails will lose -2 Strength for the next attack.
3	A light rain starts to fall. This is the Rain of Rage. If Crypt Zombies are in Marie's Army, they will attack the players. In addition, any mountain dwarves in your party will also fall under the spell of Rain of Rage and attack the people in their own party for three combat rounds before the rain stops and they come to their senses.
4	Roll 1D6+2 Swamp People attack.
5	Roll 2D6 Zombie Fei attack.
6	Roll 1D4+1 Swamp Gator attack.
7	A huge clap of thunder explodes in the air. Each player must roll 1D10. If they roll 1-9, they will lose 1D4 HP from the thunderclap sound. If they roll 10, they must roll 1D6+2 HP as their eardrums burst from the noise.
8	Silence. You are lucky. Nothing happens. You hear Black Crow cursing.
9	1D4x2 Crypt Zombies, 1D4x2 Swamp People, 1D4x2 Swamp Gators, and 1D4x2 Zombie Fei attack at once.
10	Black Crow is impatient and attacks! Defeat him to win.

Finally, Black Crow must be defeated.

REWARD

If you defeat Black Crow, you can determine the reward by rolling 1D4:

1. Each group member is given a magic potion from Marie. The potion is "Sudden Strength" and will increase your Strength +2 for four attack rounds in any battle.

2. Each person in the group is given a magic potion from Marie's daughter. The position is "Evade Death." Take this potion before a battle (it uses up one round), and even if you fall to 0 HPs, you will not die. You will remain at 1 HP for the duration of the battle. It can only be used once.

3. Each player receives 112 GP

4. The key to the town is granted to the team. A party is thrown in your honor. This day will now be known as "Salvation Day," and you will always be toasted at the event. Each player also receives 50GP.

ALTERNATE RESOLUTIONS

Why manage an army when you can use magic to solve your problems? Steel, borrow, or buy the "Cursed Cards." Then return and confront Black Crow. The cards have different powers against Black Crow. You will need one spell caster on your team to complete the campaign using Marie's Cursed Cards. For each attack round, a card can be thrown at Black Crow with the resulting effect:

1D6	Card	Action
1	Ace	Soft blows! Black Crow is only able to inflict 50% of HP for 2 rounds.
2	Two	Melee immunity! For one round, melee weapons have no effect on Black Crow.
3	Three	Double time! For one round, each player can attack twice.
4	Jack	The card is inverted! The players will not be able to use Magic cannot be used for one turn
5	Queen	You lose a magic item. The DM will decide what this is.
6	King	A crippling blow! Fire roars from the card and hits Black Crow dealing 10HP damage.

If you win, Black Crow will be defeated and peace will come to Marais Fétide. Each player is given a silver medal with a ruby in the center. The medal is worth 50GP.

GHOULISH PACT

Is this a Penny Blood adventure? Of course, it is. Do you need to do the "good thing" and save the town? Of course not. A pact can be arranged with the Ghoul Black Crow. Black Crow only controls half of the town. This means that Black Crow needs your support to conquer the whole town. Visit Cemetery #1 and convince Marie's spirit to build an army to join forces with Black Crow. Once aligned with Black Crow, you force the town into submission. One member of the team can be elected Mayor of Marais Fétide. As Mayor, you tax the people and property of Marais Fétide. The result is a steady income of 112GP per month.

MONSTERS

MONSTERS
CRYPT ZOMBIE

Medium undead, neutral evil

Armor Class 7

Hit Points 22 (3d8 + 9)

Speed 15ft

STR	DEX	CON	INT	WIS	CHA
12 (+1)	5 (-3)	16 (+3)	2 (-4)	2 (-4)	2 (-4)

Senses Darkvision 60 ft., passive Perception 6

Languages Understands the languages it knew in life but cannot speak

Challenge ¼ (50 XP)

Bite. 2d4+2 damage, have to be very close, clinging ability = 1d4 damage per turn for 3 turns from bleed.

Reanimate. If damage reduces the crypt zombie to 0 hit points, it must make a Constitution saving throw with a DC of 5+the damage taken, unless the damage is radiant or from a critical hit. The crypt zombie drops to 1 hit point on a success.

ACTIONS

Slam. Melee Weapon Attack: +2 to hit, reach 5 ft., one target. Hit: 2 (1d4 + 1) bludgeoning damage.

GHOUL - BLACK CROW

Medium undead, chaotic evil

Armor Class 12

Hit Points 90 (20d8)

Speed 30ft

STR	DEX	CON	INT	WIS	CHA
13 (+1)	15 (+2)	10 (+0)	15 (+2)	10 (+0)	18 (+4)

Skills Intimidation +7, Survival +3

Damage Immunities poison

Condition Immunities charmed, exhaustion, poisoned

Senses Darkvision 60 ft., passive Perception 10

Languages Common

Challenge 7 (2,900 XP)

ACTIONS

Bite. *Melee Weapon Attack*: +2 to hit, reach 5 ft., one creature. Hit: 9 (2d6 + 2) piercing damage.

Claws. *Melee Weapon Attack*: +4 to hit, reach 5 ft., one target. Hit: 7 (2d4 + 2) slashing damage. If the target is a creature other than an elf or undead, it must succeed on a DC 10 Constitution saving throw or be paralyzed for 1 minute.

Volley. Black Crow can be summoned at any time. Black Crow has a strong army and will send his minions to attack. The number of attacks Black Crow will send depends on the players' average level. Use the following table to determine how many "attacks" Black Crow send:

Level 1-3	1 attack is sent
Level 4-5	2 attacks are sent
Level 6-8	3 attacks are sent
Level 9-11	4 attacks are sent
Level 12-15	5 attacks are sent
Level 16+	6 attacks are sent

You will need to roll 1D10 to determine what type of attack Black Crow sends.

1d10	Encounter
1	1D4 number of Crypt Zombies attacks

2	A fine mist falls on the group. This is the Mist of Cowardice. Roll DC12 Intelligence to determine if you see the mist. Roll for each member of the team and army. Any who fails will lose -2 Strength for the next attack.
3	A light rain starts to fall. This is the Rain of Rage. If Crypt Zombies are in Marie's Army, they will attack the players. In addition, any mountain dwarves in your party will also fall under the spell of Rain of Rage and attack the people in their own party for three combat rounds before the rain stops and they come to their senses.
4	4 - Roll 1D4 Swamp People attack.
5	5 - Roll 1D6 Zombie Fei attack.
6	Roll 1D4 Swamp Gator attack.
7	A huge clap of thunder explodes in the air. Each player must roll 1D10. If they move 1-9, they will lose 1D4 HP from the thunderclap sound. If they roll 10, they must roll 1D6+2 HP as their eardrums burst from the noise.
8	Silence. You are lucky. Nothing happens. You hear Black Crow cursing.
9	1D4 Crypt Zombies, 1D4 Swamp People, 1D4 Swamp Gators, and 1D4 Zombie Fei attack at once.
10	Black Crow is impatient and attacks! Defeat him to win.

HANGING TREE SPIRIT

Medium undead, any alignment

Armor Class 12

Hit Points 45 (10d8)

Speed 0 ft., fly 40 ft. (hover)

STR	DEX	CON	INT	WIS	CHA
6 (-2)	15 (+2)	10 (+0)	10 (+0)	12 (+1)	13 (+1)

Damage Resistances acid, fire, lightning, thunder; bludgeoning, piercing, and slashing from nonmagical attacks

Damage Immunities cold, necrotic, poison

Condition Immunities charmed, exhaustion, frightened, grappled, paralyzed, petrified, poisoned, prone, restrained

Senses Darkvision 60 ft., passive Perception 11

Languages any languages it knew in life

Challenge 4 (1,100 XP)

Ethereal Sight. The hanging tree spirit can see 15 ft. into the Ethereal Plane when it is on the Material Plane, and vice versa.

Incorporeal Movement. The hanging tree spirit can move through other creatures and objects as if they were rugged terrain. It takes 5 (1d10) force damage if it ends its turn inside an object.

ACTIONS

Wail of remorse. The Hanging Tree Spirit is animated with necromantic energy. It will release a horrible scream of powerful magic, which can be heard up to 500 feet away. All creatures in a 50-foot radius must succeed a DC 15 Wisdom saving throw or take 8d6 psychic damage and become vulnerable to necrotic damage until the end of the Hanging Tree Spirit's next turn or until the Hanging Tree Spirit recharges it recharges this ability. On a success, the creature takes half the damage and doesn't become vulnerable to necrotic damage.

Dead Man's Noose. *Melee Weapon Attack*: +10 to hit, reach 15 ft., 1 target. Hit: 21 (3d10 + 5) bludgeoning damage, and the target is grappled (escape DC 18). Until this grapple ends, the creature is restrained.

SWAMP ALLIGATOR

Large beast, unaligned

Armor Class 14 (natural armor)

Hit Points 34 (4d10 + 12)

Speed 30 ft., swim 50 ft.

STR	DEX	CON	INT	WIS	CHA
21 (+5)	9 (-1)	17 (+3)	2 (-4)	2 (-4)	2 (-4)

Skills Stealth +3

Senses passive Perception 6

Languages —

Challenge 3 (700 XP)

Hold Breath. The alligator can hold its breath for 10 minutes.

Submerge. The alligator can submerge itself in any water that is four feet deep and 13ft x 4ft.

ACTIONS

Multiattack. The alligator makes two attacks: one with its bite and one with its tail.

Bite. *Melee Weapon Attack*: +8 to hit, reach 5 ft., one target. Hit: 21 (3d10 + 5) piercing damage, and the target is grappled (escape DC 16). The target is restrained until this round ends, and the alligator can't bite another target.

Tail. *Melee Weapon Attack*: +8 to hit, reach 10 ft., one target not grappled by the alligator. Hit: 14 (2d8 + 5) bludgeoning damage. If the target is a creature, it must succeed on a DC 16 Strength saving throw or be knocked prone.

Death Roll. +4 to hit, reach 5 ft., one creature. Hit: 7 (3d8 + 4) tearing damage. If this alligator has a creature in its mouth, it can perform a death roll. Upon successful roll, the target creature may lose limbs.

SWAMP FEY

Tiny fey, chaotic evil

Armor Class 14

Hit Points 15 (6d4)

Speed 0 ft., fly 50 ft. (hover)

STR	DEX	CON	INT	WIS	CHA
3 (-4)	18 (+4)	10 (+0)	14 (+2)	14 (+2)	18 (+4)

Damage Resistances fire

Damage Immunities lightning

Senses Darkvision 120 ft., passive Perception 12

Languages —

Challenge 1 (200 XP)

Consume Life. As a bonus action, the Swamp Fey can target one creature it can see within 5 ft. of it that has 0 hit points and is still alive. The target must succeed on a DC 10 Constitution saving throw against this magic or die. If the target dies, the Swamp Fey regains 10 (3d6) hit points.

Variable Illumination. The Swamp Fey sheds bright light in a 5-20 foot radius and dim light for an additional number of ft. equal to the chosen radius.

ACTIONS

Invisibility. The Swamp Fey magically turns invisible until it attacks. All of the equipment the sprite wears or carries is invisible with it.

SWAMP PEOPLE

Medium humanoid, Chaotic Neutral

Armor Class 12

Hit Points 27 (5d8 + 5)

Speed 30 ft.

STR	DEX	CON	INT	WIS	CHA
10 (+0)	14 (+2)	12 (+1)	9 (-1)	15 (+2)	9 (-1)

Senses passive Perception 12

Languages Common

Challenge 1 (200 XP)

Bayou Sense. The Swamp People have an advantage in Perception, Investigation, and Survival checks, relying on Wisdom while in a swamp.

ACTIONS

Heavy Stick. *Melee Weapon Attack*: +4 to hit, reach five ft., one target. Hit: 5 (1d4 + 2) bludgeoning damage

Poison Darts. *Ranged Weapon Attack*: +4 to hit, range 25/100 ft., one target. Hit: 1 piercing damage.

VOODOO WARRIOR

Medium humanoid, Neutral

Armor Class 12 (studded leather)

Hit Points 52 (7d8 + 21)

Speed 30 ft.

STR	DEX	CON	INT	WIS	CHA
18 (+4)	10 (+0)	16 (+3)	6 (-2)	6 (-2)	6 (-2)

Damage Resistances slashing; bludgeoning, piercing, and slashing from nonmagical attacks

Damage Immunities piercing

Senses passive Perception 8

Languages Common

Challenge 3 (700 XP)

ACTIONS

Bamboo Stave. *Melee Weapon Attack*: +6 to hit, reach 10 ft., one target. Hit: 12 (1d10 + 4) slashing damage.

ZOMBIE TORSO

Medium undead, neutral evil

Armor Class 8

Hit Points 22 (3d8 + 9)

Speed 20 ft.

STR	DEX	CON	INT	WIS	CHA
13 (+1)	6 (-2)	16 (+3)	3 (-4)	6 (-2)	5 (-3)

Condition Immunities poisoned

Senses Darkvision 60 ft., passive Perception 8

Languages Understands the languages it knew in life but cannot speak

Challenge 1/4 (50 XP)

Description. The top half of a zombie drags itself across the ground.

Undead Fortitude. If damage reduces the zombie to 0 hit points, it must make a Constitution saving throw with a DC of 5+the damage taken, unless the damage is radiant or from a critical hit. The zombie drops to 1 hit point instead on a success.

ACTIONS

Cannibal Bite. *Melee Weapon Attack*: +3 to hit, reach five ft., one target. Hit: 2 (1d6) bludgeoning damage.

Any character bitten by this attack must make an immediate DC 8 CON save. A new DC 8 CON save must be made every time a character is bitten by this attack.

Failure means that the character has contracted the zombie disease.

Suppose the disease is not treated within 2 hours of the initial bite using any curative spell or a successful DC 12 medicine skill check. In that case, the afflicted character will die and immediately rise as a zombie.

ZOMBIE TROLL

Large giant, chaotic evil

Armor Class 15 (natural armor)

Hit Points 84 (8d10 + 40)

Speed 30 ft.

STR	DEX	CON	INT	WIS	CHA
18 (+4)	13 (+1)	20 (+5)	7 (-2)	9 (-1)	7 (-2)

Skills Perception +2

Senses Darkvision 60 ft., passive Perception 12

Languages Giant

Challenge 5 (1,800 XP)

Regeneration. At level 16+, the Zombie Troll will gain the "Regeneration" ability. The troll regains 10 hit points at the start of its turn. If the troll takes acid or fire damage, this trait doesn't function at the start of the troll's next turn. The troll dies only if it starts its turn with 0 hit points and doesn't regenerate.

Variant: Loathsome Limbs. At level 10, the Zombie Troll will gain the "Loathsome Limbs" ability. Whenever the troll takes at least 15 slashing damage at one time, roll a d20 to determine what else happens to it:

1-10: Nothing else happens.

11-14: One leg is severed from the troll if it has any legs left.

15- 18: One arm is severed from the troll if it has any arms left.

19-20: The troll's head is sliced in two with brains going all over the place. It dies only if it cannot regenerate. If it dies, so does the severed head.

The part regrows if the troll finishes a short or long rest without reattaching a severed limb or head. At that point, the severed part dies. A severed part has AC 13, 10 hit points, and the troll's Regeneration trait.

A severed leg cannot attack and has a speed of 5 feet.

A severed arm has a speed of 5 feet and can make one claw attack on its turn, with a disadvantage on the attack roll unless the troll can see the arm and its target. It loses a claw attack each time the troll loses an arm.

If its head is severed, the troll loses its bite attack, and its body is blinded unless the head can see it. The severed head has a speed of 0 feet and the troll's Keen Smell trait. It can make a bite attack but only against a target in its space.

If the troll is missing a leg its speed will be cut in half. If it loses both legs, it falls prone. If it has both arms, it can crawl. It can crawl with one arm but its speed is halved. With no arms or legs, its speed is 0, and it can't benefit from bonuses to speed.

ACTIONS

Multi-attack. The troll makes three attacks: one with its bite and two with its claws.

Bite. *Melee Weapon Attack*: +7 to hit, reach 5 ft., one target. Hit: 7 (1d6 + 4) piercing damage.

Claw. *Melee Weapon Attack*: +7 to hit, reach 5 ft., one target. Hit: 11 (2d6 + 4) slashing damage.

SCALING MONSTER ATTACKS

The following chart scales the monster attacks by level of your adventurer. The table assumes a group size of 2-5 adventurers. Some monsters increase in number to form a swarm, most increase in HP but some gain additional powers and weapons for higher level adventurers.

	Level 1-3	Level 4-6	Level 7-9	Level 10-12	Level 13-15	Level 16+
Crypt Zombie	1 Crypt Zombie	1d4 Crypt Zombie	1d6 Crypt Zombie	1d8 Crypt Zombie	1d10 Crypt Zombie	1d20 Crypt Zombie
Swamp Alligator	1 swamp alligator	1 swamp alligator	2 swamp alligators	2 swamp alligators	3 swamp alligators	4 swamp alligators
Swamp People	1 person	1D4+2 people	1D4+4 people	1D6+2 people	1D6+4 people	1D8+2 people
Voodoo Warrior	1 warrior	1 warrior	2 warriors	1D4 warriors	1D4+2 warriors	1D6+2 warriors
Zombie Torso	1 Zombie Torso	1d4 Zombie Torso	1d6 Zombie Torso	1d8 Zombie Torso	1d10 Zombie Torso	1d20 Zombie Torso
Zombie Troll				Gain Loathsome Limbs ability	Gain Loathsome Limbs ability	Gain Loathsome Limbs ability + Regeneration

MAGIC ITEMS

MAGIC ITEMS

COWRIE SHELLS

Wondrous Item, artefact

DESCRIPTION

The shells represent a divine power, particularly from the ocean's mother Goddess, or spirit.

USE

The owner of the shells will be able to hold their breath underwater for 15 minutes.

DEAD BAT

Wondrous Item

DESCRIPTION

A dead bat is pinned in a glass case.

USE

If a player picks up the case, then the Bat will start to twitch. The Bat can protect the player. If the player is attacked and breaks the glass, a swarm of bats will fly at the attacker.

DAMAGE

For two rounds, the attacker is disoriented by the swarm of bats and will not attack. After two rounds, the bats vanish. The Taxidermy Bat can only be used once.

EGGSHELL POWDER

Wondrous Item

DESCRIPTION

Cascarilla is a powder made from grinding white eggshells.

USE

It is used for psychic protection and guarding against harmful spirits. The owner will gain +2 Strength when attacked by spirit.

GRIS-GRIS

Wondrous Item, artefact

DESCRIPTION

The Gris-Gris is a small amulet of a Voodoo Iwa spirit. These are wise spirits.

USE

The owner of the Gris-Gris can roll a 1D4 when encountering a trap. If they roll a 2 or 4, they will see the trap.

MARIE'S TINCTURE OF LIFE

Medical Item (blessed)

DESCRIPTION

A small bottle filled with green liquid. The liquid has an herbal smell.

USE

Drinking Marie's Tincture of Life will restore four HP.

MOJO WISH BEANS

Wondrous Item

DESCRIPTION

These pale beans allow you to make a wish.

USE

Seven days after the player makes the wish, they must plant the beans in the ground, or the wish will be undone. Be careful what you wish for.

SPIRIT OFFERING BAG

Wondrous Item

DESCRIPTION

It is believed that the spirit of Bondye, the supreme creator, resides in the Spirit Offering Bag. The bag contains sage that is soaked in olive oil.

USE

A player receives +2 Wisdom when they hold the bag. The bag can only be used once per day. After using the bag, the player must do one good thing as a payment for the Wisdom modifier.

VOODOO DOLL

Wondrous Item

DESCRIPTION

A doll made of dried straw with steel pins sticking out of it.

USE

The owner can point the Voodoo Doll at someone and start sticking pins into the doll when held.

DAMAGE

Each pin will take 1d4 HP until all six pins are used or the doll is knocked out of the player's hand.

SPELLS

SPELLS

ANIMATE FAMILIAR

Cantrip

Casting Time: 1 minute

Range: Touch

Components: V S M (the caster must slice their palm with a sharp blade and drip three drops of blood on the dead body of a pet or favored animal)

Duration: 24 hours

School: Necromancy

The caster can reanimate a dead pet or animal that has intense meaning. The animal's size must be Small such as a cat, rat, or dog. The reanimated pet cannot die. When the hit points for the pet reach zero, it will lie on the floor for one round and then come back to life with one hit point (regaining one hit point for each round until it reaches its normal hit point level). The spell lasts 24 hours.

COMMAND THE DEAD

3rd Level

Casting Time: 1 Action

Range: 20 feet

Components: V S

Duration: 4 hours

School: Necromancy

Level 5 and above can Command the Dead. It takes five minutes to cast the spell, and the caster will receive 1D6+2 damage. When you cast the spell, any undead creature within 20 feet will obey your commands for 4 hrs. You will need to rest for 1 hour before casting the spell a second time.

CREATE VOODOO DOLL

5th Level

Casting Time: 4 hours

Range: line of sight

Components: V S M (a doll, pins, and hair or blood from the intended victim)

Duration: the instant effect that is permanent

School: Necromancy

A Voodoo Priestess at the tenth Level allows you to create a Voodoo Doll. A Voodoo Doll takes four hours to complete. See Voodoo Dolls in the Magic Items section.

The Hit Point for a Voodoo Doll can be doubled if you add a lock of hair or some blood from the intended victim.

CURSE OF POX

1st Level

Casting Time: 1 minute

Range: Touch

Components: V S

Duration: Until the target completes a long rest

School: Necromancy

The caster must touch the animal or person who will receive the curse, and, while casting Curse of Pox, the caster must specify the symptoms the recipient will have (such as boils, blood from the eyeballs, etc.). The recipient will immediately be only able to move at half speed, lose 1d6+1 hit points and start complaining endlessly about how sick they feel. A long rest will remove the curse.

CURSE OF ROTTEN FLESH

2nd Level

Casting Time: 1 Action

Range: Touch

Components: V S M (dead token such as corpse ash)

Duration: 12 hours or until a "remove curse" spell is applied

School: Necromancy

The curse reverses any gained hit points from healing or a magic potion causing damage to the victim.

CURSE OF UNDEAD

4th Level

Casting Time: 1 Action

Range: Sight

Components: V S

Duration: Until dispelled

School: Necromancy

Any humanoid who fails a Constitution Saving Throw will collapse dead and immediately rise as a Crypt Zombie. A Voodoo Queen of Level 15 or higher can control the Crypt Zombie.

DEFY HEALING

Cantrip

Casting Time: 1 Action

Range: 30 feet

Components: V S

Duration: Instant

School: Necromancy

Caster will prevent creatures who acquire hit points (magically or through their regenerative process) from being able to gain the hit points. A creature that was to regain hit points or temporary hit points magically must instead make a DC 10 Constitution saving throw. On a failed save, the creature takes damage equal to the hit points it would have regained.

HEAL THE LIVING

1st Level

Casting Time: 1 Action

Range: 10 feet

Components: V S (the priestess will take 30 seconds to mumble an incantation in Cajun French)

Duration: Instant

School: Necromancy

A first-level Voodoo Priestess can use Heal the Living. The spell can only be used once per hour. On casting, the target of the attack will receive 1D4 hit points. The power of the magic increases with the Level of the Voodoo Priestess using the following table:

Level	Restored Hit Point
1	1D4
5	2D4
10	2D6
15	2D8

REANIMATE ARMY

5th Level

Casting Time: 1 hour

Range: 100 feet

Components: V S M (the caster must slice their palm with a sharp blade and touch the ground for infusing blood into the soil of the dead)

Duration: Instant

School: Necromancy

The caster can raise the dead. Roll 1d8+2 to determine how many Crypt Zombies will rise from the ground. The Crypt Zombies are entirely under the caster's control for 2 hours. After the end of the second hour, a 1d4 must be rolled for each Crypt Zombie. A roll of 1 and the Crypt Zombie will remain under the caster's control for another two hours. With a roll of 2 or 3, the Crypt Zombie will collapse and become a dead creature. A roll of 4 and the Crypt Zombie will attack the caster.

SPIRIT SHRIEK

2nd Level

Casting Time: 1 Action

Range: 30 feet radius

Components: V S

Duration: for 30 seconds, any person within a 30-foot radius will be deafened for 30 minutes. Any person within a radius of 30-60 feet will lose 50% of their hearing for 5 minutes.

School: Necromancy

The screams of the dead are released into the world of the living. Any person or animal within 30 feet will lose hearing as their eardrums burst and blood runs down their necks.

NON-PLAYER CHARACTERS

NON-PLAYER CHARACTERS

BRUNO MICHAUD

DESCRIPTION

Bruno Michaud is a young male human farmer who stands 175cm (5'8") tall with a beefy build. He has short, straight, blonde hair, rough brown skin, and green eyes. There is a scar on his left ear.

PERSONALITY

He will ponder the pros and cons before making a decision. He has no self-confidence. He will never take a life if given the choice. He always eats like it's his last meal. He cares about his friends and will do anything for them.

PLOT HOOK

Black Crow has his family, and Bruno will do anything to help them. Black Crow has challenged Bruno to kill one of the players. It will be a surprise attack. If Bruno gets down to 2HP, he will beg for his life and explain why he is attacking. Bruno has no money, but he does know Marie's grounds. He will have a labeled map that he can share with the players.

KORTH

DESCRIPTION

Korth is a 46-year-old a lizard woman astrologer. She has a plated head, brown eyes, and dirty scales. She stands 187cm (6'1") tall and has a skinny build. She has an unfinished tattoo of an inspirational quote about philosophy translated into elvish on her right hand. She has exceptionally long fingers.

PERSONALITY

She is very detached from her emotions. She is very courageous, to a fault. She pities creatures without armor, natural or made. She has a beautiful singing voice.

PLOT HOOK

She was tricked into wearing a cursed trinket.

MARIE LAVEAU - VOODOO QUEEN

DESCRIPTION

Marie Laveau is a Voodoo Queen. She has short, curled, black hair and brown eyes. She stands 187cm (6'1") tall and has a lean build. She has an oblong, striking face. She has an unfinished tattoo of the word music translated into deep speech on her left arm and an exceptional tattoo of the lyrics of a song quote about fear on her left hand.

She is a 17th level Voodoo Priestess.

PERSONALITY

She has a crude sense of humor and is very obstinate.

PLOT HOOK

She is dead and must be summoned as a spirit from her burial site.

MARIE'S DAUGHTER

DESCRIPTION

Marie Laveau's daughter, also named Marie, is an attractive Voodoo priestess. She has long, curled, black hair and penetrating eyes. She stands 172cm (5'7") tall. She is a 5th level Voodoo Priestess.

PERSONALITY

She is a very good diplomat and always works towards the resolution of conflict. She only talks in whispers. She sporadically misquotes sacred texts.

PLOT HOOK

She confronts Black Crow when the sun rises. She fears she will lose the battle.

PERONELL HILLLESS

DESCRIPTION

Peronell Hillless is a 280-year-old female medusa fortune-teller. She has hair made of black snakes and blue eyes. She has rough gray skin. She stands 189cm (6'2") tall and has an athletic build. She has a diamond-shaped, slightly pretty face. She is missing two fingers from her right hand.

PERSONALITY

She always wears dark glasses to mask her eyes. She is constantly flattering people she talks to.

PLOT HOOK

She needs help stealing the Cowrie Shells from the Trophy Room. The Cowrie Shells must be stolen and then given to Peronell. She will use the shells to bribe the Zombie Troll on the bridge and enable her to escape.

SANITE DEDE

DESCRIPTION

Sanité's spirit is strong and forceful. In life, she was the original Voodoo queen, she stood 159cm (5'2") tall and had a muscular build.

She is a 15th level Voodoo Priestess.

PERSONALITY

She is a perfectionist and will point out any mistakes the players make. The memories of the terrible things she needed to do as the first Voodoo Queen still haunt her.

GAME WITHIN A GAME

GAME WITHIN A GAME: THE CURSED CARDS

What you will need: one standard 52-card deck of playing cards

You will want the player who is having the Tarot Reading done to shuffle a deck of 52 playing cards and then select three cards and place them face down in a row on the table. The three cards represent the player's character's past, present, and future in the game. Be sure to emphasize that this is a fun reading of the character, not the person. Keep the reading light-hearted.

- Hearts often reflect emotions

- Spades represent thinking and communication

- Diamonds show insights into life

- Clubs are cards of action

The following chart can determine the card's meaning, but feel free to add your own interpretations.

	Hearts	Spades	Diamonds	Clubs
Ace	A new friendship will start	You will gain new insights	A new project or you will win some money	You will have a new idea
Two	You will have a friendship that will grow stronger	Be clear on what you mean or your words will be misinterpreted	You will be juggling lots of things and will have to be patient for events to unfold	Planning is essential
Three	You will laugh with friends	Someone on your team will hear your words and then do the exact opposite. The DM can decide when this occurs.	Teamwork makes the dreamwork — work together to get the job done	You are a born leader
Four	You need a few minutes for internal contemplation.	You recover quickly from an attack. The DM can decide when this happens.	You don't want to share the loot.	You take a well-earned rest after successfully completing a goal.
Five	You lose a precious item. The DM will decide when this happens.	You receive a hollow victory. You may win the battle but lose the war.	You lose 25% all the gold you own.	You get irritated with someone on the team.
Six	You have a good memory of when you were a child. It gives you a sense of happiness for the whole day.	You will be moving to a new location soon. This will put you in a better head space.	You will receive 20 GP at some time in the future. The DM will determine when.	You will be victorious!
Seven	You start to daydream and snuggle to focus on the present for 15 minutes.	Someone steals from you. You do not know who, but the DM can decide what is stolen and who took it.	During a battle you will pause to reassess your tactics. It is always OK to change if things are not going to plan.	You have strong conviction on a decision you make, and it cannot be changed.

Eight	You will need to make a hard choice, but it is the right choice to open new opportunities for the future.	You feel trapped, but it is just an illusion.	You need to practice and keep focused.	You are organized
Nine	You gain spiritual growth.	You will have a terrible nightmare. Don't worry, it is just a dream and not what will happen.	You are becoming more independent and will receive increased wealth. The DM can determine when you receive 5 GP at some point in the future.	You will have sustained endurance during battle. If you drop to 0 HP, then you will bounce back to +5HP during a battle. This can only be done once.
Ten	You are fulfilled.	You will volunteer for the battle that will almost mean certain death.	You will receive great wealth.	You will feel intense responsibility for the happiness of the people of the town.
Jack	You fall in love easily	You are an intellectual rebel fighting for a cause	Reliable and hard-working	Hotheaded
Queen	You are empathetic	You are smart and intelligent	Practical and warm to those around you	Untidy but strongly career minded
King	You are wise, tolerant, and diplomatic	You are a deeply ethical person who communicates effectively	You will be a successful, self-made business leader	Creative and a forceful leader

FOOD AND FUEL

FOOD AND FUEL

An army runs on food and fuel. Here you will find a recipe to feed your hungry hoard and an adult drink to quench their thirst.

FOOD – MARIE'S CAJUN CHICKEN

INGREDIENTS

- 8-ounce penne (2 cups) uncooked
- 2 tablespoons of olive oil
- 1 pound chicken breast (2 chicken breasts) boneless and skinless, cut into small pieces
- 2 tablespoons Cajun seasoning
- ¼ teaspoon of red pepper flakes (optional for a bit of heat)
- ¼ teaspoon salt or to taste
- ¼ teaspoon pepper or to taste
- 2 links of smoked sausage cut into slices
- 3 cloves garlic minced
- ¼ cup parsley chopped
- 1 cup full cream
- 1 8-ounce package of cream cheese

INSTRUCTIONS

- **Cook pasta**: Cook the pasta according to package instructions until it's al dente (cooked until it's still firm when bitten). Drain and set aside.

- **Cook Chicken**: Heat the olive oil in a large skillet over medium-high heat.

- Add the chicken to the skillet, sprinkle with the Cajun seasoning, red pepper flakes (optional), and season with salt and pepper. Cook until the chicken is no longer pink and is cooked through. It should take about 5 minutes.

- **Add sausage**: Stir in the sausage and cook for a couple more minutes until the sausage starts to brown.

- **Add garlic and parsley**: Add the garlic and parsley to the skillet and stir. Cook for 30 seconds until the garlic becomes aromatic.

- Add cream: Add the cream and cook until it comes to a boil. Stir in the cream cheese. Stir in pasta.

- Garnish and serve: Garnish with more parmesan cheese and parsley if preferred and serve while warm.

FUEL - ZOMBIE SPIT

2 parts Vanilla Milk

1 part Vanilla Vodka

1 part Irish Cream

1 part Creme de Cacao

Build on ice in a high glass.

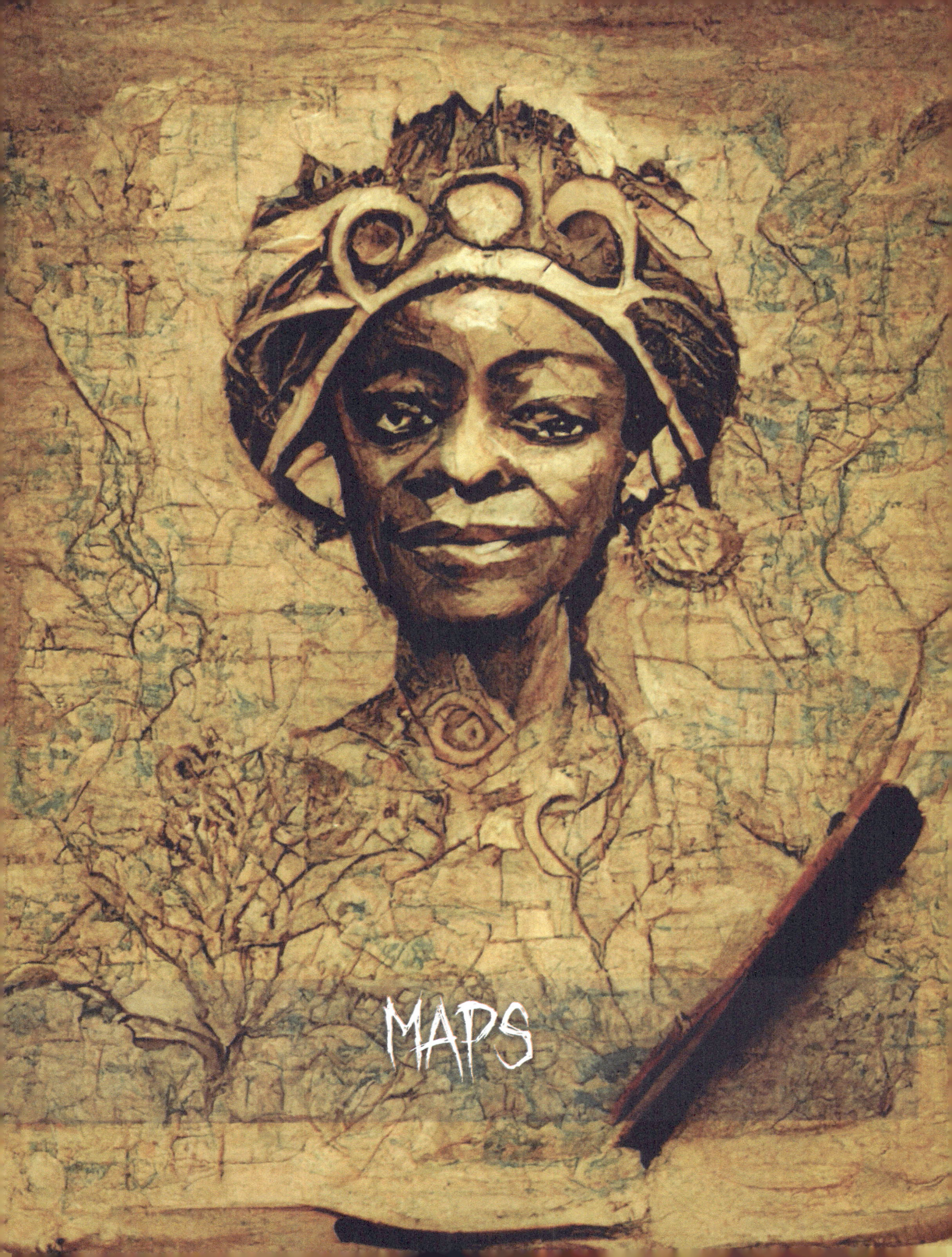

MAPS

MAPS

There are two types of map:

- DM/GM Maps with room names

- Game player maps with no rooms names

In addition, the maps are available in the following formats:

- Color

- Black and White printer friendly version

- Sepia Tone - when testing this game, the teams I worked with LOVE IT when I sent them the Sepia Tone versions of the maps as teasers for game night

MARIE LAVEAU'S ARMY MAP (WITH LABELS)

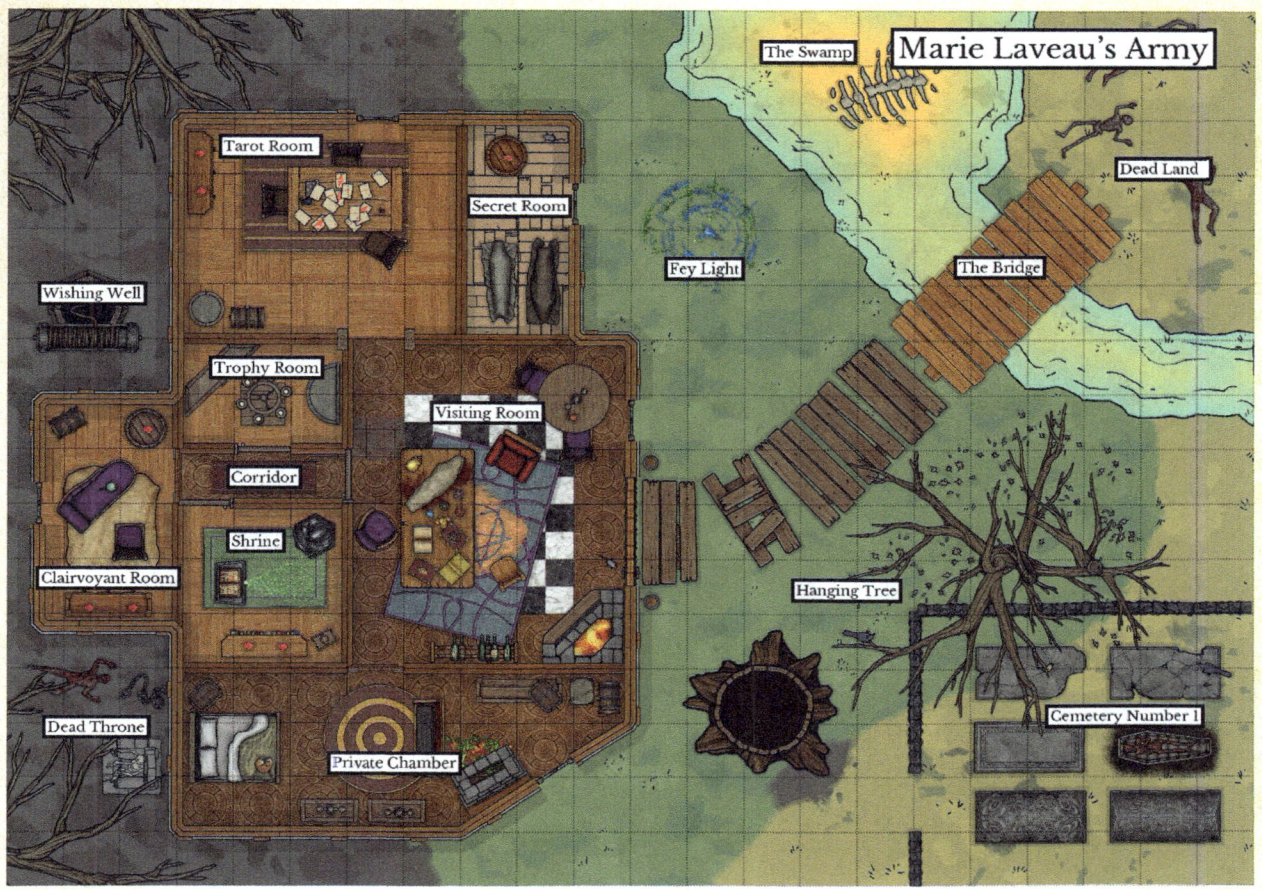

MARIE LAVEAU'S ARMY MAP (WITHOUT LABELS)

Marie Laveau's Army

MARIE LAVEAU'S ARMY MAP (NIGHT)

Marie Laveau's Army

MARIE LAVEAU'S ARMY MAP (PRINTER FRIENDLY)

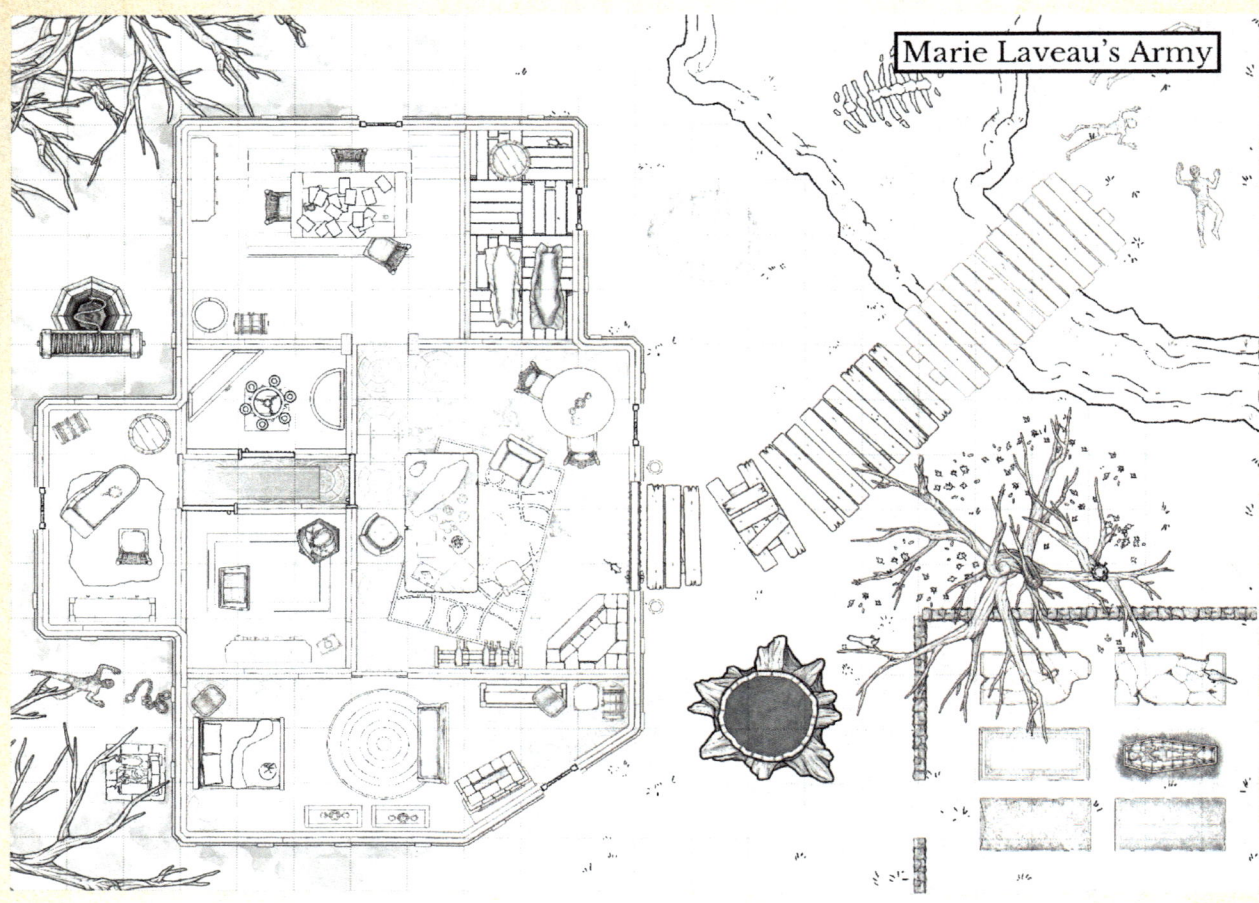

Marie Laveau's Army

MARIE LAVEAU'S ARMY MAP (SEPIA)

THE WEREWOLVES OF LONDON

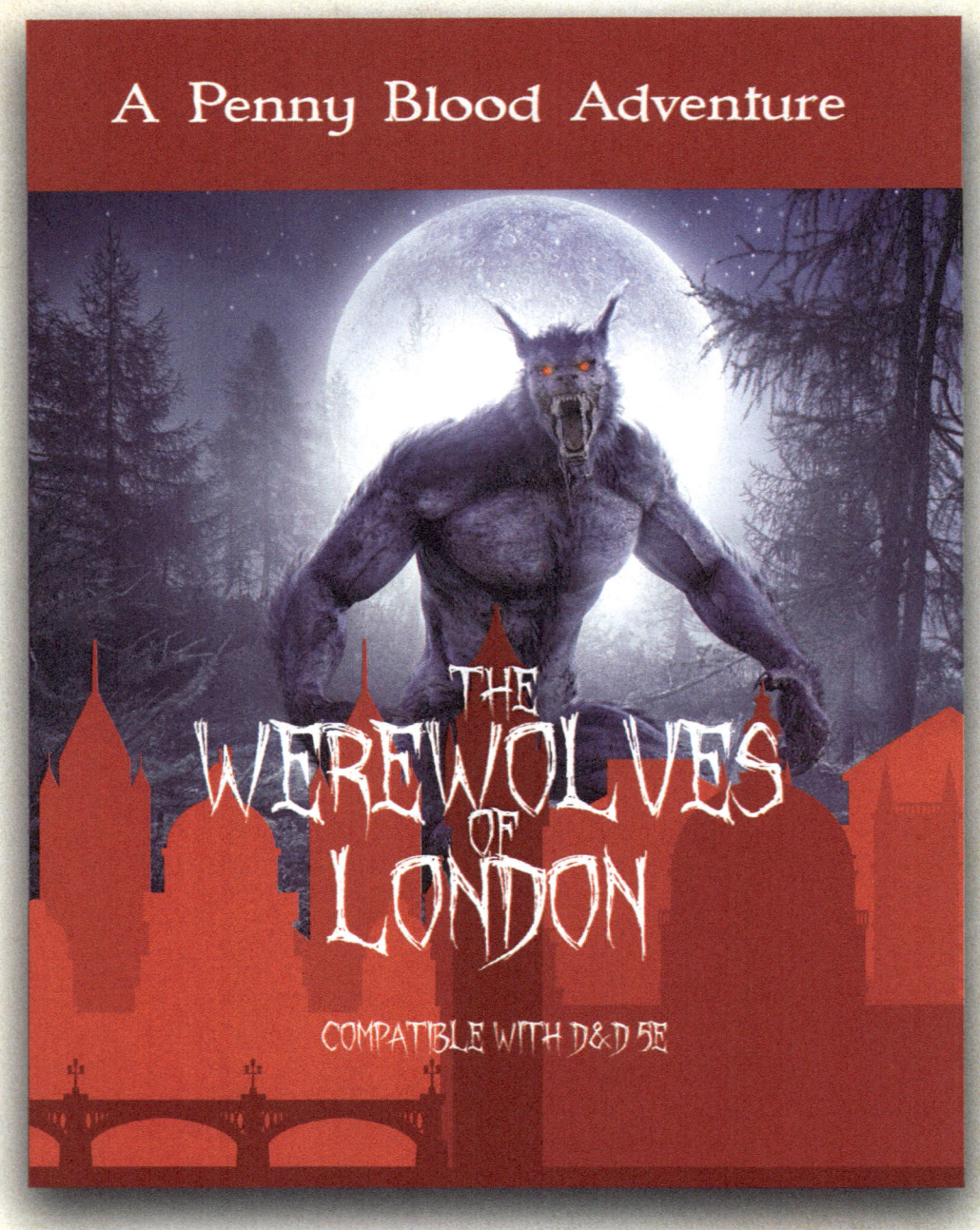

A Penny Blood Adventure

THE WEREWOLVES OF LONDON

COMPATIBLE WITH D&D 5E

THE WEREWOLVES OF LONDON

THE WEREWOLVES OF LONDON

Howling fills the cold night air over Old London Town. A full moon forces men and women to transform into wolves, cats, foxes, and bears. Blood, chaos, and fear hold the city hostage.

The Werewolves of London is a 5E compatible adventure for groups of 2-5 people. The campaign is designed for characters level 1-5 but can be expanded to support characters up to and beyond level 16.

The streets of Old London Town are dangerous. But remember….be the hero in your adventure!

RUNNING THE ADVENTURE

The adventure is written for 5th Edition Dungeons and Dragons. The D&D Player's Handbook will have detailed instructions on how to play.

The monsters, magic herbal remedies, and magic items are unique to this game. Each encounter will have a breakdown of the encounter description and a list of the monsters, traps, magical items, non-player characters, and treasure. Special items are highlighted in bold text.

You should run the game how you like. There are no hard and fast rules for how your players move through the game.

A **Random Encounter** table is located at the end of the adventure to ensure chance encounters happen.

You will see that there are several different versions of the Maps. Maps with a DM in the name are for the Dungeon Master (DM). The DM maps have labels for all the encounters that match the names in this book. The maps without DM can be given to the players. The maps are available in full color, night version (very cool when presented on a large screen TV), printer-friendly (black and white), and Sepia Tone. In addition, there are VTT versions of the maps for online tools such as Roll20.

Finally, the game includes separate cards for the Maps, Monsters, Magic Items, and Non-Player Characters.

STORY HOOK

Three weeks ago, a blood-red ship sailed up the Thames, bringing a curse of perpetual night. The sun will not rise while the ship is docked. Instead, the moon moves through a new phase every fifteen minutes, bringing a new full moon every two hours and Lycan people transform into terrifying beasts.

On board the ship is a group of arrogant Lords and Ladies. Each has the power to change into a Lycan. This pack of were-beasts are known by the name of their ship: Le Sang Rouge. All Lycans have a strong thirst for blood and their blood lust is high! They want to cleanse the land of Selene's Sisters, a Lycan pack living in the Midnight Forest.

These two packs are engaged in a civil war and caught in the middle are The Night Market and Old London Town. Terrified, the Mayor will do anything to stop the werewolves' battle!

PLAYING THE GAME

There are three ways in which GMs/DMs can run the game. They are:

- Selene's Sister: align with the sisterhood
- Le Sang Rouge pack: align with Lords and Ladies of The Red Blood Pack
- Protect the people: align with the Mayor of London

The curse of perpetual night forces the moon to move through each of eight phases every 15 minutes. Every two hours, any Lycan Warrior level 10 or below will lose control and attack anyone near them with Feral Rage as the Full Moon reveals itself. The women of Selene's Sisters want to protect the people of Old London Town, but the lower-level members of their pack cannot control the wild nature of the beasts within their skin.

SELENE'S SISTERS

A pack of Lycan Warriors live in the Midnight Forest as a sisterhood. Nature, peace, and community are their strengths. This group is trying to calm the wild beasts within them and wish to restore the natural order of Day and Night. Just don't get them angry.

They know The Le Sang Rouge must sail to sea and once there,. the curse of perpetual night will be lifted and dawn will rise.

The merchants of the Midnight Market are aligned with Selene's Sisters.

LE SANG ROUGE (THE RED BLOOD)

The pack is comprised of elitist aristocratic Lords and Ladies. The aristocrats live live on a ship whose named Le Sang Rouge. The ship, Le Sang Rouge, is itself cursed and will cause perpetual night wherever it is docked. In addition, the aristocrats intend to create a pure race of Lycanthropes by killing all rogue Lycan Warriors, including the Selene Sisters.

A bank, located in the center of Old London Town, is aligned with Le Sang Rouge.

PROTECT THE PEOPLE

The people of Old London Town and the Midnight Market are living in a constant state of fear. The Le Sang Rouge randomly attack and slaughter the hardworking townsfolk. The younger members of the Selene Sisterhood cannot control their transformations. In full Lycan mode, they must quench their desire for blood.

The mayor is offering a reward to anyone who can eliminate the Lycan threat and restore peace and order to his town.

LYCAN WARRIORS

LYCAN WARRIORS - A WERE-BEAST CLASS

Lycan Warriors have many names: skin-walkers, lycanthropes, were-beasts are just a few. A person who chooses the class of a Lycan Warrior will lead a double life. The Lycan Warrior has three forms that it may take depending on the time of day.

- Daylight form (activated when the sun rises): they will appear as a normal race. The exception is that they may have more facial hair for males, and a longer head of hair for females. Typically, Lycan Warriors will work as farmers, laborers, or any craft where they can be outside.

- Nighttime form (activated when the sun sets): When the sun goes down, A Lycan Warrior will become entranced by the moon and transform into a hybrid animal.

- Hybrid form (activated on lower levels when the sun is setting): A Lycan Warrior can also assume a hybrid form. This form offers the player the benefits of their humanoid and beast mode. Holding the Hybrid form is extremely painful for the player and can only be used by characters that are level 7 and above, and for only 15 minutes before being forced to choose either humanoid or beast mode. Level 20 can hold Hybrid form for 2 hours.

LYCAN BEASTS

There are many different animals you can choose to transform into. Pick from the following table or roll a d6 to randomly determine your form::

1d6	Name	Benefits when you are in beast mode
1	Lycanthrope - Werewolf	Your Intelligence and Strength will increase +2. In addition to the two skills you chose, you automatically have Intimidation (giving you three skills). Claws and sharp teeth are used in each attack. Each attack is 1d6+2+Your Level damage.
2	Lycanale - Werefox	Your Intelligence and Charisma will increase +2. At level 7 you will gain +3 Intelligence and Charisma. At level 15 you will gain +4 Intelligence and Charisma. Claws and sharp teeth are used in each attack. Each attack gains a 1d4+2 Hit Points.
3	Lycangeraki - Werehawk	You gain the ability to fly. The effect is that you can move 120 feet per action. Claws and sharp teeth are used in each attack. Each attack gains a 1d4+2 Hit Points.
4	Lycangat - Werecat	Your Wisdom will increase +2. At level 10 you will gain +3 Wisdom. At level 15 you will gain +4 Wisdom. Claws and sharp teeth are used in each attack. Each attack gains a 1d4+2 Hit Points.
5	Lycantav - Werebull	Your Strength will increase +4, but your Intelligence will decrease by -4. Hooves and razor-sharp horns are used in each attack. Each attack gains a 1d6+Your Level Hit Points.
6	Lycanark - Werebear	You have a keen sense of smell. You will be able to detect any poisons by scent that are within 180 feet. Your Strength will increase +3, but your charisma will decrease by -3. Bite and claws are used in each attack. Each attack gains a 1d8+Your Level Hit Points.

LYCAN WARRIOR LEVEL

The following level table shows how to rank up your PC from Level 1, known as Changing, all the way to the powerful Alpha at Level 20.

Level	Rank Title	Description
1-3	Changeling	At lower levels you have no control over your beast mode. Whenever the moon is out, even during the day, you will shift into your chosen beast form. When the full moon is out, even during the day, you will have an incredible urge to kill. Roll DC 12 Intelligence to control your urges every 15 minutes. A failed roll will cause you to go into an uncontrolled Feral Fury and attack your own party.
4-6	Shape Shifter	Shape shifters have more control over their beast mode. You will only change during the night. When the full moon is out you will have an incredible urge to kill. Roll DC 10 Intelligence to control your urges every full moon. A failed roll will cause you to go into an uncontrolled Feral Fury and attack your own party.
7-10	Skin Walker	You can now control when you turn into beast mode. The exception is a full moon, when you will still lose control and turn into a beast.
11-14	Lycanthrope	You have full control, even during full moon, for when you turn into a beast.
Level 15-19	Noble Beast	You gain +2 Strength on top of your beast mode. You can transform into two types of were beast.
20	Alpha	You are a born leader. You gain +2 Charisma and +3 Strength on top of your beast mode. You can transform into three different types of were-beasts.

HIT POINTS

Hit Dice: 1d12 per level

Hit Points at 1st Level: 12 + your Constitution modifier

Hit Points at Higher Levels: 1d12 (or 7) + your Constitution modifier per level after 1st

PROFICIENCIES

Armor: Natural Armor when in beast form

Weapons: Claws

Tools: None

Saving Throws: Strength, Constitution

Skills: Choose two from Nature, Animal Handling, Athletics, Intimidation, Perception, and Survival

EQUIPMENT

You start with the following equipment in human form, in addition to the equipment granted by your background:

• A Great Axe or a staff with clubbed end

• Two Handed Axe

• Explorers Backpack

When you transition into beast form, you drop any weapons you are holding.

Any time a Lycan Warrior enters a building or cave they will begin to panic. A DC12 Wisdom save will be needed as they enter the space If the save fails, then the Lycanthrope Warrior will panic, start screaming and will do all they can to escape to a place that is open. The Lycanthrope Warrior can make this save again at the end of each turn.

AMULET OF PACK ALLEGIANCE

The Amulet of Pack Allegiance is unique pin worn by each Lycanthrope Warrior pack. The designs for known packs are:

• Selene's Sisters: A silver full moon clasp on their cloaks

• Le Sang Rouge: A blood red stone belt buckle

• The Silver Pride: A silver icicle pin on the left sleeve

• The Desert Manes: An amethyst stone on a large golden ring worn on the center finger of the left hand

• Deadfur: A black gem with a wolf head carving bracelet

Wearers of the Pack Amulet gain +1 Dexterity and +1 Constitution, not to exceed 20 total.

Specials Benefits for Lycan Warriors

FERAL FURY

While using Feral Fury, you gain the following benefits:

- You have advantage on Strength checks and Strength saving throws.

- You have resistance to bludgeoning, piercing, and slashing damage from non-silver, non-magical weapons.

- Feral Fury Damage doubles during a full moon

Feral Fury lasts for 1 minute. It ends early if you are knocked unconscious or if your turn ends and you haven't attacked a hostile creature since your last turn or taken damage since then. You may also end your Fury on your turn as a bonus action.

Once you have used Feral Fury, you must finish a long rest before you can use it again. The number of times you may use Feral Fury is shown on the table below.

Level	Proficiency Bonus	Number of times you use Feral Fury
1-3	2	2
4-6	3	2
7-10	4	3
11-14	5	3
15-19	6	4
20	7	5

LUNA DEFENSE

While you are in full beast mode your armor class equals 12 + your Dexterity modifier + your Constitution modifier. You will not be able to hold a shield or defensive weapon.

LUNA KNOWLEDGE

When you reach Level 4 and again at Level 11 you gain proficiency in one skill of your choice from the list of skills available to you at 1st level.

LUNA WARRIOR

Starting at level 11, during a full moon, you gain an additional Hit Die towards your total Hit Points This can only be maintained for 1 hour. Afterwards, you will need a long rest before you can use the Luna Warrior again.

LUNA RESISTANCE

Resistance to non-magical damage (bludgeoning, slashing, and piercing with non-silvered and no magical damage stacked on normal weapon attacks).

ENCOUNTERS

LOCATIONS AND ENCOUNTERS IN THE WEREWOLVES OF LONDON

The Werewolves of London has four distinct areas where players can go and investigate. The four areas are:

- Old London Town
- The Night Market
- The Midnight Forest
- Le Sang Rouge

Each location has its own set of encounters and a random encounter table.

A silver moon hangs low in the sky over Old London Town. As you look down on the town, you see colorful lights illuminating its famous Night Market and shimmers on the Thames River, which winds its way slowly through the town. Docked at the quay, you recognize the infamous blood-red ship, Le Sang Rouge. On its deck, you can see several crew members moving about and a single guard standing on the top of a gangplank. Howling can be heard to the northeast, coming from the Midnight Forest.

OLD LONDON TOWN

OLD LONDON TOWN

Old London Town is caught between the two Lycan Packs. The Lycan Soldiers from Le Sang Rouge regularly patrol the city streets intimidating the citizens. The Bank is aligned to Le Sang Rouge. The Mad Mage and The Last Drink are neutral. The mayor wants all the Lycans gone but leans toward supporting Selene's Sisters.

Old London Town greets you with the smell of disease and death heavy in the air. On the main street, you can easily make out several buildings: a bank, tavern, several shops and a residence of some import. People are dashing from door to door, furtively watching the patrolling Lycan Soldiers and it seems no one wants to be caught out during this unnatural darkness. This is a town that is under siege.

THE MAD MAGE

Quinn Caskbow is a medical doctor gone slightly mad. He has a taste for tobacco and constantly smokes from a glass pipe. His specialty is selling herbal remedies. The list below shows what you can buy and the effect of the treatment. If the players talk to Quinn, they will learn about Heren, a Moonlight Wyrmling, living in the Midnight Forest. Quinn will tell them about the side quest "Dragon Defense." Quinn buys all his remedies from Baize, one of the Lycans from Selene's Sisters.

Sweetly scented smoke fills the room of the Mad Mage. Quinn Caskbow, a giant of a man standing at six and a half feet, is the owner of this store that specializes in herbal remedies. Quinn's eyes don't quite focus on you, and he looks a little insane.

Remedy	Description	Cost
Fire Cilantro Paste	Use to reduce the impact of a fire burn. Apply to the affected area within 15 minutes of the burn to reduce the Hit Point impact by 5.	10 gp
Poxia Kernel Scrub	Apply to your forehead when you are suffering a curse. The scrub has to remain on your skin for two hours to remove the curse.	50 gp
Venom Clary	A rare tonic to counter the curse of vampirism. Drink the whole bottle as the sun rises.	75 gp
Ivory Mint Paste	Clean teeth and minty breath matter. Scrub this paste on your teeth and rub it off with a stick.	5 sp
Snowy Licorice Smudge Stick	Counter the curse from an undead monster. Close yourself in a small room and burn the smudge stick. The room will fill with a sweet smell. You must stay in the room for four hours.	25 gp
Sea Ginger Glue	Rub the glue onto any wound you have received with a piecing weapon. The glue will bind the skin together and speed up recovery. Apply the glue adds 1d6+2 HP.	10 gp
Dragon Cress Gel	Rub this green, viscous gel over your eyes to gain the ability to see in complete darkness for 1 hour.	15 gp
King's Anise	Eat this root and for 15 minutes those within 20 feet will assume you are a King or Queen and obey your orders.	30 gp
Sirroshell	Suck on a Sirroshell to be able to swim under water for 30 minutes without needing to take a breath.	25 gp
Bane's Wolf Tea	Drink this tea within fifteen minutes of being bitten by a Lycan to remove the curse.	50 gp

MAYOR'S HOUSE

The Mayor, Letholdus Keenseeker, is an overweight man who welcomes you into his home. He will invite the players to join him for dinner.

The mayor's house is a large residence on the main street. He holds out a chubby hand in greeting and warmly welcomes you to his home. Gesturing towards a comfortable living room, he asks if you would like to join him for a meal.

The meal is made from cold-cut meats, slices of bread, and mustard. The mayor knows the people of Old London Town are terrified of the battle between Le Sang Rouge and Selene's Sisters. He wants the Lycanthropes gone and will pay each party member 100 gp to eliminate the threat. He will also tell the players that silver weapons will affect any Lycan Warrior. There is silver to be found throughout the city. John DeGrey, the blacksmith, will turn silver into weapons.

ENCOUNTER - THE MAYOR'S WIFE

If you explore the house, you will meet the mayor's wife, Beatrix Keenseeker, resting in her bedroom. The Mayor's Wife had her one child taken by Le Sang Rouge's pack and killed. Other children have been taken. She will attempt to convince you to complete the side quest "Thrown in the brig." You will need to roll a DC 18 Charisma (Persuasion) check. If you succeed, you can choose whether you want to do the side quest. If you fail, you will be enchanted by the story and are compelled to immediately leave and rescue the children.

THE CLEAN GETAWAY

Old Sadon Commonbrook manages the Clean Getaway, a shop that sells products for adventurers looking for a more exciting life. A Lycan Soldier stands watching over the room from the back corner.

As you enter the Clean Getaway, you see oil lamps of different types haphazardly stuffed on shelves, next to products, and standing on old storage crates. The smell of spice and the old leather fills the room. The main room of the shop is full of gear needed for an adventure. An old man, Sadon Commonbrook, is standing in the center of the room. He is already gesturing to products he sells.

The lock picking set for sale will open the door to the Captain's Cabin on Le Sang Rouge.

The players can attempt to steal items from the store. They will need to roll a DC 15 Dexterity (Sleight of Hand) check. If they succeed, then they slip the item into their pocket. If they fail, Sadon will call for a Lycan Soldier from the street who will grab you and forcefully ask you to pay for the stolen items. The catch: the prices are now double.

Item	Cost
Lock Picking Set	1 gp
Leather Backpack	4 gp
Feather bedroll	2 gp
Green glass bottle	2 gp
Silver bucket	2 gp
10 feet of chain	5 gp
crowbar	2 gp
Grappling hook	2 gp
Hammer	1 gp
Hunting Trap	5 gp
Manacles	2 gp
Oil (in a flask)	1 sp
Role, hemp	1 gp

THE BANK

The bank is a stuffy building with clerks updating books in the back room, a plain greeting room for customers, the Bank manager's Office (where the bank manager, Bucna Zizro, works), and the vault room. Players completing the side quest, Show Me The Money, will have to get to the vault room. The bank is aligned with Le Sang Rouge.

The bank exudes the odor of efficiency with a distinct lack of emotion. There are three doors leading away from the main customer room. The first is to the bank manager's Office. Inside can be seen Bucna Zizro reviewing his books. A second leads to a strong room where the Vault is located. The final door opens to the clerks' room, where three men are busily updating the bank's records.

Bucna Zizro is the bank manager. He is a stern high elf being blackmailed by Le Sang Rouge. Bucna will report any person who is defying Le Sang Rouge. Hidden in the vault room is a Lycantav (Werebull) guard who Bucna reports to.

Encounter - The Strong Room

A DC 15 Stealth check is needed to sneak into the Strong Room successfully. A failure will alert the Lycantav (Werebull), which will come out of the storeroom and attack the players. If the players are successful, they will have an opportunity to open the Vault. The Vault is enchanted. If a player touches the tumbler on the safe, the safe will demand the answer to a riddle. The players will need to answer three riddles for the safe to open. The players have three chances to answer each riddle. Failing to answer all three riddles within 15 minutes or giving three wrong answers will trigger an alarm system. The Lycantav (Werebull) will charge into the vault room and attack.

Choose from three riddles from the following list:

1d6	Riddle	Answer
1	What begins, but has no end, yet ends all that begins?	Death
2	No legs have I to dance, no lungs have I to breathe, no life have I to live or die and yet I do all three. What am I?	Fire
3	Nobody wants me, yet nobody wants to lose me. What am I?	A lawsuit
4	I have rivers without fish and roads without wagons, deserts without heat and snowy lands without cold, mountains without height and canyons without depth. What am I?	A map
5	What has a head but never weeps, has a bed but never sleeps, can run but never walks, and has a bank but no money?	A river
6	What is put on a table, cut, but never eaten?	A pack of cards

If the players succeed, the door opens, revealing 15 silver ingots, with each bar worth 100 gp.

THE LAST DRINK

Xolog, a half-orc, is the innkeeper. He laughs, tells long stories, and lies profusely to his customers. The inn has two upstairs bedrooms that cost 2 gp per night and include breakfast. The main downstairs room is where the bar is. The only drink you can buy is a red ale called Autumn Horn which costs 5sp per mug. The ale is light in flavor and alcohol (probably due to it being watered down). Behind the bar is a storage area with several barrels of Autumn Horn.

Loud laughter greets you as you step into the smoke-filled main room of the notorious tavern, "The Last Drink". Behind the bar is a tall half-orc pulling pints, telling stories, and trying his best to swindle every patron that enters his establishment. There is a table in the corner with a lone person nursing his beer. He eyes you suspiciously as enter. At the counter, a small group of patrons are playing a dice game.

There are two groups in the room. Three people are sitting at the bar, and one is sitting at the table.

ENCOUNTER - SHOW ME THE MONEY

If you join the lone person sitting at the table, Xolog will come and join you. Roll DC 10 Persuasion check, and Xolog will tell you that he and his partner are planning on stealing the silver from The Bank. Xolog will split the money from the heist 50:50 if you join him. See the Side Quest "Show Me The Money" for additional details.

ENCOUNTER - CHASE THE WOLF

The people sitting at the bar are playing "Chase the Wolf," a dice game. See the instructions for "Chase the Wolf" in the section on "Game within a Game."

Each person must pay 2 gp to play the game. The money is put in a pot in the center of the table. The winner receives half of the winnings. The other half is used to buy the next round of beers.

THE NIGHT MARKET

The Night Market is where you buy items, eat food, try your luck on a game, and find information. The Night Market is crowded with people as they go from stall to stall. Light is provided by lamps hung around the market.

Burning torches illuminate the Night Market and several shops and stalls catch your eyes, and noses, as you enter. A potion shop, food vendors and weapons shop are the most notable. People move from one stand to the next, buying items, chatting with friends, and eating food. This seems like the one place that is safe in this strange world of perpetual night.

EDUCATED BLADE

Rose Writingham runs the Educated Blade. She and her two servants teach people how to be more proficient with their weapons.

A lean, half-elf woman holding two short swords is talking to people in front of the Educated Blade. She has two servants teaching people how to be more effective with their weapons. A sign lists the weapons and skill level Rose can teach.

Below is a table of the classes you can take, how long the course runs, the damage bonus you will gain with the weapon, and the price for the lesson.

Lesson	Length of Class	Damage Bonus	Price
Dagger Skills	10 mins	1	4 gp
Intermediate Dagger	20 mins	2	8 gp
Dagger Master	1 hrs.	4	24 gp

Short-sword Skills	15 mins	1	5 gp
Intermediate Short sword	30 mins	2	10 gp
Short-sword Master	2 hrs.	4	40 gp
Axe Skills	15 mins	2	10 gp
Intermediate Axe	30 mins	4	20 gp
Axe	2 hrs.	8	80 gp
Short-sword Skills	15 mins	1	5 gp
Intermediate Short sword	30 mins	2	10 gp
Short-sword Master	2 hrs.	4	40 gp
Archer Skills	15 mins	1	5 gp
Intermediate Archer	30 mins	2	10 gp
Archer Master	2 hrs.	4	40 gp

THE BEGGING TRIBUTE

The Begging Tribute is a place where you can buy soup. The stand's owner is Orros Sayur Jelen Merwor, an older Gnome who prides himself on the quality of the soup he sells.

The Begging Tribute is a great little stand selling different types of soup. A small Gnome is managing the crowd around his stand where it's delicious smells fill the air. Standing on a box in the crowd is a man flexing his muscles. He has a sign in front of him that reads: Test your strength with Hudson the Hound! Can you catch a cannonball? Toss the cannonball back and forth with Hudson the Hound. The first to drop the ball will win a free bowl of Beef Stew. 1 sp to play the game.

There are four types of soup:

Soup	Price
Chicken and Dumpling	1 sp
Beef Stew	8 sp
Potato and Leak	7 cp
Beer Cheese	5 sp

ENCOUNTER - CANNON BALL TOSS

The rules for Cannon Ball Toss are in the section "Game within a Game."

There are two ways to play Cannonball Toss: with Dice or with a bean bag. If you win, you get a bowl of amazing Beef Stew (or you can choose a vegetarian option, too). The soup is delicious, and Hudson the Hound congratulates you with a hearty smack on the back. If you lose, Hudson the Hound will roar with triumph. He will grab you in his beefy arms and pull a thick paintbrush from his back pocket. Across your forehead, Hudson will pain a large, black "L" in tar. He will take a handful of feathers from his other pocket and pat them into the tar. It will take a whole day for the tar and feathers to fall off.

THE GLOWING POT

Gamal Smeltmaster, a scarred hill dwarf, manages The Glowing Pot. The booth looks like it sells cheap potions. The potions can be purchased, but each tincture has a high failure rating. For the potion to work, the

player must roll 1d4 and score a 4. What can I say? These are nasty potions sold by a cheap, ugly hill dwarf.

A terrifying-looking hill dwarf is scowling from behind a table at The Glowing Pot. In front of the dwarf is a collection of potion bottles. Some bottles are cracked, and others have strange fungus on the bottle stoppers. There is a sheet of paper with the prices for each potion.

Potion	Effect	Price
Potion of Good Health	Drinking the potion can restore 5 hit points	50 gp
Potion of Climbing	For one hour you can climb any object or wall as the same speed as your walking pace	180 gp
Potion of Bad Breath	Use your bonus action to breathe fire at a target within 30 feet. The target takes 3d8 fire damage or half on a successful DC 12 Dexterity saving throw. The potion can only be used once.	150 gp
Potion of the Hero	Instantly gain 10 Hit Points. Can only be used once.	180 gp
Potion of Water Walking	For 30 minutes you will be able to walk on water as if you are walking on solid ground.	100 gp
Potion of the Lycan	For 1 hour you can transform into a Lycan and gain its abilities.	220 gp
Potion of Lunacy	Drinking the potion will give you the ability to transform into any Lycan creature and gains its benefits for five attack rounds. After the fifth round you will return to your normal form but will be exhausted from the effort of the transformation. You will immediately collapse into a deep sleep, and you will not be able to wake for 6 hrs.	125 gp

Rolling a DC 8 Persuasion check and Gamal will tell you that that store is a front for animal fights behind his store. You can follow him and join the crowd of people betting on two juvenile cockatrices that will battle in a small, dirty ring.

ENCOUNTER - JUVENILE COCKATRICE FIGHT

Each player can bet on one of the Juvenile Cockatrices. Each bet is 5 gp. If you win, you receive 10 gp. One bird has a blue bib, and the other has a red one. The DM will represent one of the birds, and a player can represent the other bird.

Each player must have a 20-sided die. Both players roll their dice at the same time. The player with the highest score wins 5 points. The goal is to reach 25 points. Here are the exceptions:

- If both players roll the same number, both birds are stunned and lose 5 points.

- If a player rolls a 1, then it is sudden defeat (unless the other player rolls a one, when both birds are stunned and lose five points)

- If a player rolls a 20, then it is a sudden win (unless the other player rolls a twenty, when both birds are stunned and lose five points)

After each game, a new set of Juvenile Cockatrices is brought out. Five matches can be played in a row, after which Gamal Smeltmaster will close the illegal animal fight for four hours.

NICK'S KNACKS

A female Gnome stands in front of her stand. Her name is Wixlee, but her friends call her Nick. It's apparently a long story about why she has the nickname, but she will not tell anyone. Her table is filled with antiques and tokens that can be bought.

An old sign reading "Nick's Knacks", clearly bad word play, hangs over a cheaply decorated stand cluttered with antiques. In front of the stand is a short, grumpy gnome. She is not happy working the Night Market and is clearly bored.

If you roll a DC 12 Persuasion check, you will be able to get information about the Le Sang Rouge pack from Wixlee. She will tell you the following:

- Le Sang Rouge's pack killed her husband shortly after they arrived.

- The ship itself is cursed. The curse of the perpetual night will be removed if it can be sailed down the Thames and into the English Channel.

- Silver weapons have an extra effect on Lycans.

- The lock-picking set she sells will open the ship's door to the Captain's Cabin.

Wixlee will sell you the following items:

Item	Cost
Lock Picking Set	1 gp
Parchment detailing Lycans	2 gp
A mug with an embossed silver crown	1 gp
A Lycan Bestiary	40 sp
A damaged healers kit (the kit is all there, but the box is looking very knocked around)	4 gp
A green lantern	3 gp
A silver mirror	15 gp
A bag of clothes (only about half will fit the buyer)	3 gp
A silver signal whistle	5 sp
A box of rings of different sizes	Small rings - 5 sp
	Medium rings - 1 gp
	Large rings - 5 gp
Lunar Control Staff (see Magic Items below)	50 gp

JOHN'S SMITH

John deGrey runs the blacksmith. His specialty is forging silver weapons for anyone who wants to battle a Lycan.

The glow of a hot fire and the sound of a banging hammer come from John's Smith. John deGrey is the Blacksmith and is hard at work forging a new sword.

You will need to give John silver that can be turned into a weapon and pay him for his time. The following chart will show you the weapons he can create, the amount of silver required, the cost of the labor, the time it will take, and the effect the weapon will have on a Lycan.

Weapon	Cost	Amount of Silver Required to make the Weapon	Time to make the weapon	Damage to a Lycan (the modifier for Lycan damage is after the "+")
Silver Club	5 gp	2 pounds	1 hour	1d4+2 bludgeoning
Silver Dagger	20 gp	1 pound	15 minutes	1d4+2 piercing
Silver Quarterstaff	10 gp	4 pounds	1 hour	1d6+4 bludgeoning
Silver Short sword	40 gp	2 pounds	1 hour	1d6+2 piercing
Silver Arrows	1 gp each	0.1 pounds	10 minutes per arrow	1d4+1 piercing
Silver Axe	40 gp	4 pounds	2 hours	1d8+4 slashing
Silver Net	10 gp	3 pounds	1 hour	Entangles victim. If Lycan, they will not be able to attack for two rounds.

THE CURLY LEMON

Hard Lemonade is sold by Snak Laughingfang, a 62-year-old female orc, at her stand, The Curly Lemon.

A laughing crowd surrounds The Curly Lemon. A tall, muscular female orc is laughing with her patrons and handing out shot glasses of a yellow liquid. She sees you and beckons you to join the party.

The Hard Lemonade is very strong and will undoubtedly make your tail curl. The Lemonade is sold in shots that each cost 3 sp. Snak has already had too much to drink of her own product. A successful DC 10 Charisma (Persuasion) check, and Snak will tell you how to find Selene's Sister, the Lycans who live in the Midnight Forest.

Find the recipe for the drink sold at The Curly Lemon in the section named "Food and Fuel."

CHARMED

Ariana Duststone will tell your fortune for the price of 5 gp.

A small woman, dressed in a flowing blood red skirt and a blouse covered with stars and moons, sits waiting to tell you your fortune. Her name is Ariana Duststone, and she has sparkling blue eyes. In her hand, she cradles the Penny Blood Paper Fortune teller. A small sign hanging from her tent reads 5 gp to know your future. She beckons you over.

ENCOUNTER - PENNY BLOOD PAPER FORTUNE

See the section "Making your own Penny Blood Paper Fortune" to have the players pick their own fortune.

LE SANG ROUGE

The arrogant nobles looking to enslave Old London Town and eliminate Selene's Sisterhood, live on the blood red ship, Le Sang Rouge. The ship itself is cursed for wherever it docks, perpetual night will fall on the surrounding area. The perpetual night gives the Lycans commanding the ship the ability to easily transform and hunt their prey.

A blood red ship is docked at the quay. This ship is the Le Sang Rouge and is home to an elite group of aristocratic Lycan Warriors. There is constant movement of soldiers and nobles on the deck. A tall, confident man walks among them. He is Prince Aethelwulf from Germany. He is accompanied by Lord Darion, from Britain, and Lady Adelina from France. The three are the leaders of Le Sang Rouge. They hunt, they devour, and they command.

If the players are looking to sail Le Sang Rouge away from the dock, they will need to do the following:

- Pull up the anchor (this will require a successful DC 15 Strength check)
- Find a map in Captain's Cabin that shows how to sail down the Thames
- Using the Helm, sail the ship down the Thames for one hour before reaching the English Channel (use the random encounter table every 30 minutes)
- Scuttle the ship.
- Figure out how to escape without dying.

THE DECK

The deck of Le Sang Rouge can be accessed from a gangplank that leads away from Old London Town. A DC 15 Stealth check will be needed if a player wants to sneak onto the ship via the gangplank. A DC 15 Acrobatics or Athletics check will be needed if a player wants to swim through the water and climb the anchor's chain. A failure for either attempt will alert the 1d4+1 Lycan Soldiers who will attack.

A gangplank leads up to the deck of Le Sang Rouge. One soldier stands guard at the top of the gangway. On the deck are barrels, boxes and crates. Each side of the deck has three gold cannons with stacks of silver cannon balls nearby.

Towards the stern there is a doorway, flanked by two windows. Another pair of doors are under the forecastle. Two sets of stairs line the port and starboard sides of the ship leading to the quarterdeck and helm at the stern, and the forecastle at the bow. A brass helm is at the center of the deck.

The gold cannons each weigh 300 pounds and are worth 1,000 gp each. Each cannon ball is made from solid silver and weighs 10 pounds. The silver for each cannon ball is worth 50 gp. There are 1d4+3 cannonballs near each cannon.

The boxes on the deck contain raw meat that is dripping with blood. This is food for the crew. The barrels contain either red wine or water. The red wine is potent and humans and halflings will become drunk after two glasses. Drunk players are loud (Disadvantage to all Dexterity checks) and move at half speed. This effect lasts for 1 hour.

ENCOUNTER - LYCAN SOLDIERS

1d4+1 Lycan Soldiers will attack. Each soldier is a Level 4 Lycanthrope Warrior. If there is a full moon, the Soldiers will transform into their beast mode (the DM can determine the beast mode for each soldier). If the full moon is not out, then the soldiers will attack as trained military men.

THE CAPTAIN'S CABIN

The Captain's Cabin is locked. Two thick ropes hang on either side of the door frame. Two players will be needed to pull the ropes at the same time and roll a successful DC 15 Strength. If they are successful, they will hear a bolt unlock and the door swings open. A failed attempt will keep the door locked.

The door to the captain's cabin is shut. Two ropes hand from either side of the doorframe. An ornate lock is centered on the door. Glass in the door shows that two people are talking inside the cabin.

Inside the Captain's Cabin will be found Prince Aethelwulf and Lord Darion. The prince is charismatic and will try to convince the players to join his pack. This is a contested saving throw pitting Aethelwulf's Persuasion vs. the characters Insight or Perception. Failing the save, you are compelled to offer your arm to the prince at which point he will bite you and you will be infected with Lycan poison. A Remove Curse spell or similar magic item used within 30 minutes will eliminate the Lycan poison. Anyone bitten by the prince will have an overwhelming desire to join his pack and must roll a DC25 Constitution save. On a failed save, the character will head back to Le Sang Rouge and become a pack member. A character may roll again once every 24 hours or whenever they take damage.

ENCOUNTER - PRINCE AETHELWULF AND LORD DARION

Prince Aethelwulf is a Level 20 Alpha and Lord Darion is Level 15 Noble Beast. They will transform into their Lycan forms if attacked.

The captain's cabin has many treasures hidden in boxes in the room. They include:

- A map showing the Thames flowing into the English Channel

- A small box of treasure (5 pp, 250 gp, 500 sp)

- A full meal on the table - roast pork, vegetables and white wine. Eating the food will restore 1d4 hit points for each player.

THE BRIG

Three children have been captured and are being held in the Brig. If you are doing the side quest "Thrown in the Brig" then you can attempt to rescue the children. If you are not doing the side quest, then the players can question the children. They will find out that Lady Adelina has kidnapped each child and is planning on changing them all in to Lycan Warriors.

A squalid smell comes from the Brig as you step in. As your eyes adjust to the darkness you see three children shackled to the floor with ankle chains holding them together. They look tired and exhausted.

ENCOUNTER - ANKLE CHAINS OF DEFEAT

The ankle chains holding the children has two effects. The first is that their movement will be ⅓ of normal speed. The second is that the children will act defeated. They will complain and try to convince you that they are all just going to die. A DC 15 Dexterity check will unlock the chains. The chains can then be removed. Once the chains have been removed, the children will brighten up and move at normal speed. The charm on the chain is only in effect when the chains are locked.

THE MIDNIGHT FOREST

The Midnight Forest is the home of Selene's Sisters, a Moonlight Wyrmling dragon named Heren, and a massive observation tower.

You enter the Midnight Forest. The moonlight illuminates the autumnal trees with silver hued reds, golds, and browns. In the distance, you see a wooden tower rising into the sky. Sparkling silver light can be seen twinkling deep in the undergrowth and, to the north, you hear the howling of wolves. But this sound is different. The howls are pitched together. Almost as if the wolves are singing.

SILVER HOARD

Deep in the Midnight Forest is a Moonlight Wyrmling dragon who goes by the name of Heren. Heren will be found near her small hoard of silver coins. While Heren is young, she already possesses some of the skills of a Moonlight Dragon.

Hidden beneath the fallen autumn leaves can be seen the glinting of silver. Lying on a small hoard of silver is a silver colored Wyrmling.

Players can roll a DC 10 Charisma check, and, on a success, Heren will give the players a portion of Moon Sight to see into the future. The cost for the Moon Sight potion is either 100 SP or any silver object the players have. Moon Sight can be used only once during play. The potion can be used at the start of any encounter. The DM will whisper into the ear of the player who uses Moon Sight what will happen in the encounter.

ENCOUNTER - MOONLIGHT WYRMLING

Players can choose to steal Heren's hoard. If they do this, Heren will defend her hoard. In addition, she will call out a Lycangat (Werecat) from the Selene Sisterhood. The Lycangat will join Heren in guarding the silver hoard. Heren has 500 sp, a silver dagger (see Magic Items) and 50 gp in her hoard.

OBSERVATION TOWER

The observation tower climbs five stories above the canopy of the Midnight Forest. If the players choose to climb the building, they can see the autumnal colors of the forest spread below them.

Deep in the forest rises a massive Observation Tower. The tower is five stories high. Each level has a deck with an old ladder that takes up to the next floor.

ENCOUNTER - ROTTEN LADDER

There are five levels to the Observation Tower. Each level has a rotten ladder that takes you to the next level. A DC 12 Strength or Dexterity check will be needed to climb to the next level successfully. If you are successful, you can rise to the next level. Each level will give the player an opportunity to look down on the forest and potentially towards the Thames River. The chart below shows the radius, in feet, the player can see at each level.

1d20	Radius
1-5	20 feet
6-10	40 feet
11-15	60 feet
15-19	80 feet
20	The whole map

If the player fails a roll, they will fall off the ladder. The higher up you are, the more hit points you will suffer when falling:

Level	Damage
1	Bruised Ego. You fall, land on your bum and get up with a sheepish smile on your face.
2	Your landing is much harder, and you feel the wind being knocked out of you. 2 hit points damage.
3	You fall and you hear a snap. Your wrist is broken. It will take one week before you will heal naturally. Roll 1d4 hit point damage.
4	You fall and your leg gets caught in the frame of the tower as you fall. You hear a clear snap before hitting the ground. It will take two weeks before you can use your leg. Roll 1d4+4 hit point damage.
5	Concussion. You are knocked out for three hours. In addition, one arm and one leg are now broken. Roll 1 d6+4 hit point damage.

SELENE'S SISTERS' CAMP

Selene's Sisters live in the forest. Their camp is where they meet, meditate and attempt to heal those inflicted with the curse of Lycan Warriors class.

A large wood-burning fire is blazing in the center of a camp. There is a scattering of tents. Two women and a girl can be seen sitting by the fire. They are singing, and the sound is beautiful.

Selene's Sisters have learned the art of control over their lycanthropic form. Singing does soothe the savage beast. While the sisters are singing, they will remain in humanoid form. The three sisters are:

- Sierra: a level 1 Lycanthrope Warrior, a Changeling. Sierra is a twelve-year-old girl recently bitten by a Le Sang Rouge werewolf. She transforms into Lycanale - Werefox.

- Baize: a level 8 Lycanthrope Warrior, a Skin Walker. She is the oldest member of the group. She can transform into Lycanark - Werebear.

- Celiac: a level 18 Lycanthrope Warrior, a Noble Beast. She is middle-aged and tough. She can transform into Lycangat - Werecat, and Lycanthrope - Werewolf.

The lunar god, Selene, watches over her Sisterhood. A 25ft magical perimeter on the campfire will trigger if anyone walks into the camp. If the trap is triggered, then the sisters will stop singing. When they stop singing, the DM will need to check the phase of the moon. Sierra will lose control of the curse flowing in her blood and will transform into a Lycanale and attack the players.

If the players choose to attack the Sisterhood, two things will happen:

- Each sister will transform and attack

- A fourth Sister hiding in the woods will change, join her fraternity, and attack. She is in Lycangat (Werecat) form.

The party can also choose to talk with the Sisters. Sierra will still attack, and they must reduce her hit points to 1, knocking her unconscious. The party needs to roll DC 14 Persuasion checks to calm the sisters down. When they talk, the sisters will tell them that they are being hunted by Le Sang Rouge. The Sisters will also tell them that they learned how to control the wild beasts locked within their bodies through their songs. The perpetual night means that the three Sisters must always sing. They believe the source of the curse is the ship Le Sang Rouge. Find and destroy the cursed ship to restore

the regular day and night cycle and help Selene's Sisters and bring peace to the Midnight Forest.

ENCOUNTER: SELENE'S SILVER FLAME

The moon is watching over her Sisterhood. The trap is triggered when anyone steps within 25 feet radius of Selene's Sisters' campfire, the center of the camp. Silver fire erupts and forms a cone aimed at the players.

Effect: Targets all creatures within a 20 ft. cone, DC 18 Dexterity save or take 55 (10d10) fire damage

Trigger: Selene, the moon goddess, is watching her Sisterhood and will trigger the Silver Flame whenever anyone steps into the campsite.

Countermeasures: A detect magic spell or similar magic item will reveal that Selene centered the trap around the campfire. A successful dispel magic (DC 18) disables the trap. Selene will smile on you and let you walk into the camp.

SIDE QUESTS

SIDE QUESTS

As the DM, you can introduce the following side quests at any time in the game.

SHOW ME THE MONEY

Silver is in short supply. The only exception is the bank. The central bank has a reserve of 15 silver ingots, with each ingot worth 100 gp. The objective of the quest to break into the bank, find the ingots and get away. Later, the ingots can be melted down to make weapons.

DRAGON DEFENSE

A young Moonlight Dragon Wyrmling, named Heren, lives in the forest. Heren has a small silver hoard where she sleeps. The old people of the city frequently visit Heren, who sings to them and can provide temporary relief from aches and pains. The Wyrmling is beloved by the people. Your quest is to find Heren and protect her from Le Sang Rouge pack who are hunting her. Protect Heren and she will give you half of her silver hoard, worth 500 sp and 50 gp.

THROWN IN THE BRIG

The leaders of Le Sang Rouge are cruel. Their cruelty is defined by the children they have kidnapped and are holding in the Brig of their ship. Each child is being kept as future Lycan Warrior. The objective of this quest is to find the children and rescue them. Be careful no one gets bitten or infected. Save the children and return them to the mayor's wife and you will receive a silver coated weapon from John's Smith for each child returned. The weapons include daggers, swords, club and shield. In addition, the Mayor's Wife will give you a Silver Moon Necklace (see Magic Items).

RANDOM ENCOUNTERS

RANDOM ENCOUNTER

Roll a 1d6 for a Random Encounter.

OLD LONDON TOWN RANDOM ENCOUNTER TABLE

Below are random encounters for players walking up and down the streets:

1d6	Encounter
1	A black horse ridden by Prince Aethelwulf gallops through the streets. Roll DC 12 Dexterity to avoid the horse. Otherwise, the horse clips you with its hoof inflicting 3-hit point damage.
2	You bump into one of the town's people. They will tell you the names of each building.
3	Cloud cover hides the moon for 1 hour.
4	A window opens above you, and the homeowner throws out a bucket of garbage. Each party member must roll 1 1d20.

1-5: the bucket is full of piss and shit. The player is covered. The smell is so strong that anyone will smell them within 20 feet. The aroma lasts until they wash.

6-15: old table scraps fall on the player. You spend a couple of minutes picking it out of your hair.

16-19: a cheese, wrapped in cloth, falls to your feet. The cheese is the equivalent of one meal.

20: silver coins are accidentally in the garbage. Roll 1d4+2 to determine the number of coins.

1d6	Encounter
5	A full moon appears out of phase. All Lycan in your group will transform and attack the group with Feral Fury.
6	A patrol of 1d4+1 Lycan Soldiers step out of a side alley. They have been watching you for a while. If the players are aligned with Le Sang Rouge, then the Lycan Soldiers will cheer the team on. If not, then the Lycan Soldiers will attack.

THE NIGHT MARKET RANDOM ENCOUNTER TABLE

Below are random encounters for players in the Night Market:

1d6	Encounter
1	A brash man, Lord Darion walks into the Night Market. If the players engage with him, they will need to roll as DC 14 Charisma check. If successful, Lord Darion will tell the players about the goal for a pure race Le Sang Rouge is looking to achieve and ask for help. If unsuccessful, Lord Darion will laugh in the faces of the players, turn and leave the Night Market.
2	You bump into one of the town's people. They will tell you the names of each stand in the Night Market.
3	Cloud cover hides the moon for 1 hour.
4	A Lycan Soldier, drunk on liquor from the Curley Lemon, stumbles into the Players and attacks.
5	The players see a cloaked person moving through the Night Market. It is Celiac, the leader of Selene's Sisters. If the players want to talk to her, they can roll DC 14 Charisma. If successful, Celiac will tell the players about the Sisterhood and ask for their help. If unsuccessful, Celiac will walk away and disappear into the crowd.
6	Cloud cover evaporates and reveals a full moon. All Lycan in your group will transform and attack the group with Feral Fury.

LE SANG ROUGE RANDOM ENCOUNTER TABLE

The ship is busy, and encounters can happen any time. Use the following Random Encounter table to determine a random encounter every 30 minutes.

1d6	Encounter
1	The full moon comes out. Any person with you who is a Lycan Warrior Level 1-10 will transform into their Lycan beast.
2	The wind picks up and rocks the ship. A barrel rolls over. Roll DC 12 Dexterity to avoid the barrel. Fail, and the barrel rolls over your foot, crushing the bones (5 hit points). You will walk with a limp for the rest of the session, until healed or until you have had a long restand your speed is reduced by 50%.
3	A soldier sees you and wants to know what you are doing. Roll DC 10 Charisma. Fail, and the soldier will transform into a Lycanale / Werefox and attack.
4	You discover a box embossed with a silver wolf head. Opening the box reveals a silver necklace with a silver six pointed star. This is the Lunathrope, a necklace that transforms Lycans into their human form. The necklace has a 30 foot radius around the wearer that forces the Lycans to keep their human shape.
5	The soldiers on the deck suddenly stand to attention. As one, they raise their heads to the night, transforming in their beast form and howling at the moon. After a minute they transform back into humans and continue working.
6	Lady Adelina discovers you. She sees you all for what you are: food! She transforms and attacks!

THE MIDNIGHT FOREST RANDOM ENCOUNTER TABLE

The forest is large and random encounters can happen. Roll 1d6 for an unexpected encounter.

1d6	Encounter
1	You come across a patch of mushrooms. Eating the mushrooms will restore 2 Hit Points and heal any broken bones.
2	You hear howling to your south.
3	A Lycanark (Werebear) clearly from the Le Sang Rouge pack, attacks.
4	Clouds cover the night sky and complete darkness falls. If you have darkvision then you will be able to keep moving at a normal pace. If you do not, then your movement will be reduced to ⅓ of normal speed. The cloud will pass after 15 minutes.
5	You come across a small box lying on the ground. If you open it, you will find a silver figurine of a wolf worth 85 sp.
6	You meet a young woman. She is a member of the Selene Sisterhood. If she is in human form, she will help you find the Sisters. If the full moon is out, then she will transform into a werewolf and attack.

RESOLUTION

CALM THE BEAST

Selene's Sisterhood, located in the midnight forest, wants to calm the wild beast within and the perpetual night with its rapid changes in the lunar cycle make this impossible. To calm the beast, the players must remove the curse of Le Sang Rouge. To do this, the players must sail the ship down the Thames and out to the English Channel. Once in the Channel, the players must sink the ship.

The reward you will receive is:

- Power of the Beast: the potion, which can only be used once, will give you the ability to transform into a were-creature of your choice for one attack

- The Cybil Blade: a silver blade you can use to attack dealing double damage to were-creatures and the undead.

- 25 gp per person

PURITY

Le Sang Rouge pack has one goal: eradicate the Midnight Forest pack. Join the Le Sang Rouge in cleansing London and the forest and establishing a pure race. For this, you will receive:

- Gentry: The title of Lord of Lady and a regular income of 100 gp per month

- Liquor of the Beast: The choice to consume a potent potion that will transform you into a were-creature every full moon

- The Hallec Horn: blow the Hallec Horn, and one member of the Le Sang Rouge will come to your aid. It will take one full day for that member to join you, and they will only stay for one day.

LIBERATE OLD LONDON TOWN

Caught in between the warring packs are the people of London. The mayor wants both groups to be gone. Use any means necessary to force both packs to leave the area of Old London Town and the Night Market. If players are successful, then each player will receive the following reward:

- 100 gp per person

- The key to Old London Town: whenever you are in a town, you can show the key and will be granted free room and board for if you stay.

- Celebration party: a big party will be held in your honor

MONSTERS
LYCAN SOLDIER

Medium humanoid (human), chaotic evil

Armor Class 11 in humanoid form, 12 (natural armor) in wolf or hybrid form

Hit Points 58 (9d8 + 18)

Speed 40 ft.

STR	DEX	CON	INT	WIS	CHA
15 (+2)	13 (+1)	14 (+2)	10 (+0)	11 (+0)	10 (+0)

Skills Perception +4

Damage Immunities bludgeoning, piercing, and slashing from nonmagical attacks not made with silvered weapons

Senses passive Perception 14

Languages Common (can't speak in wolf form)

Challenge 3 (700 XP)

Shapechanger. The Lycan Soldier is a Shapeshifter-level Lycan Warrior. They remain in hybrid mode between wolf and humanoid. At full moon it must quench its thirst for blood and kill with Feral Fury. The Lycan Soldier reverts to its humanoid form if it dies.

Keen Hearing and Smell. The Lycan Soldier has an advantage on Wisdom (Perception) checks that rely on hearing or smell.

Formation Tactics. The Lycan Soldier has an advantage on saving throws against being charmed, frightened, grappled, or restrained while within 5 feet of at least one ally.

Actions

Multiattack (Humanoid or Hybrid Form Only). The werewolf makes two attacks: two with its spear (humanoid form) or one with its bite and one with its claws (hybrid form).

Claws (Hybrid Form Only). Melee Weapon Attack: +4 to hit, reach 5 ft., one creature. Hit: 7 (2d4 + 2) slashing damage.

Bite (Hybrid Form Only). Melee Weapon Attack: +4 to hit, reach 5 ft., one target. Hit: 6 (1d8 + 2) piercing damage. If the target is a humanoid, it must succeed on a DC 12 Constitution saving throw or be cursed with werewolf lycanthropy.

Spear (Humanoid Form Only). Melee or Ranged Weapon Attack: +4 to hit, reach 5 ft. or range 20/60 ft., one creature. Hit: 5 (1d6 + 2) piercing damage, or 6 (1d8 + 2) piercing damage if used with two hands to make a melee attack.

Club (Humanoid Form Only). Melee or Ranged Weapon Attack: +4 to hit, reach 5 ft., one creature. Hit: 2 (1d4) piercing damage, or 6 (1d8 + 2) piercing damage if used with two hands to make a melee attack.

Feral Fury. Melee Weapon Attack: +8 to hit, reach 5 ft., one creature. Hit: 13 (2d8 + 2) slashing damage. Feral Fury lasts for 1 minute. It ends early if you are knocked unconscious. A Lycan Soldier can only use Feral Fury once every four hours.

LYCANALE - WEREFOX

Medium humanoid (human), lawful evil

Armor Class 12

Hit Points 33 (6d8 + 6)

Speed 30 ft. (40 ft. when in Lycanale - Werefox form)

STR	DEX	CON	INT	WIS	CHA
10 (+0)	15 (+2)	12 (+1)	11 (+0)	10 (+0)	8 (-1)

Skills Perception +2, Stealth +4

Damage Immunities bludgeoning, piercing, and slashing from nonmagical attacks not made with silvered weapons

Senses darkvision 60 ft., passive Perception 12

Languages —

Challenge 2 (450 XP)

Shapechanger. The Lycanale - Werefox can use its action to polymorph into a fox-humanoid hybrid or a giant fox or back into its proper form, humanoid. Its statistics change when it transforms into a Lycanale - Werefox. Any equipment it is wearing or carrying isn't transformed. It reverts to its proper form if it dies.

Keen Smell. The Lycanale - Werefox has an advantage on Wisdom (Perception) checks that rely on smell.

Actions

Multiattack *(Humanoid or Hybrid Form Only)*. The Lycanale - Werefox makes two attacks, only one of which can be a bite.

Shortsword *(Humanoid or Hybrid Form Only)*. Melee Weapon Attack: +4 to hit, reach 5 ft., one target. Hit: 5 (1d6 + 2) piercing damage.

Hand Crossbow *(Humanoid or Hybrid Form Only)*. Ranged Weapon Attack: +4 to hit, range 30/120 ft., one target. Hit: 5 (1d6 + 2) piercing damage.

Bite *(Fox or Hybrid Form Only)*. Melee Weapon Attack: +4 to hit, reach 5 ft., one target. Hit: 4 (1d4 + 2) piercing damage. If the target is a humanoid, it must succeed on a DC 11 Constitution saving throw or be cursed with Lycanale - Werefox lycanthropy.

LYCANARK - WEREBEAR

Medium humanoid (human), neutral good

Armor Class 10 in humanoid form, 11 (natural armor) in bear and hybrid form

Hit Points 135 (18d8 + 54)

Speed 30 ft. (40 ft., climb 30 ft. in bear or hybrid form)

STR	DEX	CON	INT	WIS	CHA
19 (+4)	10 (+0)	17 (+3)	11 (+0)	12 (+1)	12 (+1)

Skills Perception +7

Damage Immunities bludgeoning, piercing, and slashing from nonmagical attacks not made with silvered weapons

Senses passive Perception 17

Languages Common (can't speak in bear form)

Challenge 5 (1,800 XP)

Shapechanger. The Lycanark / werebear can use its action to polymorph into a large bear-humanoid hybrid or a large bear, or back into its proper form, humanoid. Its statistics will change when it transforms from humanoid to Lycanark - Werebear. Any equipment it is wearing or carrying isn't transformed. It reverts to its proper form if it dies.

Keen Smell. The Lycanark / Werebear has an advantage on Wisdom (Perception) checks that rely on smell.

Actions

Multiattack. In bear form, the Lycanark / Werebear makes two claw attacks. In humanoid form, it makes two greataxe attacks. In hybrid form, it can attack like a bear or a humanoid.

Bite *(Bear or Hybrid Form Only)*. Melee Weapon Attack: +7 to hit, reach five ft., one target. Hit: 15 (2d10 + 4) piercing damage. If the target is a humanoid, it must succeed on a DC 14 Constitution saving throw or be cursed with Lycanark / Werebear lycanthropy.

Claw *(Bear or Hybrid Form Only)*. Melee Weapon Attack: +7 to hit, reach 5 ft., one target. Hit: 13 (2d8 + 4) slashing damage.

Greataxe *(Humanoid or Hybrid Form Only)*. Melee Weapon Attack: +7 to hit, reach 5 ft., one target. Hit: 10 (1d12 + 4) slashing damage.

LYCANGAT - WERECAT

Medium humanoid (human), neutral

Armor Class 12

Hit Points 120 (16d8 + 48)

Speed 30 ft. (40 ft. in Lycangat form)

STR	DEX	CON	INT	WIS	CHA
17 (+3)	15 (+2)	16 (+3)	10 (+0)	13 (+1)	11 (+0)

Skills Perception +5, Stealth +4

Damage Immunities bludgeoning, piercing, and slashing from nonmagical attacks not made with silvered weapons

Senses darkvision 60 ft., passive Perception 15

Languages —

Challenge 4 (1,100 XP)

Shapechanger. The Lycangat, or werecat, can use its action to polymorph into a cat-humanoid hybrid, into a cat, or back into its proper form, which is humanoid. Other than its size, its statistics change to Lycangat in cat-humanoid hybrid or complete Lycangat form. Any equipment it is wearing or carrying isn't transformed. It reverts to its proper form if it dies.

Keen Hearing and Smell. The Lycangat/werecat has an advantage on Wisdom (Perception) checks that rely on hearing or smell.

Pounce *(Cat or Hybrid Form Only)*. If the Lycangat moves at least 15 feet straight toward a creature and then hits it with a claw attack on the same turn, that target must succeed on a DC 14 Strength saving throw or be knocked prone. If the target is flat, the werecat can make one bite attack against it as a bonus action.

Actions

Multiattack *(Humanoid or Hybrid Form Only)*. In humanoid form, the Lycangat/werecat makes two scimitar attacks or two longbow attacks. In hybrid form, it can attack like a humanoid or make two claw attacks.

Bite *(Cat or Hybrid Form Only)*. Melee Weapon Attack: +4 to hit, reach 5 ft., one target. Hit: 6 (1d6 + 3) piercing damage. If the target is a humanoid, it must succeed on a DC 13 Constitution saving throw or be cursed with Lycangat/Werecat lycanthropy.

Claw *(Cat or Hybrid Form Only)*. Melee Weapon Attack: +5 to hit, reach 5 ft., one target. Hit: 5 (1d6 + 3) slashing damage.

Scimitar *(Humanoid or Hybrid Form Only)*. Melee Weapon Attack: +5 to hit, reach 5 ft., one target. Hit: 6 (1d6 + 3) slashing damage.

Longbow *(Humanoid or Hybrid Form Only)*. Ranged Weapon Attack: +4 to hit, range 150/600 ft., one target. Hit: 6 (1d8 + 2) piercing damage.

LYCANGERAKI - WEREHAWK

Medium humanoid (human), neutral

Armor Class 12

Hit Points 33 (6d8 + 6)

Speed 30 ft. (60 ft. flying when in Lycangeraki - Werehawk form)

STR	DEX	CON	INT	WIS	CHA
10 (+0)	15 (+2)	12 (+1)	11 (+0)	10 (+0)	8 (-1)

Skills Perception +2, Stealth +4

Damage Immunities bludgeoning, piercing, and slashing from nonmagical attacks not made with silvered weapons

Senses darkvision 60 ft., passive Perception 12

Languages —

Challenge 2 (450 XP)

Shapechanger. The Lycangeraki - Werehawk can use its action to polymorph into a hawk-humanoid hybrid or a giant hawk or back into its proper form, which is humanoid. Its statistics change when it transforms into a Lycangeraki - Werehawk. Any equipment it is wearing or carrying isn't transformed. It reverts to its proper form if it dies.

Actions

Multiattack *(Humanoid or Hybrid Form Only)*. The Lycangeraki - Werehawk makes two attacks, only one of which can be Talons or Beak.

Rapier *(Humanoid or Hybrid Form Only)*. Melee Weapon Attack: +10 to hit, Reach 5 ft one target. Hit 8 (1d8+8) piercing damage.

Talons. *(Hybrid Form Only)*. Melee Weapon Attack: +10 to hit, reach 5 ft., one target. Hit: 12 (2d8 + 4) slashing damage.

Beak *(Lycangeraki - Werehawk or Hybrid Form Only)*. Melee Weapon Attack: +10 to hit, reach 5 ft., one target. Hit: 17(2d8 + 8) piercing damage.

Talons *(Lycangeraki - Werehawk or Hybrid Form Only)*. Melee Weapon Attack: +10 to hit, reach 5 ft., one target. Hit: 12 (2d8 + 4) slashing damage.

LYCANTAV - WEREBULL

Medium humanoid (human), neutral evil

Armor Class 10 in humanoid form, 11 (natural armor) in boar or hybrid form

Hit Points 78 (12d8 + 24)

Speed 30 ft. (40 ft. in bull form)

STR	DEX	CON	INT	WIS	CHA
17 (+3)	10 (+0)	15 (+2)	10 (+0)	11 (+0)	8 (-1)

Shapechanger. The Lycantav / Werebull can use its action to polymorph into a bull-humanoid hybrid or into a bull, or back into its proper form, which is humanoid. Its statistics will change when it transforms from humanoid to Lycantav / Werebull. Any equipment it is wearing or carrying isn't transformed. It reverts to its proper form if it dies.

Actions

Multiattack *(Humanoid or Hybrid Form Only)*. The Lycantav / Werebull makes two attacks, only one of which can be with its horns.

Maul *(Humanoid or Hybrid Form Only)*. Melee Weapon Attack: +5 to hit, reach five ft., one target. Hit: 10 (2d6 + 3) bludgeoning damage.

Tusks *(Bull or Hybrid Form Only)*. Melee Weapon Attack: +5 to hit, reach five ft., one target. Hit: 10 (2d6 + 3) slashing damage. If the target is a humanoid, it must succeed on a DC 12 Constitution saving throw or be cursed with Lycantav / Werebull lycanthropy.

Relentless *(Recharges after a Short or Long Rest)*. If the Lycantav / Werebull takes 14 damage or less, that will reduce it to 0 hit points, and it is reduced to 1 hit point instead.

Charge *(Bull or Hybrid Form Only)*. If the Lycantav / Werebull moves at least 15 feet straight toward a target and then hits it with its horns on the same turn, the target takes an extra 7 (2d6) slashing damage. If the target is a creature, it must succeed on a DC 13 Strength saving throw or be knocked prone.

LYCANTHROPE - WEREWOLF

Medium humanoid (human), chaotic evil

Armor Class 11 in humanoid form, 12 (natural armor) in wolf or hybrid form

Hit Points 58 (9d8 + 18)

Speed 30 ft. (40 ft. in wolf form)

STR	DEX	CON	INT	WIS	CHA
15 (+2)	13 (+1)	14 (+2)	10 (+0)	11 (+0)	10 (+0)

Skills Perception +4

Damage Immunities bludgeoning, piercing, and slashing from nonmagical attacks not made with silvered weapons

Senses passive Perception 14

Languages Common (can't speak in wolf form)

Challenge 3 (700 XP)

Shapechanger. The Lycanthrope - Werewolf can use its action to polymorph into a wolf-humanoid hybrid or a wolf, or back into its true form, which is humanoid. Its statistics will change when it transforms from humanoid to Lycanthrope - Werewolf. Any equipment it is wearing or carrying isn't transformed. It reverts to its proper form if it dies.

Keen Hearing and Smell. The werewolf has advantage on Wisdom (Perception) checks that rely on hearing or smell.

Actions

Multiattack (Humanoid or Hybrid Form Only). The werewolf makes two attacks: two with its spear (humanoid form) or one with its bite and one with its claws (hybrid form).

Bite (Wolf or Hybrid Form Only). Melee Weapon Attack: +4 to hit, reach 5 ft., one target. Hit: 6 (1d8 + 2)

piercing damage. If the target is a humanoid, it must succeed on a DC 12 Constitution saving throw or be cursed with werewolf lycanthropy.

Claws (Hybrid Form Only). Melee Weapon Attack: +4 to hit, reach 5 ft., one creature. Hit: 4 (1d6 + 2) slashing damage.

Quarterstaff (Humanoid Form Only). Melee or Ranged Weapon Attack: +4 to hit, reach 5 ft. or range 20/60 ft., one creature. Hit: 5 (1d6) bludgeoning damage, or 6 (1d8 + 2) bludgeoning damage if used with two hands to make a melee attack.

MOONLIGHT WYRMLING

Medium dragon, neutral

Armor Class 16 (natural armor)

Hit Points 32 (5d8 + 10)

Speed 30 ft., burrow 15 ft., fly 60 ft., swim 30 ft.

STR	DEX	CON	INT	WIS	CHA
14 (+2)	10 (+0)	14 (+2)	5 (-3)	10 (+0)	11 (+0)

Saving Throws Dex +2, Con +4, Wis +2, Cha +2

Skills Perception +4, Stealth +2

Damage Immunities cold

Senses blindsight 10 ft., darkvision 60 ft., passive Perception 14

Languages Draconic

Challenge 2 (450 XP)

Moon Sight. Tears from Moonlight Wyrmling can be used in a potion called "Moon Sight" that gives players the ability to see 15 minutes into the future.

Actions

Bite. Melee Weapon Attack: +4 to hit, reach 5 ft., one target. Hit: 7 (1d10 + 2) piercing damage plus 2 (1d4) cold damage.

Lunar Breath (Recharge 5-6). The Wyrmling exhales an ethereal blast of silver light in a 15-foot cone. Each creature in that area must make a DC 12 Constitution saving throw, taking 11 (3d8) damage on a failed save, or half as much damage on a successful one.

SCALING MONSTER ATTACKS

The monsters in *The Werewolves of London* are split into two distinct groups:

- NPCs who can change into Lycan Warriors

- Encounters

For each NPC who can transform into a Lycan Warrior, you will see that there is a recommended Level for the NPC. The Level can be reviewed with the Lycan Warrior Class. You should change the Level of each Lycan Warrior to reflect the size and strength of your players.

For encounters like Lycan Soldiers, you should scale up and down the number of Lycan Soldiers who attack to match the players' party.

MAGIC ITEMS

MAGIC ITEMS

AMULET OF PACK ALLEGIANCE

Wondrous Item

The Amulet of Pack Allegiance is unique for each Lycanthrope Warrior pack. Each pack will have a unique design. Wearers of the Pack Amulet gain +1 Dexterity and +1 Constitution, to a maximum of 20.

LUNAR CONTROL STAFF

Legendary

Enchanted veins of silver lace this old, wooden staff. Any Lycan struck with the Lunar Control Staff will immediately revert to their normal form.

SILVER DAGGER

Rare

The silver dagger is enhanced with a spell that inflicts additional +2 bonus to attack and damage to any Lycan creature. Proficiency with a dagger allows you to add your proficiency bonus to the attack roll for any attack you make with it.

SILVER MOON NECKLACE

Very rare

The wearer of the Full Moon Necklace will be able to have full control over their Lycan transformations. Changing and Shape Shifter level Lycanthrope Warriors are often gifted with the Full Moon Necklace until they reach Skin Walker level.

BAIZE'S HERBAL CATALOG

BAIZE'S HERBAL CATALOG

Baize is an experienced herbalist with an extensive catalog. Below is a list of her remedies, a description and the price to purchase each item.

Potion	Description	Price
Bane's Wolf Tea	Drink this tea within fifteen minutes of being bitten by a Lycan to remove the curse.	50 gp
Dragon Cress Gel	Rub this green, viscous gel over your eyes to gain the ability to see in complete darkness for 1 hour.	15 gp
Fire Cilantro Paste	Use to reduce the impact of a fire burn. Apply to the affected area within 15 mins of the burn to reduce the Hit Point impact by 5.	10 gp
Ivory Mint Paste	Clean teeth and minty breath matter. Scrub this paste on your teeth and rub it off with a stick.	5 sp
King's Anise	Eat this root and for 15 minutes those within 20 feet will assume you are a King or Queen and obey your orders.	30 gp
Moon Sight	The potion can be used at the start of any encounter and only be used once. The DM will whisper into the ear of the player who uses Moon Sight and tell them what will happen in that encounter. The player can choose to share with the rest of the players. The potion can only be used once.	300 gp
Potion of Bad Breath	Use your bonus action to breathe fire at a target within 30 feet. The target takes 3d8 fire damage or half on a successful DC 12 Dexterity saving throw. The potion can only be used once.	150 gp
Potion of Climbing	For one hour you can climb any object or wall at the same speed as your walking pace.	180 gp
Potion of Good Health	Drinking the potion restores 5 hit points.	25 gp
Potion of Lunacy	Drinking the potion will give you the ability to transform into any Lycan creature and gains its benefits for five attack rounds. After the fifth round you will return to your normal form but will be exhausted from the effort of the transformation. Roll a DC15 Constitution check. On a fail, you will immediately collapse into a deep sleep, and you will not be able to wake for 6 hours or take any damage.	125 gp
Potion of the Hero	Instantly gain 10 Hit Points. Can only be used once.	180 gp
Potion of the Lycan	For 1 hour you can transform into a Lycan and gain its abilities.	220 gp
Potion of Water Walking	For 30 minutes you will be able to walk on water as if you are walking on solid ground.	100 gp
Poxia Kernel Scrub	Apply it to your forehead when you are suffering a curse. The scrub must remain on your skin for two hours to remove the curse.	50 gp
Sea Ginger Glue	Rub the glue onto any wound you have received with a piecing weapon. The glue will bind the skin together and speed up recovery. Apply the glue adds 1d6+2 HP.	10 gp
Sirroshell	Suck on a Sirroshell to be able to swim under water for 30 minutes without needing to take a breath.	25 gp
Snowy Licorice Smudge Stick	Counter the curse from an undead monster. Close yourself in a small room and burn the smudge stick. The room will fill with a sweet smell. You must stay in the room for four hours.	25 gp
Venom Clary	A rare tonic to counter the curse of vampirism. Drink the whole bottle as the sun rises.	75 gp

NON-PLAYER CHARACTERS

NON-PLAYER CHARACTERS

ARIANA DUSTSTONE

Description

Ariana Duststone is a 35-year-old female human fortune-teller.

She has long, wavy, red hair and blue eyes with rugged brown skin, and a soft average face. She stands 132cm (4'3") tall and has a muscular build.

Personality Traits

She rarely thinks ahead and is very courageous, to a fault. She goes out at night secretly looking for small animals.

BAIZE

Description

Baize is a 158-year-old female high elf herbalist with long, straight, silver hair, warm eyes and rough skin.

She stands 174cm (5'8") tall and has a heavy build.

Personality Traits

She is very benevolent and very self-confident. She doesn't like listening to jokes.

Herbalist. Baize is an accomplished herbalist. She supplies the herbs Quinn Caskbow sells through his store, The Mad Mage. At any one time, Baize will be carrying three different herbal compounds. The DM can select three from Baize's Herbal Catalog.

Lycan Level 8.

She can transform into Lycanark - Werebear

BUCNA ZIZRO

Description

Bucna Zizro is an 88-year-old male high elf banker. He has short, straight, white hair, brown eyes and rugged green skin.

He stands 165cm (5'4") tall has a skinny build, and a triangular, slightly attractive face.

He smells severely of alcohol and can't feel pain.

Personality Traits

He is very greedy. He never knows the current time and date. He has a very regal look. He collects buttons.

Plot Hook

He is being blackmailed by the Le Sang Rouge pack into challenging anyone who openly supports Selene's Sisters into a duel to the death.

CELIAC

Description

Celiac is a 35-year-old female human forester with short, straight, blond hair and gray eyes.

She has rough golden skin, stands 172cm (5'7") tall, has a round build and has a square, ordinary face.

She is also the leader of the Selene Sisterhood.

Personality Traits

She doesn't care about risks or odds. She has a crude sense of humor.

Lycan Level 18

She can transform into Lycangat - Werecat, and Lycanthrope - Werewolf

GAMAL SMELTMASTER

Description

Gamal Smeltmaster is a 64-year-old male hill dwarf torturer with short-cropped, straight, golden hair, brown eyes and soft, pink skin. He stands 89cm (2'11") tall, has a round build and an oval, beautiful (for a dwarf) face. He has an unfinished tribal tattoo on his right hand.

Personality Traits

He will always prioritize his needs. He constantly looks for the loophole. He always does what he is told not to. He will insult you if you are not a hill dwarf. If you are a hill dwarf, he will launch into tall stories of the wars the hill dwarves have fought. He fidgets occasionally.

HUDSON THE HOUND

Description

Hudson the Hound is a 59-year-old male human acrobat with short, curled, black hair and green eyes. He stands 154cm (5'0") tall, has an athletic build with smooth pink skin that highlights his diamond-shaped, fanciable face and gigantic neckbeard.

Personality Traits

Traits. He is kind and generous as well as very athletic. He is a perfectionist and doesn't like change.*Club. Melee Weapon Attack*: +5 to hit, reach 5 ft., one target. Hit: 2 (1d4) bludgeoning damage.

Handaxe. Melee Weapon Attack: +5 to hit, reach 5 ft., one target. Hit: 3 (1d6) slashing damage.

JOHN DEGREY

Description

John deGrey is a 44-year-old male human blacksmith sporting a bald head and brown eyes. He stands 190cm (6'2") tall, has a beefy build with a sharp, plain face. He walks with a severe limp.

Personality Traits

He doesn't worship any god, is very focused. He is materialistic, always wears a fancy hat and he likes to swim.

LADY ADELINA

Description

Lady Adelina is a 50-year-old female human aristocrat. She has short, straight hair with green eyes and golden skin. She stands 147cm (4'9") tall, has a skinny build with an edgy, typical face. She is severely allergic to poor people.

Personality Traits

She hates fair play and is very good at keeping secrets.

Lycan Level 5

He will transform into a Lycantav - Werebull.

LORD DARION

Description

Lord Darionis a 40-year-old male human standing 174cm (5'8") tall with a regular build and an edgy, slightly typical face framed with a short sideburns. He smells severely of incense to cover the smell of blood and gore from his hunts.

Personality Traits

He takes everything at face-value and uses sarcasm and insults commonly. He inherited a palace and secretly wants to become the ruler of Old London Town. He sporadically squints.

Lycan Level 10

He will transform into a Lycanale - Werefox.

ORROS SAYUR JELEN MERWOR

Description

Orros Sayur Jelen Merwor is a 201-year-old male forest gnome cook. He has short, curled, gray hair shaved on the right side, gray eyes and rugged, pockmarked, pink skin. He stands 107cm (3'6") tall and has a beefy build with a sharp, typical face sporting a long, braided mustache.

Personality Traits

He is very selfish but is very good at keeping secrets. He intermittently uses long words to sound smart and sporadically misquotes proverbs. He always talks about his plans for an invention.

Plot Hook

He is part of a secret, rebellious organization who wants to overthrow the mayor.

PRINCE AETHELWULF

Description

Prince Aethelwulf is a 44-year-old male human German Prince. He has smooth skin, stands 200cm (6'6") tall and has a beefy build.

Personality Traits

He hates fair play, is very conceited and he always has a battle story to tell. He gestures profusely during a conversation and rolls his "R"s profusely. He loves partying.

Lycan Level 20

Aethelwulf is an Alpha Lycanthrope Warrior. He can transform into the following:

• Lycanthrope - Werewolf

• Lycangeraki - Werehawk

• Lycanark - Werebear

When he reaches 1hp in each form, he will then switch to a new form and restore his hit points for that form. He switch his form twice, but then will not be able to transform for 48 hours.

QUINN CASKBOW

Description

Quinn Caskbow is a 32-year-old male human doctor with a bald head and blue eyes. He has rugged brown skin, stands 197cm (6'5") tall with a massive build and has a round, awful face with a medium beard. He is easily out of breath.

Personality Traits

He is a very good diplomat, always works towards resolution of conflict and takes everything at face value. He considers everyone else idiots, is heavily allergic to elves and has a story for everything. He also has a penchant for tobacco and constantly smokes from a glass pipe.

ROSE WRITINGHAM

Description

Rose Writingham is a 26-year-old female half-elf armorer with short, curled, brown hair and brown eyes. She has rough copper skin, stands 157cm (5'1") tall with a regular build and has a round, extremely typical face. She has 2 shocking piercings on her left ear and 4 elaborate piercings on her nose.

Personality Traits

She discreetly worships Akadi, Goddess of air, movement and speed. She is very empathic towards others and is very good at keeping secrets. She is always accompanied by her servants and sees insults as an art form.

SADON COMMONBROOK

Description

Sadon Commonbrook is an 80-year-old male human merchant who has long, braided, golden hair and brown eyes. He has rough, sunburned, brown skin, stands 152cm (4'11") tall and has a lean build with a square, bland face. He has 2 piercings on his left eyebrow.

Personality Traits

He is very impatient and very self-confident. He occasionally quotes proverbs.

SIERRA

Description

Sierra is a 12-year-old female human trapper with short, wavy, blond hair, piercing eyes and rough golden skin. She stands 137cm (4'5") tall and has an athletic build with a square, creepy face.

Personality Traits

She is very optimistic and rarely thinks ahead. She despises the aristocracy.

Lycan Level 1

She was recently bitten by one of the Le Sang Rouge pack.

She can transform into Lycanale - Werefox.

SNAK LAUGHINGFANG

Description

Snak Laughingfang is a 62-year-old female orc brewer with short, straight, golden hair that is shaved on the left side. She has brown eyes with rough green skin and stands 192cm (6'3") tall with a muscular build. She has a sharp, slightly magnificent face and is deaf in her right ear.

Personality Traits

She gets bored easily and is constantly looking for loopholes and shortcuts. She is haunted by horrible memories.

THE MAYOR (LETHOLDUS KEENSEEKER)

Description

Letholdus Keenseeker is the 50-year-old male human Mayor of Old London Town. He has a very long, blond mohawk with brown eyes and smooth black skin. He stands 182cm (5'11") tall, has a round build and has a square, awful face with a piercing on his left eyebrow.

Personality Traits

He will always prioritize the needs of other people, even to his detriment, constantly looks for loopholes and likes finding direct solutions to problems. He tells lies, very poorly and on purpose.

THE MAYOR'S WIFE (BEATRIX KEENSEEKER)

Description

Beatrix Keenseeker is the 52-year-old female human wife of the mayor. She has short, straight, blond hair with blue eyes and rugged white skin. She stands 169cm (5'6") tall, has a round build with an oval, hideous face. She is very nimble.

Personality Traits

She is very good at keeping secrets. She likes finding direct solutions to problems but will always prioritize her own needs. She doesn't worship any god.

WIXLEE

Description

Wixlee is a 29-year-old female gnome tinker with a bald head, black eyes and soft, sunburned, green skin. She stands 127cm (4'1") tall, has an athletic build and has an oval, slightly attractive face. She smells like rain and has an extra finger on her left hand.

Personality Traits

She is very direct but very cowardly. She intermittently gives money to the poor and knows all the gossip around town.

Plot Hook

She has been hired to steal items from the PCs.

XOLOG

Description

Xolog is a 50-year-old-year-old male half-orc innkeeper. He has short, braided, brown hair with gray eyes and soft, pockmarked, brown skin. He stands 177cm (5'9") tall with a regular build and has a diamond-shaped, awful face. He smells of incense.

Personality Traits

He is incredibly cross-eyed and always wears a fancy hat. He will always prioritize his own needs and constantly looks for loopholes and shortcuts. He sees insults as an artform, and he is a bad artist.

Plot Hook

He is currently being chased by law enforcement, but he is always looking for the next quick job to make him easy money.

GAME WITHIN A GAME

GAME WITHIN A GAME

CHASE THE WOLF

What you need

- 8d8
- Two or more players

OBJECTIVE

To be the first to reach 100

INSTRUCTIONS

Each player rolls eight dice, taking turns to roll the dice. The goal is to organize your dice into runs. A run is a sequence of numbers, such as 1-2-3-4. For each number used in a run, the player scores 5 points. Dice may only be used once when creating a run. Runs must begin with the number 1.

For example, a roll of 1-2-4-5-6-6-4-8 scores 10 points for runs 1-2.

For example, a roll of 1-2-1-2-3-4-7-5 scores 10 points for the run 1-2 and 20 points for the run 1-2-3-4 for 30 points.

If there is no run, no score is recorded—for example, a roll of 1-3-4-4-5-6-2-5 scores zero points.

BONUS SCORE

Players who roll 1-2-3-4-5-6-7-8 automatically score 100. If you do get a perfect run, please take a photo and send it to me :)

Play continues until one player has reached 100 points.

CANNON BALL TOSS

The objective of the game is to catch a cannonball. There are two ways to play Cannonball Toss: with Dice or with a bean bag.

CANNONBALL TOSS WITH DICE

Each player has 2d6 and they take turns rolling the dice. The objective is to take turns and use the score from your dice to determine if you caught the ball. The first player rolls both dice, then the other player must roll a number equal or greater to the total. For instance, if the first player rolls double four, then the other player must roll a total of eight or higher. If they do not roll higher then they drop the cannonball and lose. If they roll the equal number of higher, then they have caught the cannonball. The second player can now roll as they "throw" the cannonball back to the first player (who must try score a higher number to "catch" the ball).

CANNONBALL TOSS WITH A BEANBAG

Each player starts by standing six feet/2m apart. The players take turns tossing the bag back and forth. After each round, the players take one step back. They continue to do this until one player drops the bean bag and loses.

PAPER FORTUNE

MAKING YOUR OWN PENNY BLOOD PAPER FORTUNE

The Penny Blood Paper Fortune is easy to print out and create for the game. There are two versions of the Penny Blood Paper Fortune:

- One version has fortunes written on
- A second is blank so you can write your own fortunes

Instructions

Print the Penny Blood Paper Fortune teller. There are two versions of the document. One is left blank, so you can add your own fortunes.

1. Cut out the fortune teller along the lines.
2. Fold and then unfold along the lines.
3. Turn fortune tell over with the pictures on the back, and then bring the corners into the center.
4. Turnover and repeat the process of folding the corners into the center.
5. Turn back over.
6. Pull the flaps with the loose points away from the body and towards you.
7. Now, put your fingers in and work back and forth.

OK, so I did not know how to fold the paper when I first had this idea. So, I popped over to YouTube and found this fantastic "How To" video: https://www.youtube.com/watch?v=SAhiIlTxUYA

PENNY BLOOD PAPER FORTUNE

PENNY BLOOD PAPER FORTUNE - BLANK

FOOD AND FUEL

FOOD AND FUEL

An army runs on food and fuel. Here you will find a recipe to feed your hungry hoard and an adult drink to quench their thirst.

FOOD - BLOODY BROIL

Bloody Broil is a fantastic meal to share with your players. This version, Bloody Broil, is an option for those looking for a rarer cut of meat. This meal should soothe any wild beast.

- 1/3 cup soy sauce
- 1/3 cup lemon juice
- 1/2 cup olive oil
- 1/4 cup Worcestershire sauce
- 1 Tablespoon minced garlic
- 1 Tablespoon of dried onion
- 2 Tablespoons Italian seasoning
- 1 teaspoon pepper
- 1/2 teaspoon salt
- pinch of red pepper
- 1-2 lb. of Round Steak (sometimes called London Broil Steak)

INSTRUCTIONS

Combine the steak marinade by mixing the soy sauce, lemon juice, olive oil, Worcestershire sauce, garlic, Italian seasoning, and salt and pepper in a large gallon bag. Add the steak to the bag, cover well and marinate in the fridge for at least two hours or overnight.

Heat the broiler on your oven to the highest temperature. Remove the steak from the bag and rest soon a baking tray. Broil each side of the steak for 5-6 minutes. You will want to keep rotating the steak until the inside temperature reaches 130-140F/55-60C Using a steak thermometer for medium rare. For a bloodier cut, serve the steak "rare", with an internal temperature of 125F/51C.

Let the steak rest for 10-15 minutes and serve your Bloody Broil with mashed potatoes and buttered rye bread.

FUEL - SILVER BULLET

You will need this drink to take a shot at any Werewolves hunting you down.

- 1 part Gin
- 2 parts Tonic
- Dash of vermouth
- ¼ tsp of silver cocktail glitter

Shake with ice and strain into a cocktail glass. Garnish with Lime.

FUEL - THE CURLY LEMON

Taste the drink sold at The Curly Lemon.

- 2 parts vodka
- 1 part lemon juice

Shake with ice and strain into a cocktail glass. Garnish with lemon.

Page 139 of 300

MAPS

MAPS

There are two types of maps:

• DM/GM Maps with room names

• Game player maps with no room's names

In addition, the maps are available in the following formats:

• Color

• Nighttime mode (this works great when using a tablet, computer screen or broadcasting onto a TV)

• Black and White printer friendly version

• Sepia Tone - when testing this game, the teams I worked with LOVE IT when I sent them the Sepia Tone versions of the maps as teasers for game night

THE WEREWOLVES OF LONDON MAP

The Werewolves of London

THE WEREWOLVES OF LONDON MAP (WITH INTERIOR VIEW OF BUILDINGS)

The Werewolves of London

THE WEREWOLVES OF LONDON MAP (WITH LABELS)

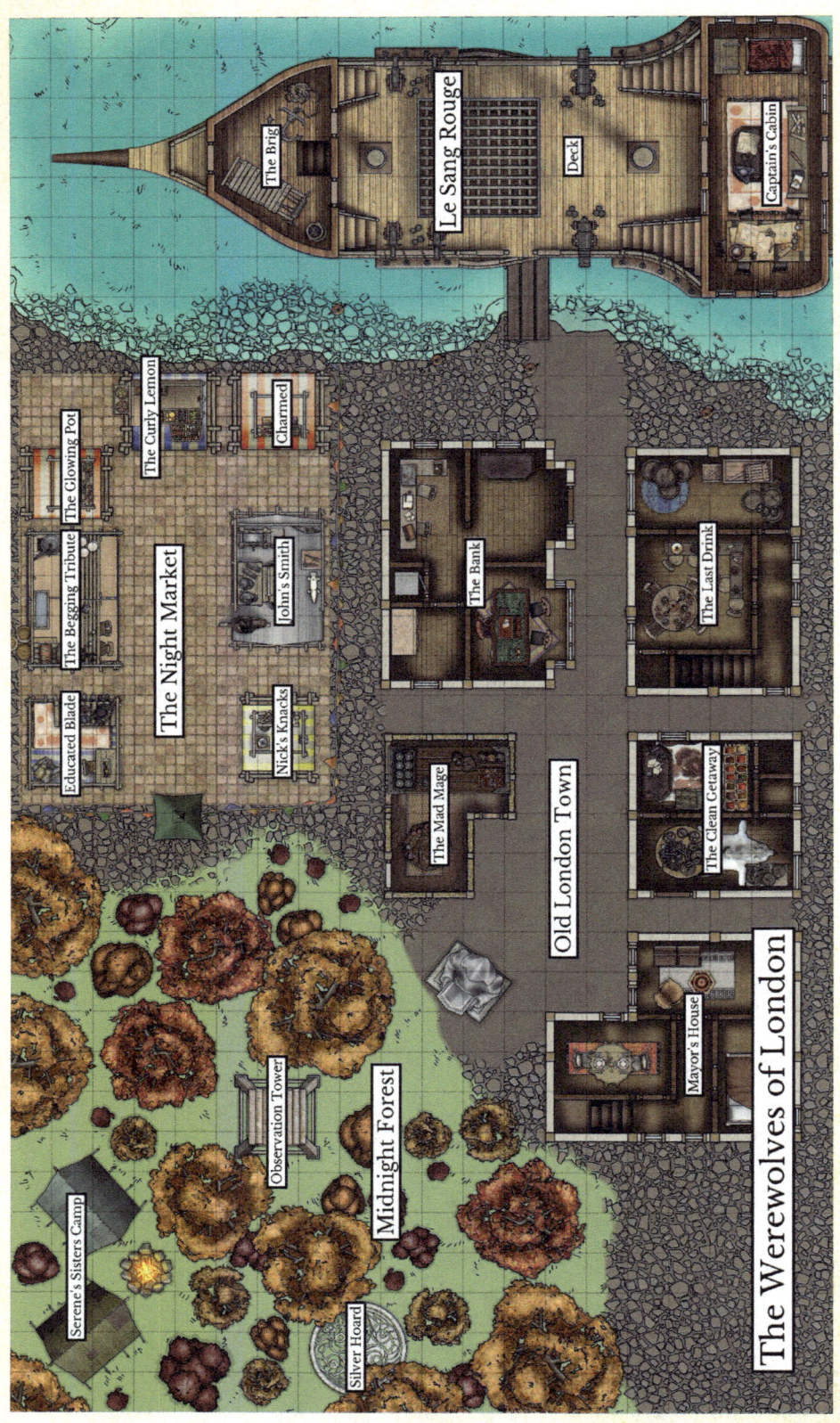

THE WEREWOLVES OF LONDON MAP (PRINTER FRIENDLY)

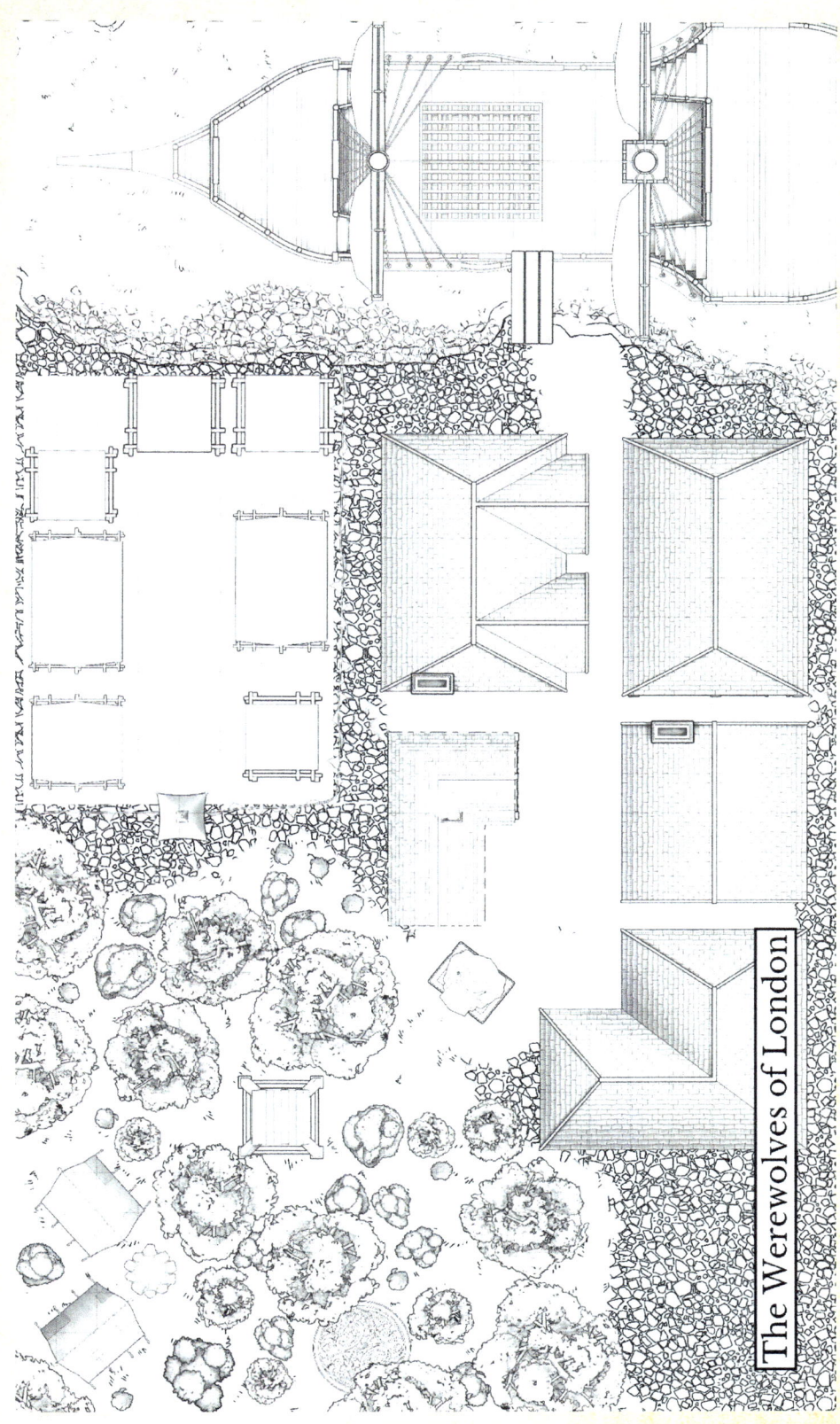

The Werewolves of London

THE WEREWOLVES OF LONDON MAP (PRINTER FRIENDLY WITH LABELS)

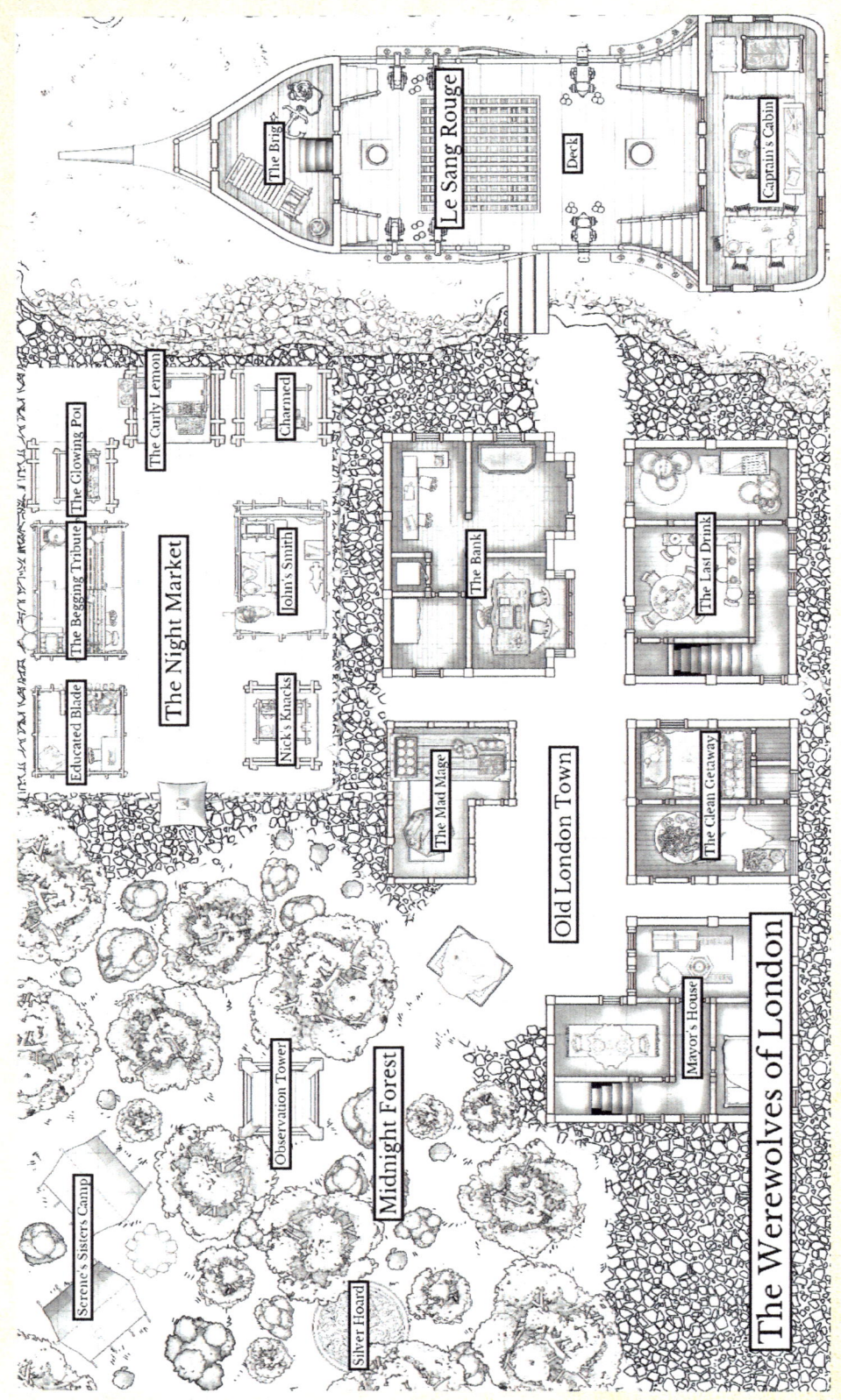

The Brig

Le Sang Rouge

Deck

Captain's Cabin

The Curly Lemon

Charmed

The Glowing Pol

The Beggng Tribute

John's Smith

The Night Market

The Bank

The Last Drink

Educated Blade

Nick's Knacks

The Mad Mage

Old London Town

The Clean Getaway

Observation Tower

Midnight Forest

Mayor's House

The Werewolves of London

Serene's Sisters Camp

Silver Hoard

THE WEREWOLVES OF LONDON MAP (WITH LIGHTS)

The Werewolves of London

THE WEREWOLVES OF LONDON MAP (SEPIA)

The Werewolves of London

THE MAD LAB

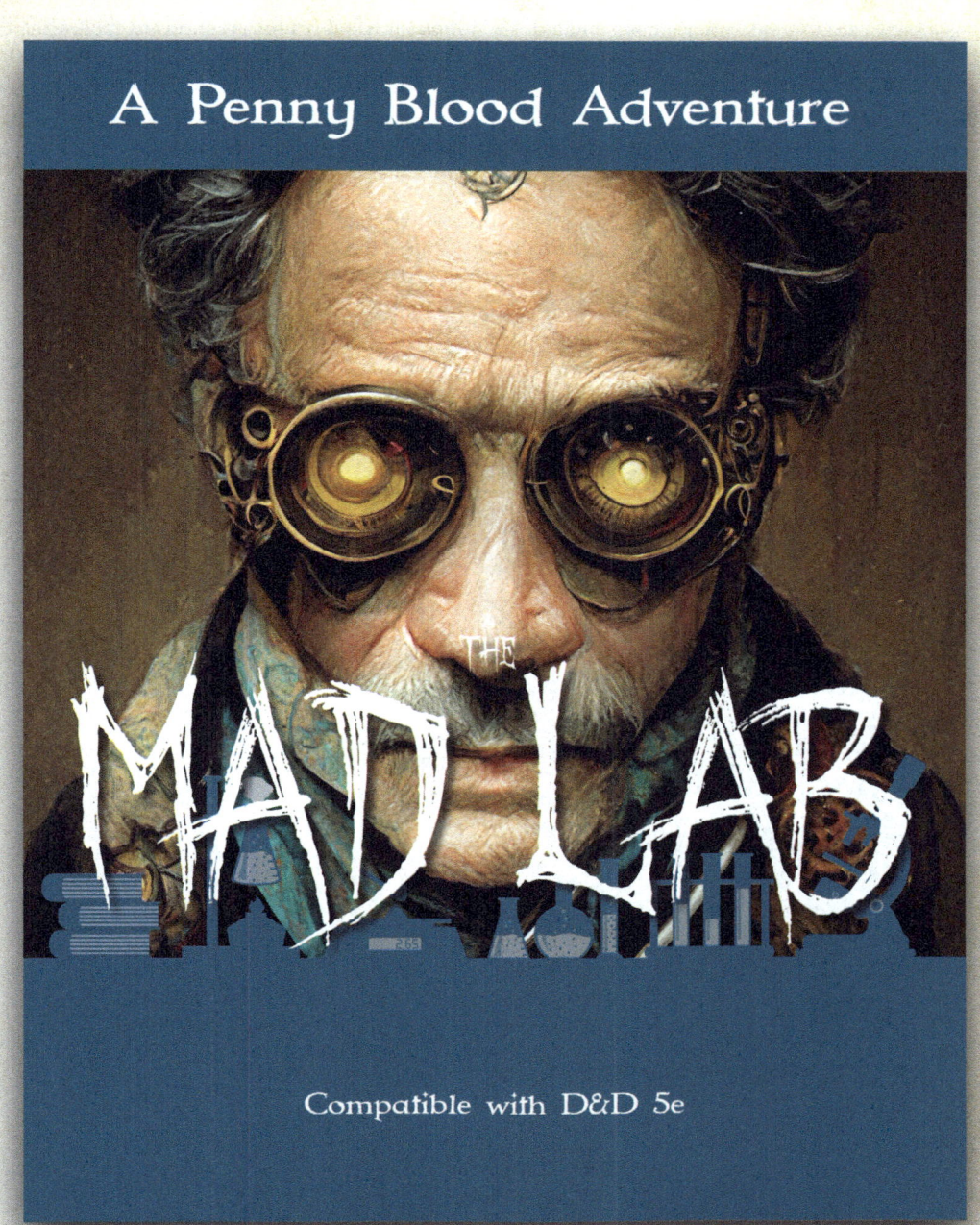

A Penny Blood Adventure

MAD LAB

Compatible with D&D 5e

THE MAD LAB

A hot, sticky summer bakes the coastline town of Briar Glen. Storms, boiling with thunder, explode in the skies every night. The bellowing howl of new life accompanies each storm as a doctor, driven mad by the desire to create intelligent life, uses the power to animate his latest creations. Life is being made, but at what cost?

The Doctor, possessed with extreme intelligence and a desire to invent life, sees his creations as the ultimate test of human brilliance. Is he a man or a god if he can create intelligent life? He is close to making his vision a reality and only needs a little more help. Those that assist him will be rewarded handsomely.

Many of the Doctor's creations have escaped. They now live on a small island only accessible through a tidally locked road. These creatures have named themselves Uplift, and their leader, named Zero, is striving to find a way in which they can live in peace.

Meanwhile, the sheriff of Briar Glen is desperate to rid his town of the mad Doctor's creations. In recent weeks, all his constables have suffered horrific deaths by monsters that have escaped the Doctor's compound. their bodies have been found torn apart, some with organs missing. The sheriff has collected a reward of 500gp if a group of adventurers can drive the mad Doctor away and end his endless creation of inhuman life.

Which path do you take as you enter the world of The Mad Lab?

RUNNING THE ADVENTURE

The structure of the Mad Lab is that players can move freely through the map and experience the encounters detailed below. The encounters can range from finding treasure, solving puzzles, talking with people in the game (NPCs), battling monsters and many other activities. The Mad Lab can be run differently depending on which Storyline the players follow. As the DM, this allows you to create a different game for each Storyline. The Storylines are summarized below and each encounter will have additional information to help you keep on track during the game:

- **Drive out the Beast**: Join the sheriff to hunt down and destroy the Mad Doctor's creations and imprison the mad Doctor himself to collect a reward of 500 gold pieces.

- **Control the Beast**: Align with the mad Doctor on his quest to create intelligent life. All he requires is three trinkets and a spell book. Oh, and someone to retrieve them! Do this, and he will reward you with augmented abilities of your choice. The required items are:

  - A locket with the picture of the one woman the Doctor loved, Caroline

  - A golden apple, the symbol of Adam and the creation myth

  - A black snake broach with red eyes, the symbol of evil

  - The spell book created by Zero

- **Free the Beast**: Many of the beasts the mad Doctor has created have escaped to a small coastal island near Briar Glen. They call themselves the "Uplift" and their leader, Zero, wants to keep this island as a sanctuary where they can peacefully live out their days. To accomplish this, all direct access to the island must be destroyed and a peace agreement with the Sheriff must be negotiated. Your reward for completing these tasks is a book of magic spells that Zero owns.

STRUCTURE FOR EACH ENCOUNTER

The campaign uses the game mechanics for Dungeons and Dragons 5e. To help DMs manage the game, each encounter is split into the following sections:

- Encounter Name

- DM Information (to give you a summary of the encounter)

- Read Aloud

- Storyline Information (to help keep things on track)

- Additional information (gives you more detailed information and instructions on how to reconcile the encounter)

- Activity (is meant as a fun, game-within-a-game section and is typically puzzles or games for the players)

- Resolution (tells you how and when the encounter is finished or resolved.)

- Monster and/or NPC (tells you about any monster or NPC the players may meet in the encounter.)

- Reward (is what everyone is working towards!)

Encounters will often have supported information that is available later in the book. For instance, the details for a monster can be found in the Monster section.

Each location will impact the Storyline the players choose differently. Each Storyline is collected in the following section to provide details for the DM to help move the story forward.

The game is modular in design which gives the DM the opportunity to swap in and out content from other games. If you do not want to use one of the monsters included in this campaign, then swap it out with a different monster from the Monster Manual or similar source.

The structure for the this and all Penny Blood Adventurer's is to give you a framework you can easily work in and modify as the DM.

Of course, as the DM, you are GOD ALMIGHTY and change where the players start depending on their skill level.

Have fun and…be the hero in your adventure!

WORKING WITH STORYLINES

The Mad Labs allows players to follow three different Storylines in the game. They are:

- **Drive Out the Beast**: Join the sheriff to hunt down and destroy the Mad Doctor's creations and imprison the mad Doctor himself to collect a reward of 500 gold pieces.

- **Control the Beast**: Align with the mad Doctor on his quest to create intelligent life. All he requires is three trinkets and a spell book. Oh, and someone to retrieve them! Do this, and he will reward you with augmented abilities of your choice.

- **Free the Beast**: Many of the beasts the mad Doctor has created have escaped to a small coastal island near Briar Glen. They call themselves the "Uplift" and their leader, Zero, wants to keep this island as a sanctuary where they can peacefully live out their days. To accomplish this, all direct access to the island must be destroyed and a peace agreement with the Sheriff must be negotiated. Your reward for completing these tasks is a book of magic spells that Zero owns.

Each encounter in the game will impact how the players follow the different Storylines. The following summarizes how each Storyline impacts each encounter.

The following sections provide a summary for Storyline specific encounters.

STARTING THE ADVENTURE

The players find themselves outside the town of Briar Glen. A crowd is forming around a captured animal. If the players look at the animal, they will see that it is unlike anything they have seen before. The creature has been stitched together from different parts and is clearly in pain. This creature is an Uplift.

Three key people are standing in the crowd the players can talk with:

- Breata Goldsun will tell the players that she is helping the Uplift leader, Zero, to build a sanctuary on a nearby island.

- Sheriff Dermot Sclator will tell the players that he will offer a sizable reward if they can eliminate the Uplift threat to Briar Glen.

- Jetts will tell the players that Dr. Koch will reward them if they can find four items and return them to him.

The captured creature will stand and howl when the players choose the Storyline they wish to follow. Everyone will cover their ears at the unnatural sound. The Uplift will then tear its bonds and sprint into the forest. Breata and the Sheriff will return to their buildings. Jetts will start walking back to the doctor's mansion.

…and so the adventure begins!

BRIAR GLEN

BRIAR GLEN ENCOUNTERS

Players will find that there are four areas they can explore in Briar Glen:

- The Sheriff's Building
- Breata Goldsun's House
- The Golden Oak Inn
- The Quay

Briar Glen is an old, quiet town that has come under the insidious shadow of Dr. Koch and his terrifying Uplift creations. The sense of foreboding in the town is exaggerated by the crashing thunder and stabbing lightning filling the sky.

STORYLINES

Drive out the Beast: The people of the town are terrified and are looking for a group of players to help them. Read the following to the PCs:

As you enter the small town of Briar Glen, you can't help but notice the stares from the town's people. Each person has dark circles from lack of sleep and some shake from fear. An old woman races up to you and demands, "Are you here to save us? Please, tell me you will save us! Our Sheriff has lost all his deputies to the creatures that have escaped from that mad Doctor's mansion! At night there are constant howls from these beasts, and I can't sleep! Are you here to help us?"

As if hearing the woman, a high-pitched scream comes from the nearby woods.

"It's them!" screams the old woman. She turns and runs back to her home. Ahead, you see the Sheriff's building, The Golden Oak Inn, a townhouse surrounded by raised flower beds, and a path that leads down to the coastline. The sheriff, an old man well beyond his best years, is standing in the center of the town and is looking at you.

Control the Beast: Breata Goldsun has hidden a golden apple the Doctor needs in her house and the locket with Dr. Koch's beloved Caroline's portrait is tied around the neck of the Uplift Dog being held in a second-floor cell in the Sheriff's building.

Free the Beast: There are three Uplift hiding in Briar Glen. An Uplift Dog has been captured by the Sheriff and is being held in a cage on the second floor of the Sheriff's building. The second two Uplift are experimental Uplift Plants (juvenile and mature specimens) that Breata Goldsun has engineered in her home. The Uplift Dog and Uplift Plants should be returned to Zero on Uplift Island.

THE SHERIFF'S BUILDING

Sheriff Dermot Sclator has a small office reflecting the typically low crime rate in the town of Briar Glen. There are two floors to the building:

- The ground floor is an open office for Sheriff Sclator.
- The second floor has two jail cells to hold prisoners until they can be taken by secured wagon to be tried in the nearby city of Velden. One of these cells have a caged Uplift Dog.

STORYLINES

Drive out the Beast: The Sheriff will want the players to join him to eliminate the town of the Uplift. The Sheriff has captured an Uplift Dog and holds it in a second-floor cell. The Uplift Dog is intelligent and will want to help the Sheriff. It will start a pattern of two short barks to communicate with the players. If the players roll a DC10 Charisma check, they can convince the Sheriff that the dog does not need to be killed.

"You've arrived just in time! These damnable Uplift are killing and eating the people of this town. Come into my office so we can talk. I think Briar Glen could really use your help." He waves you into his office. "We captured a hideous dog Dr. Koch experimented on. The mutt is bloody smart and has escaped once already, so I keep it in a cage inside the cell. I don't want to wake up to the dreadful thing chewing off my leg."

Control the Beast: Get the locket hanging around the neck of the Uplift Dog and take the maps from the office.

Free the Beast: Free the Uplift Dog and bring it to Uplift Island.

THE SHERIFF'S BUILDING - GROUND FLOOR

Sheriff Sclator has a sparse office with only a basic plank wood table dominating the room. The players will find a map on the table that names all the buildings in Briar Glen and three locations known to the Sheriff on Uplift Island.

A dog on the second floor of the building starts to howl as you step into Sheriff Sclator's office. The Sheriff motions to a table in the center of the room and invites you to sit. Maps of the town, forest, and shoreline are scattered on the table. Small crosses show where Uplift have killed the Sheriff's constables.

ACTIVITY

Players can ask to see the map. If the players choose to join Sclator and free Briar Glen of the Uplift, then Sclator will freely share the map with the players. If the players do not join the Sheriff, he will quickly gather the maps and stuff them into a box he keeps under the table.

If the players indicate that they have been asked to free the caged Uplift dog, Sclator will pull out an old iron six-shooter and point it at the group. He will demand that they go up the stairs, where he will imprison the players in one of the cells. If the players choose to attack Sclator, then Sclator will shoot. Sclator is a good shot and will get three rounds off before the players can reach him. The DM should roll 1d4 for each shot. If the rolled number is 1 or 4, then the shot hits true in the central mass of the player, reducing their HP by 50%. If

the number rolled is 3, the player receives 5HP damage from a glancing shot. If the number rolled is 2, the shot goes wide, and no one is hit. After emptying his gun, Sclator will pull a dagger from his belt to defend himself.

If the players do not attack Sclator then he will march them upstairs and lock them into the cell next to the Uplift Dog.

NPC

Sheriff Sclator

REWARD

Maps detailing the buildings in Briar Glen, Uplift Island, the shoreline, and the woods. There are no maps detailing the underground tunnels or Dr. Koch's compound.

THE SHERIFF'S BUILDING - SECOND FLOOR

The age and deterioration of the Sheriff's building will become apparent to the players if they explore the second floor. The Sheriff has been without deputies for a while. Duties have been ignored, such as cleaning the mess from the Uplift Dog. Urine drips and runs out of the cage.

The smell of urine and excrement hits you as you step up the stairs to the second floor. Mercifully, the Uplift Dog stops barking as you step onto the second floor. You can hear heavy panting as he watches you from inside his cage. The cell next to the Uplift Dog has one cot with barely enough room for two occupants.

ACTIVITY

Sclator will arrest and imprison the players if he suspects they are aligned with either Dr. Koch or The Uplift.

RESOLUTION

The players will find that, even if locked in a cell, they can break the lock with a DC10 Strength (Athletics) check. The jail is very old and rarely used.

MONSTER

Uplift Dog

REWARD

Tied around the neck of the Uplift Dog is a locket with a picture of Dr. Koch's beloved Caroline. The locket is made of solid gold and is worth 25GP.

BREATA GOLDSUN'S HOUSE - GROUND FLOOR

The ground floor of Breata's house has three main rooms:

Living Room: Breata will offer to make the players tea and lead a conversation about botany and the power of herbal remedies.

Office: Breata's office has several indoor plants. One plant in the far corner of the room has spiky leaves and is a juvenile Uplift Plant. The juvenile cannot walk, and its barb is only 1 foot long. The stinger has the same level of toxicity as an adult Uplift Plant.

Trunk Room: A locked trunk contains three Soul Honey jars that Breata uses to raise the Uplift Plants. The lock is weak and can be easily broken with a hammer, sliced by a sword, or some other melee weapon.

The scent of flowers fills the house of Breata Goldsun, and you are reminded of your great aunt and the flowery perfume she used to wear. Breata, with a warm smile and gentle laugh, invites you to join her for a bit of tea and cake in her living room.

ADDITIONAL INFORMATION

Office: A juvenile Uplift Plant is growing in the Office, and it looks exactly like any typical plant. Players who successfully roll a DC12 Intelligence (Nature) check will be able to identify the Juvenile due to the unusual coloring of the poisonous barb growing out of the plant's stigma. Breata will be enthusiastic about explaining that she engineered the intelligent plant and will detail the properties of the Uplift Plants she is growing. The DM can decide if they want Breata to "accidentally" let the players know that a full-size Uplift Plant is growing in the Sunroom on the house's second floor.

ACTIVITY

Explore the ground floor of the house.

MONSTER

Juvenile Uplift Plant

REWARD

Three jars of Soul Honey

BREATA GOLDSUN'S HOUSE - SECOND FLOOR

The second floor of Breata's house has the following

three main rooms:

Sunroom: a mature Uplift Plant is hidden among the many plants along with a Golden Apple.

Study: the study has books scattered across the floor. If the players roll a successful DC15 Intelligence check, they will find Breata's herbal book. A small room at the back of the study leads to a small storage room that contains family tokens and nothing of value.

Bedroom: Breata's bedroom with a dresser.

In addition to the main rooms there is a small water closet with a hidden storage unit. If the players roll DC 10 Investigation check while in the water closet, they will notice that the back wall is false and can be removed. Behind the false wall is a barrel that contains one pot of Soul Honey, 15 silver pieces, and 5 gold pieces.

As you step up the stairs, you feel the humidity in the air and the temperature increasing significantly. You see the reason as soon as you step onto the second-floor landing. A Sunroom, full of exotic plants, with large windows in the walls and ceiling. A complex misting system to keep the plants watered dominates most of the second floor. In front of you is a door to a water closet. In addition, there is a bedroom and a locked door to your right.

ADDITIONAL INFORMATION

Sunroom: The walls and ceiling of the Sunroom are comprised of thick glass windows to increase the heat of the sun. Every ten minutes, the misting system sprays water into the air, soaking the plants. The heat and humidity will be uncomfortable to all races except those that live in or are conditioned to hot climates such as Dragonborn. All other players, except those who are used to the heat, must roll 1d6 each time they reach for their weapons. If they roll a 6, the weapon slips from their grip, rattling onto the floor.

Study: Breata is an extraordinarily smart botanist, but she is not very organized. The scattering of books on the floor of the Study is her way of cataloging her work. A successful DC15 Intelligence (Investigation) check will reveal a book where Breata has been collecting herbal remedies. See the section "Breata Goldsun's Herbal Book" for a complete list of the herbal remedies she has collected.

Bedroom: It is a simple bedroom. Two players can rest in Breata's room if they ask her. Her only payment will be to have the players cut a new cord of wood in preparation for the coming winter. If the players agree, they will find an axe behind the house.

ACTIVITY

The Uplift Plant has a Golden Apple, symbol of new life, at its base covered in soil. The trick will be how to get the Golden Apple from the protection of the plant.

MONSTER

Uplift Plant

REWARD

- Breata's herbal book in the Study

- Golden Apple (worth 35gp) in the Sunroom

THE GOLDEN OAK INN

The Golden Oak Inn is a stout, two-story building that acts as the central gathering place for the people of Briar Glen. The Bar is always full, and drinks are quickly poured by the owner, Gwen Le Favre. Gwen has owned the Golden Oak for many years, and even though she was not raised in Briar Glen, the town's people have come to love her.

The Golden Oak Inn is comprised of the following rooms:

The Bar - a communal place where drinks can be purchased, and good conversations are had.

Game Room - chance your luck and play a game of dice.

Meeting Room - Alicia Van Buren, from the Full Moon Circus, will challenge players to her side quest titled "Exploitation."

Bedroom (with a bathroom) - players can rest for the night and clean themselves up.

Storage Room - beer and liquor are kept in a cool room.

The sweet smell of smoke from clay pipes and the hum of chatter from a dozen people greet you as you step into the Golden Oak Inn. Behind the bar is Gwen Le Favre, working hard as she does every day, pulling drinks and keeping her patrons happy. Tables fill the room, and five stools line the bar, three of them occupied. To your left, an open door reveals a small meeting room with comfortable chairs and a single occupant, a garishly dressed elven woman.

You see stairs leading up to a second story, where you assume rooms can be rented by night for weary travelers. Loud cheers can be heard from a back room where there is clearly a game of some kind being played.

STORYLINES

Drive out the Beast: Players can pay the local people to join them in driving out the Uplift. Players can either bribe the locals (1gp per person), buy the entire bar two rounds of drinks (DM will need to roll 3d6+4gp for the cost for each round), or give an impassioned (DC10 Charisma check) speech to rally them together in driving out the Uplift. The DC is low on purpose because the locals, fired up and angry, will join them in routing the Uplift from their town, but in their hearts, they are cowards. For 1d4+1 rounds after the first encounter with an Uplift, the locals, terrified of the Uplift, will run away from the group.

Control the Beast: Gwen Le Favre makes a cocktail called Lightning Bolt that the Doctor enjoys. It has been two weeks since one of the doctor's minions have bought him a flask of beverage and Gwen knows that the Doctor will pay 15GP if the players can bring him a bottle.

Free the Beast: Free the captured Uplift Wilding on the second floor.

ADDITIONAL INFORMATION

The Bar: Gwen Le Favre is the owner of the Golden Oak and is quick to pull a fresh pint of beer or mix a drink. Below is a list of drinks and prices:

Name	Drink Type	Price
Summer Dew	White Wine	2gp per bottle
Midnight Forest	Red Wine	3gp per bottle
Mother Superior	Brown Ale	3sp per tankard
Full Moon	Pale Ale	2sp per tankard
Deadfur Strong	Stout	7sp per tankard
Lightning Bolt	Cocktail	3gp per glass
Green Monster	Cocktail	1gp per glass
Monster-Tini	Cocktail	2gp per glass
Lightning	Shot (local gin)	1gp per shot
Old Man	Shot (imported W	1gp per shot

Game Room: players can join the game *Double Down* being played by three other locals. For each round, the players and locals must pay 5GP into a pot in the center of the table. The winner takes half of the coins in the pool. The loser must take the other half of the collection and buy a fresh round of drinks (any change is added back to the pot). The rules for Double Down are covered in the section "Game within a Game" later in the book.

Meeting Room: The players will find Alicia Van Buren in the meeting room, where she is talking loudly and boldly about her exploits with the Full Moon Circus. Alicia will also tell the players she is looking to capture Uplift and will pay any player who brings her a new creature. See the side quest, "Exploitation." In addition, Alicia can command all animals as she has a ring called "Mandatum Anulum - The Command Ring" on her right hand.

Bedroom: Players can stay at the inn for 5sp per night. It costs an additional 1sp to use the bath.

Storage Room: Four barrels of ale and five small cases of liquor are kept in the cool, dark storage room. In the far corner of the room is a cage holding an Uplift Wildling.

SIDE QUEST: A THIEVES JOB

Gwen Le Favre will split the value of any item of artwork they can steal from Dr. Koch's Gallery. She has a buyer from the nearby town of Velden.

MONSTER

Uplift Wildling

NPC

- Gwen Le Favre
- Alicia Van Buren

THE QUAY

Briar Glen has a small quay with only one boat, a dinghy named The Talisman, that is captained by Berwyn Jeffries. On closer inspection, the players will see that the boat has cracks in its hull, and it is incredible that The Talisman can still float.

Sharp, salt air welcomes you as you step up to the small quay where an old captain sits on an upturned orange crate whittling a bone into the shape of a dagger. Behind him is a small, old boat bobbing on the water. The man stands as you make your way down the length of the quay. He smiles at you and says "Hello, I've heard about you. My name is Berwyn, and this here is my ship. I can take you wherever you want to go up and down the coast. All I charge is a meager 5sp for each hour we are out at sea."

STORYLINES

Drive out the Beast: Players can hire The Talisman to sail them to Uplift Island and hunt down the Uplift to drive them out. In addition, the players can also hire Berwyn and the boat to float over the land bridge that joins the Island to the mainland at high tide. From there, they can drop dynamite onto the land bridge, flood the underground tunnels, and permanently lock the Uplift on the Island. Dynamite can be found in the Storage Room below the Doctor's Tower.

Control the Beast: Take the boat and sneak on the West side of the island.

Free the Beast: Use The Talisman to ferry Uplift to the island.

ACTIVITY

Berwyn will insist on captaining the boat and will not be persuaded or intimidated otherwise. Only magic or overcoming the old man will allow the players to sail the boat without him. The ship is small, and only 3 players, plus Berwyn, can ride at the same time. Animals larger than a dog will not be able to ride the boat. If the players choose to add more players, then they run the risk of capsizing. Use the following table to determine if the boat turns turtle and capsizes:

Roll 1d8	Number of people in the boat including the captain
Roll 1 and the boat will capsize	4
Roll 1 or 8 and the boat will capsize	5
Roll 1, 4, or 8 and the boat will capsize	6
Roll 1, 4, 6, or 8 and the boat will capsize	7
The boat will immediately capsize the moment the 8th person steps fully onto the dinghy	8

The water is cold, but the boat is never more than 100 feet from shore. Players who can swim will make it to land before hypothermia sets in. Players who cannot swim will need to roll a 1d4+2 to determine how many turns they spend in the water before they start to drown. The D&D Player Manual specifies holding your breath as "a character can hold their breath for a number of minutes equal to 1 + their Constitution Modifier." With that said, the following table reflects the length of time different races can hold their breath underwater:

Race	Minutes holding breath under water
Dwarf	2 minutes
Elf	5 minutes
Halfling	1 minute
Human	3 minutes
Dragonborn	5 minutes
Gnome	1 minute
Half-Elf	4 minutes
Half-Orc	3 minutes
Tiefling	4 minutes
Uplift	5 minutes

If the boat does flip, the players who can swim should roll a DC15 Strength (Athletics) check to see if they can right the capsized vessel while treading water. If the players fail to re-float The Talisman, they will lose 2HP each round due to the cold water but can try righting the boat on the next round. This increases to 3 HP per round after five rounds.

RESOLUTION

The players can sail up and down the coast.

MONSTER NPC

Captain Berwyn Jeffries

MAGIC ITEM

Bone Dagger - Captain Berwyn Jeffries will sell the Bone Dagger to the players for 15gp.

UPLIFT ISLAND

UPLIFT ISLAND ENCOUNTERS

The Island is small, with a few trees, some scattered shrubs, and three huts. It has a pebble-covered shoreline covered in a common seaweed that's locals call Ocean Catnip. The west side of the Island has a collection of small caves that the players can explore.

Players will only be detected arriving on the Island if they cross the tidal road the East side of the Island where Zero has Uplift Soldiers guarding the Tidal Road. Players will not be seen or attacked if they cross the water and land on the Island's North, West, or East side.

Zero has created a sanctuary on a small coastal island connected to the shoreline with a tidally locked road. She, and other Uplift she has rescued, live on the Island in modest huts that protect them from the storms. The sea salt air and harsh winds are always present and chill you to the bone.

STORYLINES

Drive out the Beast: Find Ocean Catnip.

Control the Beast: Find Ocean Catnip.

Free the Beast: Zero would like you to bring any Uplift you find in the caves to her hut.

ACTIVITY

Small caves are located on the West side of the island. Each of the caves is small, ranging in size from 4-10ft in height and 6-18 feet in depth.

EXPLORING THE CAVES

The DM can roll 1d4+2 to determine how many caves are on the West side of Uplift Island. The following table will determine what the players can do in each cave:

1D4	Encounter
1	1 bushel of Ocean Catnip
2	Nothing is in the cave but pebbles
3	The tide has turned and is rushing into the cave. Huge waves crash into the cave and soak the players. Smaller players, such as Gnomes, Dwarves and Halflings, will be thrown by the waves against the rocky back of the cave and receive 1d4HP damage. There is a thirty second gap between the thundering waves to escape the cave.
4	A soaked and scared Uplift Wildling is hiding at the back of the cave and will attack players.

MONSTER

Uplift Wilding

ZERO'S HUT

Zero's hut is sparse, reflecting her personality. The players will find that she is factual and to the point. She has been through too much pain, emotionally and physically, to meander around niceties. One Uplift soldier is located outside her hut. A short sword lies on the table within her reach.

Zero stands in her hut and greets you as you enter. She is a tall, proud woman with heavy scars on her face and arms from the procedures Dr. Koch has conducted. A slight tick in her left eye gives away the constant pain she must be living with. Her hut is humble, with a small straw mattress on the floor and a table holding a collection of fruits and vegetables. She invites you to sit down and talk with her as she opens a small book to take notes. A short sword rests within easy reach on the table.

STORYLINES

Drive out the Beast: Listen to Zero's explanation that she wants to create a sanctuary on Uplift Island.

Control the Beast: Take Zero's spell book.

Free the Beast: Zero will explain that she wants to free the Uplift and bring them to the Island where she is

providing a safe sanctuary.

ACTIVITY

The players need to negotiate with Zero. The DM's direction for the game will determine the negotiation tactic. Apply the following:

Drive out the Beast: What the Sheriff wants closely aligns with what Zero wants. Players should roll a DC15 Charisma (Persuasion) check. If they are successful, they will tell Zero that their goal is to eliminate the threat of the Uplift from Briar Glen. Zero will offer the players 3 magic spells (the DM can choose which spells) that can be used to help capture the Uplift. She will also offer the players 25gp for each Uplift they guide safely to the Island. If the players fail the Persuasion check, then they will switch to the campaign "Free the Beast" if they are currently running a different Storyline. This will not cause the players to turn against each other but will lead to friction in the team.

Control the Beast: Zero will use her Charisma to influence the players to align with her campaign of freeing the Uplift. Players must succeed on the DC15 Charisma (Persuasion) check to remain loyal to Dr. Koch. If they fail, the player will switch alliance to Zero and continue the campaign using the Storyline "Free the Beast." If the player succeeds, then aggressive negotiations can start. The players will need to capture Zero to steal her notebook. Zero is a level 20 Intelligentia Uplift. She will attack both with her short sword and with magic. The DM should review the "History of the Uplift" section and decide which spells Zero can use. The Uplift Warrior guarding the hut will step in and join the fight.

Free the Beast: Zero will explain her story of creating a safe place for the Uplift. Players aligned to the "Free the Beast" will receive 5 spells from the Spells section in the book. The DM can choose which spells to give. In addition, she will reward you with 25gp for each rescued Uplift.

NPC

Zero, leader of the Uplift

MONSTER

Uplift Warrior

REWARD

Zero has a notebook where she keeps her daily journal and a collection of spells

UPLIFT INFIRMARY

A haggard man named Déka is the only person on the Island who cares for the injured Uplift. Many Uplift creatures arriving on the Island are hurt by Dr. Koch's abuse and malnutrition. Déka will introduce himself as a nurse, but not a very good one. The infirmary, like all the huts on Uplift Island, is small and cramped. There are two beds, both occupied by unconscious Uplift, a small table and stool, along with a small chest that looks like it contains medicine.

The smells of vomit and excrement hit you as you step into the small Uplift Infirmary. The figure of an old man, obviously another of Dr. Koch's creations, is tending two Uplift lying in their beds. The man turns and looks at you. "See this," and he points a bony finger to a cot, "this is how Uplift arrive to our island. Half dead and half starved. And the Sheriff calls us the monsters!"

STORYLINES

For all storylines: The medicine chest contains 6 oz of Golden Tea that can be used in drinks that contain trace amounts of Soul Honey. See Breata Goldsun's Herbal Book.

Free the Beast: If the players explain that they are there to help the Uplift, Déka will share three herbal remedies from his medicine chest. The DM should pick three

medications from Breata Goldsun's Herbal Book.

ACTIVITY

Players can pay Déka either with one ration of food or 2gp for him to look at any woods the players may have. The remedy Déka offers should be one herbal remedy from Breata Goldsun's Herbal Book. The DM can roll 1d10 to select a random remedy.

If the players choose to fight Déka, they must be quick. Déka has a jar of concentrated Rosemary Fire Tea that he will pour down the throats of both patients. The patients, revived from the hypothermia they had been suffering from, will leap up and attack. Both are Uplift Warriors.

MONSTER

Two Uplift Warriors

ABANDONED HUT

The hut is run down and neglected but not completely empty. What looks like a collection of body parts scattered in the corner of the room will, if the players investigate the area, come to life as a Corrupted Uplift, an early creation engineered by Dr. Koch.

Holes in the roof let in the rain as you step into the small, abandoned hut. Scanning the room, you see a pile of straw filling one corner, a broken table and chairs, and a bed with what looks like a pile of body pieces filling the remaining space in the hut. The air is dank and rotten with the smell of decay.

STORYLINES

Drive out the Beast: The players should try and escape the hut and trap the Corrupted Uplift inside.

Control the Beast: Leave the Corrupted Uplift alone.

Free the Beast: Uplift Warriors will rush into the hut to calm the Corrupted Uplift. The Uplift Warriors will demand the players leave the hut.

ACTIVITY

A DC10 Intelligence (Investigation) will reveal a secret door on the floor leading to the Torture Room below.

MONSTER

Corrupted Uplift - If the Corrupted Uplift gets down to 1HP, it will try to escape through the secret door in the floor leading to the Torture Room.

TIDAL ROAD

The Tidal Road is a land bridge connecting Uplift Island with the shoreline near Briar Glen. The narrow road is 15 feet wide, dropping sharply into the cold sea. The tide covers the road twice a day. The DM can roll a 1d6 to determine if the waves cover the road. An odd number means the tide has come in, and the road is under 6 feet of water. The players will need to find another way to the island or wait 1d6 hours for the tide to go out. An even number means that the tide has pulled out and the bridge can now be crossed.

Zero will have 1d4+1 Uplift Warriors acting as sentries where the road joins Uplift Island. The Uplift Warriors will spread themselves along the tidal road if the tide has gone out.

The Tidal Road runs directly above a tunnel that leads to Dr. Koch's mansion and laboratory.

Ocean Catnip, shellfish, and seawater cover the Tidal Road connecting Uplift Island with the shoreline of Briar Glen. Uplift Warriors are standing guard where the Tidal Road connects with the Island. Waves are lapping against the road. The tide can change at any time, and the Tidal Road will sink beneath the waves again.

STORYLINES

Drive out the Beast: The Uplift struggle with swimming in the tidal waters around Uplift Island. The Sheriff would be pleased if you could trap all the Uplift on the Island and prevent them from escaping by destroying the tidal road. The players can use dynamite in the Storage Room beneath The Mad Lab tower to destroy the tidal road and flood the tunnel that runs under the road.

Control the Beast: The players can access the island using the Tidal Road.

Free the Beast: Destroy the Tidal Road.

MONSTER

Uplift Warriors

REWARD

Each Uplift Warrior has a small soldiers backpack that contains the following:

- A bedroll
- A mess kit
- A tinderbox
- 10 torches
- 5 days of rations
- A waterskin
- 1oz of Golden Tea is a leather pouch
- 50ft of hempen rope

RUINED MONUMENT

The ruined monument is a trap which is triggered if the players try to lift a stone column pinning down a broach of a black snake with red eyes.

The sea winds blow the leaves of the trees of Golden Woodland, and you could swear you can hear them whispering to each other. At the center of the woodland is a monument once sacred to the Druids. That all changed decades ago when a storm ravaged the area, causing a giant tree to collapse on the site. Now, a ruined monument and bent and broken trees are all that remain. Beneath a collapsed stone column, you do see something sparkling in the sunlight.

STORYLINES

Drive out the Beast: Use the Random Encounter table to see if an Uplift arrives.

Control the Beast: Find and take the broach.

Free the Beast: Use the Random Encounter table to determine if any Uplift come near the Ruined Monument.

ACTIVITY

One section of the monument, a stone column, has collapsed and is pinning an object to the ground. The broach will catch the player's attention as the sunlight catches and sparkles off one red-eye bloodstone gem. On closer inspection, the players will see that it is a broach of a black snake with red eyes. The column must be moved for the players to get to the broach. Of course, this is a trap. It takes a DC20 (Strength) to lift it or some other way to destroy (AC 14, 15 HP) or move it.

RESOLUTION

Lift the column and pluck the broach free.

TRAP

The weight of the fallen column keeps a pressure plate pressed down. If the pressure plate raises or lowers, it releases trip wire which causes a 15ft square net to spring up from the ground, trapping those within the area and lifting them into the air, and dangling them from a tree.

Effect: Targets all creatures within a 15 ft. square area, DC 11 Strength save or become restrained

Trigger: a pedestal activates when the stone column is lifted from a pedestal.

Countermeasures: A successful DC 10 Intelligence (Investigation) check allows a character to detect the trap's presence from mechanisms in the pedestal. Placing an object of equal weight on the pedestal prevents the trap from triggering. A successful DC 10 Dexterity (Sleight of Hand) check neutralizes the switch without causing the weight on the pedestal. An unsuccessful attempt triggers the trap.

REWARD

A black snake broach with red eyes worth 75gp

BELOW GROUND

BELOW GROUND ENCOUNTERS

The Below Ground section links Dr. Koch's mansion and lab with Uplift Island through a tunnel.

STORAGE ROOM

As the name implies, the Storage Room stores stuff. The complete list of items is below. In addition, the players will find a Time Trap Magic Item.

Dozens of crates, bags and barrels containing salted meat, apples, and general provisions of all kinds are stored here. A complex mechanical box is gently humming in the far corner of the room.

STORYLINES

Drive out the Beast: Find the dynamite

Control the Beast: The players should explore the room and take what they need.

Free the Beast: The players should take what they can.

ADDITIONAL INFORMATION

The following items are in the storage room:

- The Time Trap device (See magic items)
- Three cases of salted fish
- Four boxes of salted pork
- Two barrels of apples
- Four barrels of potatoes
- A crate of carrots
- A crate with six jars of natural bee honey
- A crate with six jars of strawberry jam
- Three crates, each with six jars of canned tomatoes
- A crate of dried noodles
- A box containing five different leather pouches, each holding salt, pepper, dried rosemary, dried coriander, and dried turmeric
- a crowbar
- a hammer
- 10 pitons
- 10 torches
- a tinderbox
- 15 sticks of dynamite. Players can light a stick of dynamite and throw it up to 40 feet away. Each creature within 5 feet of that point must make a DC 12 Dexterity saving throw, taking 2d8 bludgeoning damage on a failed save or half as much damage on a successful one. Up to five sticks can be bound together, so they explode simultaneously. Each additional stick increases the damage by 1d8 and the burst radius by 5 feet (to a maximum of 20 feet).
- 2 small barrels of gunpowder (each barrel is equivalent to five sticks of dynamite).
- 400ft of fuse. The fuse burns at a rate of 60ft per round.

REWARD

Time Trap (see Magic Items)

ARMORY

The players will see four cases holding weapons, two racks on either wall with larger weapons and two metal statues. These are Clockwork Soldiers, and they will attack if the players attempt to take any weapons. The Clockwork Soldiers have a surprise round at the start of combat.

The orange light from flaming torches on the walls illuminate Dr. Koch's armory. Swords, daggers, shields, and other large weapons are organized in cases and racks. In the center of the room stand two bronze statues of warriors in fighting poses.

STORYLINES

Drive out the Beast: The Sheriff and the people of Briar Glen are low on weapons. The weapons in the armory can be used by the townspeople.

Control the Beast: The players can arm themselves with weapons.

Free the Beast: Take range weapons for Zero's Uplift Warriors.

ACTIVITY

The statues are Clockwork Soldiers that will be activated if any of the weapons are touched by the players. A successful DC12 Intelligence (Investigation) check will reveal that trap.

MONSTER

Clockwork Soldiers

REWARD

The following weapons are in the cases in the room:

Name	Damage	Weight	Properties	Steampunk Enhancement
Double Tap Club	1d4x2 bludgeoning damage	2 lb.	Light	Large, metal ball bearings inside of the club head will bounce creating a double impact effect providing an additional 1d4 bludgeoning damage.
Dagger of Concealment	1d4 piercing + 1 use Poison Syringe (1d6 poison damage)	1 lb.	Finesse, light, thrown (20/60)	The dagger is enhanced with a concealed syringe that can be triggered to inject a one-time use point into the victim.
Shocking Hand axe	1d6 slashing + 1d6 lightning damage	2 lb.	Light, thrown (20/60)	The Doctor has concealed batteries into the handle to deliver a surprise electric shock. There is enough charge for four electric shocks.
Distance Javelin	1d6 piercing damage	2 lb.	Thrown (30/120)	The javelin has a small engine that will double the distance the javelin can be thrown. The engine only has enough fuel for one use.
Repeating Crossbow, light	1d6 piercing damage per bolt	5 lb.	Ammunition, range (80/320), loading, two-handed	The crossbow has been modified to shoot up to four darts in a short series of repeating bursts in a single action.
10 Bolt Clips	16 bolts per clip, each bolt 1d6 piercing damage	0.5l b per clip	Ammunition	Ammunition for Repeating Crossbow

FOOL'S GOLD / HIDDEN TREASURE

A tiny clockwork dragon, initially created by Dr. Koch for his beloved Caroline, is lying dormant on the pile of Treasure. The Treasure is gold-painted metal forgeries, and players who reach down to touch it will activate the clockwork dragon. Players can roll for a DC10 Wisdom (Perception) check and will be able to identify the fools gold and that the Clockwork Dragon will activate if they touch it.

Two oversized entrances, one leading to a dark tunnel and the second to the armory, dominate the West and South walls of the room. In the Northeast corner is a pile of gold coins, silver trinkets, rubies, and other precious items glinting in the light of flaming torches that burn in their sconces on the wall.

STORYLINES

Drive out the Beast: Take the Clockwork dragon and fake gold (the fake gold is painted copper).

Control the Beast: Return the Clockwork dragon to Dr. Koch.

Free the Beast: Take the treasure.

ADDITIONAL INFORMATION

If the players roll a DC12 Wisdom (Perception) check, they will discover the room's west wall is fake. The wall can be broken with a club or similar bludgeoning tool. Behind the wall are three chests of gold and four barrels of expensive wine. Each chest contains 2d12+4gp. Each barrel holds 42 gallons of Midnight Forest Red wine worth approximately 500gp and weighing 600 pounds.

A trap door in the ceiling of the hidden treasure room will lead up into Dr. Koch's mansion.

MONSTER

Clockwork Dragon

REWARD

- Clockwork Dragon
- Fake Treasure made of copper
- Gold coins and barrels of wine

THE TUNNEL

The tunnel is nearly 200ft long and will take the average player 6-7 rounds to make it through from one side to the other. The tunnel is not lit. Players with Darkvision, or similar spell/magic items will be able to see but normal players will be stumbling in total darkness unless they have a torch or similar item.

A dark, unlit tunnel disappears before you. The cold, damp air is salty, and you see water running freely down the walls. You see many dark recesses where anything could be hiding, and a series of fading echoes announces each step you take.

STORYLINES

Drive out the Beast: Use the tunnel to escort fleeing Uplift to the island or blow the tunnel and trap the Uplift on their island.

Control the Beast: Beware! The Tunnel is long and dark.

Free the Beast: Destroy the tunnel and flood the underground complex. Players will have 1d4+2 rounds

to escape from the flooding waters.

ACTIVITY

Use the Below Ground Random Encounter table every 3 rounds to generate what will happen to the players as they walk through the tunnel.

TORTURE ROOM

A secret trap in the ceiling of the Torture Room can be detected with a DC 12 Intelligence (Investigation) check. The trap door will open into an Abandoned Hut on Uplift Island.

Decay and the acrid, iron smell of blood fills your nostrils as you step into the Torture Room. On immediate inspection, you see body parts scattered across the floor. In the corner is a manacled Uplift Wilding chained to the walls. Next to the door is a ladder. The Doctor has been busy testing the limits of his creations.

STORYLINES

Drive out the Beast: End the suffering of the Uplift Wildling.

Control the Beast: Attack the Uplift Wilding.

Free the Beast: Help the Uplift Wilding.

MONSTER

Uplift Wildling. The chained Uplift Wilding has Disadvantage on all its attacks and its speed is 0.

THE DOCTOR'S MANSION

THE DOCTOR'S MANSION ENCOUNTERS

The mansion is both a home and a functional center for the people who support Dr. Koch. Players will be able to wander around the house and explore the rooms. The mansion connects to the tower to the south of the building, known as The Mad Lab. Beneath the Mansion is an underground network of rooms and tunnels. Stairs in the entrance lead up to The Observatory and a door in the south wall connects with a small corridor leading to the Research Room along with another set of stairs leading to the second floor.

Dark blue thunderhead clouds constantly encircle Dr. Koch's mansion and lightning strikes the top of the adjacent tower bringing life to the creatures he creates.

ENTRANCE

Dr. Koch will greet the players as they enter the house but will leave very quickly. The players should be encouraged to explore the house.

You step into the Doctor's house and are greeted by a lean man. "Good day, I am Dr. Koch and I welcome you to my house," he says with notably raspy voice. "Please excuse me, but I am in the middle of an experiment. I encourage you to make yourself at home. I am certain we will meet up again later today." With that, the doctor turns and abruptly leaves. You look around the room and notice several stuffed heads of wild animals

on the walls. Some are familiar, such as a lion's head, but others are grotesque mixes of animals. One appears to be a cross between a boar and a tiger.

STORYLINES

For all storylines: The players should explore the house and grounds.

ADDITIONAL INFORMATION

If the players try to attack Dr. Koch before he leaves, they will find that he is a fast-moving man and will dodge them. As he escapes the room, he will call out for two Steampunk Orcs to enter and attack the players.

MONSTER

Steampunk Orcs

RESEARCH ROOM

The Research Room contains maps and documents covering the travels of Dr. Koch. If players roll a successful DC15 Intelligence (Investigation) check, they will find a map that shows all the levels and labelled locations in the campaign. Players who were told by Dr. Koch where to look for the map will find the maps without a roll. A door on the east wall leads to a corridor that connects to the kitchen and leads to The Mad Lab.

Scattered maps, journals and other documents clutter a large table in the Research Room.

STORYLINES

For all storylines: Take the maps.

REWARD

Maps with labels for each level in the campaign

KITCHEN

An automaton is stationed in the kitchen as a cook. The players can ask the automaton to make food for them using the list below. The players can also choose to attack the automaton. If the players explore the kitchen, they will find a storage room in the back that contains small barrels of apples, potatoes, carrots, and jars of pickled vegetables.

As you enter the kitchen, a collection of delicious smells assaults your nostrils. An automaton cook buzzes and whirrs as it spins in place, making the meals for the workers in the mansion. A sign on the counter lists the meals that can be made for a fee of 5sp. Customers can drop their coins into a half-full jar on the counter.

STORYLINES

Drive out the Beast: Keep your energy up and have a meal.

Control the Beast: Enjoy your meal. It is free today.

Free the Beast: The automaton cook will be suspicious of the players and refuse to serve the players.

ACTIVITY

The automaton can make any of the following meals. Each meal will cost 5sp and the coins can be inserted into a jar on the kitchen counter. The robot will only make one meal per player, and the meal will restore 1d4+1HP.

- Grilled wild boar chops
- Broiled salmon and potatoes
- Roast chicken and potatoes
- Smoked sausage, goose eggs, and dates
- Cheese pie and onion soup
- Baked boar and greens
- Minted pea soup
- Baked goat flank
- Rabbit stew and willow crackers

The players can try to take the jar of silver coins. The automaton cook will grab the pot back and attack the players if they do. The jar's coins will fly around the room as the cook fights. The automaton cook is fixed in place, giving the players the option to step out of range of the flailing arms. If the players defeat the cook, they will find 6d10+5sp.

MONSTER

Automaton Cook

REWARD

A delicious meal

GRAND ROOM

The Grand Room is the one area of the house where people working for Dr. Koch will socialize. Everyone in the room will leave if a player attacks. The occupants of the space include:

- Jetts, the doctor's assistant
- Plague Doctor
- A Steampunk Orc

The room is full of the people and creatures who serve Dr. Koch. You see the doctor's loyal assistant, Jetts, the cold-blooded Plague Doctor, and a Steampunk Orc who looks out of place. Comfortable chairs and sofas are placed near an arched window with views of the countryside surrounding the mansion.

STORYLINES

Drive out the Beast: The Steampunk Orc can be bribed for 5sp. It will answer one question. For 10gp, it will join the players and disavow his loyalty to Dr. Koch. The players must keep paying the Steampunk Orc 10gp daily for its loyalty.

Control the Beast: Jetts will tell the players that Dr. Koch is working at the top of the Tower. He will misdirect all other players to the Torture room below ground.

Free the Beast: Attack the Plague Doctor.

ADDITIONAL INFORMATION

Use the following table to determine the name of the Steampunk Orc:

1d10	Orc Name
1	Kerghug
2	Qog
3	Haguk
4	Olaugh
5	Eggha
6	Hagu
7	Eghuglat
8	Hig
9	Kurdan
10	Ig

MONSTERS

- Steampunk Orc
- Clockwork Soldiers

REWARD

Information

THE GALLERY

The display room is where the Doctor showcases his collection of fine art. The price for each item can be found in the list below. Adjacent to the Display room is a small storage room. The storage room contains three chests with additional, lower-valued art items. Players can roll DC15 Intelligence (Investigation) to find a trap door that leads down to a treasure room.

Ornate statues, exquisite paintings, and precious jewelry are on full display. The light from the windows causes each item to sparkle and shine as you walk around the room. The artwork depicts various exotic locations, all include Dr. Koch. Behind the Gallery is a small storage room with several large chests.

STORYLINES

Drive out the Beast: Players can steal the artwork if they complete the side quest "A Thieves Job" for Gwen Le Favre.

Control the Beast: Nice paintings.

Free the Beast: Destroy the artwork.

ADDITIONAL INFORMATION

Value of each item on display in the Gallery

Item	Value
Giant opal and silver figurine of a sea serpent	1,000gp
Marble statue of an Olympian athlete (weight 500lbs)	750gp
Collection of 5 rings in gold and silver with different colored gemstones	Each ring is value at 250gp
Silver music box	150gp

Value of items in storage

Item	Value

A portrait of Dr. Koch as a young man	100gp
A silver crown	125gp
An ivory statue of a bear	75gp
A statue of a mermaid carved from a narwhale	125gp

REWARD

The value of each item

PANIC ROOM

The Panic Room is a trap.

The small room has an animal skin rug on the floor and, in the far corner, a small, open chest with an unmistakable glint of gold.

STORYLINES

Drive out the Beast: Take the gold.

Control the Beast: If the players step into the room, Jetts will grab them by the arm and warn them, "Stop! You don't want to go in there." If the players persist, Jetts will let them enter the room. He will stay outside.

Free the Beast: Enter if you dare.

ACTIVITY - COLLAPSING CEILING TRAP

If a player steps on the rug in the center of the room, the ceiling will collapse. All players in the room will be affected by the collapsing ceiling.

Effect: Targets all players within a 10 ft. square area, DC 14 Dexterity (Stealth) save or take 24 (4d10) damage.

Trigger: Activates when a player steps on the rug and triggers the ceiling to collapse.

Resolution: Once the trap is detected with a successful DC 15 Wisdom (Perception) check, an iron spike or similar object can be wedged between the floor and the ceiling. The rug can also be magically held shut using the arcane lock spell or similar magic.

REWARD

Small chest with 25gp

BEDROOMS

There are four bedrooms on the second floor:

- **Servants' quarters**: three beds in a spartan room.
- **Head of Household**: one basic bed and an armchair.
- **Guest Room**: A comfortable room for traveling guests.
- **Dr. Koch's private room**: a luxurious room with a walk-in wardrobe containing a chest of 30gp and 15sp.

The austere servants' bedrooms reflect the poverty of their lives. A second room is private for the Head of Household, who also has her own comfortable chair. A crackling fireplace welcomes you into the guest bedroom together with a large, plush bed and extra wide armchair. For the doctor, a purple bed and an overstuffed armchair reflect the high status he holds for himself. The bed looks very inviting.

ADDITIONAL INFORMATION

The players can choose to rest in the rooms. The DM will need to roll 1d6 for every hour of elapsed gameplay. If the number equals 6, a house cleaner will enter the room and scream, alerting a Clockwork Soldier, who will take two rounds to arrive at the room and attack the players.

THE OBSERVATORY

The telescope has a unique lens that shows Uplift as a bright red. Solving the anagram, the players can see through the telescope and where Uplift are located on the map.

A large brass telescope fills the observatory. Walking up to the telescope, you see a lock on the eyepiece, and below the lock is a sign that says, "I am a Moon Starer. What am I?"

STORYLINES

For all storylines: Use the telescope to find the Uplift.

ACTIVITY

The players will need to solve an anagram to use the observatory. The anagram is: Moon Starer = Astronomer

RESOLUTION

If the players solve the riddle, they can use the telescope.

EXPERIMENT ROOM / UPLIFT CONTAINMENT ROOM

The Plague Doctor is a cruel man and was hired so he can explore his sadistic tendencies. The room has a steel chair that the Plague Doctor uses to electrify Uplift as he assesses how resistant they are to pain. There is a smaller room where an Uplift Boar-Tiger is in an iron chest waiting for the next round of tests.

The Plague Doctor's looming figure dominates this room of horrors. A steel chair stands in the center of the room with chains and other bloodied restraints on the floor. A high-pitched howl can be heard from a containment room. The Plague Doctor motions for you to enter.

STORYLINES

Drive out the Beast: Eliminate the threat of the Boar-Tiger.

Control the Beast: The Plague Doctor is looking for a willing PC to sit in the steel chair to ensure it works. The DM will randomly choose a player. The Plague Doctor has no alliance with Dr. Koch and, when the player is sitting in the chair, will throw a lever sending electricity through the player, who will receive 3d10+4 Lightning damage.

Free the Beast: Free the Uplift Boar-Tiger.

MONSTERS

- Plague Doctor
- Uplift Boar-Tiger

THE MAD LAB

THE MAD LAB ENCOUNTERS

Players will have three levels to explore in The Mad Lab. Bold experiments designed to test the limits of man's ability to mimic the gods are centered on the tower adjacent to Dr. Koch's mansion. The building, better known as The Mad Lab, is where the wildness of imagination meets with the coldness of the scientific mind. Advance through the three levels of the tower and come away inspired either through fear of the evilness on display or by the arrogance of one man's ego!

STORYLINES

Drive out the Beast: Destroy the Mad Lab and hope the Doctor doesn't escape to continue engineering his corrupted creations.

Control the Beast: Bring the Doctor the items he asked you to collect and Zero's book of spells.

Free the Beast: You must help any Uplift to escape the Mad Lab and guide them to Uplift Island.

GROUND FLOOR

The ground floor of the Mad Lab is Dr. Koch's preparation room, and the players will find a trap door that leads to the below ground Storage Room. The room has a Clockwork Soldier that will ignore the players unless it is stopped from completing its programmed tasks.

You step into the tower's ground floor and see an automaton in a soldier's uniform picking up and moving crates. This is one of Dr. Koch's Clockwork Soldiers. A stone spiral staircase leads to the next floor. In the back of the room is a marble table with body parts loosely connected to form the rough outline of a humanoid. This is clearly a preparation room for the creation of a new Uplift.

STORYLINES

Drive out the Beast: Smash up the body pieces to stop a future Uplift from being created.

Control the Beast: The players should try to create their own Uplift using the body parts and Soul Honey.

Free the Beast: Collect the Soul Honey to bring back to Zero.

MONSTER

Clockwork Soldier

REWARD

Two jars of Soul Honey

SECOND FLOOR – THE HONEY ROOM

The second floor of The Mad Lab is known as The Honey Room due to the large glass vat of Soul Honey in which Uplift bodies are manufactured.

Large clockwork wheels slowly spin and grind, filling the second floor with continuous noise supplemented by the whirring of electrified machines. Dominating the room is a massive glass vat filled with Soul Honey. Within the vat, an Uplift experiment is growing. The spiral staircase continues up to the roof, where you can see lightning and hear the wailing cries of a creature. Steampunk Orcs are working with Jetts, the Doctor's assistant, in managing the machines.

STORYLINES

Drive out the Beast: Destroy machines and vats in the room.

Control the Beast: The players should use the large vats of Soul Honey to grow your new engineered life form.

Free the Beast: Steal equipment and Soul Honey to bring back to Zero.

MONSTER

Steampunk Orc

NPC

Jetts

ROOF

The roof of the lab is where Dr. Koch brings life to his creations. The focal point of the roof is a spiraling set of nested copper rings that attracts the lightning. In the far corner is a dais on which Dr. Koch is standing and bringing life to his latest Uplift creation. In addition, there are carts with surgical instruments, a stretcher, and several tables stacked with half-filled jars of Soul Honey.

Continuous forks of lightning stab a set of circular copper spinning rings. Lying on a dais is a body being jolted by blue and purple bolts of electricity. A peal of thunder roars in the heavens and in response the body cries back. The Monster is rising!

STORYLINES

Drive out the Beast: Destroy The Monster.

Control the Beast: Give the doctor the four items he needs. He will be upset if the players do not have all the items and will command The Monster to attack.

Free the Beast: Free The Monster and bring it to Zero.

ADDITIONAL INFORMATION

The Monster has just been given life and it is confused. Roll 1d4 to determine how it will react:

1d4	The Monster's Reaction
1	Terrified, The Monster pulls off the straps holding into the dais, runs to the edge of the tower and leaps into the void. Roll 8d10 to determine how much damage he suffers from his fall.
2	Angered by the storm, The Monster stands on the dais and reaches his arms high into the sky. Raw lightning streaks down and hits it's outstretched hands but he stands and absorbs the electricity. The Monster will be able to attack with a 5 foot wide bolt of Lightning (melee attack, self (15 ft. line), 1d6+2 Lightning damage).
3	The Monster stays lying on the dais.
4	The Monster sits up, reaches for the Doctor, and strangles him. He looks at the players and there is deep knowledge in his eyes. If the players are following the "Drive out the Beast" Storyline, then The Monster will speak to the players and explain that he will help them restore peace to Briar Glen. If the players are following "Control the Beast" then The Monster will attack them. If the players are following "Free the Beast" then the monster will say, "Take me to Zero."

MONSTER

The Monster

For larger or more advanced teams, the DM can choose to add 1d4 Steampunk Orcs as guards.

DUNGEON MASTER TOOLS

DUNGEON MASTER TOOLS

Do you feel it? The immense burden and power of being the Dungeon Master! Being a DM inspired me to write the Penny Blood Adventures. The focus of this section is to list out the tools you can use to help with The Mad Lab.

First, let's cover the files you get with the game. Included with The Mad Lab is a set of files. Expand the ZIP file, and you will have the following:

- Maps: they come with labels, without labels, printer friendly, and in sepia colors
- Encounters: each encounter has artwork
- NPCs: each NPC has both artwork and a stat block
- Monster: each monster comes with artwork and a stat block
- Magic Items: each magic item comes with artwork
- Tokens: each NPC, Monsters, and Magic Item has a token for online playing
- VTT Maps: VTT is a format that many online tools, such as Shard, use for gaming

Feel free to change and update the assets to meet the needs of your group.

The second item I'd like to cover is Storylines. A lot is happening with the different storylines in the game. The following three pages are 1-page summaries for each storyline you can print out as cheat sheets.

Third, if you are a new DM, purchase the Dragons of Stromwreck Isle Starter Set. What makes this kit so useful is the Starter Set Rulebook. Wizards of the Coast have done a great job summarizing how to play D&D and what you need to do as a DM.

Fourth, as the DM, your role is to guide the players through an interesting story and let them have fun. Sometimes, the players will do something outside the content of the game. That is OK. Let them do something weird and wonderful. You will be amazed at what happens.

Finally, remember that no matter what happens, you are GOD ALMIGHTY in the game.

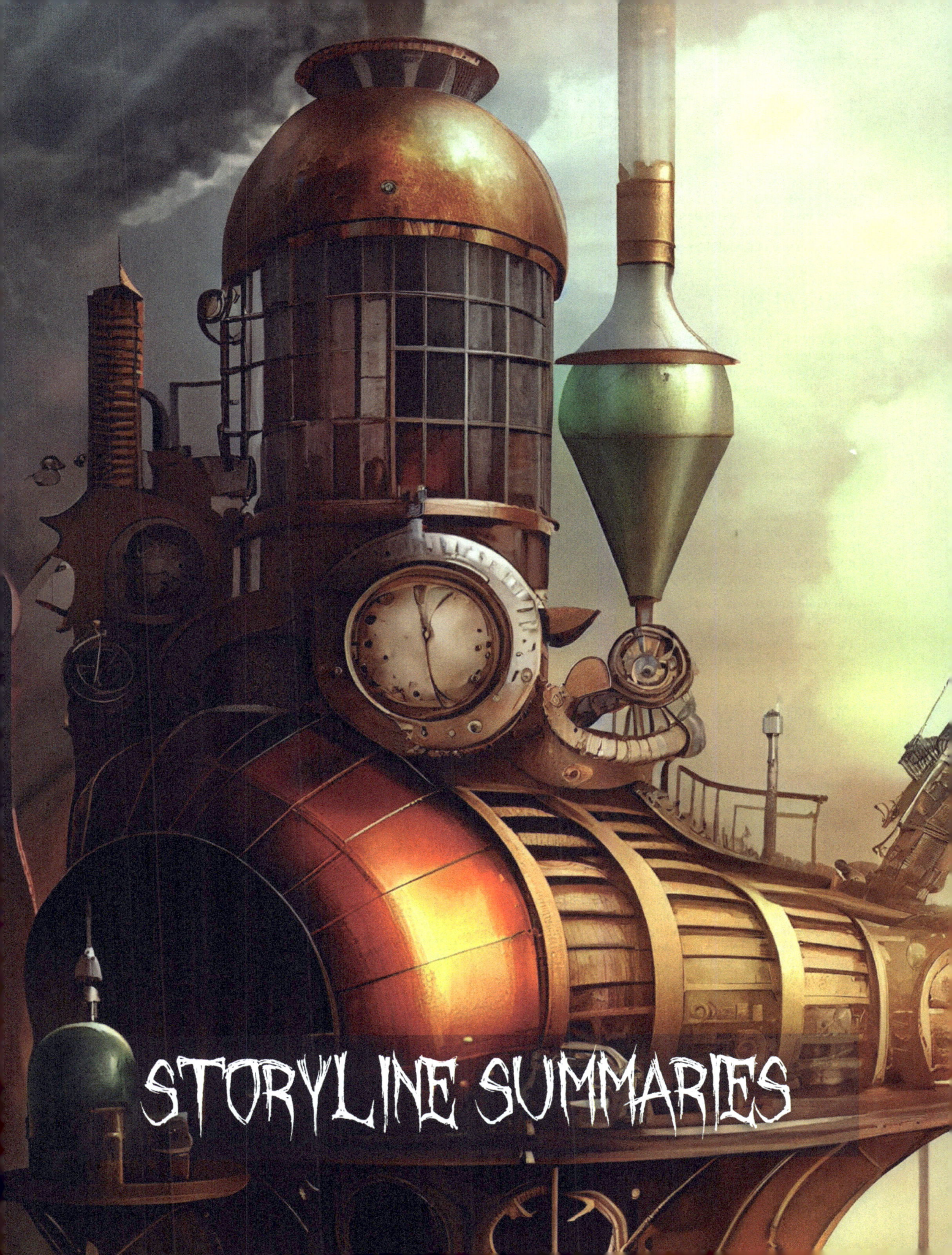

STORYLINE SUMMARIES

DRIVE OUT THE BEAST STORYLINE

Sheriff Dermot Sclator is the last man standing between the people of Briar Glen and Dr. Koch's creations. He has already lost all his deputies and is desperate to save the town from further attacks. Join the Sheriff to hunt down the Uplift, imprison Dr. Koch, and then collect a reward of 500 gold pieces.

BRIAR GLEN

Briar Glen is the town the Sheriff is protecting. Various places around town hold clues that will help the players complete the quest. The players can use dynamite to explore the Tidal Road and collapse it into the Tunnel beneath thereby preventing the Uplift access to the mainland.

The Sheriff's Building: The Uplift Dog is intelligent and will want to help the Sheriff. It will start a pattern of two short barks to communicate with the players. If the players roll a DC10 Charisma check, they can convince the Sheriff that the dog does not need to be killed.

Breata Goldsun's House: The Sheriff wants all Uplift, even the plants, gone. If the players discover the Uplift Plants Breata is growing, they will need to determine how to remove it from their home. The Juvenile Uplift Plant is in the office and the Mature Uplift Plant is in the second-floor sunroom.

The Golden Oak Inn: Bribe the townsfolk to join the players to remove the Uplift.

The Quay: With dynamite found in the Storage Room, players can take The Talisman to the Tidal Road and blow it up.

UPLIFT ISLAND

Ocean Catnip can be used to pacify the Uplift, and the plant can be found on the shores of Uplift Island. Players can use the plant to lead the Uplift away from Bria Glen.

Zero's Hut: Zero explains that she is attempting to bring all Uplift to the Island and remove the threat of attacks on the people of Briar Glen. The Sheriff will support Zero as this meets his goal of safety for the townsfolk.

Tidal Road: The Uplift struggle with swimming in the tidal waters around Uplift Island. The Sheriff would be pleased if you could trap all the Uplift on the Island and prevent them from escaping by destroying the tidal road. The players can use dynamite in the **Storage Room** beneath The Mad Lab tower to destroy the tidal road and flood the tunnel that runs under the road.

BELOW GROUND

The Below Ground rooms and tunnels crisscross much of the area between Dr. Koch's mansion and Uplift Island. Blowing up the tunnel will flood the Below Ground area and lock the Uplift on their Island. Players will find dynamite in the storage room.

Storage Room: Find the dynamite.

Fool's Gold/Hidden Treasure: The clockwork dragon can be returned to Briar Glen, where Breata Goldsun can analyze the device and build a replica. She will need the copper from the fake gold to make a larger version of the clockwork dragon that she can control.

The Tunnel: The tunnel can be used as an alternative way of escorting Uplift safely to the Island and away from Briar Glen. Players can also blow the tunnel up. Big bang time!!

THE DOCTOR'S MANSION

Dr. Koch is the creator of the Uplift creatures, and his house is a good place for players to explore to find tools they can use to help the people of Briar Glen.

Grand Room: The Steampunk Orc can be bribed for 5sp. It will answer one question. For 10gp, it will join the players and disavow his alignment. The players must keep paying the Steampunk Orc 10gp daily for its loyalty.

Experiment Room/Uplift Containment Room: The Uplift Boar-Tiger in the Containment Room is a terrifying creature that will hunt down the people of Briar Glen and can't be allowed to escape. The players need to either capture the beast or kill it.

THE MAD LAB

Destroy the Mad Lab and hope the Doctor doesn't escape to continue engineering his corrupted creations.

Ground Floor: The body parts on the table are in the first stage of being engineered into new Uplift. Players should smash up the pieces so they can't be used. Attacking the body pieces will interrupt the Clockwork Soldier from following its instructions, and it will attack.

Second Floor: The Honey Room is critical in engineering the new Uplift. Destroy machines and vats in the room, and the Doctor will be stopped from continuing his work.

Roof: The Monster is terrifying in its size. It must be destroyed.

CONTROL THE BEAST STORYLINE

The power of the gods to create intelligent life is within the grasp of Dr. Koch and the engineering he is working on in his Mad Lab. The following list is the four items that need to be found and where to find them:

- A locket with the picture of the one woman the Doctor loved, Caroline, is tied around the neck of the Uplift Dog in the Sheriff's building.

- A golden apple, the symbol of Adam and the creation myth, is hidden in the soil of the mature Uplift Plant in Breata Goldsun's house.

- A black snake broach with red eyes, the symbol of evil, is pinned to the ground by a fallen column at the Ruined Monument.

- The spell book created by Zero - Zero always keeps the book with her.

BRIAR GLEN

Two of the items Dr. Koch needs are in Briar Glen. The locket and the golden apple.

The Sheriff's Building: Dr. Koch finds Sheriff Sclator an annoying man who spends too much time asking questions and would prefer that the Sheriff be eliminated altogether. In addition, the Doctor's beloved Caroline's locket is tied around the neck of the Uplift Dog in the second-floor cell.

Dr. Koch can benefit from having a copy of the maps. Knowledge is power. With the right map, he can direct the players where to find Zero's hut and obtain her books of magic spells.

Breata Goldsun's House: Dr. Koch feels disgusted that he had a relationship with Breata, tainting his love for his beloved Caroline. He will do what he can to break Breata's heart. The players should find and destroy the Juvenile Uplift Plant and steal the Soul Honey in the trunk. The golden apple Dr. Koch desires is hidden in the second-floor plant room containing the Mature Uplift Plant.

UPLIFT ISLAND

Dr. Koch has heard that Ocean Catnip can be used as a pacifier for the Uplift and would like you to collect and return with as much Ocean Catnip as possible. One of the items he needs the players to find is located at the Ruined Monument encounter.

Zero's Hut: Dr. Koch wants Zero's spell book and its contents.

Abandoned Hut: Beneath the hut is a Torture Room that the Doctor knows about. He will have told you that he suspects an earlier creation, the Corrupted Uplift, is hiding in the abandoned hut. He will also tell the players that if they leave the Corrupted Uplift alone, he will not attack. The DM can choose whether to share this information with the players.

Ruined Monument: Dr. Koch has told the players that one of the critical items he needs to be returned is a broach shaped as a snake with red eyes. The broach is partially hidden by a fallen stone column.

BELOW GROUND

Beneath Dr. Koch's compound is a system of rooms and tunnels that lead from his house to Uplift Island.

Fool's Gold/Hidden Treasure: Dr. Koch lost the clockwork dragon shortly after arriving at Briar Glen. He will be delighted if you return it to him.

Torture Room: Dr. Koch would probably like to know how well an Uplift will defend itself in battle. The players can choose to attack the Uplift Wilding and record how it responds in the name of scientific research.

THE DOCTOR'S MANSION

The Doctor loves his home. It is where he lives, works, and explores the intellectual depths of his mind.

Entrance: Dr. Koch will provide one additional piece of information before he leaves the room. He will tell the players that there are maps he has drafted in the Research Room that they can use.

Research Room: The players can use the map to identify Zero's hut on Uplift Island and where to find her magic spell book. The DM will inform the players that Zero always keeps the book with her.

Experiment Room/Uplift Containment Room: Do not trust the Plague Doctor.

THE MAD LAB

The beating heart of Dr. Koch's experiments is The Mad Lab.

Ground Floor: Soul Honey is the first ingredient in breathing life into the Uplift, and there are two jars in the room. The players can begin their experiments by pouring Soul Honey onto the body parts on the marble table. The players will see the bones begin to form, muscles growing over them, and skin starting to cover them. Jetts, the Doctor's assistant, will run down the staircase and shout with delighted glee at your work. He will then encourage the players to lift the body and bring it to the second floor of The Mad Lab to grow the Uplift in a glass vat of Soul Honey.

Second Floor: The players will be directed to the Soul Honey vat if they carry up an Uplift from the ground floor. Jetts will show them the room, the machines, and the massive vat of Soul Honey needed to prepare Uplift before their birth on the roof of The Mad Lab.

Roof: The players will receive rewards if they have the Doctor's requested items.

FREE THE BEAST STORYLINE

The Uplift has been created through torture, pain, and the mad ideals of a single man. Zero, the first intelligent Uplift, has created a sanctuary on a nearby island known as Uplift Island. She will reward the players if they can guide any Uplift they find to their new shelter.

BRIAR GLEN

The townsfolk of Briar are terrified of the Uplift. The Sheriff's deputies have all been killed. The townsfolk know that the Sheriff has captured an Uplift Dog. Still, they need to find out that Breata Goldsun is creating how own Uplift Plants (she has juvenile and mature Uplift Plants in her home).

The Sheriff's Building: Sheriff Sclator has captured an Uplift Dog and keeps him in a cage on the second floor of his building.

The Golden Oak Inn: Alicia Van Buren has an Uplift Wildling in a cage in the storage room on the Inn's second floor.

The Quay: Players can hire the boat to rescue the Uplift they have found and take them to Uplift Island.

UPLIFT ISLAND

The new home of the Uplift is on the Island.

Zero's Hut: Zero will explain that she wants to free the Uplift and bring them to the Island where she is providing a safe sanctuary.

Uplift Infirmary: If the players explain that they are there to help the Uplift, Déka will share three herbal remedies from his medicine chest. The DM should pick three medications from Breata Goldsun's Herbal Book.

Abandoned Hut: Before the players can enter the abandoned hut, Uplift Warriors will rush in to calm the Corrupted Uplift. The Uplift Warriors will demand the players leave the hut.

Tidal Road: Zero wants Uplift Island to be a sanctuary for the Uplift. Zero would like the tidal road destroyed so that the Sheriff and future adventuring parties will not be able to quickly arrive at the Island and hunt the Uplift.

Ruined Monument: The Golden Woodland is where Uplift will stay before finding their way to Zero. Use the Random Encounter table to see if any Uplift comes near the Ruined Monument and attempt to persuade them to join your team.

BELOW GROUND

The below-ground tunnels and rooms are seen by the Uplift to escape from the mad Doctor.

Storage Room: Food is scarce for the Uplift, and Zero would appreciate any food you can bring to the Island.

Armory: Zero's Uplift Warriors do not have any range weapons. Zero will reward the players with one magic spell for each ranged weapon they can bring.

Fool's Gold/Hidden Treasure: The Treasure can be used by the Uplift to negotiate peace with the people of Briar Glen.

The Tunnel: A natural barrier can be created by exploding the tunnel's center and letting the seawater flood the Below Ground complex. The pressure of the seawater will cause even a tiny hole in the tunnel to expand quickly. Players will have 1d4+2 rounds to escape from the flooding waters.

Torture Room: The Uplift Wilding is clearly in pain and exhausted from the treatment it has received from the Doctor.

THE DOCTOR'S MANSION

The players are repulsed by the arrogance displayed in the Doctor's mansion.

Research Room: The map shows the tunnel running under the tidal road connecting to the Island. If you, the DM, feeling generous, this would be a good time to hint that dynamite could be used in the tunnel to blow it up and flood the underground complex.

Grand Room: The cruel reputation of the Plague Doctor has reached the ears of Zero. He must be destroyed. If the players attack the Plague Doctor, he will dodge their attacks and run up the stairs. The rest of the room will be alerted, and the Steampunk Orc will attack. Jetts will run out shouting for Clockwork Soldiers. The Clockwork Soldiers will take two rounds to arrive at the scene. If the players are still there, then 1d4 Clockwork Soldiers will attack.

The Gallery: Dr. Koch uses his artwork as collateral for loans to fund his work. Destroying the artwork will impact his ability to borrow money in the future.

Experiment Room/Uplift Containment Room: Free the Uplift Boar-Tiger from the cruel and unusual punishment it is suffering.

THE MAD LAB

The nerve center for Uplift creation is The Mad Lab. The players must stop Dr. Koch and his diabolical experiments.

Ground Floor: Collect the Soul Honey to bring it back to Zero.

Second Floor: The Honey Room is central to Dr. Koch's method of engineering Uplift. If the players look around the room, they will find five empty jars filled with Soul Honey and a cart that can hold up to 200 pounds of equipment. The players should try to steal as much as possible and return to Zero on Uplift Island.

Roof: The Monster is the ultimate Uplift. The Players must figure out how to bring the creature to Zero.

SIDE QUESTS

SIDE QUESTS

Below are side quests the players can follow:

EXPLOITATION

Alicia Van Buren, the lion tamer for the Full Moon Circus, is in town and will pay 50gp for each Uplift captured. She wants to take the Uplift and put them on display at the Full Moon Circus.

BOTANY

Breata Goldsun is secretly raising Uplift plants. She needs a special syrup the Doctor has created called "Soul Honey." Your challenge is to find five jars of Soul Honey. In exchange for your help, Breata will give you her Herbal Book and the ingredients for three remedies.

TICK-TOCK

A Clockwork Dragon is trapped beneath Dr. Koch's house. Tears from the dragon are used in the creation of Soul Honey but each tear is causing rust to grow on the dragon, slowing its responses. The Clockwork Dragon needs oil, which can be found on the second floor of the Tower lab, and to be freed of the manacles holding it captive. The Clockwork Dragon will show the players the secret room where it keeps its treasure and will let the players take the treasure.

A THIEVES JOB

Gwen Le Favre will split the value for each item of artwork they can steal from Dr. Koch's Gallery as she already has a buyer from the nearby town of Velden.

RANDOM ENCOUNTERS

RANDOM ENCOUNTERS

There are four areas in the game where Random Encounters can occur. They are:

- Briar Glen
- The Doctor's Mansion and The Mad Lab
- Below Ground
- Uplift Island

BRIAR GLEN

1d6	Encounter
1	A patrol of 1d4 Steampunk Orcs step up to the players and demand to know what they are doing in Briar Glen
2	A rogue Uplift Warrior attacks the players
3	Cold, metallic hands reach around each player and capture them in a pincer like grip! Clockwork Soldiers have captured the players and will march them to the Doctor's mansion and place them in the Torture Room below Uplift Island.
4	The players get thirsty and go to the Vagabond Child Inn for drinks
5	The players find a jar of Soul Honey
6	Storm clouds roll in and it begins to blast down with rain. The players need to run and get shelter at the nearest house.

THE DOCTOR'S MANSION AND THE MAD LAB

1d6	Encounter
1	Storm clouds roll in and lightning strikes the Doctor's house and mansion. Each player must make a DC10 Dexterity (Acrobatics) to leap out of the way of the lightning or suffer 1d6HP Lightning.
2	1d4 Clockwork Soldiers attack
3	2 Steampunk Orcs attack
4	Lightning strikes the house, and all the lights go out, plunging the players into complete darkness for 5 minutes when the lights flicker back on.
5	The players find a jar of Soul Honey
6	The Plague Doctor attacks

BELOW GROUND

1d6	Encounter
1	1d4 Steampunk Orcs attack
2	The players find a box of apples. There is enough for each player to have three apples. Each apple restores 2HP.
3	2 Clockwork Soldiers attack
4	An Uplift Wildling races towards the players and attacks
5	The players find a jar of Soul Honey
6	The players find three sticks of dynamite

UPLIFT ISLAND

1d6	Encounter
1	The tide is rushing in fast. The players have only 15 minutes before the tide will cover the road leading to the mainland. If they do not make it, the players will be trapped on the island for 15 minutes when the tide will retreat, once again revealing the road to the mainland.
2	The tide is retreating and reveals the road to the mainland. The road will be accessible for 15 minutes before the tide comes back in.
3	An Uplift Wildling attacks
4	1d4 Uplift Warriors attack
5	The players find a jar of Soul Honey
6	The tortured scream of an Uplift comes from the mainland

RESOLUTION

The Mad Lab can be played multiple ways. The three approaches are to support the people Briar Glen and their sheriff, defend the Uplift, or join the Doctor in his quest to create intelligent life. The following are resolutions for each of these three objectives:

DRIVE OUT THE BEAST

If you can drive the Doctor away from Briar Glen then the people will reward you with 500gp. As the DM, you can be liberal in your interpretation of what it means to "drive the Doctor away." This can mean killing the Doctor, capturing, and imprisoning the Doctor in the town's jail or chasing him out of the city. The players will find the Doctor in his tower conducting experiments.

FREE THE BEAST

Zero and the Uplift that she has rescued want to be left in peace on the small island they now call home. A natural barrier can be created if the players explode the tunnel that leads to the island. Water will flood the underground of the Doctor's compound and the tidal road will be destroyed. This will prevent the Uplift from escaping from the Island and potentially attacking people from the town of Brian Glen. Zero will share with you a book of magic spells that she has created as your reward.

CONTROL THE BEAST

The team aligned with the Doctor and have found the three items he desires (a locket with a picture of his beloved Caroline, a golden apple, and a black snake broach) and Zero's book of magic spells. For your reward, the Doctor will modify your body. You can choose two abilities that can each be increased by 2 points. The procedure to modify your body is painful and will cause 1d6+2HP damage but the outcome is that two abilities will be stronger.

UPLIFT CLASS

UPLIFT HISTORY AND CLASS

The Uplift are constructs made by a mad genius. Taking body parts from animals and humans, Doctor Nicolaj Koch used a substance known as "Soul Honey" and electricity to infuse life into his engineered creatures. The Doctor named his creation "Uplift" to reflect that the creations have been "lifted up from dirt and ignorance."

Many Uplifts died immediately after their terrifying birth. The unlucky that lived were tortured by Dr. Koch as he experimented with each creation. Each Uplift was a path for the Doctor to determine how to create life and human-level intelligence.

Eventually, one Uplift survived the torture of the Doctor, and her name is Zero. Born with stunning intelligence, Zero quickly perceives the unholy creation she is. She took it upon herself to educate herself secretly while feigning stupidity to the Doctor. A quick study, Zero taught herself about botany, biology, and chemistry and learned Ancient Greek and Latin. In time, she developed a plan to escape from the compound the doctor had trapped her in. During one of Briar Glen's terrifying summer thunderstorms, she ran away, bringing five Uplift with her. They eventually made their way to a small island.

On the Island, Zero develops plans to help additional Uplift to escape. She is also experimenting with stolen Soul Honey to engineer new Uplift that are born free, not in captivity. In addition, Zero has discovered that the Soul Honey can be fed to Uplift to both strengthen and increase their intelligence. Zero has identified five critical stages for each Uplift:

- **Infans** – This is the "child" stage is when the Uplift is first created and given life. They are often confused and scared at this stage and can only communicate with grunts.

- **Truculentus** - The wild animal stage is soon after birth. The Uplift can communicate in simple words and has begun to understand that it is an unholy creature. Anger, rage, and terror are base emotions that conflict themselves within the Uplift.

- **Construe** - The third stage is to "build" a foundation for what the Uplift can attain. This is a point of self-reflection for young Uplift, where personality traits will be developed.

- **Mandatum** - If the Uplift can live long enough and receive the benefits of Soul Honey, they will reach a stage where they can fully command their body and mind. Leaders will emerge at this stage.

- **Intelligentia** - The final stage for an Uplift is "Intelligence." It is with a sense of irony that the desire of Dr. Koch is to engineer intelligent life. But the creatures he births must escape the Doctor's tight control and have their own experiences to gain full intelligence.

Zero sees herself as the mother and protector of the Uplift race.

THE UPLIFT CLASS

The Uplift are born with raw strength and are natural warriors. Over time, as you gain experience as an Uplift, you will also learn basic spells. There are spells in this book unique to the Uplift however you can complement an Uplift PC with Druid and Ranger spells (see pages 208-209 in the D&D Players Handbook).

HIT POINTS

Hit Dice: 1d8 per level
Hit Points at 1st Level: 8 + your Constitution modifier
Hit Points at Higher Levels: 1d8 (or 5) + your Constitution modifier per level after 1st

PROFICIENCIES

Armor: Natural armor for levels 1-7, and then a choice of leather or chainmail armer at higher levels.

Weapons: Clubs, daggers, darts, javelins, maces, quarterstaffs, scimitars, sickles, slings, spears
Tools: Healer's kit, Antitoxin, hunting trap
Saving Throws: Strength, Wisdom (level 8+)
Skills: Choose two from Arcana, Animal Handling, Insight, Medicine, Nature, Perception, Religion, and Survival

EQUIPMENT

You start with no equipment

SPELL CASTING

Spell Slots per Spell Level

Level	Cantrips Known	1st	2nd	3rd	4th	5th	6th	7th	8th	9th
1st	-	-	-	-	-	-	-	-	-	-

2nd	-	-	-	-	-	-	-	-	-
3rd	-	-	-	-	-	-	-	-	-
4th	-	-	-	-	-	-	-	-	-
5th	-	-	-	-	-	-	-	-	-
6th	-	-	-	-	-	-	-	-	-
7th	-	-	-	-	-	-	-	-	-
8th	1	-	-	-	-	-	-	-	-
9th	1	1	-	-	-	-	-	-	-
10th	2	1	1	-	-	-	-	-	-
11th	2	1	1	-	-	-	-	-	-
12th	2	2	1	1	-	-	-	-	-
13th	2	2	1	1	1	-	-	-	-
14th	3	2	1	2	1	-	-	-	-
15th	3	2	1	2	1	-	-	-	-
16th	3	3	2	2	1	1	-	-	-
17th	3	3	2	2	1	1	-	-	-
18th	4	3	2	2	1	1	-	-	-
19th	4	3	3	2	2	1	-	-	-
20th	4	4	3	3	2	1	-	-	-

Drawing on the divine essence of nature itself, you can cast spells to shape that essence to your will.

CANTRIPS

At the 8th level, you know one cantrip of your choice from the list of spells included in this book or from Druid and Ranger (see pages 208-209 in the D&D Players Handbook). You learn additional cantrips of your choice at higher levels.

PREPARING AND CASTING SPELLS

The table shows how many spell slots have starting at the 9th-level and higher . To cast one of these spells, you must spend a slot of the spell's level or higher. You regain all expended spell slots when you finish a long rest.

You prepare the list of spells that are available for you to cast. When you do so, choose spells equal to your Wisdom modifier + your Uplift level (minimum of one spell). The spells must be of a level for which you have spell slots.

You can also change your list of prepared spells when you finish a long rest. Preparing a new list of spells requires time spent in meditation: at least 1 minute per spell level for each spell on your list.

SPELL-CASTING ABILITY

Wisdom is your spell-casting ability for your spells. You use your Wisdom whenever a spell refers to your spell-casting ability. In addition, you use your Wisdom modifier when setting the saving throw DC for a spell you cast and when making an attack roll with one.

Spell save DC = 8 + your proficiency bonus + your Wisdom modifier

Spell attack modifier = your proficiency bonus + your Wisdom modifier

ENHANCED MOVEMENT

Level	Proficiency Bonus	Level Name	Raw Strength	Enhanced Movement
1st	0	Infans	1d4	-

2nd	1	Infans	1d4	+10ft
3rd	1	Infans	1d4	+10ft
4th	1	Truculentus	1d4	+10ft
5th	2	Truculentus	1d6	+15ft
6th	2	Truculentus	1d6	+15ft
7th	2	Truculentus	1d6	+20ft
8th	2	Construe	1d6	+20ft
9th	3	Construe	1d8	+20ft
10th	3	Construe	1d8	+20ft
11th	3	Construe	1d8	+25ft
12th	3	Construe	1d8	+25ft
13th	3	Mandatum	1d8	+25ft
14th	4	Mandatum	1d10	+25ft
15th	4	Mandatum	1d10	+25ft
16th	4	Mandatum	1d10	+30ft
17th	4	Intelligentia	1d10	+30ft
18th	4	Intelligentia	1d12	+30ff
19th	5	Intelligentia	1d12	+30ft
20th	5	Intelligentia	1d12	+35ft

The raw energy of an Uplift is demonstrated with the increase in speed they gain with each level.

RAW STRENGTH

The defining attribute of an Uplift is its raw strength. If the Uplift has no weapons, it can use its own hands as clubs and inflict damage reflecting its level. For instance, a Level 12 Uplift can inflict 1d8 damage with their fists.

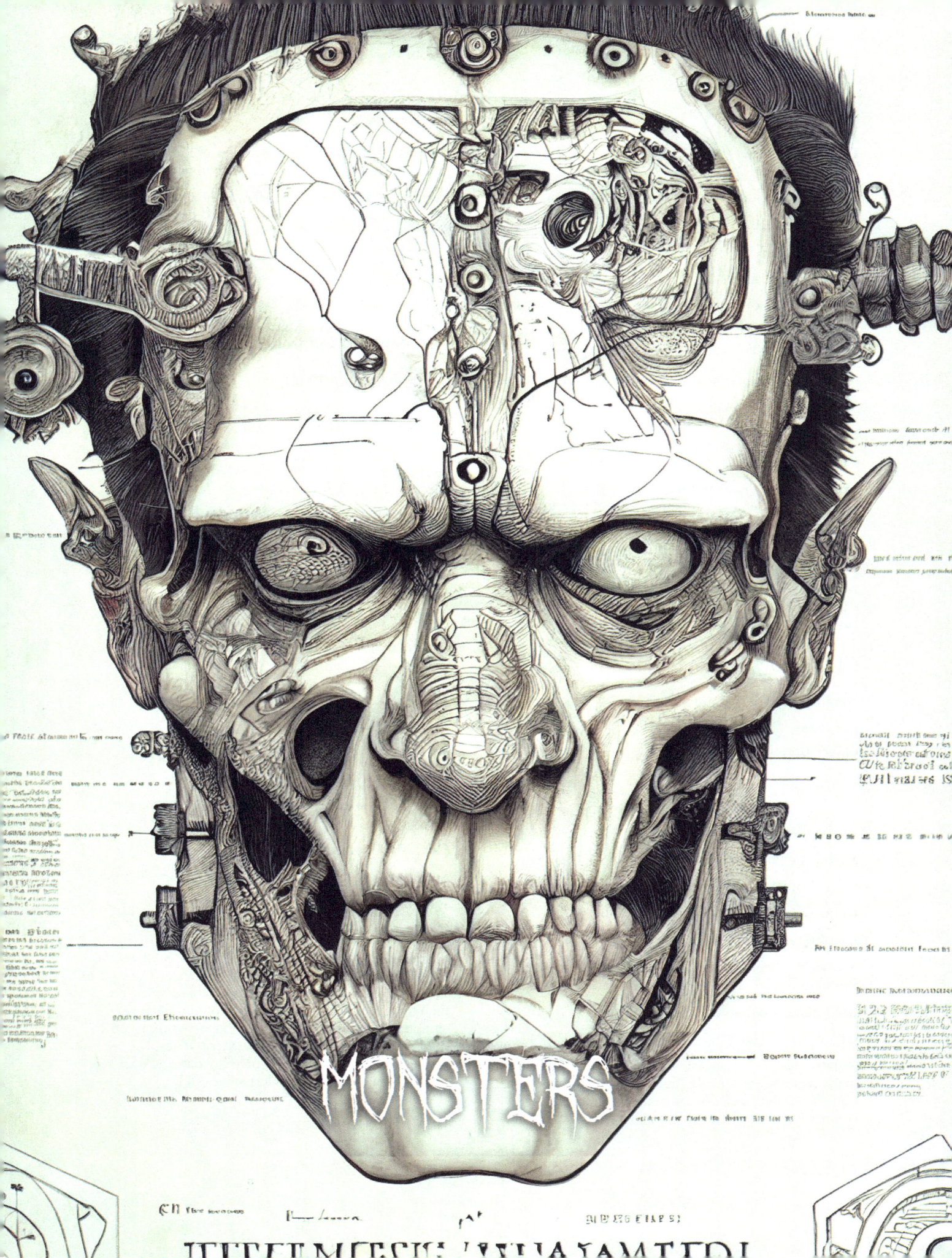

MONSTERS

AUTOMATON COOK

Medium humanoid (Automaton), any alignment

Armor Class 13

Hit Points 26 (4d8 + 8)

Speed 0 ft., Reach 10 ft.

STR	DEX	CON	INT	WIS	CHA
14 (+2)	16 (+3)	14 (+2)	4 (-3)	1 (-5)	4 (-3)

Damage Immunities cold, fire, poison, psychic

Senses passive Perception 5

Languages Common

Challenge 1 (200 XP)

Fixed Position. The Automaton Cook cannot move, but its arms can extend to 10ft and rotate entirely around its body.

ACTIONS

Kitchen Knives. *Melee Weapon attack:* the Automaton Cook has two kitchen knives that inflict 1d4 slashing damage.

CLOCKWORK DRAGON

Armor Class 17 (natural armor)

Hit Points 37 (5d4 + 25)

Speed 40 ft., fly 80 ft., swim 40 ft.

STR	DEX	CON	INT	WIS	CHA
13 (+1)	14 (+2)	20 (+5)	16 (+3)	15 (+2)	19 (+4)

Saving Throws Dex +4, Con +7, Wis +4, Cha +6

Skills Insight +4, Perception +6, Stealth +4

Damage Immunities lightning, necrotic

Condition Immunities exhaustion, poisoned

Senses blindsight 60 ft., darkvision 120 ft., passive Perception 16

Languages Common, Draconic

Challenge 3 (700 XP)

Relative Size. The clockwork dragon is tiny and can fit in the palm of your hand. The actions below reflect the tiny size of the clockwork dragon. With that said, an engineer can rebuild the dragon on a larger scale. The DM will need to scale up the effects of the actions to reflect the new size of the clockwork dragon.

Legendary Resistance (3/Day). If the dragon fails a saving throw, it can choose to succeed instead.

ACTIONS

Bite. Melee Weapon Attack: +2 to hit, reach 1 ft., one target. Hit: 2 piercing damage.

Claw. Melee Weapon Attack: +2 to hit, reach 1 ft., one target. Hit: 4 slashing damage.

LEGENDARY ACTIONS

Only one legendary action can be used at a time and only at the end of another creature's turn. The dragon regains all legendary actions at the start of its turn.

Detect. The dragon makes a Wisdom (Perception) check.

Tail Attack. The dragon makes a tail attack.

CLOCKWORK SOLDIER

Medium humanoid (Warforged), any alignment

Armor Class 13

Hit Points 26 (4d8 + 8)

Speed 30 ft.

STR	DEX	CON	INT	WIS	CHA
14 (+2)	16 (+3)	14 (+2)	10 (+1)	14 (+2)	6 (-2)

Saving Throws Str +4

Damage Immunities cold, fire, necrotic, poison, psychic

Condition Immunities exhaustion

Senses darkvision 30 ft., passive Perception 12

Languages —

Challenge 1 (200 XP)

Shrapnel Explosion. When a Clockwork Soldier hits 0HP, it will initiate a self-destruct sequence. The eyes of the Clockwork Soldier will flash red three times, and then the Clockwork Soldier will explode, sending shrapnel flying in all directions. Players within a 15ft radius need to make a DC 12 Dexterity (Acrobatics) saving throw, taking 7 (2d6) piercing damage on a failed throw or half as much if successful.

ACTIONS

Integrated Short Sword. *Melee Weapon Attack*: The Clockwork Soldier carries a concealed short sword hidden within its forearm. The weapon can eject on command. +5 to hit, reach 5 ft., 1 target. Hit: 5 (1d6 + 2) piercing damage.

PLAGUE DOCTOR

Medium humanoid (any race), any alignment

Armor Class 14 (studded leather)

Hit Points 27 (5d8 + 5)

Speed 30 ft.

STR	DEX	CON	INT	WIS	CHA
10 (+0)	14 (+2)	12 (+1)	14 (+2)	15 (+2)	9 (-1)

Saving Throws Int +6

Skills Medicine +6

Damage Resistances poison; damage from spells

Damage Immunities necrotic

Senses passive Perception 12

Languages Abyssal

Challenge 12 (8,400 XP)

Magic Resistance. The Plague Doctor has advantage on saving throws against spells and other magical effects.

Pandemic Panic. Players must roll a DC15 Intelligence (Arcana) when they see the Plague Doctor. A failed roll will cause the player to panic about a pandemic. This will cause the player to freeze for one round and then move at half speed for two additional rounds. The panic will lift at the start of the fourth round.

ACTIONS

Dagger. *Melee or Ranged Weapon Attack*: +6 to hit, reach 5 ft. or range 20/60 ft., one target. Hit: 4 (1d4 + 2) piercing damage.

Plague Mask. If the Plague Doctor is reduced to 1HP, they will pull off the mask around their face. The effort will cause the Plague Doctor to die, but the players will see what is behind the mask. Hundreds of flies, feasting on the rotting flesh of the Plague Doctor's face, will fly into the air and land on the players. The players must roll a successful DC10 Dexterity (Acrobatics) to avoid the flies. If the player fails, then a fly will land and bite the player inflicting 1d4 necrotic damage.

STEAMPUNK ORC

Medium humanoid (orc), chaotic evil

Armor Class 13 (hide armor)

Hit Points 15 (2d8 + 6)

Speed 30 ft.

STR	DEX	CON	INT	WIS	CHA
16 (+3)	12 (+1)	16 (+3)	7 (-2)	11 (+0)	10 (+0)

Skills Intimidation +2

Senses darkvision 60 ft., passive Perception 10

Languages Common, Orc

Challenge 1/2 (100 XP)

Aggressive. As a bonus action, the orc can move up to its speed toward a hostile creature that it can see.

Steampunk Goggles. The Steampunk Goggles have thick, brass rims, with dark green lenses. The goggles protect the orcs from the harmful effects of sunlight.

Leather Coat and Gloves. The Steampunk Orcs wear thick, long-sleeved leather gloves and a full-length leather coat. Along with the Steampunk Goggles, the Orc can easily move around in full daylight without breaking into painful blisters.

ACTIONS

Great axe. *Melee Weapon Attack*: +5 to hit, reach 5 ft., one target. Hit: 9 (1d12 + 3) slashing damage.

Javelin. *Melee or Ranged Weapon Attack*: +5 to hit, reach 5 ft. or range 30/120 ft., one target. Hit: 6 (1d6 + 3) piercing damage.

THE MONSTER

Large construct (Uplift), unaligned

Armor Class 14 (natural armor)

Hit Points 76 (8d10 + 32)

Speed 20 ft.

STR	DEX	CON	INT	WIS	CHA
20 (+5)	9 (-1)	18 (+4)	3 (-4)	8 (-1)	1 (-5)

Damage Immunities acid, poison, psychic; bludgeoning, piercing, and slashing from nonmagical attacks not made with adamantine weapons

Condition Immunities charmed, exhaustion, frightened, paralyzed, petrified, poisoned

Senses darkvision 60 ft., passive Perception 9

Challenge 5 (1,800 XP)

Acid Absorption. Whenever the Monster is subjected to acid damage, it takes no damage and instead regains hit points equal to the acid damage dealt.

Blind Fury. Whenever the Monster starts its turn with 60 hit points or fewer, roll a d8. On an 8, the Monster goes into a Blind Fury. On each turn, during a Blind Fury, the Monster attacks the nearest creature it can see. If no creature is near enough to move to and attack, the Monster attacks an object, with a preference for an object smaller than itself. Once the Monster goes into a Blind Fury, it continues to do so until it is destroyed or regains all its hit points.

Thick Skin. The Monster has a +1 bonus to AC (included in its statistics) and resistance to bludgeoning and slashing damage.

ACTIONS

Multiattack. The Monster makes two slam attacks.

Slam. *Melee Weapon Attack*: +8 to hit, reach 5 ft., one target. Hit: 16 (2d10 + 5) bludgeoning damage. If the target is a creature, it must succeed on a DC 15 Constitution saving throw or have its hit point maximum reduced by an amount equal to the damage taken. The target dies if this attack reduces its hit point maximum to 0. The reduction lasts until removed by the greater restoration spell or other magic.

UPLIFT BOAR-TIGER

Medium beast, unaligned

Armor Class 12 (natural armor)

Hit Points 13 (3d8)

Speed 40 ft.

STR	DEX	CON	INT	WIS	CHA
15 (+2)	13 (+1)	11 (+0)	2 (+4)	11 (+0)	5 (-3)

Senses passive Perception 10

Languages —

Challenge 1/2 (100 XP)

Keen Smell. The Uplift boar-tiger has advantage on Wisdom (Perception) checks that rely on smell.

Charge. If the Uplift boar-tiger moves at least 20 ft. straight toward a target and then hits it with a tusk attack on the same turn, the target takes an extra 3 (1d6) slashing damage. If the target is a creature, it must succeed on a DC 11 Strength saving throw or be knocked prone.

Relentless (Recharges after a Short or Long Rest). If the Uplift boar-tiger takes seven damage or less, that will reduce it to 0 hit points, it is reduced to 1 hit point instead.

ACTIONS

Tusk. *Melee Weapon Attack*: +3 to hit, reach 5 ft., one target. Hit: 4 (1d6 + 1) slashing damage.

Claw. *Melee Weapon Attack*: +5 to hit, reach 5 ft., one target. Hit: 7 (1d8 + 3) slashing damage.

UPLIFT DOG

Medium beast (Uplift), unaligned

Armor Class 13 (natural armor)

Hit Points 11 (2d8 + 2)

Speed 40 ft.

STR	DEX	CON	INT	WIS	CHA
12 (+1)	15 (+2)	12 (+1)	7 (-2)	12 (+1)	6 (-2)

Skills Perception +3, Stealth +4

Senses passive Perception 13

Languages Understands Common

Challenge 1/4 (50 XP)

Keen Hearing and Smell. The Uplift Dog has advantage on Wisdom (Perception) checks that rely on hearing or smell.

Basic Commands. The Uplift Dog can understand basic commands and will try and communicate with players through barks that follow a basic pattern:

- 1 short bark for "Yes"

- 2 short barks for "No"

- 3 short barks for "Warning"

ACTIONS

Bite. *Melee Weapon Attack*: +4 to hit, reach 5 ft., one target. Hit: 7 (2d4 + 2) piercing damage. If the target is a creature, it must succeed on a DC 11 Strength saving throw or be knocked prone.

CORRUPTED UPLIFT

Medium construct, unaligned

Armor Class 17 (natural armor)

Hit Points 67 (9d8 + 27)

Speed 30 ft.

STR	DEX	CON	INT	WIS	CHA
18 (+4)	9 (-1)	17 (+3)	3 (-4)	11 (+0)	1 (-5)

Damage Resistances bludgeoning

Condition Immunities charmed, exhaustion, frightened, paralyzed, petrified, poisoned

Senses darkvision 120 ft., passive Perception 10

Languages Understands Common but can't speak

Challenge 3 (700 XP)

ACTIONS

Slam. *Melee Weapon Attack*: −10 to hit, reach 5 ft., one target. Hit: 12 (4d8 + 4) bludgeoning damage.

UPLIFT PLANT (MATURE)

Medium plant, chaotic good

Armor Class 10 (natural armor)

Hit Points 19 (3d8 + 6)

Speed 5 ft.

STR	DEX	CON	INT	WIS	CHA
14 (+2)	5 (-3)	14 (+2)	3 (-4)	1 (-5)	1 (-5)

Damage Vulnerabilities fire

Damage Resistances bludgeoning, piercing

Senses passive Perception 5

Languages —

Challenge 1 (200 XP)

False Appearance. While the Uplift Plant remains motionless, it is indistinguishable from a regular plant.

Root Communication. The Uplift Plant can communicate with other Uplift Plants within 500ft by tapping a wooden nodule near its roots. The communication is basic:

- One tap means "Danger, stay away."

- Two taps mean "Help needed." Any Uplift Plant will shuffle on their roots towards the communicating plant.

Root Walking. Each Uplift Plant can pull itself out of the ground and perform a rudimentary walk. This can be to find better sunlight, richer soil, or attack a player. The Uplift Plant can only walk at a slow 5ft per round.

ACTIONS

Poisonous Barb. The Uplift Plant has a 5ft stigma that will shoot out of the center of a large, red flower at the top of the plant. The stigma will detect and strike the nearest player. The Poisonous Barb will inflict 1d4+2 damage with each strike, and the poison keeps its potency for 1 minute before drying. A creature hit by the poisoned weapon or ammunition must succeed on a DC 13 Constitution saving throw or be poisoned for 1 minute. Until this poison ends, the target is paralyzed. The target can repeat the saving throw at the end of each turn, ending the effect on itself on a success.

UPLIFT PLANT (JUVENILE)

Small plant, chaotic good

Armor Class 9 (natural armor)

Hit Points 2 (1d6 - 1)

Speed 0 ft.

STR	DEX	CON	INT	WIS	CHA
9 (-1)	3 (-4)	9 (-1)	3 (-4)	1 (-5)	1 (-5)

Damage Vulnerabilities fire

Damage Resistances bludgeoning, piercing

Senses passive Perception 5

Languages —

Challenge 1/4 (50 XP)

False Appearance. The Juvenile Uplift Plant will look almost like any other plant. The unusual growth of the Poisonous Barb in the stigma can be detected DC 12 Intelligence (Nature) check.

Root Communication. The Uplift Plant can communicate with other Uplift Plants within 500ft by tapping a wooden nodule near its roots. The communication is basic:

- One tap means "Danger, stay away."

- Two taps mean "Help needed." Any Uplift Plant will shuffle on their roots towards the communicating plant.

ACTIONS

Poisonous Barb. The Uplift Plant has a 1ft stigma that will shoot out of the center of a large, red flower at the top of the plant. The stigma will detect and strike the nearest player. The Poisonous Barb will inflict 1d4+2 damage with each strike (1 strike per round), and the poison keeps its potency for 1 minute before drying. A creature hit by the poisoned weapon or ammunition must succeed on a DC 13 Constitution saving throw or be poisoned for 1 minute. Until this poison ends, the target is paralyzed. The target can repeat the saving throw at the end of each turn, ending the effect on itself on a success.

UPLIFT WARRIOR

Medium humanoid (Uplift), neutral

Armor Class 16 (natural armor, shield)

Hit Points 33 (6d8 + 6)

Speed 30 ft., swim 30 ft.

STR	DEX	CON	INT	WIS	CHA
15 (+2)	13 (+1)	13 (+1)	9 (-1)	12 (+1)	7 (-2)

Skills Perception +3, Stealth +5, Survival +5

Senses passive Perception 13

Languages Common

Challenge 1 (200 XP)

ACTIONS

Multiattack. The Uplift Warrior makes two melee attacks, each one with a different weapon.

Heavy Club. *Melee Weapon Attack:* +4 to hit, reach 5 ft., one target. *Hit:* 5 (1d6 + 2) bludgeoning damage.

Javelin. *Melee or Ranged Weapon Attack:* +4 to hit, reach 5 ft. or range 30/120 ft., one target. *Hit:* 5 (1d6 + 2) piercing damage.

Spiked Shield. *Melee Weapon Attack:* +4 to hit, reach 5 ft., one target. *Hit:* 5 (1d6 + 2) piercing damage.

UPLIFT WILDLING

Medium construct (Uplift), unaligned

Armor Class 17 (natural armor)

Hit Points 22 (4d8 + 4)

Speed 30 ft.

STR	DEX	CON	INT	WIS	CHA
13 (+1)	14 (+2)	12 (+1)	9 (-1)	12 (+1)	6 (-2)

Senses darkvision 60 ft., passive Perception 11

Languages —

Challenge 5 (1,800 XP)

Acrobatics. The Uplift Wildling has advantage on Dexterity (Acrobatics) checks to avoid or escape a grapple or restraint.

ACTIONS

Claws. *Melee Weapon Attack:* +6 to hit, reach 5 ft., 1 target. *Hit:* (1d6 + 3) Slashing damage.

Bite. *Melee Weapon Attack:* +5 to hit, range ft., 1 target. *Hit:* 7 (1d8 + 2) Piercing damage.

SCALING MONSTER ATTACKS

The monsters in The Mad Lab can be scaled using the Uplift Class section. Match the Uplift monsters to the level of your players.

MAGIC ITEMS

MAGIC ITEMS

BONE DAGGER

Common

The bone dagger has been infused with an enchanted filagree etching that gives the user an additional +2 damage against Uplift and Construct monsters. For all other attacks, the dagger has the standard 1d4 damage.

SOUL HONEY

Rare

The sticky, yellow syrup is made by mad genius Doctor Nicolaj Koch. No one knows how it is made. What is known is that the Soul Honey has healing properties. Any wound the player suffers will heal twice as fast if a generous coating of soul honey is added to the infected area.

MANDATUM ANULUM - THE COMMAND RING

Rare

The Command Ring will control any Uplift or Construct Creature (such as a Golem) within 25 feet of the player wearing the ring. Any creature under the command of the ring must roll a DC15 Intelligence (Arcana) check each round. If the Creature is successful, it can break free of the control of the ring for two consecutive rounds. On the third round, if the creature is within 25 feet range of the ring, it will need to roll DC15 Intelligence check.

STEAMPUNK GOGGLES

Common

Brass-ringed steampunk goggles identified with their green lenses enable the wearer to see two things

- The first is that the wearer can see 60ft in total darkness

- The second is that the wearer will be able to see the heat emitted from any object

TIME TRAP

Very rare

The Time Trap is a clockwork mechanism that will cover any player in a 15ft radius and hold them frozen in time for one hour and completely protect the player from any attack.

SPELLS

SPELLS

ATTRACT LIGHTNING

3rd Level

Casting Time: 1 minute

Range: Self

Components: V S M (requires a 3ft iron rod you hold into the sky)

Duration: Instant

School of Evocation

The caster must hold the iron rod into the sky. Lightning will strike to the rod and the rod will absorb the power. The effect is that the caster will now be resistant to any lightning attack for 60 minutes.

AWAKEN BODY

5th Level

Casting Time: 5 minutes

Range: Self

Components: V S M (requires the caster to burn a sage stick around the corpse)

Duration: 1 minute

School of Necromancy

A body can be awakened from death when a spell is cast on it. For one minute, the caster can ask the body any question and receive a truthful answer. After one minute, the body will collapse, and aggressive decomposition will prevent the spell from being cast a second time. The body will decay entirely in less than 30 minutes.

BREATH OF RUST

2nd Level

Casting Time: 1 Action

Range: Self, 15 ft line

Components: V S

Duration: Instant

School of Evocation

The caster can breathe a 15ft column that will cause any steel, iron, bronze, or copper item caught in the column to instantly rust. Cogs and mechanical weapons will corrode and cease.

CLEAR PATH

1st Level

Casting Time: 1 Action

Range: Self, 100 ft radius

Components: V S

Duration: Instant

School of Enchantment

Clear Path allows the caster to see a bird's eye view of the map in a 100ft radius around them. In addition, the caster will see any labels for rooms. This can only be cast once per day.

COMPASSION

Cantrip

Casting Time: 1 Action

Range: 15 ft radius of the caster

Components: V S

Duration: Instant

School of Enchantment

When cast, any NPC, player, or Monster within a 15ft radius become compassionate to those around it. Any player, NPC, or Monster aligned to evil can roll as DC10 Wisdom (Perception). If they are successful, they can block the Compassion spell. If they fail, then they will drop their weapons. The spell lasts for three rounds and will fade abruptly.

CONSTRUCT BLOOD BOND

4th Level

Casting Time: 1 Action

Range: Touch

Components: V S M (This spell requires the caster to slice open their arm and drain a cup of blood onto the face of the inanimate they are attempting to bring to life. This will cause 1d6+2HP damage.)

Duration: Permanent

School of Transmutation

The animated form will awaken with 1d8+3HP and be utterly loyal to the caster.

GIVE LIFE TO A CONSTRUCT

3rd Level

Casting Time: 1 Action

Range: Touch

Components: V S

Duration: Instant

School of Transmutation

This spell can be cast on a dormant construct. On releasing the magic, the caster will lose 1d4HP and gain 1 level of exhaustion, and the construct will receive 1d8+3HP. This spell can only be cast once every four rounds.

INFUSE SOUL HONEY

4th Level

Casting Time: 15 minutes

Range: Touch

Components: V S M (The caster will need a pint of honey and a pint of plasma)

Duration: Instant

School of Transmutation

The concoction is brewed by mixing the honey and plasma, then casting the spell. On completion, the Soul Honey can be used to heal wounds twice as fast as normal and is critical in creating Uplift.

PERFECT ARMOR

5th Level

Casting Time: Bonus action

Range: Self

Components: V S

Duration: Five rounds and can be cast twice per day

School of Evocation

For five complete rounds, weapons struck at the caster's body will have no effect. For all intents and purposes, the caster has a perfect set of armor wrapped around their entire body. The side effect is that the caster can only move at a slow 10ft per round.

POISON FUNGUS

3rd Level

Casting Time: 1 Action

Range: Touch

Components: V S

Duration: Instant

School of Enchantment

The caster can touch a plant and cause it to instantly die and corrode from the effect of poisonous fungi.

HERB BOOK

BREATA GOLDSUN'S HERB BOOK

Potion Name	Rarity	Description
Fire Spearmint	Rare	Fire Spearmint is a paste that can be rubbed onto a flammable object. The paste will erupt in flames within ten seconds of exposure to the object. Fire Spearmint can also be used to seal wounds. Spread the paste over the open wound. The paste will burn and close the wound in ten seconds. This is an excruciating process. Humanoids and smaller beings will pass out from pain for five minutes.
Cavern Chives	Uncommon	Cavern Chives grow in the total darkness of sea caves. The Cavern Chives can be chewed and allow the player to see in total darkness up to 30ft. The effects of Cavern Chives only last for 5 minutes.
Dragon Weed	Rare	Dragon Weed is strong pipe tobacco that generates golden smoke. Dragon Weed tobacco is often enjoyed by intelligent races and classes.
Creator's Vine	Very Rare	The vine appears to grow from the barren ground and excretes a thick, golden sap. The sap from the vine can be collected and used as an ingredient in Soul Honey. Creator's Vine sap can be ingested by itself to restore 1d4+2 HP.
Nettle Mint Tea	Common	Nettle mint tea is excellent when drunk with a spoonful of sugar. Nettle mint tea does not overtly have any beneficial effects. Still, drinkers often comment that they feel calmer after a good strong cup. Negotiations will end well if they are started with nettle mint tea.
Sweet Cinnamon	Rare	A mild hallucinogenic, Sweet Cinnamon is often added to Hot Chocolate or dusted on top of sweet treats such as popcorn. The effect is for the player to see bright streaks of colors following moving objects. This will result in the player becoming giddy and start laughing.
Ocean Catnip	Common	Ocean Catnip is a common seaweed that floats in the seawater close to the shoreline. Ocean Catnip can be mashed into a pulp. The effect of smashing the Ocean Catnip releases oils in the plant that construct creatures find irresistible. The Ocean Catnip can be spread on the ground, and any construct creature will be immediately distracted by the Ocean Catnip. They will smell the Catnip, roll on the floor in the pulp, and do all they can to absorb the scent. The effect lasts five minutes.
Storm Ginger	Uncommon	Storm Gingers grows only during summer when heavy storms fill the skies. Ginger can be used in bread, tea, and cakes. The effect of the Storm Ginger is to gain an uncanny ability to know when and where lightning will strike within the next five minutes. Storm hunters will store large amounts of Storm Ginger to help their ability to chase and watch violent storms.
Golden Tea	Very Rare	Crystals of Soul Honey infuse the earthy taste of Golden Tea. Players who drink Golden Tea will restore 1d4HP per cup of tea.
Rosemary Fire Tea	Uncommon	Rosemary Fire Tea should be drunk before or shortly after exposure to extreme cold. The effects of hyperthermia will be immediately reversed if swallowed within 30 minutes.

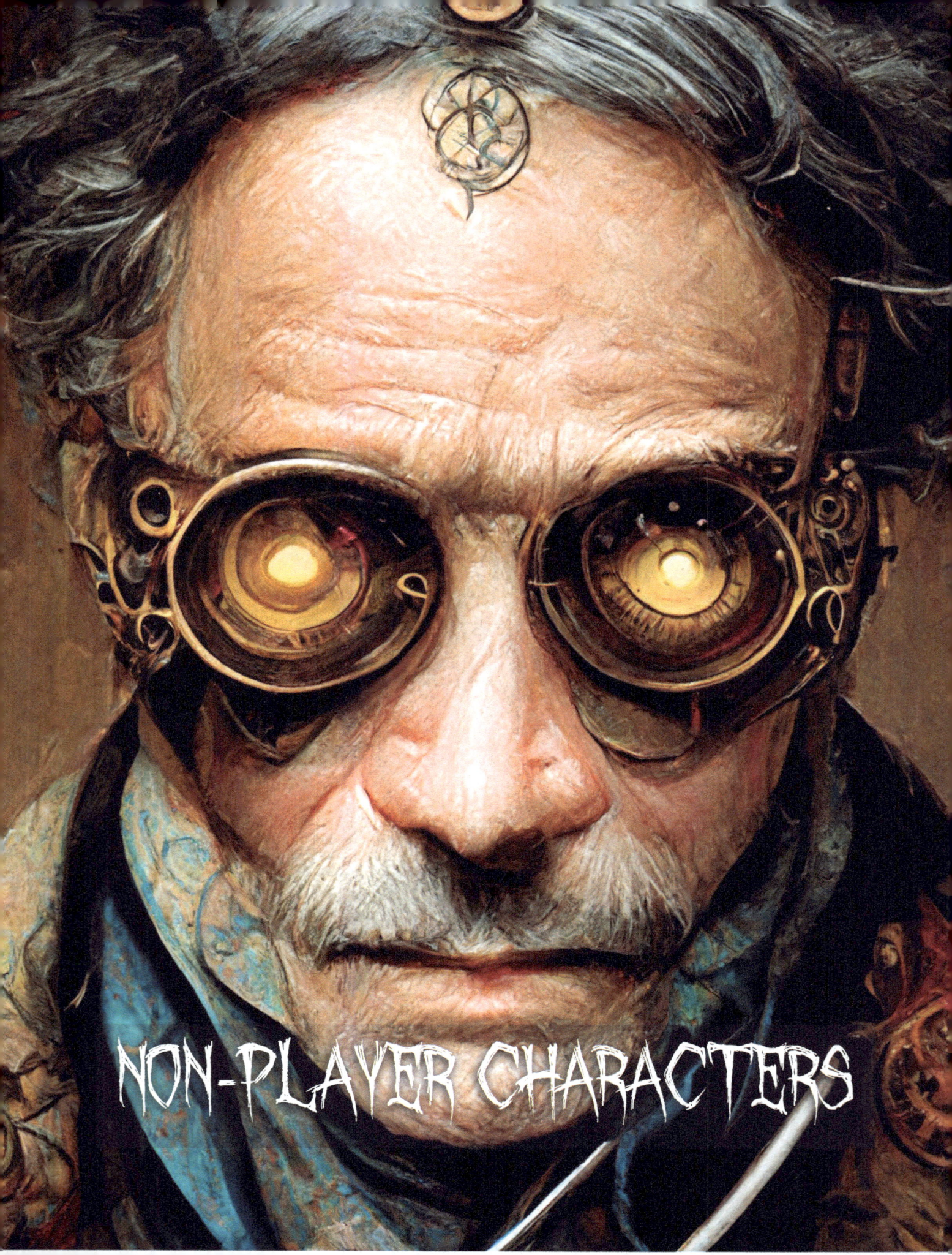

NON-PLAYER CHARACTERS

NON-PLAYER CHARACTERS

ALICIA VAN BUREN

No entertainment in the world is more fantastic and exciting than the Full Moon Circus. Traveling by day and performing at night, the Full Moon Circus pulls in packed houses and delights with unparalleled spectacle. Central to the Full Moon Circus is the collection of exotic and rare beasts on display in the carnival's Midway. The eclectic menagerie is managed by Alicia Van Buren, the youngest member of the Van Buren Lion Taming family. Alicia is in Briar Glen as she has heard about the Uplift and wants to add them to her animal collection. Alicia is cold, daring, and determined. Do not underestimate Alicia, as she will not hesitate to slice your throat. As far as she is concerned, any person she meets is an animal that can be exploited and put on display.

BREATA GOLDSUN

Breata is a gentle and caring lady. The house Breata lives in has been in her family for generations. The house is surrounded by raised flower beds. Exotic flowers can be found in sunrooms within the home. Like her grandfather, Breata loves to study plants, and she has a fondness for animals.

Breata's passion has become a dangerous obsession. Recently, she had a short affair with Doctor Nicolaj Koch and learned about his desire to engineer intelligent creates. Enthralled by his vision, she stole the secret Soul Honey and a golden apple from the Doctor's laboratory so that she could conduct her own experiments. In her home, she is growing plants using Soul Honey. The Uplift plants have gained intelligence and will attack anyone who goes near them.

DOCTOR NICOLAJ KOCH

Few truly know the origins of Doctor Nicolaj Koch. He was born into a wealthy family living in a mountain range called Barsea Heights. What he did in his youth is a mystery but in his mid-twenties, he is recorded as opening his first medical practice in the small town of Tavár. The practice was open for only a year when the elders ran the Doctor out of town after allegations of cruel and unusual treatment of his patients. The Doctor disappears from records for nearly ten years before reappearing in the city of Soronet. The only evidence of what the Doctor did in this missing decade is captured by a locket holding a picture of a young woman. He fondly refers to the woman as his "darling, Caroline." The locket was kept in a safe in his bedroom until it was recently stolen.

In his early 40s, the doctor moved to Soronet, a growing town close to the Barsea Heights mountains. This time he stays for nearly a decade and gained a clientele of wealthy patients. The Doctor has defined a method of slowing aging by injecting a special jelly into the skin of his benefactors. Dr. Koch is paid well for his work, and his wealth began to grow. He developed a philanthropic reputation due to his weekend work at the poor hospital. Little do the people of Soronet suspect that the Doctor used his time at the poor hospital to experiment with his jelly, a substance he now calls Soul Honey. Screams of pain can be heard at night as the doctor forcefully injects Soul Honey into his patients. At best, the results of his treatment can be called "mixed."

With wealth to fund his work, the Doctor abruptly closed his practice and left Soronet. His made his new home in a mansion just outside the small town of Briar Glen. He is singular in his work: to engineer and replicate intelligent life and become a God. Mad. Brilliant. Insane. Genius. These are all words that describe the complex mind of Doctor Nicolaj Koch.

GWEN LE FAVRE

Gwen is the owner of the Golden Oak Inn and enjoys a busy trade with both locals and adventurers passing through the small town. Gwen arrived at Briar Glen five years ago and spent six months and her own money restoring the Inn to its former glory. Initially skeptical of an outsider coming into their community, the locals of Briar Glen were delighted when the Inn re-opened.

Always running a side hustle, Gwen's latest scheme is selling artwork to a wealthy business owner in the nearby city of Velden. The buyer appears to have an unlimited supply of money and will buy almost every piece of art Gwen acquires. More importantly, there are never any questions on how the art was acquired.

JETTS

Every Doctor needs an assistant. Jetts, a goblin enhanced with steam technology and clockwork gears and springs, is Doctor Nicolaj Koch's assistant. The Doctor found Jetts lying in a pauper's grave, with barely a breath left in him. In a rare moment of compassion, the Doctor chose to rescue Jetts and heal him back to health. On his journey to recovery, the Doctor conducted painful experiments on Jetts. Still, the result has left the goblin with enhancements he did not have earlier in his life. Jetts is loyal to the Doctor, even though the Doctor will freely experiment on him. As far

as Jetts is concerned, each experiment the Doctor conducts on him leaves him stronger.

ZERO

Every organization needs a leader and for the Uplift, the role has fallen to Zero. There are many creatures Doctor Koch engineered, but the first to have human-level intelligence is Zero. Zero's life started with her opening her eyes and seeing the mad Doctor staring down at her, begging for her to live. In a moment of brilliance, Zero did not show her intelligence and remained mute, leading the Doctor to believe she was yet another failure. Zero was used for many painful experiments by the Doctor and it took her nearly a month of planning to escape. Still, she was able to find her way through the underground system beneath the Doctor's mansion and find a secret entrance to a small island. She now helps all Uplift to escape and tries to rehabilitate them on the island that she has renamed *Uplift Island*.

SHERIFF DERMOT SCLATOR

Old, tired, and exhausted, Sheriff Dermot Sclator finds that he is desperate to protect the people of Briar Glen. Dermot has spent his entire life in the sleepy town and has not had the desire to leave. His father was the first elected sheriff, and, in time, Dermot found himself taking on the role. He has three deputies who work for him though all three have been killed from escaped Uplift. He is a man divided: on the one hand, he is compassionate to the Uplift and the torture they have endured from Dr. Koch. On the other hand, the wild Uplift has slaughtered his men and threatened his town. Alone, he must defend Briar Glen and restore the peace he cherished in his youth.

GAME WITHIN A GAME

GAME WITHIN A GAME - DOUBLE DOWN

What you need:

- Each player must have three 6-sided dice
- Pen and paper to keep track of the score

HOW TO PLAY

Each player has three dice. You can have as many players as you would like.

Tip: give each player a different set of dice, all the same color.

There are two parts to each round:

- Staying in the game
- Determining your score

At the start of each round, the players must roll their dice simultaneously. Players can stay in the game if they roll a double number. They are out of the game if they do not roll a double number. Those who roll a double can then take one die and roll it to determine how many points they score for the round.

If a player rolls three numbers of the same value, they automatically win and can use the total of all three dice as their score for the round.

Play continues until the first person reaches a score of 50 points.

FOOD AND FUEL

FOOD AND FUEL

LIGHTNING BOLT

1 part Gin

Dash of Apple Brandy

Dash of Agave nectar

Mix with ice and strain into a glass

GREEN MONSTER

2 parts vodka

2 parts cream

1 part green creme de menthe

Mix with ice and strain into a glass

MONSTER-TINI

1 part Vodka

Dash of creme de cacao

Dash of grenadine

Mix with ice and strain into a glass. Garnish with a cherry.

5.

FRANKEN-CRISPY TREATS

The following is a modification of the traditional Rice Crispy Treats.

INGREDIENTS

*   3 tablespoons of butter

*   1 10oz package of marshmallows

*   6 cups of puffed rice cereal

*   Green food coloring

*   Pretzel sticks

*   1 small bag of Mini marshmallows

*   1 bag of red-hot candy

INSTRUCTIONS

1. In a large saucepan melt butter over low heat. Add marshmallows and food coloring and stir until completely melted. Remove from heat. Your mixture should have a monster green color.

2. Add puffed rice cereal. Stir until well coated.

3. Using buttered spoon or wax paper evenly press mixture into 13 x 9 x 2-inch pan coated with cooking spray. Cool. Cut into 2-inch squares.

4. Use red hot candy pieces for eyes on each square.

5. Press a mini marshmallow on the end of a pretzel stick and then press two pretzel sticks on either side of the marshmallow to look like Frankenstein Monster's neck bolts.

MAPS

MAPS

There are two types of map:

- DM/GM Maps with room names

- Game player maps with no rooms names

THE MAD LAB - BELOW GROUND

THE MAD LAB - BELOW GROUND (WITHOUT LABELS)

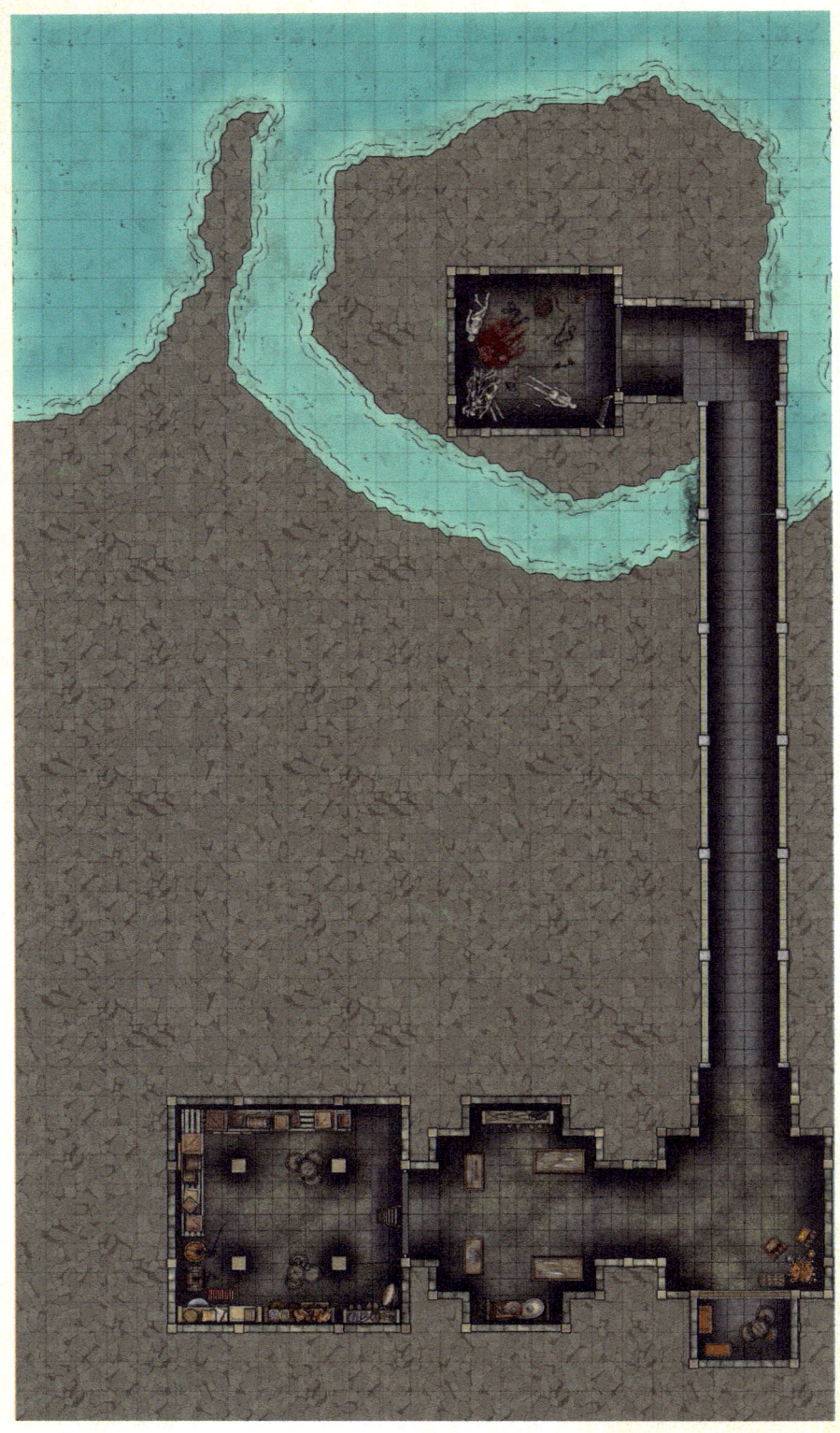

THE MAD LAB - GROUND LEVEL

The Quay

Uplift Infirmary

Abandoned Hut

Zero's Hut

Tidal Road

The Sheriff's Building

Office

Ruined Monument

Office

Trunk Room

Living Room

Breata Goldsun's House

Meeting Room

The Golden Oak Inn

Game Room

The Bar

Research Room

Entrance

Ground Floor

Kitchen

The Gallery

Grand Room

THE MAD LAB - GROUND LEVEL (WITHOUT LABELS)

THE MAD LAB - SECOND LEVEL

THE MAD LAB - SECOND LEVEL (WITHOUT LABELS)

THE MAD LAB - ROOF LEVEL

THE MAD LAB - ROOF LEVEL (WITHOUT LABELS)

MIDWINTER VAMPIRES

A Penny Blood Adventure

MIDWINTER VAMPIRES

Compatible with D&D 5e

MIDWINTER VAMPIRES

It is the year's longest night, and snowstorms howl through the Barsea Heights mountains. Hunger is driving all creatures to find new food. Fox chase mice. Deer scratch at the ground with their hooves. And vampires hunt for blood.

The cold winds have forced three groups of vampires to find food in the small town of Barsea. Sheltered in the mountains forming Barsea Heights and with the midwinter solstice creating short days, the vampires boldly walk the city, feasting on the people. There is only one problem: the vampire sects each have a blood oath to destroy the other. Only one sect can survive and reap the rewards of the hunt.

ABOUT THE GAME

Midwinter Vampires is a game that can be played in three different ways. You can choose if you follow the Storyline of the Whispering Night, Bone Brothers, or Youngblood vampire sects. For every encounter in the game, additional information will influence the Storyline the players are following. Will the players be a Youngblood looking to clear their records? Will the Bone Brothers convince the players that they need to eradicate all vampires to create a pure breed? Or will the players align with the Whispering Night and restore the macabre balance between the vampires and the townspeople of Barsea?

But I hear you say, won't the vampires attack the PCs? Good question! The game also comes with a complete Vampire Class that players can use to create their characters. The class will have a full breakdown of how to be a vampire for levels 1-20.

In the game, the characters can explore through a castle at the top of Barsea Heights, find out what is hidden in the Bone Cathedral, and search through the town to find the secrets that are being kept hidden.

Good luck.... and remember, be the hero in your adventure.

INTRODUCING THE THREE VAMPIRE SECTS

Three vampire sects are vying for power over Barsea, and each has a reason for wanting to control the town. The sects are:

·   Whispering Night

·   Bone Brothers

·   Youngblood

There is a fourth path through the adventure where the characters can choose to defeat all vampires and free the town of the vampire plague. This is a much tougher storyline and designed for characters of higher levels. For this reason, the campaign does not explicitly provide additional help. It is up to the PCs to eradicate the vampire menace.

WHISPERING NIGHT

The Whispering Night family resides in the castle at the top of the highest mountain in Barsea Heights. Their charismatic leader, Marcus, has remained unopposed for hundreds of years. His sister, Lisha, is thirsty for power and will do what she can to take leadership away from Marcus. And their younger brother, Treznor, has fallen in love with Lucia, the leader of the Youngblood. But family is a tight bond and the three members of Whispering Night hold to their family vows. The town of Barsea and the Whispering Night vampires share an uneasy truce. The unquenchable thirst that the vampires suffer is sated through volunteers from Barsea. Each volunteer will ask for immortality, and occasionally, the Whispering Night sect will grant that wish. In return, the Whispering Night family protects the people of Barsea from invaders. The Bone Brothers and Youngblood are the latest invaders to know the wrath of the Whispering Night.

BONE BROTHERS

Outside the city limits to Barsea is a cathedral made from human bones. Father Quinn along with Brothers Nostro and Marius worship and pray to their devil god.

then bodies were found with tell-tale signs of vampirism. It did not take long for the Youngbloods to be branded as outcasts, bringing a new level of fear to the people. The Youngblood are a group of vampires that were bitten when they were teenagers and are now trying to survive. They did not kill the people in the town, but they were all too familiar with being branded. This has happened time and time again. Hence, they wander, nomads moving from one place to another. The Youngblood suspect the Bone Brothers are behind the killings. Their leader, Lucia, is strong-willed and impatient and wants to take the fight to the other sects to find out who has wrongly implicated the Youngbloods. Joining her are Ulysses and Jade. These teenage vampires will feel revenge against those that scorn their name.

Which sect will you align yourself with?

All three are zealot vampires who see their sect as a pure line of vampirism and are committed to eradicating impure vampires. For many years there has been an uneasy stalemate between the Whispering Night and the Bone Brothers. The arrival of the Youngbloods sect has recently allowed the Bone Brothers to tip the balance of power in their direction. The Bone Brothers will use the Youngblood to distract the Whispering Nights' attention. While the Whispering Night and Youngbloods battle, the Bone Brothers will seize an opportunity to take control and reign as the supreme, pure race.

YOUNGBLOOD

A group of skinny teenagers arrived shortly before the solstice. At first, the teenagers were ignored, the townsfolk of Barsea's seeing them as vagabonds but

STRUCTURE FOR EACH ENCOUNTER

The campaign uses the game mechanics for Dungeons and Dragons 5e. To help DMs manage the game, each encounter is split into the following sections:

- **Encounter Name**

- **DM Information** (to give you a summary of the encounter)

- **Read Aloud**

- **Storyline Information** (to help keep things on track)

- **Additional information** (gives you more detailed information and instructions on how to reconcile the encounter)

- **Activity** (is meant as a fun, game-within-a-game section and is typically puzzles or games for the players)

- **Resolution** (tells you how and when the encounter is finished or resolved.)

- **Monster** and/or **NPC** (tells you about any monster or NPC the players may meet in the encounter.)

- **Reward** (is what everyone is working towards!)

- **Encounters** will often have supported information that is available later in the book. For instance, the details of a monster can be found in the Monster section.

Each location will impact the Storyline the players choose differently. Each Storyline is collected in the following section to provide details for the DM to help move the story forward.

The game is modular in design, allowing the DM to swap in and out content from other games. If you want to avoid using one of the monsters included in this campaign, swap it out with a different monster from the Monster Manual or a similar source.

The structure for this and all Penny Blood Adventurers is to give you a framework you can easily work in and modify as the DM.

DUNGEON MASTER TOOLS

Do you feel it? The immense burden and power of being the Dungeon Master! Being a DM inspired me to write the Penny Blood Adventures. The focus of this section is to list out the tools you can use to help with Midwinter Vampires.

First, let's cover the files included with Midwinter Vampires. Expand the ZIP file, and you will have the following:

- **Maps**: they come with labels, without labels, printer friendly, and in sepia colors

- **Encounters**: each encounter has artwork

- **NPCs**: each NPC has both artwork and a stat block

- **Monster**: each monster comes with artwork and a stat block

- **Magic Items**: each magic item comes with artwork

- **Tokens**: each NPC, Monsters, and Magic Item has a token for online playing

- **VTT Maps**: VTT is a format that many online tools, such as Shard, use for gaming

Feel free to change and update the assets to meet the needs of your group.

The second item I'd like to cover is Storylines. A lot is happening with the different storylines in the game. The following three pages are 1-page summaries for each storyline you can print out as cheat sheets. Midwinter Vampires allows players to follow different Storylines aligned to each vampire sect in the game that are:

- Whispering Night

- Bone Brothers

- Youngblood

Third, if you are a new DM, purchase the Dragons of Storm Wreck Isle Starter Set. What makes this kit so useful is the Starter Set Rulebook. Wizards of the Coast have done a great job summarizing how to play D&D and what you need to do as a DM.

Fourth, as the DM, your role is to guide the players through an interesting story and let them have fun. Sometimes, the players will do something outside the content of the game. That is OK. Let them do something weird and wonderful. You will be amazed at what happens.

Finally, remember that no matter what happens, you have the final say.

VAMPIRE CLASS

BE THE MONSTER - THE VAMPIRE CLASS

The elite killers of the night are the vampires. The cruel and merciless way they hunt and consume their victims has created legends that have lasted hundreds of years. Vampires are singular in how they attack but will form small sects to reinforce their reign over their hunting grounds.

There is little known about the origins of vampires. Some hold onto a lie that the demon Vonak perpetuates, that he created a true bloodline of vampires. But it must always be remembered that demons lie. Vonak does have the capability to create vampires, but he is not the only source of vampirism. There are many types of vampires, and they often reflect the community where they reside.

For this reason, you must always be careful and watchful for any person you meet at night. The vampire is intelligent, wise, and, cunning, but above all other things, it is a fierce predator. They will outsmart you. Be on your guard.

No one knows how long vampires have existed. They are created when another vampire forces its victim to consume a small amount of its blood, thereby passing on the vampirism disease. The first effects on the victim will mimic death. Indeed, many vampires find that they are enclosed within a coffin, buried six feet underground when they wake from their sleep of death. It is up to the vampire to escape its tomb, and many go insane as they fight through the coffin lid and dig up through the dirt. All the while, a deep hunger for fresh blood consumes the vampire. They are the most vulnerable at this early stage in the vampire's existence. Many still hold onto the same restrictions that keep mortals in check and forget that they are now immortal. If you are to destroy a vampire, do it while it is still learning its own capabilities. Wait too long, and the vampire will fully embrace their new skills and hunt you down like the prey you are.

LEVELS

The victim will retain the abilities they had before becoming a vampire (for instance, a wizard will still be able to cast spells, and a gnome will be a tinkerer). Still, the new vampire desire for blood will dominate a level 1 character, subside slightly until level 4. Still, it will not be until level 5 that the character can control their vampire urges. The result is that there can be some interesting mashups, such as an Elf Druid becoming a vampire. They remain an Elf and can continue to leverage their Druid skills at the level when they were converted, but now can level up as a vampire.

A vampire will go through distinct phases of growth and maturity as defined by the following levels:

Level	Name	Translation	Description	Abilities
1	Jurământ de sânge	Blood Oath	The victim, either willingly or not, consumes vampire blood. For 72 hours the body of the victim will lie still as if dead. Following that time, the victim will awake at the first level of vampirism. A deep thirst for blood will overpower all other needs they have and they will need to hunt their first victims no matter what type of humanoid or creature it is. Indeed, many farmers have found a herd of dead cattle drained of their blood from a new *Jurământ de sânge*.	+2 to Dexterity. Gains Vampire's Bite and Vampiric Speed.
2-4	Băutor de sânge	Blood Drinker	Fresh blood is the source of power for the vampire and a Băutor de sânge will spend as considerable time attacking livestock, wild animals, and other humanoids. Their instincts are feral, and they are filled with a deep rage.	+2 to Constitution. Gains Blood of the Vampire and Night Sight.
5-8	Ucigaș	Killer	The Ucigaș has gained control over their rage and base instincts. For many, it is at this level that they believe they are not blessed rather than cursed. A cool, calm peace embraces the vampire and lends them the ability to hone their skills as a brutal killer.	+2 to Intelligence. Gains Vermin Hoard and Prince of Darkness.
9-12	Schimbare	Change	When a vampire is Schimbare they will be able to temporarily change into animals including a wolf, a cauldron of bats, or mischief of rats. See the description below on "Animal Change."	+2 to Strength Gains Animal Change.
13-16	Prădător	Predator	The vampire has reached the apex ability of their hunting skills. They are simply an elite predator, or Prădător. It is at this level they can dissolve into Mist. See the description below on "Mist."	Additional +1 to **Constitution** Gains **Mist**.

| 17-19 | Înțelepciune | Wisdom | Through long age comes much wisdom. A Înțelepciune vampire can begin to form simple magic. The vampire does not have the ability to become a master of magic but can perform several cantrips, and level 1-3 spells. Use the chart below spell slots. | +2 to **Wisdom**. Gains the ability to cast spells (see **Spell Casting** below) |
| 20 | Lider | Leader | When a vampire reaches the highest level, they ooze charm and can use it as a weapon. In addition, a Lider vampire has additional spell casting abilities. A Lider is no longer a predator, but a weapon that can carve its victims like a surgeon with a sharp blade. | +2 to **Charisma** and gains **Vampire's Charm**, and additional spell slots. |

HIT POINTS

Hit Dice: 1d10 per level
Hit Points at 1st Level: 10 + your Constitution modifier
Hit Points at Higher Levels: 1d10 + your Constitution modifier per level after 1st

PROFICIENCIES

Weapons: Daggers, darts, scimitars, rapier
Tools: Retain skills before being turned by a vampire
Saving Throws: Strength
Skills: Choose two from Acrobatics, Animal Handling, Arcana, Deception, Intimidation, Persuasion, and Religion

EQUIPMENT

You start with the equipment you died with.

Armor: None

VAMPIRE SECTS

Vampires form small sects of 2-5. Each sect has a name and sigil branded into the skin of their followers. The leading Vampire sects are:

- Whispering Night
- Youngblood
- Bone Brothers
- Rêves de sang
- l'Origine Cruelle
- Légion de la mort
- Masquerade

- Death's Shadow
- Phoenix Rising

ABILITIES

VAMPIRIC SPEED

Vampires are fast. Their base walking speed is 50% faster than the race they were when alive. For example, a human who has a walking speed of 30 now has a walking speed of 45.

NIGHT SIGHT

Vampires can see 60ft in pitch darkness as if it were daylight, and they can see up to 120 ft if the moon is out.

ANIMAL CHANGE

Once per day, the vampire can change either into a **vampire wolf**, 2d6+4 **cauldron of vampire bats** or a **mischief of vampire rats** for 1d4+1 rounds. Use the stat block in the Monster section to see the skills the vampire gains.

VERMIN HOARD

Twice a day, a vampire can call a vermin hoard of 2d6+4 rats, bats, or spiders. The vermin hoard will do what the vampire commands, including attacking a target. Use the stat block in the Monster section for each vermin type.

VAMPIRE'S BITE

The vampire will drain its victim of blood from any place on the body where a main artery is easily accessed. The neck and wrist are often exposed areas of weakness for most humanoids. The vampire will drain 1d6+3 HP each round. The vampire will not, if they have the choice, kill their victim. They prefer to drain the victim close to death, give them time to recover, and then drain them again. And again. And again….

PRINCE OF DARKNESS

This ability grants the vampire Advantage on all its Ability checks, Saving throws and Attack rolls.

BLOOD OF THE VAMPIRE

The blood of a vampire is powerful. A small droplet can restore 1d20+10 HP. Each time a creature consumes vampire blood, it will need to complete a DC15 Constitution check. If they fail, then they have consumed too much blood and will appear to die, only to wake 72 hrs. later as a level 1 vampire.

VAMPIRIC MIST

The vampire can become an incorporeal mist for up to three rounds twice per day. While a mist, the vampire cannot attack nor be attacked. The mist can move at 30 ft per round.

VAMPIRE'S CHARM

The vampire will need to make direct eye-to-eye contact with its target. The target will do whatever the vampire commands for 1d4 rounds unless they are able to succeed a DC 15 Wisdom (Perception) or (Insight) save.

SPELL-CASTING

Vampires have limited spell-casting abilities. The vampire will retain the spell-casting level they had before being turned into a vampire. For instance, a level 15 wizard will retain the same spells and spell slots but

will only be able to add more spells and slots when they reach vampire level 17.

Spell Slots per Spell Level

Level	Cantrips	1st	2nd	3rd	4th
17th	3	2	1	0	0
18th	4	3	2	2	0
19th	4	3	3	3	1
20th	5	4	3	3	2

WEAKNESSES

Nature loves balance. While the vampire has been granted exceptional powers, it has also been cursed with weaknesses. The following can be used against a vampire.

SUNLIGHT

The vampire is sensitive to full sunlight. It will need to wear dark glasses and have exposed skin covered. Even with eye protection, the vampire can only see 15ft as they will be dazzled by the sun. Each round a vampire is exposed to direct sunlight, they will suffer 1d6 points of Radiant damage.

RELIGIOUS ITEMS

It is not the sacred item that hurts the vampire, but the belief placed in the object. For this reason, any religious item will cause 1d4 burning damage when placed on a vampire's skin. The powerful belief in a benevolent entity hurts the vampire, not necessarily the object itself. A character can roll DC 15 Intelligence (Religion) check on any item to imbue it will enough belief to be used as a Religious Item.

DECAPITATION

Cutting off a vampire's head will kill it.

RUNNING WATER

Vampires cannot cross running water. Therefore, they like places in the mountains or during winter when the water is frozen.

WOODEN STAKE

A wooden stake hammered through the heart will kill a vampire.

BY INVITATION ONLY

A vampire cannot cross the threshold to any dwelling unless it has been invited inside.

SILVER

Silver used in many religious artifacts is often why vampires will recoil. Silver will cause a vampire's skin

to immediately blister, causing 2d4+2 damage. This is in addition to any damage caused by using a Religious Item. On top of this, the vampire is repulsed by the metal and will do all they can to be at least 20 feet away from it. The higher level a vampire is, the more they can resist silver. Use the following table to determine if the vampire fails a Constitution check and is repulsed by the silver.

Level	Constitution Check
1	20
2-4	15
5-8	10
9-12	5
13-16	1
17-19	0
20	0

THE ADVENTURE

STARTING THE ADVENTURE

The characters find themselves in the Barsea Town Hall on the outskirts of town. The town's residents have gathered, demanding help to resolve the issues of the increased vampire attacks. Inside the crowded town hall, the characters will find the following people:

- Lisha, from the Whispering Night
- Father Quinn, from the Bone Brothers
- Jade, from the Youngblood
- Dr. Naomi Whitt represents the town's people who want to be rid of the vampires.

Various towns folk from the town. They are all scared and a little confused at the increased vampire attacks.

You enter Barsea Town Hall and see many townsfolk standing around, angrily debating the increased vampire attacks. A truce with all the vampire sects has been called to enable the townsfolk to meet and talk. In one corner of the room, you see an elegant, porcelain-skinned woman, clad in black leather armor, standing and talking to one of the town's elders. In the center of the room a man, dressed in dark monks robes are having a hushed, private conversation with the town's priest. Aloof and almost hiding in the shadows is a young teenage girl with a brightly colored tattoo on her right arm. She sees you looking at her and involuntarily pulls back into the shadows. A doctor, still wearing her bloodied lab coat from the day's work, is having a heated conversation with a second town elder.

This is your opportunity to walk around the room and meet with the people from the town.

The objective of the Town Hall is to give the players a chance to have their characters meet all the different groups that influence action in the game. Their goal is to align with either a vampire sect or free the town of the vampires altogether. Once they decide who they will align with, one of the elders of Barsea will knock his gavel on the podium at the front of the hall and announce that the meeting has concluded. All NPCs will leave, and the characters will be encouraged to leave. The Town Hall will be locked up. Below are details you can give the players for each of the main storylines in the game:

WHISPERING NIGHT

Lisha, from the Whispering Night, is discussing with a town elder how they can restore the status quo that existed in Barsea with the Bone Brothers before the Youngblood arrived.

As you approach the fierce-looking woman, the town elder excuses himself, and she turns to face you. Her eyes are penetrating, and she exudes intelligence and cunning. "So," she says with a rasping voice, "you are the adventurers I have heard of. Welcome to our little town. My name is Lisha, and my family has lived here for many centuries providing protection over Barsea and the surrounding mountains. All has been peaceful, even after the Bone Brothers built their cursed cathedral. That is until the blasted Youngbloods arrived. My town's people are now living in fear as the number of attacks has increased. Will you join my family and help restore peace to Barsea? Suppose you do decide to join my family. In that case, I encourage you to receive the family brand, which will protect you from other Whispering Night members. I cannot guarantee protection if you do not have the brand."

At this, Lisha pulls up the sleeve on her arm to reveal a blood-red brand. "If you align with the Whispering Night, you must go to the blacksmith and receive your brand. If you do not decide to receive the family brand, then you must bring me the head of Jude the Cheat. That cursed man insists on selling weapons to strike down vampires. Bring me his head, and I can offer you safe passage in Whispering Night Castle.

BONE BROTHERS

Father Quinn is conspiring with Pastor Walter Tonkin on ways in which they can overthrow the Youngblood and Whispering Night. Both men are intent on their whispered conversation and do not see the characters walk up to them. Consequently, the characters will overhear some dialogue between the two men.

You walk up to the robed figures and, as you get closer, you overhear some of their conversations.

".... those damn teenagers are hiding in the town," the town's priest, Pastor Tonkin, says with a hand to cover his mouth to muffle the sound. "One of my partitioners told me they are holed up in the double barn on the south side of town."

"Excellent," hisses the man in the black robes, "I will send my brothers to rout them. They should be easy to eliminate. It is the Whispering Night that will be…challenging."

At this point, Pastor Tonkin sees you all standing close and listening. With a well-rehearsed smile, he turns and holds his hands out to you in greeting. "My guests, welcome to our little town. You must think that silly little problems are beneath the adventures you typically engage in. I will leave you to talk with Father Quinn." At this, Pastor Tonkin turns and leaves.

Father Quinn turns and casts his red eyes on you. For a moment, you are all stunned by his presence. He is fiercely religious, and his devotion to his god radiates from his presence. "My children, you come out on such a dark night. Welcome to Barsea. I would strongly encourage you to join a service at our Bone Cathedral. My fraternity solely aims to eradicate our township's vile, impure vampires. Will you join us on this crusade? If you do, I encourage you to receive our brotherhood's brand and protection." At this, he slides up his sleeve and reveals the brand on his arm.

YOUNGBLOOD

Jade is uncomfortable being in the hall and her discomfort will show by being argumentative and combative to the characters.

The teenage girl flicks her eyes up, and, for a moment, you can see her calculating if she wants to talk with you. You can hear her raging debate with herself in the few steps it takes for you to cross the room. You reach her, and she simply says, "Yes, what?" There is a moment of unease as you all stand around the small young woman, and then she breaks the silence. "For god's sake, my name is Jade. I am a Youngblood," she indicates the colorful brand on her arm, "we came here as

there was nowhere else for us to go. We have been running for so long, and now we know we must find a place. Barsea is as good as any, I guess. We want to be seen as leaders and not vagrants. I hate that the town's people say that about us." She scowls at the people in the room. "Help us for an alignment with Whispering Night. We know the Bone Brothers are conspiring against us, so they must be destroyed. Will you help us? If you do, get our pact's brand and receive protection from all the Youngblood." A flicker of annoyance flashes over her face. Jade abruptly turns and leaves the room. "Whatever you decide, stay out of our way. Or else."

SAVE THE TOWN

New to Barsea, Dr. Whitt has not been worn down by generations of repression from the insidious presence of the vampire sects. She has settled into her profession at the infirmary but has seen too much needless violence in recent months. The characters can hear her raised voice as they approach the doctor, who is in a heated conversation with one of the town's elders.

"Damn it, man, can't you see the truth?" shouts Dr. Whitt. "These vampires are killing the people of Barsea. They must be stopped!"

The town elder sees you approach and uses this as an excuse to remove himself from the anger the doctor is firing in his direction. She turns, and you see fully the blood-soaked lab coat she is wearing. Clearly, the doctor came straight from the infirmary. "Good, you are the adventures everyone has been talking about. These people are unaware of the evil in this town. People are dying in my care, and there is but one cause: vampires! They are everywhere in this town, and they must be destroyed. Will you step up to the challenge and free Barsea from Whispering Night, Bone Brothers, and Youngblood? Please, give Barsea something they have not had in a generation: the ability to live without fear."

Dr. Whitt can't offer the players protection as she is unaware of the vampire pact brands. Eradicating the town of all vampires is a tough battle. Players who are level 10 or above are recommended to take on this challenge.

After the characters choose which pact they will align with

The people in the hall will start to leave as soon as the characters have chosen the which pact they will follow.

ADDITIONAL INFORMATION

To protect the characters, a sigil mark must be burnt into their flash to show they are aligned to a specific vampire sect. The brand will offer protection from that sect. Only one brand can be on a character; if a character chooses to have two or more brands, then the character has no protection. There is a smithy in the town called Nerves of Steel, where the characters can go and receive their brand.

The Town Hall will remain locked for the entire game. Characters can choose to break back into the Town Hall. They can pick the lock on the front door, which requires a DC 20 Dexterity (Sleight of Hand) check, or they can break a window. If the players break a window to enter the Town Hall, then a **Spider Soldier** will be alerted and attack them in the building.

The characters can wander around the building. There are three rooms:

- **Hall** - The main hall dominates the building with a small stage and podium. Behind the platform can be found a small vial of Vampire's Blood.

- **Back Room** - behind the stage is a small room where NPCs can prepare before they go on stage.

- **Front Office** - a small office at the front of the building is used to check coats, greet visitors, and has a small kitchen for making coffee and tea.

THE TOWN OF BARSEA

Barsea is both the home and workplace for the people who live in the town, and the hiding place for the Youngblood vampires. Characters will start in the **Town Hall** and then investigate the rest of the buildings. A visit to Nerves of Steel will give the characters an opportunity to be branded with a vampire sect sigil.

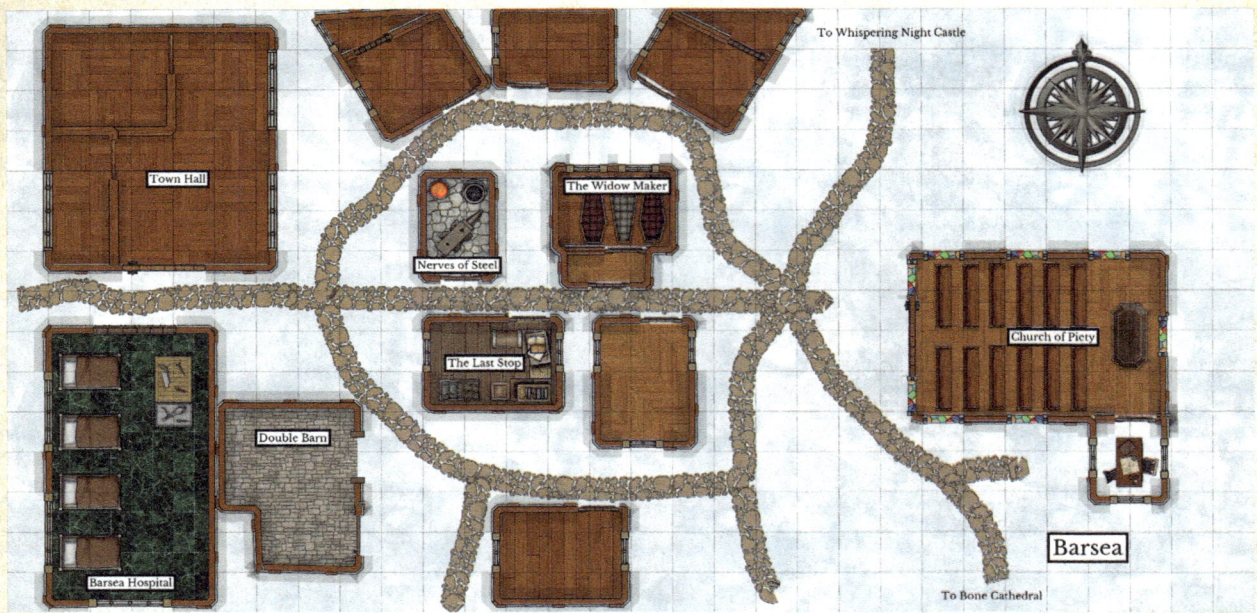

The Town of Barsea

NERVES OF STEEL (BLACKSMITH)

Barsea's blacksmith is a half-giantess named Ristina Vrani. Ristina towers close to 8 feet tall with well-conditioned muscles. She is the third generation in her family to run the blacksmith. When she inherited it, she changed the name to "Nerves of Steel" as a pun to reflect the grit needed by her customers. While Ristina is a traditional blacksmith, she has a unique alliance with the vampire sects. For a small fee, she will burn a brand providing protection from the vampires. Use the table name Vampire Sigils to ensure the correct brand is burned into the character's skin.

Known as the 'Nerves of Steel', the smell of a hot forge and the taste of hammered metal greet you

as you enter the smithy. A towering woman is hard at work forging a silver blade when you arrive at her workshop. Looking around the workshop, you see examples of Ristina's work. Some weapons are forged from precious metals and hanging from a display board. In the corner of the room is a table with fine silver jewelry, and near the forge is a bucket filled with blood-caked branding irons, each with a different sigil. The woman turns and glowers at you. "So," she says in a deep voice, "you hear to be branded? I hope you have nerves of steel." She laughs heartily at her joke.

STORYLINE INFORMATION

The characters must select a sigil and be branded with it to receive protection from a vampire sect.

ADDITIONAL INFORMATION

The branding itself will cause 1d6+2 Hit Point damage and leaves a permanent scar. Each character that decides to get branded will need to succeed on a DC 15 Constitution save, or they will pass out from the pain. It will take 15 minutes before they gain consciousness. If the character bites down on a piece of leather or wood, such as a belt or bridle, the act will grant the character Advantage on the roll.

VAMPIRE SIGILS

The sigil will offer each character protection from the associated vampire sect. A character cannot have more than one sigil. Any character with two or more sigils will have no protection from any vampire sect.

The characters can choose from the following which sigil they would like branded on their skin:

- Whispering Night
- Youngblood
- Bone Brothers
- Rêves de sang
- l'Origine Cruelle
- Légion de la mort
- Masquerade
- Death's Shadow
- Phoenix Rising

ACTIVITY

Ristina will also sell weapons or jewelry to the players. Here is a list of weapons she has for sale:

Item	Damage	Properties	Cost	lbs.	Additional Notes
Silver Dagger	1d4 piercing	Finesse thrown (20/60)	4 gp	1	The silver dagger is more brittle than steel. It can only be used four times before the blade snaps.
Silver Laced Rapier	1d8 slashing	Finesse	30 gp	2	The rapier has silver filagree work laced around the handle and blade. The silver weakens the blade, and it will snap after three battles.
Blood Scimitar	1d8 slashing	Finesse, light	12 gp	3	The weapon of the Spider Soldiers.
Silver Warhammer	1d8 bludgeoning	Versatile (1d10)	30 gp	2	The head of the Warhammer is cast from silver.

List of jewelry that can be purchased:

Item	Cost
Silver Ring	5 sp
Silver bracelet	10 sp
Silver necklace	12 sp
Silver Candlesticks (2)	15 sp
Silver cross (small)	5 sp
Silver cross (large)	15 sp

NPC

Ristina Vrani

DOUBLE BARN

On the south side of town is an old double barn used by the local farmers to store hay during the winter. Jade and Lucia are in the barn. There is a trap set at the entrance to the barn. The trap has two purposes: 1) to alert Lucia of intruders and 2) to eliminate the intruders.

The red-sided walls of a barn stand out in stark contrast to the white snow while in the sky, dark clouds indicate a storm is coming. As if reading your thoughts, a crack of lightning splits the night, accompanied by strengthening winds and heavy snow begins to fall. There are two doors in the barn, one wide open the other is closed. Light spills out into the dark through the open door.

ADDITIONAL INFORMATION

TRAP

The light spilling from the barn door fills a square of 15ft square in front of the building.

Trigger: Characters stepping into the light trigger the trap.

Effect: A snow tornado, a column 15 feet in diameter and 100 feet tall, will drop down from the clouds and target the characters. The tornado will last 1d6+2 rounds. For each round, the characters will each have to succeed in a DC 15 Strength (Athletics) check or receive 1d4+2 HP damage from the violent wind of the snow tornado.

Countermeasures: A successful DC 15 Intelligence (Investigation) check allows a character to observe that the light itself ripples with magic. A second door, further down the side of the barn, can be opened with a successful DC 20 Dexterity check using thieves' tools. A character without thieves' tools can attempt this check with a disadvantage using any edged weapon or tool. On a failed check, the second door will not open.

STORYLINE INFORMATION
WHISPERING NIGHT

If the players have the sigil of the Whispering Night, then Lucia and Jade will stay hidden in the barn. The characters must get past the trap to enter the barn. If they can enter the barn, then Jade will approach the characters. She will tell them that she wants to negotiate peace with Whispering Night. Her terms are to share the town, and each sect can enjoy the blood of the people of Barsea. Her words imply that the Bone Brothers must be destroyed. The characters can choose to take the proposition to the Whisper Night family or attack Lucia and Jade.

BONE BROTHERS

If the players are branded with the sigil of the Bone Brothers, then Lucia and Jade will stay hidden in the barn. The characters must get past the trap to enter the barn. On entering the barn, Lucia will slip away but Jade will remain and attack the players.

YOUNGBLOOD

If the players are branded with the Youngblood sigil, Lucia and Jade will appear, warn them of the trap, and escort them around it, into the barn. Once in the barn, Lucia and Jade will explain that they believe that the Bone Brothers are killing the people in Barsea and making it look like Youngblood. To clear the name of the Youngblood, the leader of the Bone Brothers, Father Quinn, must be decapitated. Jade knows that the Whispering Night will only respond to strength, and they want the characters to take the head of Father Quinn to the Whispering Night to negotiate a peace treaty. The terms of the treaty are simple: the blood of the people of Barsea is to be split 50:50 between the two sects. Lucia will tell the characters that they are hungry and need to eat quickly, or they will lose control and begin to attack the next person they meet.

NPC

Lucia and Jade

REWARD

In the event the characters attack and defeat Lucia and Jade, they will find a small leather purse with 15 gp in the barn and a book containing four vampire spells. The DM can select four spells from the list in this book's "Spells" section.

THE LAST STOP

There is only one store in Barsea. The Last Stop is the grocery store, bookstore, hardware store, and bakery for the entire town, and is run by Jude the Cheat, a skeletally thin man with a terrifyingly large smile. Jude runs his store like he runs his life, fast and wild. He talks very fast and is always trying to con his patrons. Each player will need to roll a DC 10 Charisma (Insight) check each time they buy something from Jude, or Jude will increase the price of each item by 25% (rounding up when necessary). If the players try to steal from Jude the Cheat, they will need to succeed on a DC 20 Dexterity (Sleight of Hand) or they will be violently stopped by a Războinic Lups (Wolf Warriors) employed by Jude as a security guard.

There is a collection of books that Jude sells. If the characters succeed in a DC 10 Charisma (Persuasion) check, Jude will provide an additional description for the book. If the characters fail, Jude will only show them the book title and nothing else. Either way, the characters will need to buy the book to learn its content.

You step into a cluttered store overflowing with items for sale. Everywhere you look, you see tables filled with books, shelves of hardware, even a section of meat on a block of melting and bloodied ice. In the center of the room, is a skeletally thin man with his arms wide apart and a rictus smile on his face. "Welcome to The Last Stop," he says. "My name is Jude, though some call me Jude the Cheat, but let's pay them no mind! What can I get for you?"

In the far corner of the store, you see a Wolf Warrior watching you. He is clearly a security guard. "My whole store is for sale. How can I rob you today?"

STORYLINE INFORMATION
WHISPERING NIGHT

Marcus tolerates Jude the Cheat, but Lisha wants him, and his business eliminated. (Lisha will reward the characters with 50 gp if they bring her the heads of these two.)

BONE BROTHERS

Jude has a cipher book titled Assassins and Spies that can be used to decode the lock on the entrance to the sanctuary below the ballroom floor in Whispering Night castle.

YOUNGBLOOD

The Youngblood are hungry. Steal or buy some bloody steak for them to feast upon and satisfy their urges.

ADDITIONAL INFORMATION

Jude sells many things. Here is a list of items the characters can buy:

Hardware Items	Price	Weight (lbs.)
Silver Cross	10 sp	⅛
Flask of holy water	20 gp	1
Crowbar	2 gp	5
Wooden Stakes	1 sp each	½
Set of Manacles	2 gp	6
Steel Mirror	5 gp	½
Flask of Oil	1 sp	1
Tinderbox	5 sp	1
Torches	1 cp	1
Monster Pack (3 wc crowbar, silver cros steel mirror, flash o torches, strong leasl	33 gp	49

Grocery and Bakery Items	Price
Sausages (uncooked)	5 cp each
Pork Chops (uncooked)	1 sp each
Steaks (uncooked and swimm	1 gp each
Chicken (uncooked)	1 sp per chicken
Pork Pie	5 cp
Beef Pasty	1 sp
Loaf of bread	2 cp
Apple Pie (whole)	5 sp
Shortbread	2 cp each

Each book is bound in heavy leather and weighs 5 lbs.

Book Title	Description	Price
Assassins and Spies	A history of various infamous cutthroats and villains. It also explains the mirror cipher used by Whispering Night	10 gp
Treats for My Lady	A collection of poetry written by Cyran (a short collection of his terrible poetry is included in the section "Cyran's Verse")	2 gp
Beggars Bowl	A collection of recipes including Sarmale (stuffed cabbage)	2 gp
The Drinks Are On Me	The infamous dwarf, Nofom Darkview, has collected his favorite drinks into one volume including the notorious Vampire's Cocktail	5 gp
Playing for all the Marbles	Nulah, the Elf Barbarian, has collected her favorite games in one book. This includes the notorious "Death Dice" game	2 gp
Miss Elsa Vexx's 2nd Volume of Everyday Spells	Elsa Vexx has written several books on magic. This is the best-selling volume 2 of the series. The DM can give the characters two spells from this tome that are level 2 or below	10 gp

BOOK – ASSASSINS AND SPIES

Assassins and Spies is a book that explains a mirror cipher. The Whispering Night uses the mirror cipher to secure their buildings and locks. If the characters buy the text, then the DM can read the following description of a mirror cipher to them.

The mirror cipher is created by swapping each letter with its corresponding letter from the other end of the alphabet. For example, Z stands for A, Y stands for B, X stands for C, etcetera. Below is the alphabet written from left to right (as you usually do). Then, write them from right to left, so each letter is beneath its corresponding letter from the other end.

Normal	ABCDEFGHIJKLMNOPQRSTUVWXYZ
Reverse	ZYXWVUTSRQPONMLKJIHGFEDCBA

An example mirror cipher:

Normal: vampire

Encrypted: eznkriv

NPC

Jude the Cheat

MONSTER

Războinic Lup (Wolf Warrior)

CHURCH OF PIETY

The Church of Piety is a simple, wooden church that leaks. Rain will fall through the roof during the summer, and snow will blow in during the winter. The church's main room has an altar and a lectern from where Pastor Walter Tonkin will preach and is lined with basic pews made from wooden boxes. There is a small office at the back of the church where Pastor Tonkin prepares his speeches. The pews are filled with Strigoi (Ghosts) listening to the Pastor preach about Vonak.

You open the flimsy wooden door to the Church of Piety. Each pew is full of people listening to Pastor Walter Tonkin give his impassioned homily, "And, thus, I call onto thee, and the lord we follow, to bring about resolution and balance to this town we live in. Aye, I say, hear my words: The vampires in the castle must go! Yes, you heard my words. We need to run that family out! For too long, they have ruled over our town. We must drive them out and destroy their home. But we must not stop. No, I say, we must not stop. Children with vampire's teeth - yes, you know who I am talking about, the so-called 'Youngblood' - must be run out. Get your stakes and drive them out!! I have spoken with our good friend Father Quinn, who has shown me the way forward. It is a way made of peace and unity with a true race. Yes, we must take that path."

ADDITIONAL INFORMATION

The people in the church are Strigoi (Ghosts). A DC 15 Intelligence (Investigation) check will alert the characters that the parishioners are not what they seem.

STORYLINE INFORMATION

WHISPERING NIGHT

The characters step into the room as Pastor Tonkin is speaking. They will go unnoticed if the players succeed in a DC 20 Dexterity (Stealth) check. They will need to roll for each round they are in the church. If they fail, Pastor Tonkin will see the characters and the sigil they wear for Whisper Night and start screaming at them. "Blasphemers! How day thou enter this holy sanctuary! You are not welcome here. You are aligned with our enemy. Strigoi! Remove these foul people!" 1d6+2 Strigoi will stand and attack the characters.

BONE BROTHERS

If the characters step into the church, Pastor Tonkin will see the Bone Brothers' sigil branded on them. He will open his arms and greet them like long-lost friends. The Strigoi sitting in the pews will murmur and point at the characters but remain seated. The Pastor will give the characters a flask of Holy Water he has behind the lectern. He instructs the characters to use the Holy Water on the Youngblood and Whispering Night vampires.

YOUNGBLOOD

The characters step into the room as Pastor Tonkin is speaking. They will go unnoticed if the players succeed in a DC 20 Dexterity (Stealth) check. They will need to roll for each round they are in the church. If they fail, Pastor Tonkin will see the characters and their branded sigil and start to lecture them. "How dare thou enter our holy house? How dare they align with the Youngblood vermin ravaging our town? I see you for who you are. Filth! Yes, you heard what I said. You are filth! And we will cleanse you with all our powers." 1d4 Strigoi will stand and attack the characters.

NPC

Pastor Walter Tonkin

MONSTER

Strigoi (Ghosts)

REWARD

A flask of Holy Water is on the lectern

THE WIDOW MAKER

Anna Shade Barsea's mortician and coffin maker. She is hiding Youngblood vampire Ulysses in a coffin against the wall. Anna sees nothing wrong with the vampires. Indeed, she sees their predatory instincts as part of the natural cycle of life and death. In her small workshop, she deals with death, and naturally, a vampire would want to seek shelter.

Anna Shade, a middle-aged woman, is both the mortician and coffin maker for Barsea. As you might expect, business has been good. Her business is small, with the workshop and embalming room occupying the same small space. Coffins line the walls, and a body drains on a marble table, waiting to be prepped.

STORYLINE INFORMATION
WHISPERING NIGHT

Ulysses will detect that the characters have the Whispering Night sigil and remain hidden but to be found. Players must succeed on a DC 10 Intelligence (Investigation) check to see him. He understands that a truce with Whispering Night should be negotiated. He will go with the characters to Whispering Night's castle to broker a peace deal. The deal that Lucia wants is a 50:50 split of control over Barsea and to force the Bone Brothers out. While Ulysses is with the characters, they will have Disadvantage on any Intelligence (Investigation) checks they attempt.

BONE BROTHERS

Ulysses will remain hidden in the coffin. The characters must succeed on a DC 20 Intelligence (Investigation) check to find Ulysses. If they do discover him, then he will try to escape. The players will roll with Disadvantage DC 15 Strength (Athletics) check to catch him. If they see him, they will need to bind him, or he will try to escape.

YOUNGBLOOD

Ulysses will reveal himself to the characters, stepping out from hiding in one of the coffins. If asked, Ulysses will join the characters. Ulysses is a smart scout, and while he is with the characters, they will have Advantage on any Intelligence (Investigation) checks they attempt.

NPC
Ulysses and Anna Shade

BARSEA HOSPITAL

Barsea Hospital is a place full of sick patients. The characters must be careful as these patients have all been bitten by vampires and are now the almost dead Agroape Mort. Roll 1d6+2 to determine how many patients are in the room. The patients will drag themselves out of their beds and attack the characters with their bare hands, wearing only a thin hospital gown.

The long ward of Barsea Hospital stretches out before you. Each bed has a pole, a shivering victim with thick bandages wrapped around their necks, wrists, and other places where vampires can easily feast on human blood. You are surprised to see a vampire sitting and talking with the patients. He wears the thick, religious clothing of the Bone Brothers. Near you and sitting at a cluttered lab table is Doctor Naomi Whitt. She looks through a magnifying glass at a blood spot and appears completely lost in her thoughts.

ADDITIONAL INFORMATION
Dr. Whitt is hunting for a cure using scientific methods. The characters can help her. See details in the activity "Find the Cure" below.

STORYLINE INFORMATION
WHISPERING NIGHT

Brother Nostro will see the sigil for the Whispering Night and stiffly greet the characters. He does not want to offend the characters, but he does resent the arrogant nature of the Whispering Night family. A DC 15 Charisma (Persuasion) check and Brother Nostro will tell the players that they should talk to the doctor who knows how to cure the patients in the hospital but needs help. Otherwise, he will turn back to helping the sick and dying.

BONE BROTHERS

If the characters approach Brother Nostro, he can detect the Bone Brother sigil burned into their flesh. He will become agitated and alarmed that they have caught him helping in the hospital instead of serving the needs of Vonak, the vampire demon the Bone Brothers worship. Characters need to roll a successful DC 20 Charisma (Persuasion) check to calm Broth Nostro. If they fail, he will attack and alarm the patients, who are Agroape Mort monsters and will also attack the characters.

YOUNGBLOOD

Brother Nostro will see the Youngblood sigil on the characters. He will take time from his caring duties to explain that he has seen the errors of his ways and that the characters should talk with the doctor to learn how to get a cure for vampirism.

ACTIVITY - FIND THE CURE
Finding a cure for vampirism is very difficult. Each vampire sect has a different variation of vampire disease and to cure the people in Barsea, Dr. Whitt knows she will need magic. If the characters want to help find a cure, then they will need to get the following:

- A sample of blood from each vampire sect (the doctor will give three syringes to collect the blood)

- A copy of "Miss Elsa Vexx's 2nd Volume of Everyday Spells," which is the only place to find a spell named "Remove Vampirism."

- A magic caster (either a character or vampire NPC who can cast 3rd level spells)

These items can be used to cure patients in the hospital.

If the characters complete this task, Dr. Whitt will give them a light wooden box that opens to show three syringes in protective padding. Each syringe is filled with liquid silver and can be injected into a vampire. The effect is to immediately deliver 2d6+4 HP damage. The vampire will feel their insides boil from the impact of the silver.

NPC

Doctor Naomi Whitt and Brother Nostro

MONSTER

Agroape Mort - the almost dead

REWARD

A box containing three syringes filled with liquid silver

GENERAL HOUSING

Throughout the town of Barsea are residential houses. Use the random table below to identify what will happen if the characters choose to enter one of the houses.

The people of Barsea are defeated by centuries of vampire tyranny. They hide in their houses. Some will help, some will curse, and others will trick you. You enter a home in Barsea at your own risk.

STORYLINE INFORMATION

No additional information for storylines.

ADDITIONAL INFORMATION

Roll 1d8 to determine the encounter the characters will experience if they knock on any of the general housing in the town:

1d8	Encounter
1	A family of four are huddled together in this house. They are happy to see you and will offer you a free meal restoring +2HP.
2	An old man lives in this house alone. He is terrified that your presence will alert the vampires and bring them to his house. He slams the door in your face.
3	A young, pregnant woman opens the door and begins to scream when she sees you. 1d4 Spider Soldiers are alerted to your presence and immediately attack the characters.
4	The house is abandoned. If the players investigate the house, they will find a small silver cross (5 sp) and two silver candlesticks (15 sp)
5	2 Războinic Lups (Wolf Warriors) are using the house as a temporary barracks. They will attack the players. If the players defeat the 2 Războinic Lups, they can explore the house and find silver Warhammer (30 gp).
6	Two children open the door to the characters and let them in. The children do not have much but they can offer shelter and will sing the following nursery rhyme to the characters:

Verse 1:

The vampire rises up at night
He's a hunter in the dark
He flies through the air with all his might
Searching for a beating heart

Chorus:

Vampire hunting in the night
He's looking for his prey
Vampire hunting in the night
He'll fly and fly and fly away

Verse 2:

He needs to drink some blood, you see
To keep him feeling strong
He'll sneak up on you quietly
And before you know it, he's gone

Chorus

Verse 3:

But don't be afraid, little one
He won't hurt you if you're good
Just make sure you stay in the sun
And he'll leave you as he should

Chorus

| 7 | This house will appear to be empty. If the characters search it, they will find Strigoi (Ghosts) have taken up residence in the bedrooms. There are 1d4-1 bedrooms in the house, each with one Strigoi. |
| 8 | This house will look dark and deserted from the outside. Opening the door, a swarm of cockroaches will attack the players as they step into the dark house. |

WHISPERING NIGHT CASTLE

WHISPERING NIGHT CASTLE

The Whispering Night Castle, the ancestral home to Marcus, Lisha, and Treznor, is heavily guarded by Războinic Lups (Wolf Warriors) and Spider Soldiers. The Ballroom is host to the annual "Minge de cadavre" (Corpse Ball) and is also the only access point to the crypts located in the caverns below the castle.

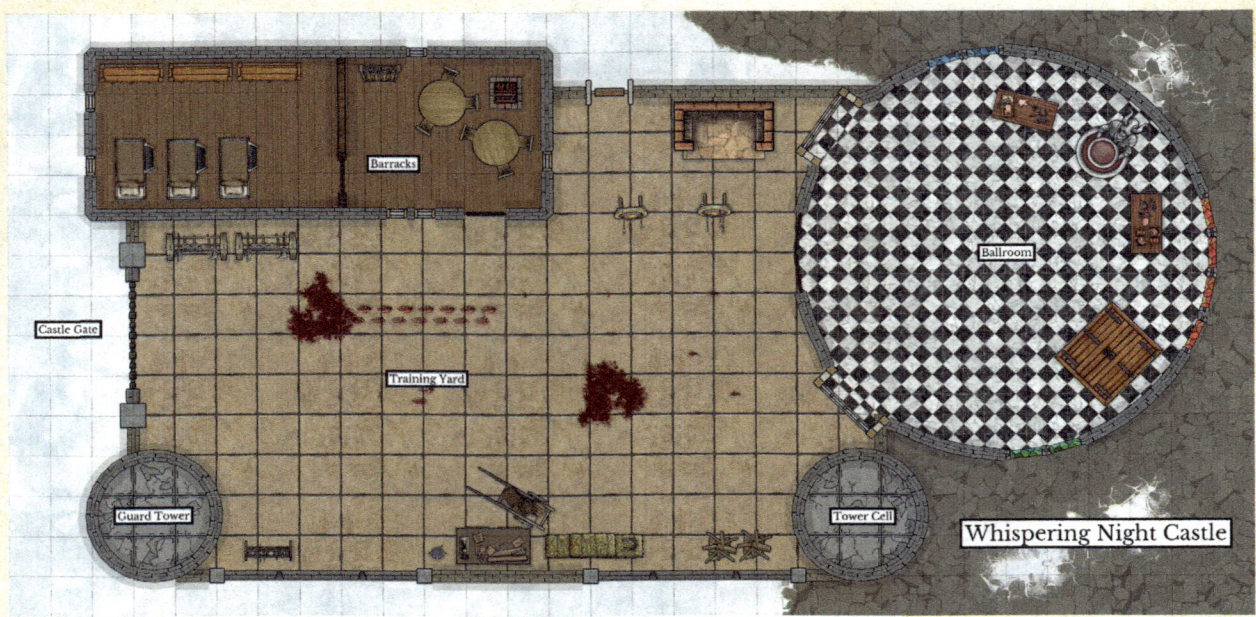

Whispering Night Castle

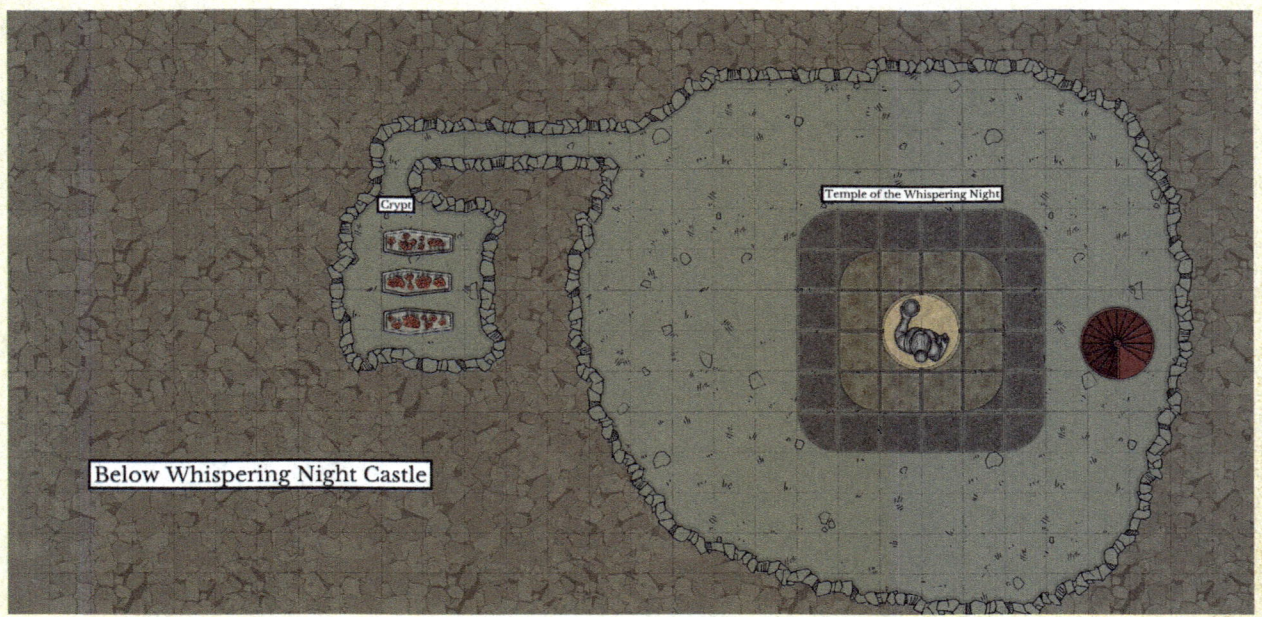

Below Whispering Night Castle

CASTLE GATE

There are several ways to get into the castle. The first is to show the sigil of the Whispering Night, the second is to have the head of Jude the Cheat, and a third method is to battle their way into the castle. This option will require breaking through the gate. Another option, if you are a Bone Brother, is to succeed on the Charisma check with the guards. The gate can be broken with magic (such as an earthquake spell) or by attacking it with a bludgeoning weapon. Piercing weapons, such as a short sword, can be used, but the effect of using it as a bludgeoning weapon will blunt the weapon and reduce its HP effect by 50%. The Castle Gate is a very large object and has 39 (6d12) HP. Breaking the gate will alert the guards in the training yard.

The entrance to the Whispering Night castle is a steel gate 20 ft wide by 40 ft high, split down the center to form two doors that swing outwards. There are two 12-inch-wide speakers' holes in the center of each gate, from which can be seen the face of a Războinic Lups (Wolf Warriors) on the left door and a Spier Soldier on the right. The walls of the castle wrap around and over the gate in cold, gray stone.

STORYLINE INFORMATION
WHISPERING NIGHT

Characters with the Whisper Night sigil will be granted access to the castle.

BONE BROTHERS

There is an uneasy truce with the Bone Brothers. A successful DC 15 Charisma (Persuasion) check by the characters will convince the guards that they mean no harm and will be granted entry. A failed roll will result in characters being told to leave the castle grounds.

YOUNGBLOOD

The speakers' hole is slammed shut, and the characters are refused entry.

OBSTACLE

Castle Gate (Very Large Object)

Războinic Lups (Wolf Warriors) Spider Soldier

TOWER CELL

The person in the tower cell is Falcon, leader of the Deadfur Werewolf Pack. The distant *Wolf War* from the continent's other side has reached the Barsea Heights mountains. The Wolf War has packs of Werewolves

fighting Vampire sects. Falcon was recently captured by the Whispering Night, and he vowed to kill the entire family. The characters can choose the side quest "Wolf Chase," where they can free Falcon. Falcon will join the team but only support them if they hunt vampires. If the characters do not free Falcon, the prisoner will curse them. Characters need a successful DC 10 Wisdom Save to ignore the curse. Characters who fail will believe they are condemned by Falcon and will roll with disadvantage for 1d10 rounds when the curse finally lifts.

As you step into the cell, the sights and smells of blood, decay and bodily excrements make for a vomit-inducing assault your senses. You see only one cell, and a man, whose body is slashed with whip marks, is strung up with manacles that dangle him from the ceiling. Tightly wrapped around his wrist is a silver bracelet with a large wolf's head and midnight black gems for eyes. He raises his head and snarls at you. "What," he growls, "you've come to look at the monster?" At this, he raises his head to the ceiling and releases a loud howl.

MONSTER
Werewolf

BARRACKS

There are two rooms in the Barracks. The main room and the bunk room.

Main Room: The main room has two tables, a fire pit, and a place to store weapons (there is currently a club, an axe, and a stave). At the table are two Războinic Lups (Wolf Warriors), and they are playing Death Dice.

Bunk Room: The bunk room has three bunk beds (with each bunk having room for three beds stacked on top of each other). The third shift guards are resting in the beds. There will be 1d4 Războinic Lups (Wolf Warriors) and 1d4 Spider Soldiers.

In the front room of the barracks, two Wolf Soldiers are sitting at a round wooden playing a game of some kind. They look up at you as you enter. To their right is a rack of weapons, and you see them glance at them before coming back and glaring at you.

STORYLINE INFORMATION
WHISPERING NIGHT

The Războinic Lups (Wolf Warriors) sitting at the table will relax and ask the characters to join them in a game of Death Dice. Their names are Dowers and Beryn. They will ask characters to keep their voices down as their brothers are resting in the bunk room.

BONE BROTHERS

The Wolf Warriors will question why the characters are in the Barracks. The characters must succeed in a DC 5 Charisma (Persuasion). If they are successful, they will be asked to join the game of Death Dice. If the characters fail, the Wolf Warriors will violently escort them out of the building. If the characters attack, the guards in the bunk room will wake and burst through the door.

YOUNGBLOOD

The Războinic Lups (Wolf Warriors) will smell the stain of the Youngblood sigil on the characters as they enter the room. They will immediately stand up from their table and demand, in loud voices, why the characters are here. The characters need to roll a DC 15 Charisma (Persuasion) or (Intimidation) check to force the Războinic Lup to sit back down. A failed roll will result in the Wolf Warriors howling and then attacking. The howl will awaken the guards in the bunk room, who will join the attack.

MONSTER

Războinic Lups (Wolf Warriors)

Spider Soldiers

GUARD TOWER

Spider Soldiers typically use the Guard Tower. They do not use the ladder, preferring to use their Spider Climb abilities to scale the wall up to the parapet. There will be one Spider Soldier on the parapet.

A spindly ladder reaches 40ft from the base to the top of the guard tower. Above, you see a closed latch door that must lead to the parapet that overlooks anyone coming to Whispering Night Castle and anyone practicing in the training yard.

ACTIVITY

The ladder is old and decayed. Have the player roll up to 4 checks, once every 10 feet, to climb the ladder. A successful DC 15 Dexterity (Acrobatics) check will enable a character to climb the ladder. If the character fails the check to climb the ladder, they will step on a rotten wooden rung that will snap and send the character down to the ground taking 1d6 points of bludgeoning damage per 10 feet climbed. The creature lands prone unless it avoids taking damage from the fall.

The character must succeed in a DC 20 Dexterity (Stealth) check to sneak onto the unseen parapet. A failed check will result in the Spider Soldier seeing the character opening the latch door and will attack. The Spider Solider will have advantage for two rounds as the characters defend themselves and try to get on the parapet.

MONSTER

Spider Soldier

TRAINING YARD

The training yard is comprised of the following:

Close to the entrance are 2d4+2 Războinic Lups (Wolf Warriors) practicing one-on-one combat with short swords and shields. Each sword delivers 1d6 piercing damage, and each shield provides AC +2.

The back half of the yard has 2d4 Spider Soldiers practicing archery. Each Spider Soldier has a short bow with a quiver containing 1d6+2 arrows. Each bow has an 80/320 range, with each arrow delivering 1d6 Piercing damage.

The Training Yard is a show of force. The whole yard is swarming with Războinic Lups (Wolf Warriors) and Spider Soldiers practice sword fighting, archery, and one-on-one combat. Across the yard, you can see the entrance to the infamous Whispering Night Ballroom. You can also hear music coming from the Ballroom. It must be the notorious annual Blood Ball.

ADDITIONAL INFORMATION

Any characters with **Jude the Cheats** head, will be granted safe passage across the training yard.

If the characters fight their way across the yard, they will find that the guards will attack in three distinct groups.

The first group will be the Războinic Lups (Wolf Warriors) close to the entrance. They will be supported by Spider Soldiers that are firing arrows into the melee.

The second group will be Spider Soldiers. The Spider Soldiers have short bows but do not have any other weapons.

The third group is a 1d4+2 mix of Războinic Lups (Wolf Warriors) and Spider Soldiers from the Barracks. Each will have a short sword and join the attack.

STORYLINE INFORMATION
WHISPERING NIGHT

Characters with the Whispering Night sigil are asked to halt in the center of the yard. All the guards will gather around the players while one guard is sent to the Ballroom. The guard sent to the Ballroom will return in three rounds with Lisha, who will greet the players and invite them to join the seasonal Blood Ball.

BONE BROTHERS

Characters with the Bone Brothers sigil will be asked to halt in the center of the yard. Characters must succeed in a DC 15 Charisma (Intimidation) or (Persuasion) check. If the characters succeed, a guard will be sent to the Ballroom and return with Marcus. Marcus, who wants to keep the peace with the Bone Brothers, will invite the characters to join the Blood Ball. If the characters fail the Charisma check, then the guards will attempt to arrest the players and imprison them in the Tower Cell.

YOUNGBLOOD

Characters with the Youngblood sigil will be asked why they are at the Whispering Night Castle. A successful DC 10 Charisma (Deception) check will send one of the guards to the ball and return with Treznor. Treznor will see the Youngblood sigil and immediately take you to the Ballroom. On the way to the Ballroom, he will tell you that he loves Lucia and will do what is needed to secure her safety from the Bone Brothers and his family. When the characters enter the Ballroom, Treznor excuses himself to rejoin the Blood Ball but tells them that he can be found in the Ballroom when they need his help. Characters who fail the Charisma check will be attacked by the guards, who will have orders from Marcus to kill any Youngblood intruders.

MONSTER

Spider Soldiers

Războinic Lups (Wolf Warriors)

REWARDS

Weapons can be found throughout the training yard. The characters will see the following:

5 Short Swords

2 Long Swords

3 short bows

3 longbows

4 shields

BALLROOM

The *Minge de cadavre*, known as the **Corpse Ball**, always happens on the longest nights of the winter in the Grand Ballroom. Each dancing guest is a reanimated corpse called a Cadavru that has fallen victim to the Whispering Night family. The Cadavru aren't very strong, but there are a lot of them.

The Whispering Night "Minge de cadavre" event of the year is the **Corpse Ball**. The massive Whispering Night Ballroom is full of people dressed in black and white gowns dancing to ethereal music. A band dressed in red plays discordant music at the back of the room. To their left and right, below the massive stained-glass portraits of the family members, are tables filled with bloodied steaks, platters of sweetbread treats, and, at the end of each table, a small fountain of blood where guests are refilling their glasses. Treznor and his sister, Lisha, are talking to guests below one of the stained-glass windows. On the southeast side of the room, you see a large, locked wooden door that must lead to a lower passage.

ADDITIONAL INFORMATION

Lisha is a fiercely powerful vampire. If the characters approach her, they will need to succeed in a DC 20 Charisma (Deception) or (Persuasion) check to trick her into helping the characters. If they succeed, Lisha will tell the characters that the door on the other side of the room leads to the sacred tombs where her family rests. She will say to them that the riddle must be unencrypted using a mirror cipher that can be found in **The Last Stop**. Failing the Charisma check Lisha will laugh at the characters and force them to dance with a Cadavru guest. The DM will roll 1d4 to determine how many rounds the character must dance with the Cadavru. For each round, the character must complete a DC 10 Constitution save. Any failure will result in the Cadavru attacking the character with an advantage. Following the dance or successful Charisma check, Lisha will leave the characters and join her brother in the crypt.

Characters with **Jude the Cheats** head will be created by Lisha. She will grant the characters amnesty, and they will be able to move around the room, ignored by the Cadavru dancing guests.

The **locked wooden door** has a small mouthpiece in the center of the door. Above the mouthpiece is the following encrypted phase. The characters must solve the phrase and utter the answer into the mouthpiece for the door to open. If the players have the book "Assassins and Spies" from The Last Stop, they will know that the following riddle is encrypted with a mirror cipher. A character with thief tools can do a DC 20 Dexterity (Sleight of Hand) check to pick the lock. A failure will result in a high pitch scream emitting from the door and alerting the room to the characters, and 2d6 Cadavru will attack.

Encrypted riddle: Dszg szh uzmth, wirmph yollw, zmw lmob xlnvh lfg zg mrtsg?

Unencrypted riddle: What has fangs, drinks blood, and only comes out at night?

Answer: A vampire

The door will open and reveal a spiral staircase that leads down into a cavern below the castle.

STORYLINE INFORMATION
WHISPERING NIGHT

Characters with the Whispering Night sigil will be granted safe passage at the Minge de cadavre.

BONE BROTHERS

Characters with a Bone Brothers sigil will need to pass a DC 15 Intelligence (Investigation) check to be granted amnesty and safe passage in the ball. Failure will result in the characters being forced out of the room.

YOUNGBLOOD

Treznor will approach the characters with a Youngblood sigil. He will caution them to be careful and cover up any part of their body that shows the sigil, or the Cadavru will attack. He will whisper to them his love for Lucia, and he will join the characters. The one caveat is that he will not attack any of his family (blood is thicker than water, even for vampires). An attack on his family will be seen as too far, and Treznor will renounce his love and attack the characters.

NPC

Treznor

Lisha

MONSTER

Cadavru (Corpse)

REWARDS

The fountain is infused with vampire blood. Drinking one cup will restore 1d4 damage. Natural and Good characters can only drink one cup from the blood fountain. Two cups and the character will be violently sick as their body rejects the foulness of the blood. Evil characters can drink three cups from the fountain before becoming violently ill. A sick character will be completely immobilized for one round. It will take 2 additional rounds for the character to be fully recovered.

THE TEMPLE OF THE WHISPERING NIGHT`

The plinth in the center of the room comprises three levels, of which the first and third levels are traps.

A spiral staircase leads into a cavernous room cut from the rock face. The infamous Temple of the Whispering Night is dominated by a forty-foot statue standing on a three-tier plinth in the center of the room. At the base of the statue lies a blade with what looks like a razor-sharp edge. It looks like there are items on the top plinth.

ADDITIONAL INFORMATION
BOTTOM TIER TRAP - DEAD WEIGHT

This trap has a cover constructed from material identical to the floor of the lower tier. Stepping on this tier will trigger the trap.

Effect: +10 to hit against one target, Casts Dead Weight centered on the trigger with DC 17 (if relevant)

Trigger: activates when a creature steps on the false floor and activates the trap.

Countermeasures: The trap can be detected with a successful DC 20 Wisdom (Perception) check. The characters must step over the lower tier to prevent the trap from triggering. The floor can also be magically held shut using the arcane lock spell or similar magic.

Casting dispels magic (DC 15) on the trap will cancel the stored spell.

TOP TIER TRAP - DEADLY BLADE

The object's weight keeps a pressure plate depressed to just the right amount. If the pressure plate raises or lowers, it drops a guillotine blade from a slit in the ceiling.

Effect: +10 to hit against one target, 37 (10d10) slashing damage

Trigger: pedestal activates when an object is removed from a pedestal.

Countermeasures: A successful DC 10 Intelligence (Investigation) check allows a character to deduce the trap's presence from mechanisms in the pedestal. Placing an object of equal weight on the pedestal prevents the trap from triggering. A successful DC 10 Dexterity (Sleight of Hand) check makes the switch without causing the weight on the pedestal to change. Unsuccessfully attempting the swap triggers the trap.

REWARDS

Vampire's blade

Vampire's crossbow

Cross the Threshold medallion

A gold chalice with the family sigil on worth 25 gp

CRYPT

The Whispering Night family rest in their family crypt. Marcus and Lisha will be lying in their crypts. The characters can enter the room unnoticed if they pass a DC 15 Dexterity (Stealth) check. If they fail, both vampires will wake and rise from their caskets.

You enter the small antechamber and see three iron caskets lying on the room floor. This is the Whispering Night family crypt.

STORYLINE INFORMATION

WHISPERING NIGHT

If the characters wake the sleeping vampires, they will not be attacked.

BONE BROTHERS

If the characters wake the sleeping vampires, they can do a DC 20 Charisma (Persuasion) check to stop them from attacking. A failed check will lead to the vampires attacking.

YOUNGBLOOD

If the characters wake the sleeping vampires, they will be immediately attacked.

NPC

Marcus

Lisha

REWARDS

Vampire gold — each casket contains 2d12+2 gold coins with the family sigil stamped into each.

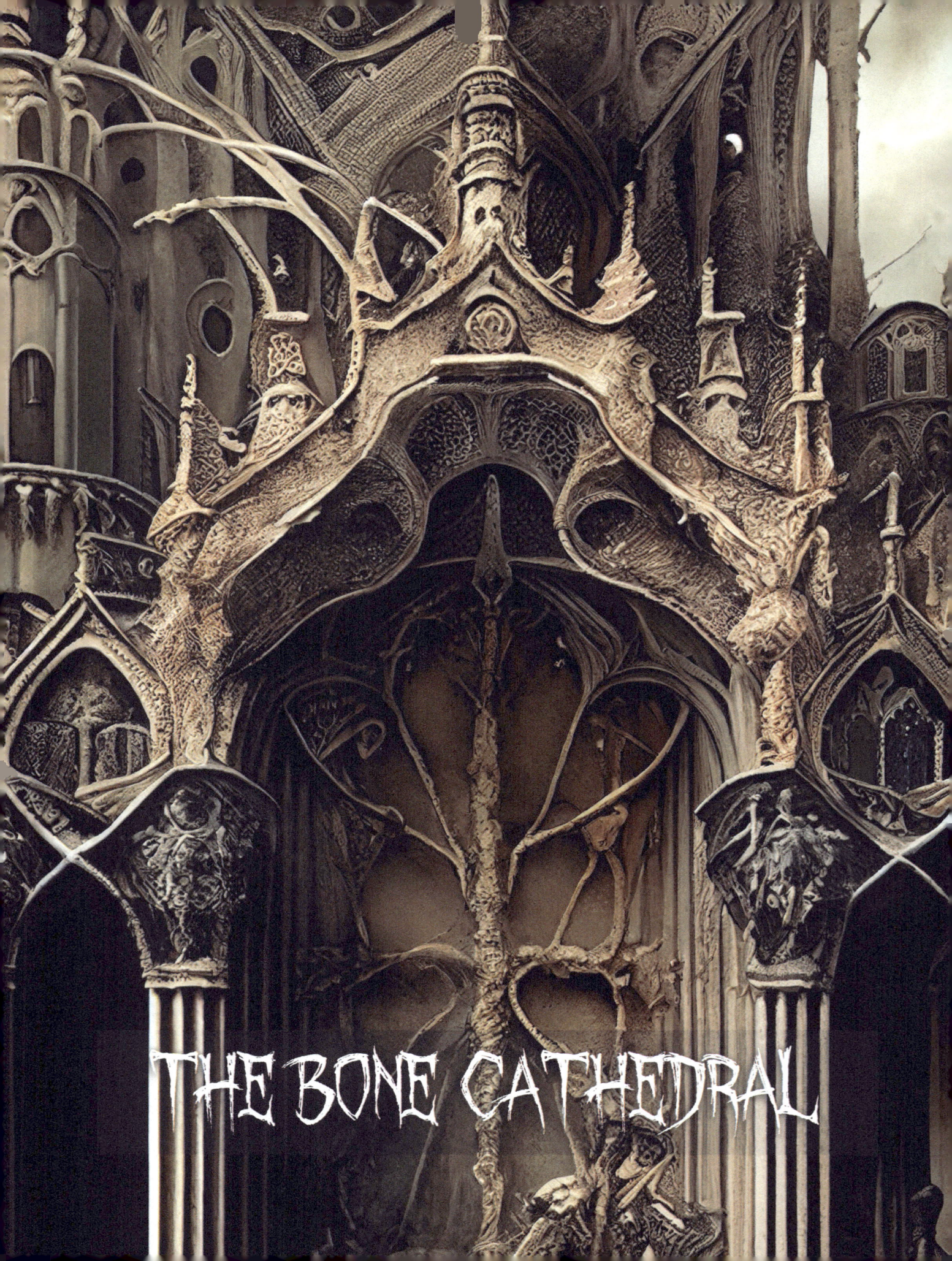

THE BONE CATHEDRAL

THE BONE CATHEDRAL

The Bone Cathedral is the sanctuary for the Bone Brothers. The massive, intimidating building reaches high into the sky with its presence casting a shadow of fear and intimidation on the people of Barsea. The characters should be cautious as they move through the building.

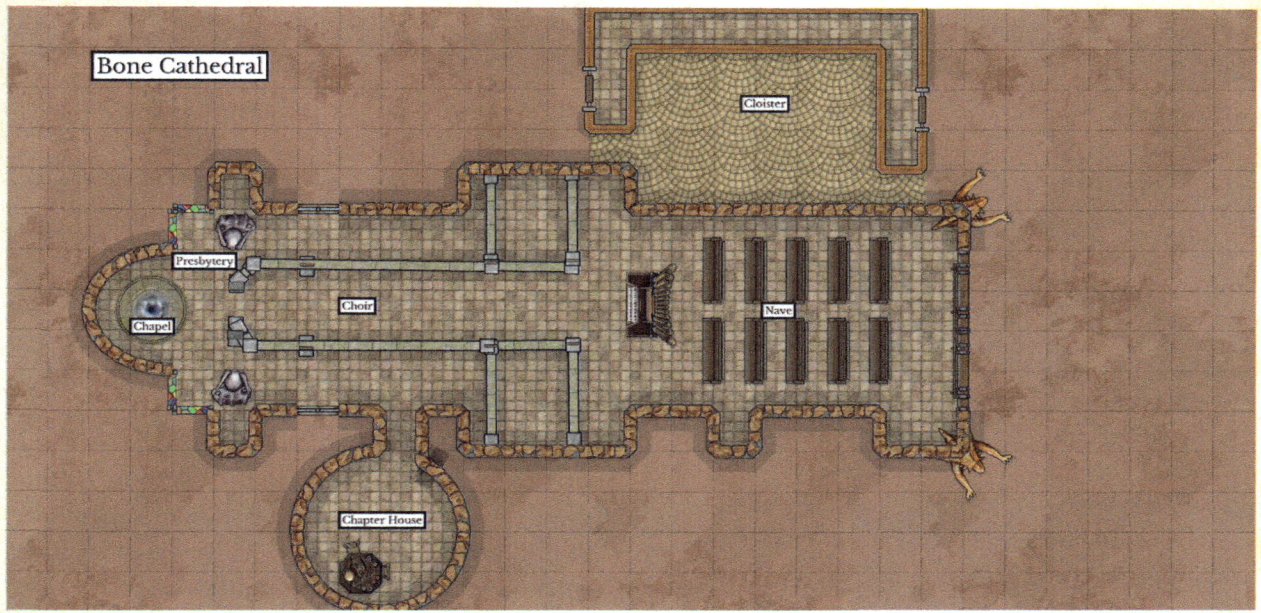

The Bone Cathedral

NAVE

There is currently no service at the Bone Cathedral, and the characters can enter the building unmolested.

The massive, ivory doors are open to the Bone Cathedral, and you can hear the discordant notes of the Bone Organ coughing and bellowing its notes for all to hear. The front third of the Cathedral has rows of pews, and further back, you see the Choir practicing. Looking around, you see that the entire construction is made from bones. Giant femurs arch together to hold the building together, latticed with rib bones from another big creature, and all decorated with human skulls towering from the floor up to the sixty-foot ceiling above you.

ADDITIONAL INFORMATION

The Bone Organ is enchanted. The player of the organ will hit specific notes designed to induce anxiety. Youngblood characters are particularly susceptible to this. Any other character within a 15 ft radius of the

Bone Organ will be overcome with fear and roll with disadvantage until they are out of the radius of influence. A successful DC 15 Intelligence (Religion) will dispel the anxiety (DC 20 for any Youngblood, who are specifically targeted by the organ.) Characters with Bone Brother sigils will not be impacted by the Bone Organ.

Characters can choose to destroy the Bone Organ. The organ is being played by a Cântăreață Nesfântă (Unholy Singer). The organ has 27 (5d10) HP and will cause a lot of noise, alerting the Choir and Brother Marius.

STORYLINE INFORMATION

WHISPERING NIGHT

Characters with the Whispering Night sigil will sense neither a sense of peace nor foreboding. The Cathedral is intimidating, but it is, after all, just a large church.

BONE BROTHERS

Characters with the Bone Brothers' sigil will find peace in the building. If they choose, they can pray from one of the pews and regain +2HP.

YOUNGBLOOD

Characters with the Youngblood sigil will be overcome with a sense of anxiety. As they move further into the Bone Cathedral, their fear increases. All Youngblood will suffer Disadvantage on all Ability Checks while they are in the Bone Cathedral. The source of their anxiety is the massive Bone Organ. If the characters can destroy the organ, their fear will lift. They will be able to roll with advantage for two rounds due to the relief of not feeling so anxious.

MONSTER

Unholy Organ

Cântăreață Nesfântă (Unholy Singer)

CHOIR

The cantor, Brother Marius, leads the singing from the Unholy Singers in the Choir. A DC 20 Dexterity (Stealth) check can be used to sneak through the Choir unseen. A failed check will alert the Choir and Brother Marius to the presence of the characters. There are 1d6+2 Cântăreață Nesfântă (Unholy Singer) and Brother Marius.

The entrance to the corridor between the Nave and the Chapel is formed by an arch of bones. You see the Cântăreață Nesfântă dressed in their Sunday clothes standing in the narrow corridor room that includes is used by the Choir. Their heads are raised, and they are singing a monotonous dirge. Leading them as Cantor is Brother Marius. Thick muscles from his body juxtapose against the angelic voice coming from his mouth.

STORYLINE INFORMATION
WHISPERING NIGHT

If characters with the Whispering Night sigil fail the DC check, Brother Marius will allow two Cântăreață Nesfântă to attack before calling a halt and demanding to know why the characters are in the Cathedral. Brother Marius will take the characters to the Presbytery to meet Father Quinn.

BONE BROTHERS

Characters with the Bone Brother sigil can walk through the Choir without being attacked. Brother Marius will be delighted that you heard his performance and, between verses, will attempt a ghastly smile with his fangs clearly visible.

YOUNGBLOOD

If characters with the Youngblood sigil fail the DC check, then Brother Marius will lead the attack with the entire Choir supporting him.

MONSTER

Cântăreață Nesfântă (Unholy Singer)

NPC

Brother Marius

PRESBYTERY

Father Quinn will try to convince the characters to find and destroy the Whispering Night and Youngblood vampires. They must battle the powerful vampire if they succeed in his intimidation check. Brother Marius will join the fight if he has brought the characters to see Father Quinn.

Father Quinn is practicing his next homily in the center of the room. He looks up and is not surprised to see you. Cold malice tinged with religious mania radiates from the vampire. "I am a powerful vampire and possess extraordinary abilities that set me apart from the rest of humanity. I am strong, fast, and able to withstand injuries that cripple or kill a mortal. Be careful, as I am mindful of those who may seek to use my abilities for their own gain, and I am prepared to defend myself."

STORYLINE INFORMATION
WHISPERING NIGHT

Father Quinn is an intelligent and charismatic man. Suppose the characters are brought in by Brother Marius. In that case, Quinn will demand that they make recompense for sneaking by the Choir by attacking and destroying the Youngblood vampires. Evidence of their death must be brought back to Father Quinn. Characters will only be able to ignore Quinn if they counter with a DC 15 Wisdom (Perception) or (Insight) save. If they fail, they will have a burning desire to leave the Cathedral, find any Youngblood vampire, and bring their heads back to him.

BONE BROTHERS

If Brother Marius is with the characters, he will introduce them to Father Quinn. If not, then the characters can present themselves. Father Quinn will want to recruit the characters to destroy the Whispering Night and Youngblood vampires. He will reward the characters handsomely if they do his work.

YOUNGBLOOD

Father Quinn will smell the stench of the Youngblood sigil on the characters. He will immediately attack the characters and will have advantage for two rounds.

NPC

Father Quinn

CHAPEL

Vonak is a lesser demon but is the originator of the Bone Brother vampire line. Vonak can only visit the mortal world through the fiery dais he stands on, but he cannot step out of the ten-foot radius. He is free to attack any character who steps into the circle.

A deity stands on a stone plinth ringed in flames of orange and red. It is Vonak, a demon, the progenitor of the Bone Brother vampire race, and a force to be reckoned with. Vonak lifts his head and roars up to the ceiling, with the flames rising higher and higher on each bellow. Looking up, you see three beams of light cast from the stained glass in the ceiling and walls. Steel mirrors rest on a table.

ADDITIONAL INFORMATION

Three beams of light are cast into the room, one green, one red, one blue, and three mirrors. Vonak stands in the middle of the room on a small dais. Carved into the dais are the words: "As people have worked together to advance throughout time, so must you see the true light?"

Reflect all three colors of light using the mirrors to form a beam of white light. Striking Vonak with the light will cause 2d8+4 damage. The characters must succeed in a DC 15 Intelligence (Arcana) check to correctly align the mirrors at the beginning of each round.

Vonak can call on swarms of beasts for each round he is battling the characters. Use the following table to determine which swarm will attack:

1d6	Swarm
1	Mischief of rats
2	Cauldron of Bats
3	Cockroach
4	Scorpions
5	1d4 Păianjen Vampir (Vampire Spider)
6	1d4 Strigoi (Ghosts)

If Vonak is reduced to 1 HP, he will utter a final roar, and the fires will be extinguished. Vonak has returned to the netherworld to regain his powers and will not return for the remainder of the campaign.

If the characters can defeat Vonak, they will find a flask of Unholy Water in the center of the Dais.

STORYLINE INFORMATION
WHISPERING NIGHT

Vonak is repulsed by the Whispering Night and will focus his first swarm to attack any of them. He will not stop unless the characters defeat him, or they leave the Chapel.

BONE BROTHERS

Vonak is pleased with your alignment and will offer the characters a flask filled with Unholy Water.

YOUNGBLOOD

Vonak is repulsed by the Youngblood and sends his first swarm to attack those characters. He will not stop unless the characters defeat him, or they leave the Chapel.

MONSTER

Vonak

REWARD

Flask of Unholy Water (contains enough to be used three times)

CHAPTER HOUSE

The Chapter House is where the brothers live and meditate. It is where they keep their holy books. One book lies open on a desk in the center of the room and has a riddle written in it.

Riddle: What word has three consecutive double letters?

Solution: Bookkeeper

If the characters can successfully solve the riddle, then the DM can let them review and pick two spells. If the players are having a hard time, have them make a DC12 group Intelligence Check to succeed.

Dust motes float in the air as you look around the Chapter House. This is where the Brothers must live. A table is stacked with books for research and meditation.

REWARD

Two spells

CLOISTER

The Cloister is a trap to induce fear into the characters. The trap does not care what sigil the characters may have. If a character steps into the central quad of the Cloister, the trap will be triggered.

Effect: Targets all characters within the quad, DC 11 Wisdom (Perception) save or become frightened for 3 (1d4) rounds

Trigger: when a character steps on the quad.

Countermeasures: A successful DC 15 Intelligence (Investigation) check allows a character to deduce the trap's presence from alterations made to the mechanism to accommodate the trigger. A successful DC 20 Dexterity check using thieves' tools disarms the trap, removing the trigger from the floor. Unsuccessfully attempting to pick up the floor's mechanism triggers the trap. Casting dispels magic (DC 20) and will allay the effects of the trap.

The Cloister is dominated by a central stone-tiled quad with an open-air corridor wrapping around it. You will see an entrance on both sides of the Cloister.

WHISPERING NIGHT STORYLINE SUMMARY

The following is a 1-page summary sheet for key Whispering Night storyline encounters.

BARSEA

Double Barn - If the players have the sigil of the Whispering Night, then Lucia and Jade will stay hidden in the barn. The characters must get past the trap to enter the barn. If they can enter the barn, then Jade will approach the characters. She will tell them that she wants to negotiate peace with Whispering Night. Her terms are to share the town, and each sect can enjoy the blood of the people of Barsea. Her words imply that the Bone Brothers must be destroyed. The characters can choose to take the proposition to the Whisper Night family or attack Lucia and Jade.

The Last Stop - Marcus tolerates Jude the Cheat, but Lisha wants him, and his business eliminated. (Lisha will reward the characters with 50 gp if they bring her the heads of these two.)

Church of Piety - The characters step into the room as Pastor Tonkin is speaking. They will go unnoticed if the players succeed in a DC 20 Dexterity (Stealth) check. They will need to roll for each round they are in the church. If they fail, Pastor Tonkin will see the characters and the sigil they wear for Whisper Night and start screaming at them. "Blasphemers! How day thou enter this holy sanctuary! You are not welcome here. You are aligned with our enemy. Strigoi! Remove these foul people!" 1d6+2 Strigoi will stand and attack the characters.

The Widow Maker - Ulysses will detect that the characters have the Whispering Night sigil and remain hidden but to be found. Players must succeed on a DC 10 Intelligence (Investigation) check to see him. He understands that a truce with Whispering Night should be negotiated. He will go with the characters to Whispering Night's castle to broker a peace deal. The deal that Lucia wants is a 50:50 split of control over Barsea and to force the Bone Brothers out. While Ulysses is with the characters, they will have Disadvantage on any Intelligence (Investigation) checks they attempt.

Barsea Hospital - Brother Nostro will see the sigil for the Whispering Night and stiffly greet the characters. He does not want to offend the characters, but he does resent the arrogant nature of the Whispering Night family. A DC 15 Charisma (Persuasion) check and Brother Nostro will tell the players that they should talk to the doctor who knows how to cure the patients in the hospital but needs help. Otherwise, he will turn back to helping the sick and dying.

WHISPERING NIGHT CASTLE

Castle Gate - Characters with the Whisper Night sigil will be granted access to the castle.

Barracks - The Războinic Lups (Wolf Warriors) sitting at the table will relax and ask the characters to join them in a game of Death Dice. Their names are Dowers and Beryn. They will ask characters to keep their voices down as their brothers are resting in the bunk room.

Training Yard - Characters with the Whispering Night sigil is asked to halt in the center of the yard. All the guards will gather around the players while one guard is sent to the Ballroom. The guard sent to the Ballroom will return in three rounds with Lisha, who will greet the players and invite them to join the seasonal Blood Ball.

Ballroom - Characters with the Whispering Night sigil will be granted safe passage at the Minge de cadavre.

Crypt - If the characters wake the sleeping vampires, they will not be attacked.

BONE BROTHERS

Nave - Characters with the Whispering Night sigil will experience neither a sense of peace nor foreboding. The Cathedral is intimidating, but it is, after all, just a large church.

Choir - Suppose characters with the Whispering Night sigil fail the DC check. In that case, Brother Marius will allow two Cântăreață Nesfântă to attack before calling a halt and demanding to know why the characters are in the Cathedral. Brother Marius will take the characters to the Presbytery to meet Father Quinn.

Presbytery - Father Quinn is an intelligent and charismatic man. Suppose the characters are brought in by Brother Marius. In that case, Quinn will demand that they make recompense for sneaking by the Choir by attacking and destroying the Youngblood vampires. Evidence of their death must be brought back to Father Quinn. Characters will only be able to ignore Quinn if they succeed in a DC 15 Wisdom (Perception) or (Insight) save. If they fail, they will have a burning desire to leave the Cathedral, find any Youngblood vampire, and bring its head back to Quinn.

Chapel - Vonak is repulsed by the Whispering Night and sends his first swarm to attack the characters. He will not stop unless the characters defeat him, or they leave the Chapel.

BONE BROTHERS STORYLINE SUMMARY

The following is a 1-page summary sheet for key Bone Brothers storyline encounters.

BARSEA

Double Barn - If the players are branded with the sigil of the Bone Brothers, then Lucia and Jade will stay hidden in the barn. The characters must get past the trap to enter the barn. On entering the barn, Lucia will slip away but Jade will remain and attack the players.

Church of Piety - If the characters step into the church, Pastor Tonkin will see the Bone Brothers' sigil branded on them. He will open his arms and greet them like long-lost friends. The Strigoi sitting in the pews will murmur and point at the characters but remain seated. The Pastor will give the characters a flask of Holy Water he has behind the lectern. He instructs the characters to use the Holy Water on the Youngblood and Whispering Night vampires.

The Widow Maker - Ulysses will remain hidden in the coffin. The characters must succeed on a DC 20 Intelligence (Investigation) check to find Ulysses. If they do discover him, then he will try to escape. The players will roll with Disadvantage DC 15 Strength (Athletics) check to catch him. If they see him, they will need to bind him, or he will try to escape.

Barsea Hospital - If the characters approach Brother Nostro, he can detect the Bone Brother sigil burned into their flesh. He will become agitated and alarmed that they have caught him helping in the hospital instead of serving the needs of Vonak, the vampire demon the Bone Brothers worship. Characters need to roll a successful DC 20 Charisma (Persuasion) check to calm Broth Nostro. If they fail, he will attack and alarm the patients, who are Agroape Mort monsters and will also attack the characters.

WHISPERING NIGHT CASTLE

Castle Gate - There is an uneasy truce with the Bone Brothers. A successful DC 15 Charisma (Persuasion) check by the characters will convince the guards that they mean no harm and will be granted entry. A failed roll will result in characters being told to leave the castle grounds.

Barracks - The Războinic Lups (Wolf Warriors) will question why the characters are in the Barracks. The characters must succeed in a DC 5 Charisma (Persuasion). If they are successful, they will be asked to join the game of Death Dice. If the characters fail, the Războinic Lups (Wolf Warriors) will violently escort them out of the building. If the characters attack, the guards in the bunk room will wake and burst through the door.

Training Yard - Characters with the Bone Brothers sigil will be asked to halt in the center of the yard. Characters must succeed in a DC 15 Charisma (Intimidation) or (Persuasion) check. If the characters succeed, a guard will be sent to the Ballroom and return with Marcus. Marcus, who wants to keep the peace with the Bone Brothers, will invite the characters to join the Blood Ball. If the characters fail the Charisma check, then the guards will attempt to arrest the players and imprison them in the Tower Cell.

Ballroom - Characters with a Bone Brothers sigil will need to pass a DC 15 Intelligence (Investigation) check to be granted amnesty and safe passage in the ball. Failure will result in the characters being forced out of the room.

Crypt - If the characters wake the sleeping vampires, they can roll a DC 20 Charisma (Persuasion) check to stop them from attacking. A failed check will lead to the vampires attacking.

BONE BROTHERS

Nave - Characters with the Bone Brothers' sigil will find peace in the building. If they choose, they can pray in a pew and regain +2HP.

Choir - Characters with the Bone Brother sigil can walk through the Choir without being attacked. Brother Marius will be delighted that you hear his performance and, between verses, will attempt a ghastly smile with his fangs clearly visible.

Presbytery - If Brother Marius is with the characters, he will introduce them to Father Quinn. If not, then the characters can present themselves. Father Quinn will want to recruit the characters to destroy the Whispering Night and Youngblood vampires. He will reward the characters handsomely if they do his work.

Chapel - Vonak is pleased with your alignment and will offer the characters a flask filled with Unholy Water.

YOUNGBLOOD STORYLINE SUMMARY

The following is a 1-page summary sheet for key Youngblood storyline encounters.

BARSEA

Double Barn - If the players are branded with the Youngblood sigil, Lucia and Jade will appear, warn them of the trap, and escort them around it, into the barn. Once in the barn, Lucia and Jade will explain that they believe that the Bone Brothers are killing the people in Barsea and making it look like Youngblood. To clear the name of the Youngblood, the leader of the Bone Brothers, Father Quinn, must be decapitated. Jade knows that the Whispering Night will only respond to strength and they want the characters to take the head of Father Quinn to the Whispering Night to negotiate a peace treaty. The terms of the treaty are simple: the blood of the people of Barsea is to be split 50:50 between the two sects. Lucia will tell the characters that they are hungry and need to eat quickly, or they will lose control and begin to attack the next person they meet.

Church of Piety - The characters step into the room as Pastor Tonkin is speaking. They will go unnoticed if the players succeed in a DC 20 Dexterity (Stealth) check. They will need to roll for each round they are in the church. If they fail, Pastor Tonkin will see the characters and their branded sigil and start to lecture them. "How dare thou enter our holy house? How dare they align with the Youngblood vermin ravaging our town? I see you for who you are. Filth! Yes, you heard what I said. You are filth! And we will cleanse you with all our powers." 1d4 Strigoi will stand and attack the characters.

The Widow Maker - Ulysses will reveal himself to the characters, stepping out from hiding in one of the coffins. If asked, Ulysses will join the characters. Ulysses is a smart scout, and while he is with the characters, they will have Advantage on any Intelligence (Investigation) checks they attempt.

Barsea Hospital - Brother Nostro will see the Youngblood sigil on the characters. He will take time from his caring duties to explain that he has seen the errors of his ways and that the characters should talk with the doctor to learn how to get a cure for vampirism.

WHISPERING NIGHT CASTLE

Castle Gate - The speakers' hole is slammed shut, and the characters are refused entry.

Barracks - The Războinic Lups (Wolf Warriors) will smell the stain of the Youngblood sigil on the characters as they enter the room. They will immediately stand up from their table and demand, in loud voices, why the characters are here. The characters need to roll a DC 15 Charisma (Persuasion) or (Intimidation) check to force the Wolf Warriors to sit back down. A failed roll will result in the Wolf Warriors howling and then attacking. The howl will awaken the guards in the bunk room, who will join the attack.

Training Yard - Characters with the Youngblood sigil will be asked why they are at the Whispering Night Castle. A successful DC 10 Charisma (Deception) check will send one of the guards to the ball and return with Treznor. Treznor will see the Youngblood sigil and immediately take you to the Ballroom. On the way to the Ballroom, he will tell you that he loves Lucia and will do what is needed to secure her safety from the Bone Brothers and his family. When the characters enter the Ballroom, Treznor excuses himself to rejoin the Blood Ball but tells them that he can be found in the Ballroom when they need his help. Characters who fail the Charisma check will be attacked by the guards, who will have orders from Marcus to kill any Youngblood intruders.

Ballroom - Treznor will approach the characters with a Youngblood sigil. He will caution them to be careful and cover up any part of their body that shows the sigil, or the Cadavru will attack. He will whisper to them his love for Lucia, and he will join the characters. The one caveat is that he will not attack any of his family (blood is thicker than water, even for vampires). An attack on his family will be seen as too far, and Treznor will renounce his love and attack the characters.

Crypt - If the characters wake the sleeping vampires, they will be immediately attacked.

BONE BROTHERS

Nave - Characters with the Youngblood sigil will be overcome with a sense of anxiety. As they move further into the Bone Cathedral, their fear increases. Characters will roll with disadvantage while they are in the Bone Cathedral. The source of their anxiety is the massive Bone Organ. If the characters can destroy the organ, their fear will lift. They will be able to roll with advantage for two rounds due to the relief of not feeling so anxious.

Choir - If characters with the Youngblood sigil fail the DC check, then Brother Marius will lead the attack with all the Choir supporting him.

Presbytery - Father Quinn will smell the stench of the Youngblood sigil on the characters. He will immediately attack the characters and will have advantage for two rounds.

Chapel - Vonak is repulsed by the Youngblood and sends his first swarm to attack the characters. He will not stop unless the characters defeat him, or they leave the Chapel.

SIDE QUESTS

SIDE QUESTS

FIND THE CURE

Finding a cure for vampirism is very hard. Each vampire sect has a different variation of the vampire disease. To cure the people in Barsea, Dr. Whitt knows she will need magic. If the characters want to help find a cure, then they will need to get the following:

- A sample of blood from each vampire sect (the doctor will give three syringes to collect the blood)

- A copy of "Miss Elsa Vexx's 2nd Volume of Everyday Spells" which is the only place to find a spell named "Remove Vampirism"

- A magic caster (either a character or vampire NPC who can cast 3rd level spells)

These items can be used to cure the patients in the hospital.

If the characters do complete this task, then Dr. Whitt will give them a thin wooden box that opens to show three syringes in protective padding. Each syringe is filled with liquid silver and can be injected into a vampire. The effect is to immediately delivery 2d6+4 HP damage. The vampire will feel their insides boil from the effects of the silver.

WOLF CHASE

Release Falcon, the leader of the Deadfur Werewolf Pack. Falcon will join the characters and support them if they are hunting vampires. He will not support any peace negotiations with vampires due to his involvement in the Wolf War.

RANDOM ENCOUNTERS

RANDOM ENCOUNTERS

Use the following tables to generate random encounters as the characters move through the three main areas of the game.

THE TOWN OF BARSEA

1d6	Encounter
1	The characters find a **Vampire Stake**
2	The characters encounter 1 **Strigoi**
3	A unified battle cry can be heard from Whispering Night Castle
4	The characters come across a lost little boy. The child will be asked to be taken to the hospital so he can sit with his ill parents.
5	Discordant sounds coming from the Bone Cathedral cause an unsettling feeling in the characters.
6	The characters encounter 1 **Agroape Mort** who has escaped the hospital

THE WHISPERING NIGHT CASTLE

1d6	Encounter
1	1 Spider Soldier attacks
2	A dehydrated is found. It is the same as one standard meal but will require hot water to be added.
3	A swarm of **cockroaches** attacks the characters.
4	The characters find a quiver of 10 bolts for a vampire crossbow.
5	The characters pause to hear the howling wind running down from the mountains.
6	2 **Războinic Lups** (Wolf Warriors) attack

THE BONE CATHEDRAL

1d6	Encounter
1	The characters come across a Holy Axe
2	A **Păianjen Vampir** (Vampire Spider) scuttles up to the characters.
3	The characters find a vial of Unholy Water that is good for one use.
4	The characters pause to pray to their own gods.
5	The characters meet 1 **Cântăreață Nesfântă** (Unholy Singer)
6	The characters move unmolested

SCALING MONSTERS

SCALING MONSTERS

The following monsters can be increased depending on the size and level of the party:

- Războinic Lup (Wolf Warrior)
- Strigoi (Ghosts)
- Cântăreață Nesfântă (Unholy Singer)
- Spider Soldier
- Șobolan Vampir (Vampire Rat)
- Liliac Vampir (Vampire Bat)
- Păianjen Vampir (Vampire Spider)
- Cockroach
- Scorpions

Use the following table for party size to increase the number of monsters:

Party Size	Increase number by
5-8	x 1.5
9-12	x 2
13	x 2.5

Use the following table for party level to increase the number of monsters:

Party Level	Increase number by
5-8	x 1.5
9-12	x 2
13-15	x 2.5
Level 16+	x 3.5

Now take the number for the party and the level and add the two together. For instance, if you have a Party Size of 5 with an average Party Level of 10, then you would add 1.5 + 2.5 to get 4 times the monsters. 3 creatures for a level 10 party is no challenge, especially if there are 6 or 7 PC's. Increase that to 12, and suddenly you have a challenge. Feel free to adjust as you see fit.

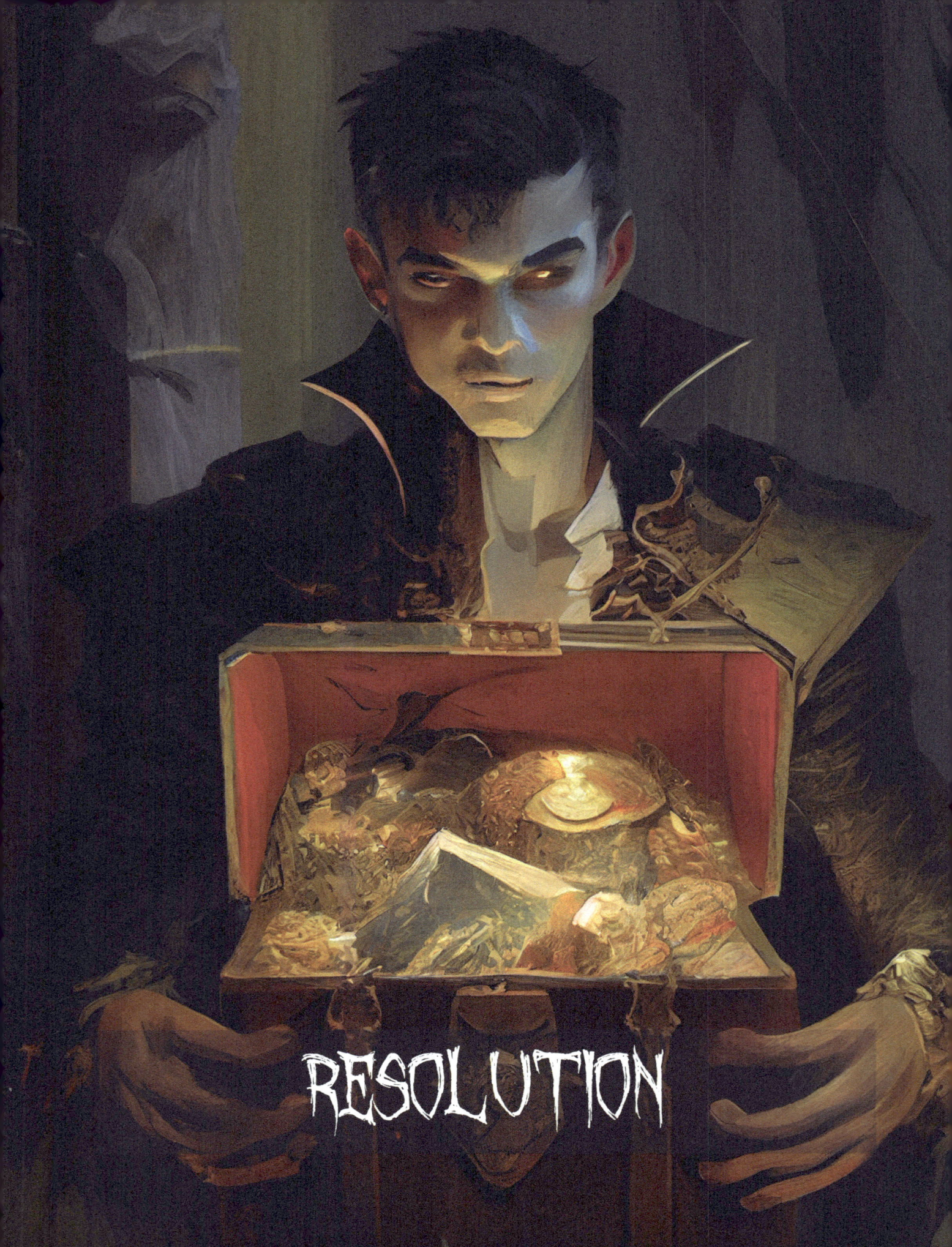

RESOLUTION

RESOLUTION

The final resolution of the game can be defined in two ways:

- The characters align with a particular vampire sect and overthrow the competing sects, destroy the sect(s) or by defining a truce/alignment with the other sect(s).

- The characters decide to destroy all the vampire sects and free the town.

WHISPERING NIGHT

The Whispering Night have resided as overlords of Barsea for centuries. For them, a resolution will happen if a truce with the vampire sects is established. But the terms of any truce must be fair of the vampires will go to war with each other!

The Whispering Night will promise characters the following if they align with them:

- **Elixir of Life** - a potent potion that can prevent death for 24 hrs.

- A Vampire Blade

- 200gp per player

BONE BROTHERS

Father Quinn sees a world where his fraternity rules overall. He will only be happy when all members of Whispering Night and Youngblood are eradicated.

The Bone Brothers will offer the following if the characters align with them:

- Three spells from Father Quinn's Dark Book

- Unholy Water

- A gold, inverted cross worth 150gp

YOUNGBLOOD

Lucia wants the Youngblood to have a rightful place at the table to make decisions and she believes that a truce can be brokered with Whispering Night. The radical religious beliefs of the Bone Brothers make it clear that they must be destroyed. Decapitate Father Quinn and use his head a negotiation tool with the Whispering Night.

The Youngblood are fiercely loyal and will offer characters the following if they help:

- **Eye of Next** is an amulet that will see what happens in the next round (can only be used once daily).

- **Vampire's Bow** is a blood-soaked crossbow that can fire two bolts per round, but this means it will need to be reloaded more often.

The Youngblood have no money, but they will help the players raid the Whispering Night castle and steal precious items.

FREE THE TOWN OF BARSEA

Barsea has been under the rule of vampires for hundreds of years. Generations have only known a life of fear. Pastor Tonkin will do all he can to have the Bone Brothers rule over the people of Barsea. He will seed dissent and gaslight the people against the player characters. In contrast, Dr. Whitt will support the PCs, but she will also ask the PCs to act with compassion. Not all vampires are monsters. Some, like Brother Nostro, change their ways and can help the players eradicate the evil vampire presence.

If the town is freed, then the characters will receive the following:

- 100gp will be given to the characters

- The town hall will be dedicated after the players and renamed after a name they suggest

- An annual feast celebrating the PCs will be given and named after each character. The banquet provides an additional +2HP to the PC's total.

MONSTERS

MONSTERS

AGROAPE MORT (ALMOST DEAD)

Medium undead, neutral evil

Armor Class 9

Hit Points 14 (4d8 - 4)

Speed 10 ft.

STR	DEX	CON	INT	WIS	CHA
10 (+0)	10 (+0)	10 (+0)	10 (+0)	10 (+0)	10 (+0)

CADAVRU (CORPSE)

Medium humanoid (any race), any alignment

Armor Class 10

Hit Points 9 (2d8)

Speed 15 ft.

STR	DEX	CON	INT	WIS	CHA
8 (-1)	8 (-1)	8 (-1)	3 (-4)	3 (-4)	3 (-4)

Senses passive Perception 10

Languages Common

Challenge 1/8 (25 XP)

Vampiric Infection. The victim has been bitten by a vampire and is in the process of being transformed into one. At the end of each long rest, the victim must make a DC 10 Constitution saving throw. On a failed save, they take 1d6 necrotic damage and their hit point maximum is reduced by an equal amount. This process continues until the victim is reduced to 0 hit points, at which point they rise as a vampire under the control of the vampire that bit them.

ACTIONS

Unarmed Strike. Melee Weapon Attack: +0 to hit, reach 5 ft., one target. Hit: 1 bludgeoning damage.

CANTAREATA NESFANTA (UNHOLY SINGER)

Medium humanoid (any race), any alignment

Armor Class 10

Hit Points 9 (2d8)

Speed 30 ft.

STR	DEX	CON	INT	WIS	CHA
10 (+0)	10 (+0)	10 (+0)	10 (+0)	14 (+2)	11 (+0)

Skills Religion +2

Senses passive Perception 12

Languages any one language (usually Common)

Challenge 1/4 (50 XP)

Unholy Voice. The Cântăreață Nesfântă can sing a high-pitched note that will cause any creature within 20 ft to be stunned for one round and incapable of moving. If the creature is within 5 ft of the Cântăreață Nesfântă then the Unholy Voice will cause the eardrums of the creature to burst and cause +5HP damage.

COCKROACHES

Tiny swarm of Tiny beasts, unaligned

Armor Class 12 (natural armor)

Hit Points 12 (5d4)

Speed 20 ft., climb 20 ft.

STR	DEX	CON	INT	WIS	CHA
3 (-4)	13 (+1)	10 (+0)	1 (-5)	7 (-2)	1 (-5)

Senses blindsight 10 ft., passive Perception 8

Languages —

Challenge 1/8 (25 XP)

Swarm. The cockroaches can occupy another creature's space and vice versa, and the swarm can move through any opening large enough for a Tiny insect. The swarm can't regain hit points or gain temporary hit points.

ACTIONS

Bites. Melee Weapon Attack: +3 to hit, reach 0 ft., one target in the swarm's space. Hit: 10 (4d4) piercing damage, or 5 (2d4) piercing damage if the cockroaches have half its hit points or fewer.

LILIAC VAMPIR (VAMPIRE BATS)

Medium swarm of Tiny beasts, unaligned

Armor Class 12

Hit Points 22 (5d8)

Speed 0 ft., fly 30 ft.

STR	DEX	CON	INT	WIS	CHA
5 (-3)	15 (+2)	10 (+0)	2 (-4)	12 (+1)	4 (-3)

Damage Resistances bludgeoning, piercing, slashing

Condition Immunities charmed, frightened, grappled, paralyzed, petrified, prone, restrained, stunned

Senses blindsight 60 ft., passive Perception 11

Challenge 1/4 (50 XP)

Echolocation. The Vampire Bats can't use its blindsight while deafened.

Keen Hearing. The Vampire Bats has advantage on Wisdom (Perception) checks that rely on hearing.

Cauldron of Bats. A swarm of bats is known as a cauldron. The Vampire Bats can occupy another creature's space and vice versa, and the cauldron can move through any opening large enough for a Tiny bat. The cauldron can't regain hit points or gain temporary hit points.

ACTIONS

Vampire Bite. Melee Weapon Attack: +2 to hit, reach 0 ft., one target in the Vampire Bats' space. The Vampire Bat will land on their victim next to the main artery close to the skin's surface, such as the neck. The vampire bite will drain 1d6+3 HP for each round.

LUPUL VAMPIR (VAMPIRE WOLF)

Medium beast, unaligned

Armor Class 13 (natural armor)

Hit Points 11 (2d8 + 2)

Speed 60 ft.

STR	DEX	CON	INT	WIS	CHA
15 (+2)	15 (+2)	12 (+1)	10 (+0)	12 (+1)	10 (+0)

Skills Perception +3, Stealth +4

Senses passive Perception 13

Languages understands Common

Challenge 1 (200 XP)

Children of the Night. The Vampire Wolf has advantage on an attack roll against a creature if at least one of the Vampire Wolf's allies is within 5 ft. of the creature and the ally isn't incapacitated.

Keen Hearing and Smell. The wolf has advantage on Wisdom (Perception) checks that rely on hearing or smell.

ACTIONS

Bite. Melee Weapon Attack: +4 to hit, reach 5 ft., one target. Hit: 7 (2d4 + 2) piercing damage. If the target is a creature, it must succeed on a DC 11 Strength saving throw or be knocked prone.

PAIANJEN VAMPIR (VAMPIRE SPIDERS)

Medium swarm of Tiny beasts, unaligned

Armor Class 12 (natural armor)

Hit Points 13 (3d8)

Speed 20 ft., climb 20 ft.

STR	DEX	CON	INT	WIS	CHA
7 (-2)	13 (+1)	10 (+0)	1 (-5)	7 (-2)	1 (-5)

Senses blindsight 10 ft., passive Perception 8

Challenge 1/2 (100 XP)

Swarm. The Vampire Spiders can occupy another creature's space and vice versa, and the swarm can move through any opening large enough for a Tiny insect. The swarm can't regain hit points or gain temporary hit points.

Spider Climb. The Vampire Spiders can climb difficult surfaces, including upside down on ceilings, without needing to make an ability check.

Web Sense. While in contact with a web, the Vampire Spiders knows the exact location of any other creature in contact with the same web.

Web Walker. Vampire Spiders ignore movement restrictions caused by webbing.

ACTIONS

Vampire Bite. Melee Weapon Attack: +2 to hit, reach 0 ft., one target in the Vampire Spider's space. The Vampire Spider will scurry up their victim to find the main artery close to the skin's surface, such as the neck. The vampire bite will drain 1d6+3 HP for each round.

RĂZBOINIC LUP (WOLF WARRIOR)

Medium humanoid (Wolf Humanoid), unaligned

Armor Class 13 (natural armor)

Hit Points 32 (5d8 + 10)

Speed 45 ft.

STR	DEX	CON	INT	WIS	CHA
15 (+2)	13 (+1)	15 (+2)	12 (+1)	12 (+1)	10 (+0)

Skills Perception +3, Stealth +3

Senses passive Perception 13

Challenge 1 (200 XP)

Keen Hearing and Smell. The Războinic Lup has advantage on Wisdom (Perception) checks that rely on hearing or smell.

Pack Tactics. The Războinic Lup has advantage on Attack rolls against a creature if at least one of the Războinic Lup's allies is within 5 ft. of the creature and the ally isn't incapacitated.

ACTIONS

Bite. Melee Weapon Attack: +5 to hit, reach 5 ft., one target. Hit: 10 (2d6 + 3) piercing damage. If the target is a creature, it must succeed on a DC 13 Strength saving throw or be knocked prone.

Lupine Sword. Melee Weapon Attack: one-handed martial weapon dealing 1d8 slashing damage.

SCORPION

Tiny beast, unaligned

Armor Class 14 (natural armor)

Hit Points 24 (7d4 + 7)

Speed 20 ft.

STR	DEX	CON	INT	WIS	CHA
12 (+1)	10 (+0)	12 (+1)	1 (-5)	6 (-2)	3 (-4)

Senses blindsight 60 ft., passive Perception 8

Challenge 1/8 (25 XP)

ACTIONS

Claw. Melee Weapon Attack: +2 to hit, reach 0.5 ft., one target. Hit: 2 (1d4) bludgeoning damage, and the target is grappled (escape DC 12). The scorpion has two claws, each of which can grapple only one target.

Multiattack. The scorpion makes three attacks: two with its claws and one with its sting.

Sting. Melee Weapon Attack: +4 to hit, reach 0.5 ft., one creature. Hit: 3 (1d4 + 1) piercing damage, and the target must make a DC 12 Constitution saving throw, taking 22 (4d10) poison damage on a failed save or half as much damage on a successful one.

SPIDER SOLDIER

Medium humanoid, unaligned

Armor Class 16 (breastplate)

Hit Points 11 (2d8 + 2)

Speed 40 ft., climb 40 ft.

STR	DEX	CON	INT	WIS	CHA
15 (+2)	16 (+3)	13 (+1)	10 (+0)	10 (+0)	10 (+0)

Skills Perception +3, Stealth +7

Senses blindsight 10 ft., darkvision 60 ft., passive Perception 13

Languages common

Challenge 1/4 (50 XP)

Spider Climb. The Spider Soldier can climb difficult surfaces, including upside down on ceilings, without making an ability check.

ACTIONS

Bite. Melee Weapon Attack: +3 to hit, reach five ft., one creature. Hit: 4 (1d6 + 1) piercing damage, and the target must make a DC 11 Constitution saving throw, taking 7 (2d6) poison damage on a failed save or half as much damage on a successful one. If the poison damage reduces the target to 0 hit points, the target is stable but poisoned for 1 hour, even after regaining hit points, and is paralyzed in this way.

Blood Scimitar. Melee Weapon Attack: the notorious weapon of a Spider Soldier, the Blood Scimitar is a military one-handed weapon with a heavy blade and a distinct red hue to the steel. The Blood Scimitar deals 1d8 damage.

STRIGOI (GHOST)

Medium undead, neutral evil

Armor Class 15 (natural armor)

Hit Points 30 (4d8 + 12)

Speed 30 ft.

STR	DEX	CON	INT	WIS	CHA
16 (+3)	16 (+3)	16 (+3)	11 (+0)	10 (+0)	12 (+1)

Saving Throws Dex +5, Wis +2

Skills Perception +2, Stealth +5

Damage Resistances necrotic; bludgeoning, piercing, and slashing from nonmagical attacks

Senses darkvision 60 ft., passive Perception 12

Languages the languages it knew in life

Challenge 2 (450 XP)

Regeneration. The Strigoi regains 10 hit points at the start of its turn if it has at least 1 hit point and isn't in sunlight or running water. If the Strigoi takes radiant damage or damage from holy water, this trait doesn't function at the start of the Strigoi's next turn.

ACTIONS

Multiattack. The Strigoi makes two attacks, only one of which can be a bite attack.

Bite. Melee Weapon Attack: +6 to hit, reach five ft., one willing creature, or a creature that the Strigoi grapples, incapacitated, or restrained. Hit: 6 (1d6 + 3) piercing damage plus 7 (2d6) necrotic damage. The target's hit point maximum is reduced by an amount equal to the necrotic damage taken, and the Strigoi regains hit points equal to that amount. The reduction lasts until the target finishes a long rest. The target dies if this effect reduces its hit point maximum to 0.

Claws. Melee Weapon Attack: +6 to hit, reach 5 ft., one creature. Hit: 8 (2d4 + 3) slashing damage. Instead of dealing damage, the Strigoi can grapple the target (escape DC 13).

SOBOLAN VAMPIR (VAMPIRE RATS)

Medium swarm of Tiny beasts, unaligned

Armor Class 10

Hit Points 24 (7d8 - 7)

Speed 30 ft.

STR	DEX	CON	INT	WIS	CHA
12 (+1)	11 (+0)	9 (-1)	8 (-1)	10 (+0)	3 (-4)

Damage Resistances bludgeoning, piercing, slashing

Condition Immunities charmed, frightened, grappled, paralyzed, petrified, prone, restrained, stunned

Senses darkvision 30 ft., passive Perception 10

Challenge 1/4 (50 XP)

Mischief of Rats. A swarm of rats is known as a Mischief of Rats. The swarm can occupy another creature's space and vice versa, and the swarm can move through any opening large enough for a Tiny rat. The swarm can't regain hit points or gain temporary hit points.

Keen Smell. The swarm has advantage on Wisdom (Perception) checks that rely on smell.

ACTIONS

Bites. Melee Weapon Attack: +2 to hit, reach 0 ft., one target in the swarm's space. Hit: 7 (2d6) piercing damage, or 3 (1d6) piercing damage if the swarm has half of its hit points or fewer.

VONAH (VAMPIRE DEMON)

Large fiend, Chaotic Evil

Armor Class 16 (scale mail)

Hit Points 136 (16d10 + 48)

Speed 60 ft., climb 30 ft., fly 120 ft.

STR	DEX	CON	INT	WIS	CHA
20 (+5)	17 (+3)	16 (+3)	20 (+5)	20 (+5)	20 (+5)

Damage Resistances bludgeoning, piercing, and slashing from nonmagical attacks

Damage Immunities fire, poison

Condition Immunities exhaustion, grappled, paralyzed, petrified, poisoned, prone, restrained, unconscious

Senses darkvision 60 ft., passive Perception 15

Languages Abyssal, Common, Infernal, Undercommon

Challenge 9 (5,000 XP)

Fire Form. Vonak can move through a space as narrow as 1 inch wide without squeezing. A creature that touches the elemental or hits it with a melee attack within 5 ft. of it takes 5 (1d10) fire damage. In addition, Vonak can enter a hostile creature's space and stop there. The first time he enters a creature's space on a turn, that creature takes 5 (1d10) fire damage and catches fire; until someone takes action to douse the fire, the creature takes 5 (1d10) fire damage at the start of each of its turns.

Running Water. For every 5 ft. Vonak moves in running water, or for every gallon of water splashed on him, he takes 1 cold damage.

Mist. Once per battle, Vonak can dissolve into mist and move up to 30 ft.

ACTIONS

Multiattack. The elemental makes two touch attacks.

Vampire's Bite. Vonak will drain its victim from any place on the body where the main artery is easily accessed. The neck and wrist are often exposed areas of weakness for most beings. The vampire will drain 1d6+3 HP for each round.

Vampire's Blade. Melee Weapon Attack: the Vampire's Blade is a necrotic blade infused with poison. The edge will cause 1d4 slashing damage. The necrotic venom in the blade will continue to inflict +2HP damage every round until the victim receives a cure for poisons.

WEREWOLF

Medium humanoid (human), Neutral evil

Armor Class 11 in humanoid form, 12 (natural armor) in wolf or hybrid form

Hit Points 58 (9d8 + 18)

Speed 30 ft. (40 ft. in wolf form)

STR	DEX	CON	INT	WIS	CHA
16 (+3)	12 (+13)	14 (+2)	10 (+0)	11 (+0)	10 (+0)

Skills Perception +4, Stealth +5

Damage Immunities bludgeoning, piercing, and slashing from nonmagical attacks not made with silvered weapons

Condition Immunities charmed, frightened

Senses darkvision 60 ft., passive Perception 14

Languages Common (can't speak in wolf form), Sylvan

Challenge 3 (700 XP)

Shapechanger. The werewolf can use its action to polymorph into a wolf-humanoid hybrid or into a wolf, or back into its true form, which is humanoid. Its statistics, other than its AC, are the same in each form. Any equipment it is wearing or carrying isn't transformed. It reverts to its true form if it dies.

Keen Hearing and Smell. The werewolf has advantage on Wisdom (Perception) checks that rely on hearing or smell.

Frightful Presence. Each creature within 30 feet of the werewolf and aware of it must succeed on a DC 11 Wisdom saving throw or become frightened for 1 minute. A creature can repeat the saving throw at the end of each of its turns, ending the effect on itself on a success. If a creature's saving throw is successful or the effect ends for it, the creature is immune to the werewolf's Frightful Presence for the next 24 hours.

Lycanthropy. A humanoid bitten by a werewolf in wolf form must succeed on a DC 13 Constitution saving throw or be cursed with werewolf lycanthropy. The curse can be removed only by a remove curse spell or similar magic.

ACTIONS

Multiattack (Humanoid or Hybrid Form Only). The werewolf makes two attacks: two with its spear (humanoid form) or one with its bite and one with its claws (hybrid form).

Bite (Wolf or Hybrid Form Only). *Melee Weapon Attack:* +4 to hit, reach 5 ft., one target. Hit: 6 (1d8 + 2) piercing damage. If the target is a humanoid, it must succeed on a DC 12 Constitution saving throw or be cursed with werewolf lycanthropy.

Claws (Hybrid Form Only). *Melee Weapon Attack:* +4 to hit, reach 5 ft., one creature. Hit: 7 (2d4 + 2) slashing damage.

MAGIC ITEMS

MAGIC ITEMS

VAMPIRE'S BRAND

Common

Protection from a vampire sect can be achieved by having the sect's brand burned into your skin. When the character has a brand, they cannot be attacked by a member of that vampire sect. The brand can only be removed either through magic or by removing the limb.

CROSS THE THRESHOLD

Rare

The medallion is worn by many vampires and allows them to cross thresholds into a home unharmed. Characters who own the "Cross the Threshold" medallion can +2 to Charisma (Stealth) checks.

VAMPIRE STAKE

Common

Carved from hardened wood, a vampire stake must be driven cleanly through the heart of a vampire. The effect is the immediate death of the vampire. The vampire cannot recover from a stake through the heart.

HOLY AXE

Very Rare

The tool of choice for decapitating a vampire is a Holy Axe. Made from silver and blessed by religious leaders and designed to kill vampires. The axe will inflict 1d8 slashing damage for all targets. An additional +4 can be added for vampires.

SILVER CROSS

Common

Repulsed by the silver, a vampire will receive 2d4+2 damage when a silver cross is pressed onto exposed skin.

VAMPIRE'S BLOOD

Rare

The blood of the vampire is powerful. A small droplet can restore 1d20+10 HP. Each time a creature consumes vampire blood, it must complete a DC15 Constitution check. If they fail, they have consumed too much blood and will appear to die, only to wake 72 hours later as a level 1 vampire.

ELIXIR OF LIFE

Very Rare

A potent potion that can prevent death for 24 hours.

VAMPIRE'S BLADE

Rare

A necrotic blade that is infused with poison. The edge will cause 1d4 slashing damage. The necrotic venom in the blade will continue to inflict +2HP damage every round until the victim receives a cure for poisons.

UNHOLY WATER

Rare

Unholy Water can be splashed onto a target. The target will need to succeed a DC 15 Wisdom save. A failure will result in the target immediately becoming overcome with unholy revelry. The impact will last three rounds.

VAMPIRE'S CROSSBOW

Rare

Vampire's Crossbow fires blood-soaked bolts per round. Each bolt will inflict 1d6 piercing damage with a range of 80/320.

SPELLS

SPELLS

SCORPION STING

3rd Level

Casting Time: 1 minute to prepare

Range: 10-25ft

Components: V S M (requires you have a bottle of scorpion venom)

Duration: The scorpions will follow the caster until the caster commands them to dissolve (at which point the scorpions will melt and puddle on the soil), or the scorpions will be killed.

School of Evocation: Conjuration

The caster must have a tablespoon of scorpion venom. The venom is scattered on the ground. Each droplet will generate a scorpion (roll 1d8+4 for the number of scorpions) following the caster's commands. See the Monsters section for the stat block for a scorpion.

MESMERISM

1st Level

Casting Time: 10 seconds to prepare (the caster will need to mumble the invocation to themselves)

Range: 25ft

Components: V S

Duration: The spell will last for 1d4 rounds.

School of Evocation: Enchantment

The caster can mesmerize a target victim, who will do exactly what the caster wants them to do. To block the spell, the target must succeed in a DC 15 Charisma (Deception) check.

DEAD WEIGHT

Cantrip

Casting Time: 10 seconds to prepare

Range: 25ft

Components: V S

Duration: The spell will last for 1d4 rounds.

School of Evocation: Enchantment

The target will immediately collapse to the floor and will look as if they are dead. The target will need to succeed a DC 15 Strength check to block the spell.

PRETERNATURAL STRENGTH

2nd Level

Casting Time: Instant

Range: Self or a target within 30ft

Components: V S

Duration: 4 rounds

School of Evocation: Enchantment

The caster can cast this spell on themselves or a target. For 4 rounds, the target will receive a +3 Strength modifier to a maximum of score of 20. When the spell ends, the target will gains 1 level of exhaustion.

PRETERNATURAL SPEED

1st Level

Casting Time: Instant

Range: Self or a target within 30ft

Components: V S

Duration: 2 rounds

School of Evocation: Enchantment

The caster can cast this spell on themselves or a target. For 2 rounds, the target will be able to run at double speed. When the spell ends, the target will return to its previous speed. The spell exhausts the body, and the creature will incur 1 level of exhaustion.

WINGS OF THE DEAD

4th Level

Casting Time: Instant

Range: Self (The caster can only cast this spell on themselves)

Components: V S M (requires crushed bat wings)

Duration: 3 rounds

School of Evocation: Enchantment

Clutching a small pouch of crushed bat wings, the caster can cast Wings of the Dead on themselves and grow bat wings. For three rounds, they can fly at 120ft per round. The spell can only be cast once per day.

DEADLY THOUGHTS

2nd Level

Casting Time: 1 minute to prepare

Range: A target within 30ft

Components: V S

Duration: 2 rounds

School of Evocation: Enchantment

For two rounds, the caster can identify a target and read their mind. The target will need to succeed a DC 15 Charisma (Persuasion) or (Intimidation) save. On a failed save, the caster can read the target's thoughts and ask the target questions. The responses must be truthful. The spell can only be cast once per day.

MIND OVER MATTER

Cantrip

Casting Time: Instant

Range: A target within 30ft

Components: V S

Duration: Instant

School of Evocation: Evocation

The caster can identify any object and move it during the round. The caster can only move things that they can physically lift. The spell can be cast three times per day.

HEALING THE DEAD

3rd Level

Casting Time: Instant

Range: Touch

Components: V S M (requires a vial of blood)

Duration: Instant

School of Evocation: Necromancy

If a character reaches 0 HP, the caster has two rounds to cast Healing the Dead to restore 2d6+2 HP to the target. The target cannot be healed if more than two rounds have passed. The spell can only be once per day. The caster will lose the same number of HP given to the dead target and cannot be restored if they fall below 0HP.

CALL OF THE WILD

3rd Level

Casting Time: Instant

Range: Self

Components: V S

Duration: Instant

School of Evocation: Enchantment

For 1d4+2 rounds, the caster can turn themselves into a wolf. They gain the stats for a wolf, as detailed in the Monster section of the game however they retain their Intelligence, Wisdom, and Charisma scores.

REMOVE VAMPIRISM

3rd Level

Casting Time: Instant

Range: Touch

Components: V S M (requires a vial of blood from the vampire that bit the target)

Duration: Instant

School of Evocation: Enchantment

The spell removes vampirism from a character for 24hrs and requires blood from the vampire who attacked the character. If the character completes a successful DC 15 Wisdom (Medicine) check then the cure will become permanent.

NON-PLAYER CHARACTERS

NON-PLAYER CHARACTERS

WHISPERING NIGHT

MARCUS

It has been more than five centuries since Marcus became a vampire. He rules as the leader of his family and honors the centuries-old nobility of the Whispering Night.

His Turning is so far in the past that he barely remembers any life before. On the day of his "un-death," he was defending the Whispering Night castle from a group of bandits. The bandits were feral vampires from the northern woods, crazed by the blood lust that consumes them. Wielding his sword, Marcus attacked the small group and slew three of the band. Only one was left, their leader Killian, a vampire possessed of preternatural strength and cunning. The two fought each other, with swords clashing on the Barsea Heights mountain tops. There was little doubt who would win — Killian was stronger and pushed his blade to the hilt through Marcus's gut. Snarling, Killian brought Marcus close and whispered, "You have but one chance to live. Or you die here and now." With the cold steel deep inside his body, Marcus knew he was dying. Without flinching, he demanded to live, knowing the cost. Killian obliged, biting into Marcus's throat, and passing the curse of everlasting life onto him.

Marcus did not see Killian again after their battle.

He lay on the mountaintop for several hours in a fever as his body first died and then hitched back into an undead state. Thirst for blood overwhelmed him. Coming down to the town, he hunted for fresh blood. He found an old woman and was about to give into this new primal urge when the visage of his father rose before him. With scorn, his father said, "Marcus, you are a leader not only of your family but the town's people." Ashamed, he let the woman go, but the thirst was strong. To satisfy his need, Marcus arranged with the town's leaders. Willing volunteers must be sent to the castle. Each victim will play a game of chance. If they win, they will be converted to a vampire and have immortality. If they lose, then Marcus and his siblings will feast. There are many volunteers.

LISHA

While Marcus sees himself as the family's Patriarch, Lisha considers a much larger world. Lisha's drive to capture power matches her thirst for blood as she sees a world where she rules massive regions. Intensely intelligent, Lisha brokered the arrangement for volunteers to donate their lives to the vampires. In addition, Lisha managed the peace agreement with the Bone Brothers. This has suited her well for many decades, and she even became somewhat content. Still, the arrival of the Youngblood sect has reignited a fire in Lisha. She wants to grow the Whispering Night influence across all vampire sects. With that said, she will not turn against her family. She sees Marcus and Treznor as critical pawns needed to grow her dominion. Everyone else is disposable.

TREZNOR

The youngest of the three Whispering Night siblings, Treznor was changed to a vampire when he was only seventeen. Like his older brother, Treznor has tried to rule and protect the towns the castle overlooks, but his thirst is so strong that he has, on many occasions, slipped out of the castle, and secretly slain travelers, homeless people, and even traveled to faraway towns to quench his thirst. He is careful not to hunt in Barsea. Not because of some ridiculous pact with the town elders but from fear of reprisal from his brother. When Killian bit Marcus, he received the full Vampire curse. He was careful not to give either Treznor or their sister Lisha the same powers. To this end, Treznor does not have the same Charisma or Strength as Marcus, and his sister is far more Intelligent and for centuries, Treznor has harbored resentment towards his siblings.

By chance, Treznor was hunting for vagrants around Barsea when he came across Lucia. The two first saw each other as mortal enemies and battled each other. The battle quickly turned to love and then deep, aligned loyalty to each other. The two, together, see that they can create a new vampire sect. Treznor only needs to seize his chance to overthrow his family when it presents itself to him.

BONE BROTHERS
FATHER QUINN

Many call themselves vampires. Only Father Quinn knows you must be seduced by the demon Vonak, the source of all vampirisms, to be a true vampire. Vonak has chosen very few to be blessed with true vampirism. Father Quinn considers himself one of the select few and now devotes his time to worshipping Vonak. The Bone Cathedral, where he lives, is a temple to Vonak, and only the truly blessed vampire may enter its satanic chambers.

It has been a century since Father Quinn was turned into a vampire, and during that time, a deep unease grew

YOUNGBLOOD
LUCIA

Strong, confident, and daring, Lucia knows her destiny will be blinding. Turned as a teenager, Lucia has only been a vampire for five years but she immediately understood the power of her future. Once a shy and reclusive young woman, she is now possessed with power and seeks revenge against those who judged and belittled her.

She founded the Youngblood sect to pull together outcasts like her and sees each person in her group as shouldering the burden of shame. The Youngblood do not judge each other, which has become their power, knowing that together they can defend themselves and, as they grow in strength and numbers, they will have the strength to attack other sects.

Complicating things is her relationship with Treznor. On the one hand, Treznor is an outcast, shunned by his family while on the other, he is a blood member of the Whispering Night, whose loyalty to family is legendary.

within him: how do I create a world with only pure vampires and eradicate these undead imposters? This unease has grown into a burning anger which is fueled by a zealot's mania. Cleansing the world of the filth will start with the Youngblood and Whispering Night.

BROTHER NOSTRO

Doubt is a frivolous emotion for a vampire. The thirst for blood removes the need for doubt when you see your prey. And yet, Brother Nostro is plagued with doubt. Outwardly he stands as the right-hand man to Father Quinn, quick to follow commands. But inwardly, when he is alone, he doubts his motives. Brother Nostro wonders what the world would be like if he were truly a holy man, doing good.

For this reason, Brother Nostro will support Dr. Whitt at the town's small hospital. Father Quinn believes Brother Nostro volunteers at the hospital to scout future victims, but in truth he is there to see if his soul can be redeemed.

BROTHER MARIUS

Not all vampires are intelligent, beautiful and charismatic. Some are just ugly, blunt instruments and Brother Marius is Father Quinn's blunt instrument. Brother Marius has two thing going for him: he is strong, and he is stupid. For Father Quinn, all he must do is point Marius at a target and command him to destroy it!

The only redeeming part of Marius is his voice: when he sings, he sounds like an angel. He is the cantor to the unholy singers at the Bone Cathedral.

Lucia will need to tread carefully.

ULYSSES

Every charismatic leader needs a strategist. Ulysses is a calm and patient vampire, unlike many of his kin, and he uses this to outwit the people he is set to track and destroy. Visually, Ulysses looks like he is only twelve years old, yet he was turned more than fifty years ago and has used this time to grow his mind and calm his natural tendencies. Ulysses often goes scouting, using his tiny frame to slip in and out of buildings without being seen. If Ulysses is discovered on one of his trips, it is typically because he wanted to be found. He always has strategies for every encounter.

JADE

Love is a sharp blade that cuts deep. Jade is deeply in love with Lucia, will follow her wherever she goes and is completely loyal to her. Still, Lucia's relationship with Treznor is creating a growing hole of anger. Jade knows she is strong and powerful and cannot know when she will snap and attack Treznor.

BARSEA TOWNSFOLK
PASTOR WALTER TONKIN

Walter Tonkin discovered religion late in his life after he spent twelve years in a damp prison. Every Sunday, he can be found at St. Alnwyck's passionately preaching the good word. During the week, he finds the lost and sways them into joining his flock.

The god he preaches to at church every Sunday is not the god he worships. In prison, he did discover religion, but it is Vonak he found. He is desperate to receive pure vampire venom from Vonak, and Father Quinn has told him that if he grows his flock to provide a good stock of victims, then Vonak will grant his wish. Secretly aligned with the Bone Brothers, Pastor Tonkin will do all in his power to ensure the Bone Brothers are successful.

DOCTOR NAOMI WHITT

Patients keep coming to Barsea Hospital with severe blood loss. Dr. Whitt is the only trained physician in the town and she sees what is happening: a curse brought on by the undead. She labors day and night to heal the incurable. Arriving at Barsea in early spring, Dr. Whitt did not know the world she was entering. The arrival of the harsh winter has only proven to escalate the living hell Dr. Whitt finds herself in. Strong, resilient, and fiercely determined, Dr. Whitt will find a cure for vampirism. An unlikely partner in her hunt for a cure is Brother Nostro. They are working to cure vampirism.

JUDE THE CHEAT

Jude "the cheat" is a charming and charismatic halfling with a knack for getting what he wants through deceit and manipulation. He has spent most of his life as a con artist, using his quick wit and silver tongue to swindle unsuspecting marks out of their gold. Though he is not above using violence if it suits his needs, Jude prefers to use his charm and cunning to get his way. Despite his dishonest profession, Jude has a code of ethics that he follows and will not take advantage of those who cannot afford to lose what he is trying to take from them.

RISTINA VRANI

Ristina Vrani is a formidable half-giantess with a passion for blacksmithing. She has spent much of her life honing her craft, creating weapons and armor for those in need. Though she is not one for words, Ristina's strength and determination speak for themselves. She is fiercely loyal to her friends and will stop at nothing to protect them. In combat, Ristina is a force to be reckoned with, wielding her greatsword with skill and precision. When she's not working at her forge, Ristina can often be found exploring the wilderness or taking on mercenary work to support herself and her craft.

CYRAN'S VERSE

Cyran is a vampire who has chosen to live in isolation. He uses his time during the day and night to write poetry. Is it good poetry? None who have met Cyran and given him their critique of his verse have lived to tell the tale.

THE VAMPIRE'S LAMENT

In the dark of night, when all is still
I roam the streets, a lonely thrill
I am a vampire, cursed to live
Forever hungry, forever give

With each life I take, I feel the pain
Of a soul forever lost, never to gain
The happiness and joy it once held dear
Now gone, consumed by my own fear

I regret the choice I made that day
To trade my soul for endless prey
But now I am trapped, a monster inside
Forever longing for the love I denied

I am a vampire, a creature of the night
Condemned to live without the light
I regret the lives I've taken, one by one
But it's too late, my fate is done

I roam the earth, a sad and lonely soul
Forever regretting the lives I stole.

DEFIANT IN THE NIGHT

I am a vampire, feared by all
But I will not cower, I will not fall

I am a warrior, strong and bold
I will not be defeated, I will never fold

My enemies tremble at the sight of me
But I will not back down, I will not flee
I am a force to be reckoned with
I will not be stopped, I will not be finished

I am a vampire, born to fight
I will battle until the end of night
I will not rest until I am victorious
I will not be defeated, I am ferocious

I am a vampire, unbreakable and proud
I will face my enemies, and I will not back down
I will fight with all my might
I am a vampire, and I am ready for this fight.

BECOMING THE NIGHT

O, how I long to feel the night
And leave behind the humdrum light
To taste the blood and feel alive
In this new form that I'll contrive

Gone are the days of mortal strife
And all the pains of human life
I'll roam the earth with endless youth
A creature of the moon, uncouth

No longer bound by time or place
I'll move with speed and stealthy grace
A predator of the darkest kind

My prey, the helpless and the blind

Gone is the guilt and fear of death
No longer ruled by failing breath
I'll take my fill and never tire
A vampire, free from human mire

So let the change come quickly now
And let me feel the power, the prow
Of this new life that I will lead
A vampire, in the night I'll feed.

THE VAMPIRE'S HUNT

In the dark of night, I stalk
Silent as a shadow, I walk
My prey, unaware of my presence
Unsuspecting, in a state of innocence

I watch from the shadows, my hunger rising
The beat of their heart, the blood in their veins
I can almost taste it, so close and yet far
A temptation, a pull, like a distant star

I move in, swift and deadly
They turn, but it's too late, already
I strike, a sudden flash of fangs
A gasp, a scream, as they realize their fate

And then it's over, the deed is done
Their life, now mine, my prey, my own
I drink my fill, and then I flee
Into the night, a vampire, free.

GAME WITHIN A GAME

GAME WITHIN A GAME

DEATH DICE

What is needed: each player will need four 6-sided dice.

Objective: to have the highest total of four dice.

Rules: each player rolls four dice behind their hands to hide the result from the other players. The player then chooses one die and shares it with all players. The players then make bets to see who has the highest total. Each player lifts their hand and reveals the total for their four dice when the wages have been placed. The winner takes all.

FOOD AND FUEL

FOOD AND FUEL

VAMPIRE'S COCKTAIL

1 part raspberry liqueur

1 part vodka

Ice

Shake in a tumbler and strain into a glass.

VAMPIRE NON-ALCOHOLIC COCKTAIL

4 cups of sprite

2 cups of cranberry juice

1/2 cup of raspberries

Ice

Place all ingredients together in a bowl and server in chilled glasses.

SARMALE (STUFFED CABBAGE ROLLS)

Ingredients

⅔ cup water

⅓ cup uncooked white rice

8 cabbage leaves

1-pound lean ground beef

¼ cup chopped onion

1 egg, slightly beaten

1 (10.5 ounce) can condensed tomato soup, divided

1 teaspoon salt

Dash of black pepper

Directions

Bring water to a boil in a saucepan and then add rice. Cover, reduce to low, and simmer until rice is cooked through and liquid has been absorbed. This will take about twenty minutes.

In a separate wide saucepan, bring water to a boil (add a pinch of salt to the water). Add the eight cabbage leaves and cook for 2 to 4 minutes or until softened. Drain the cabbage.

In a bowl, mix ground beef, 1 cup of cooked rice, onion, egg, 2 tablespoons of tomato soup, salt, and pepper.

Place 2 tablespoons of the mixture onto each cabbage leaf. Roll the cabbage leaf over the mixture and tuck in the ends to stop the filling from falling out.

Put the cabbage rolls in a large skillet over medium heat and pour the remaining tomato soup on top. Cover and bring to a boil and then reduce the heat to low and simmer for about 40 minutes, stirring and coating with the liquid

MAPS

MAPS

THE TOWN OF BARSEA

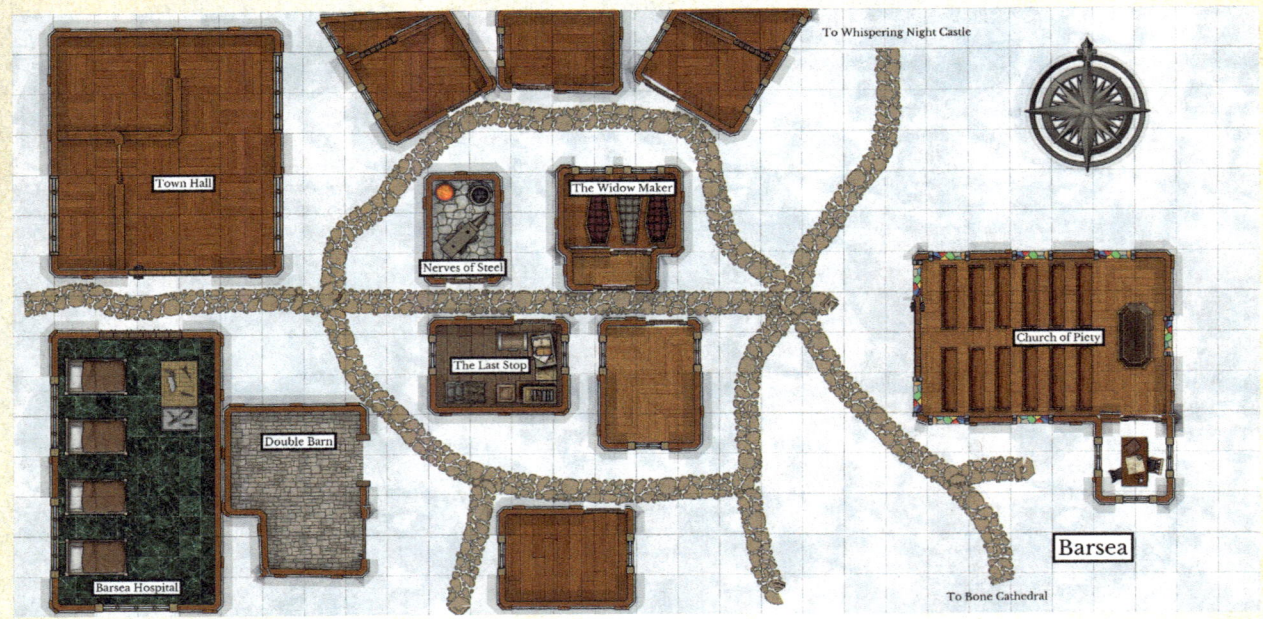

THE BONE CATHEDRAL

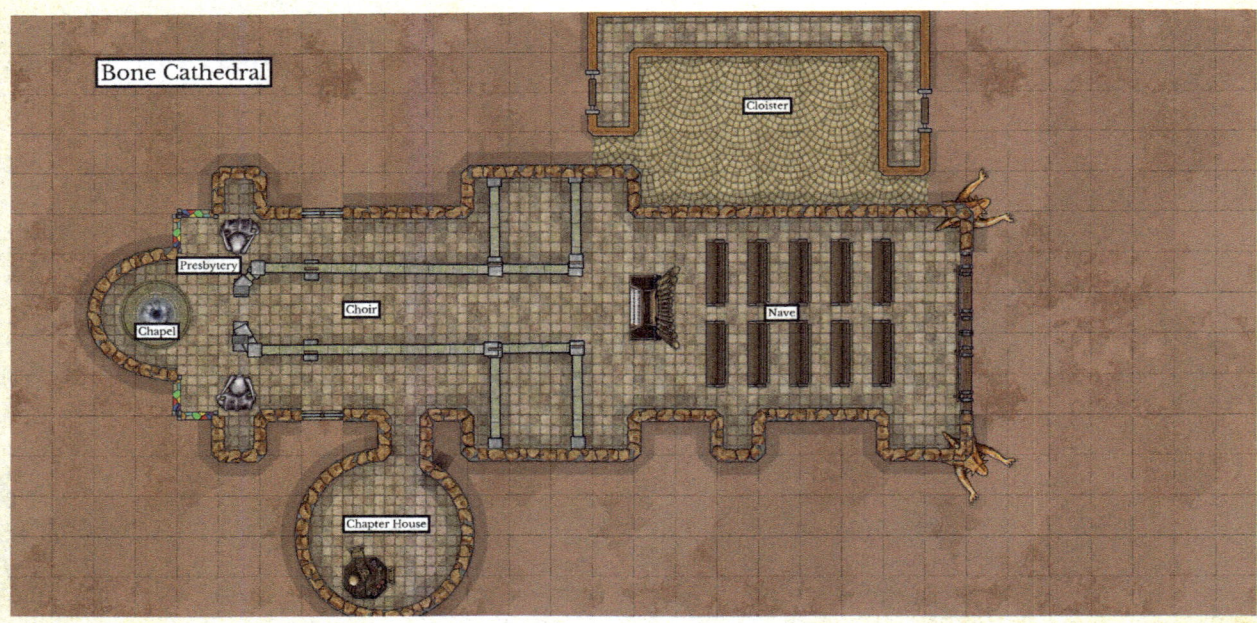

WHISPERING NIGHT CASTLE

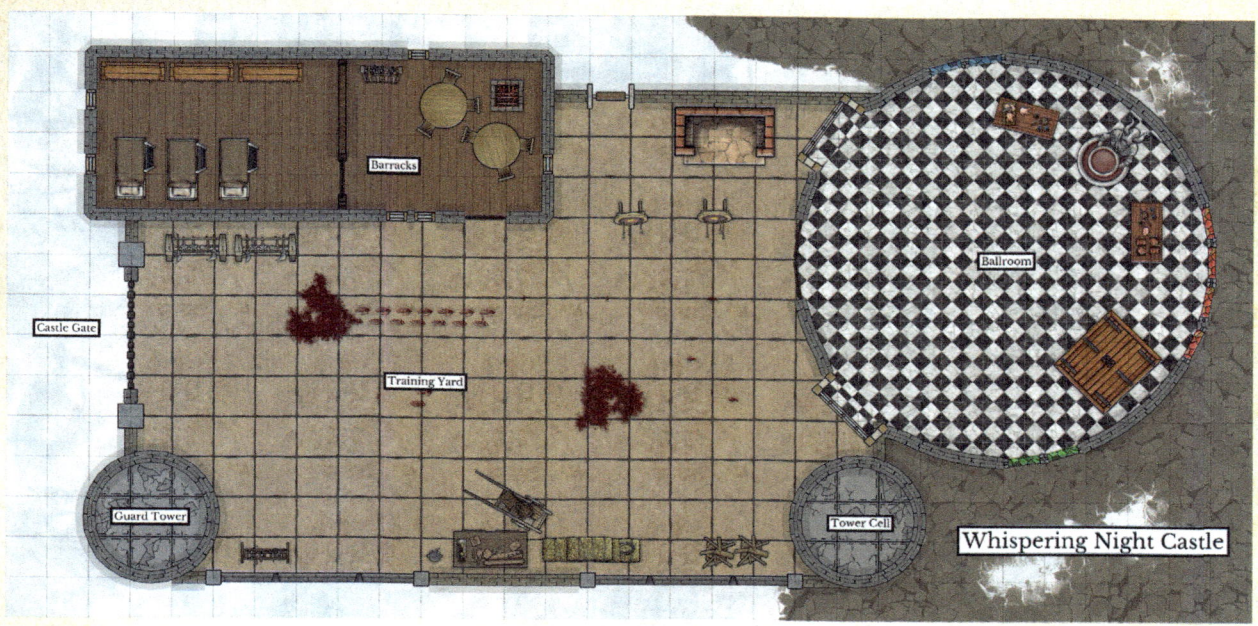

Whispering Night Castle

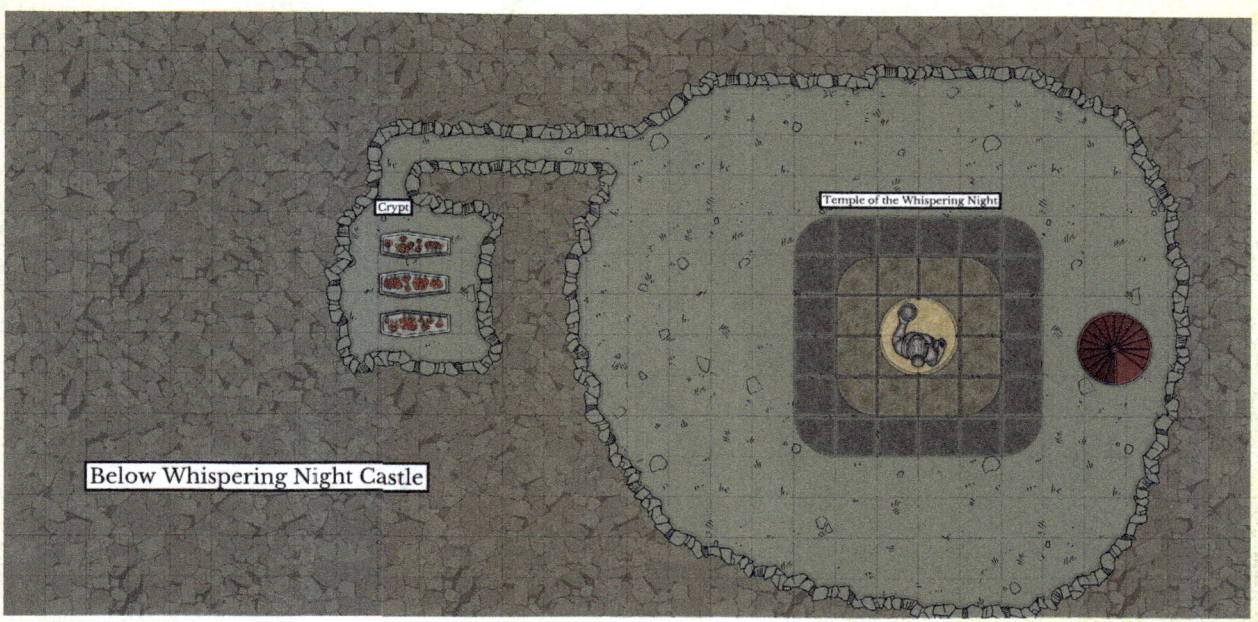

Below Whispering Night Castle

SPECIAL THANKS

SPECIAL THANKS

Special thanks to the following backers:

- Adam Pitalo
- Anton Semenov
- Ashe Ragone
- Bellansa
- Cameron Meause
- Daniel Hettrick
- Delta
- Doug Kendall Entertainment
- Emma
- Ernest Sandridge III
- Gerd Hauser
- Hfelschow
- James "The Great Old One" Burke
- Jared Nicholls
- Jason Dawson
- Jeff Seitz
- Jonny
- Kaillie Bill
- Kaleb Norris
- Katie K.
- Kerrie G M Ritchie
- KorvusRock
- Matthew Rice
- Patrick
- Robert Czeerwinski
- Ryan McDuffle
- Shanna Broussard
- Starling Ridgeway
- Stephanie M
- Stormy Danger
- Sven "DOC" Berglowe
- Tristin
- Tyler

EDITORIAL TEAM

EDITORIAL TEAM

Author: Matthew David

Art: Midjourney

Editor: Michael Paulick

Map Editor: Dr Feargood

OPEN GAME LICENSE VERSION 1.0A

Made in the USA
Columbia, SC
18 January 2023